"May I Have the First Dance?"
Maximilian Bowed.

The Emperor was an excellent dancer. He held Aimée closer than was customary. The hand against her back as he guided her about the dance floor moved almost imperceptibly, and the effect sent a deeper thrill through her body than she had ever felt before. It was deliberate, she knew, for when she dared glance up at his face, there was the faintest smile around the corners of his mouth.

Aimée could barely force herself to look away from his compelling gaze, for never had she seen eyes as blue as his. And his blond hair and beard almost gleamed with a golden quality under the lights of a thousand candles and chandeliers.

Could this man, whom she had every reason to detest and fear, really be the gilded god who held her close and sent wave after wave of sensation through her body by the merest brush of his fingers on her back . . . ?

Also published by POCKET BOOKS/RICHARD GALLEN

This Golden Rapture
  by Paula Moore

The Fire Bride
  by Julia Wherlock

THE LOVE OF THE LION

Angela Gray

PUBLISHED BY POCKET BOOKS NEW YORK

A POCKET BOOKS/RICHARD GALLEN *Original* publication

POCKET BOOKS, a Simon & Schuster division of
GULF & WESTERN CORPORATION
1230 Avenue of the Americas, New York, N.Y. 10020

ISBN: 0-671-41464-X

First Pocket Books printing November, 1980

10 9 8 7 6 5 4 3 2 1

POCKET and colophon are trademarks of Simon & Schuster.

Printed in the U.S.A.

Chapter 1

"Why are we acting like criminals, father?" implored beautiful, young Aimée Gaudin. For three days she had been held a virtual prisoner in her own father's house after he had arrived suddenly at her convent school and whisked her away. Now, at last, they were finally going out. But instead of feeling quieted, her fears only grew. "Why, father, why?" she begged again.

"Soon, Aimée, be patient," her father waved away her questions—as if she were some impertinent servant girl. Matters must be grave, indeed, if he treated her this way. And she had noted how his usually smiling face was now a stern mask etched wth fatigue and worry.

Aimée had been raised strictly as a young upper class woman, well-bred and quiet, but she was also a determined one, much like her mother. And she had decided she would no longer let her father treat her like the child she once had been. But only the clip-clop of the horses' hooves on the cobblestoned streets of Paris broke the silence. Finally, she said, "I don't understand why you, one of Louis Napoleon's most respected diplomats, who is usually busy with meetings, urgent political affairs and exciting social events, have been staying at home all day and then venturing out late at night only after some messenger arrives." Her father started, obviously surprised at her knowledge but said nothing. "Yes," she went on, "I have heard your late-night comings and goings—and all this mystery frightens me, father." The tears welled up in her eyes, causing her to look like a little girl again. "Father, I want to know what is happening. . . ."

Looking intently now at his distraught daughter, Emile Gaudin realized that she was a grown woman and that she deserved an answer.

"Things have changed," he said sharply. "And as I told you, it will all be explained later, after dinner tonight." With that he lapsed into silence again.

Aimée, contrite at having aroused her father's anger when he was clearly under so much pressure already, hugged him impulsively. "I don't mean to be so inquisitive and so angry. I know that whatever you're doing must be the best thing. Forgive me."

"It is I who should be forgiven," he said in a strained voice. "But I can't explain now." He gestured with his hand toward the carriage driver. "There are spies everywhere. This isn't the Paris you once knew—before your mother died. Everything has changed. . . . Enough. It will all be told later this evening. In the meantime, enjoy this ride through our beautiful Paris. It may be a long time before we have another such opportunity."

She was startled by that statement. "Am I not to go back to school?" Then, when she received no reply, she wheedled hopefully, "Have you been appointed ambassador to America or to Mexico again? Are we going away?"

Avoiding her gaze and smiling ruefully, Emile shook ⬤is head and replied, "No, we aren't going away. Or, if we do, not to the American continent—unless you

2

want to be caught up in their Civil War. Perhaps Italy, Switzerland or Vienna. Who knows? Enough now. Sit back and observe Paris, Aimée, and be patient."

Still puzzled, Aimée nevertheless tried to do as her father asked. They were driving through the Bois de Boulogne, which bordered on the western suburb of Neuilly-sur-Seine, a favorite pleasure ground lush with flowers and greenery and containing race courses, promenades and bridle paths. At any other time, without the worry that now occupied her mind, it would be easy to lose herself in the beauty and luxury of the living picture she surveyed from the carriage. Ladies and gentlemen dressed in the most fashionable styles of the moment strolled along the promenades. Other couples in riding habits, mounted on splendid steeds whose coats glistened with care, maintained an easy gait so that they might see and be seen as they moved along the bridle paths. Aimée often had wished to make the acquaintance of some of these elegant people. The girls had gossiped endlessly at school about *les affaires d'amour* of many so-called respectably married women and of the ladies of the theatre and society who had an endless succession of lovers. As she observed the beautifully gowned ladies, she wondered if some of them were those she had heard about.

At last, lulled by the regular clopping of the carriage horses' gait and by the murmur of distant voices in the soft evening air, Aimée sat back and gave herself up to the sights and sounds of Paris. She remembered someone had once said: "To live in Paris is to live with a lover—and though an inconstant one, a thrilling one."

They left the park and moved along the avenue, and there, too, were fashionably dressed ladies, moving at their leisure and holding their tiny, rainbow-hued parasols which, when touched by the early evening sun, gave their faces a radiant glow. Her gaze rested on an elegantly dressed and coquettish young woman whose escort had just caught her gloved hand and brought it to his lips. With a sigh, Aimée turned her attention to the buggies they passed on the avenue, wondering which of the rakish-looking young men who drove them were on their way to a love tryst. Aimée allowed her imagination free rein. . . .

Although a waning daylight still hovered over this warm mid-June evening when the carriage pulled up before the lavish facade of Mama LeFon's restaurant, it was the fashionable hour for supper. After being helped down by the doorman, Aimée took her father's arm and they entered the restaurant. The buxom, smiling Mama LeFon who was waiting at the door, greeted Emile with a kiss and Aimée with a tight, warm hug of welcome. She motioned to the maître d'hôtel who led them to a table in a far corner of the room, situated near the entrance to the kitchens. Aimée was surprised that her father had consented to sit at a table so near the waiter traffic. M. Gaudin was, after all, a very important personage, one who commanded high respect and was accustomed to the most prestigious table. Unperturbed, however, he ordered champagne and caviar. Indeed, he appeared lost in thoughts more pressing. Aimée wondered once again about the mysterious events that had transformed her father's normally cheerful and relaxed countenance into a grim, tense mask. Finally, he looked up, saw her troubled expression and nodded, as if acknowledging her unspoken thoughts.

"I know, Aimée, it was unfair of me not to tell you at once, but I didn't want to frighten you unnecessarily. Let me explain as best I can. You know, of course, that I was instrumental in Louis Napoleon Bonaparte's ascension to the throne and that I was rewarded with honors and several high diplomatic posts. But, when Louis proclaimed himself dictator of France, I was outraged and said so. I was warned then to say nothing further, and of course I followed that advice, for I knew that I had made dangerous enemies. But there are men who remember my feelings, and now . . ."

"Yes?" Aimée prompted, with growing conviction that matters were far worse than she had guessed.

"I will explain. As a former ambassador to Mexico with considerable experience in its affairs, I advised the French government to abandon its plan to take over the country by force. But the authorities ignored my advice. To make matters worse, Napoleon has sent Ferdinand Maximilian to rule Mexico. This Austrian archduke—with his leonine mane of hair and proud bearing—may look like a king of the jungle, but he is weak politically. He knows nothing of the country he was sent to rule: he has no idea of the minds and hearts of the Mexican people. Not even a strong, ruthless man could rule such a country, for there is a revolutionary force at work which ultimately will prevail and destroy us."

"But, Father," Aimée said, her voice and face now mirroring her anxiety, "can they blame you for expressing an opinion?"

"My dear Aimée, it was more than an opinion. A man in Mexico named Benito Juárez heads the new revolution. I have advised him of certain matters and . . . some of my letters to him were intercepted. They are now calling me a traitor, although I wished only to find some way to spare France the shame of this ill-advised venture, for we stand only to lose."

"If you're right, they'll have to admit it, won't they?"

"Yes, but in the meantime we must be very careful. Tonight I shall receive word from a friend. Certain people have interceded for me and perhaps I'm to be forgiven. I'll learn the results of their efforts tonight. So—"
He broke off as the waiter came to take their orders.

Although M. Gaudin, affecting his familiar charm, attempted to ease Aimée's anxiety by speaking of lighter topics, he could not distract her. Aimée had no appetite for Mama LeFon's delicious *coq au vin*. Her fears only mounted as time crept by with no sign of her father's friend. Finally M. Gaudin fell silent and Aimée, feeling helpless and vulnerable, could only sit and wait. The small man who finally arrived and joined them was a stranger to Aimée. He wore spectacles and an expression of agitation that did little to allay her fears. Emilie Gaudin did not introduce him, but merely waited expectantly for the waiter to depart so that his friend could speak freely.

At last the worried-looking little man cleared his throat and turned to M. Gaudin. "Word has not yet come," he said. "There is a meeting at the palace now, Emile, but I'm not optimistic. There's great pressure because so much money has already been spent on the Mexican venture that France must get it back or Louis will regard it as a failure. And he is not much given to admitting his errors."

"Then we're finished," Emile said decisively. "Henri, it's best you leave now, and make your way to Italy or Belgium. Anywhere safe."

"And what of you, Emile?"

"We'll try to do the same."

The man called Henri arose abruptly. "There's no time to lose. Goodbye, my friend. I'll try to contact you as soon as I'm settled somewhere."

"Godspeed, Henri," Emile said. "Go now . . . no more delay."

Henri was halfway across the restaurant when he was met by another man who had disregarded the headwaiter and plunged past the red rope guarding the entrance. He spoke no more than half a dozen words, then made a hasty exit. Henri returned hurriedly to the table.

"It seems you've been watched, Emile, and they're already on their way here. You've been secretly condemned as a traitor. Listen to me now and don't argue. I'll make a dash for it through the front door. They'll stop me, or try to, but I'll divert their attention if I can. If I'm caught, I'll swear that I fled because I learned you were a traitor and I wished no contact with you. While I keep them busy, you and your daughter might be able to get out the back way. You were seated at this table near the kitchen door by intent, to give you a chance to escape. Au revoir, my friend."

He walked briskly toward the restaurant entrance and must have reached the street, for the excitement began about a minute or so after he left the table. There were shouts, and then shots rang out.

Emile grasped his daughter's hand, pulled her to her feet and led her through the kitchen door. Cooks and scullery maids stood aside as if by command. Aimée found herself in an alley behind the restaurant. Here they looked about, saw no one. They could still hear the commotion in the street in front of the restaurant, but there was no more shooting.

"Poor Henri," Emilie said. "I think he knew what it meant to give us this chance."

"Father, there are men at the end of this alley, to your right," Aimée whispered.

Emile looked and saw the dim shapes in the darkness. He led Aimée to the left, and they moved as quietly as possible along the alley, keeping to the deeper shadows close to the buildings. They were almost at the other end of the alley when a dark form blocked their exit to the street.

Emile grasped Aimée's hand again and pulled her into a doorway. He tried the door but it was locked. As they looked wildly from one end of the alley to the other, they heard a shot which seemed to come from the street in front of Mama LeFon's. Then there was a second shot. Emile quickly broke a small glass pane in the door but, fortunately for them, the sound of shattering glass was lost in the confusion of voices that broke out after the gunfire. Quickly, he reached through the empty square to unlock the door.

They could hear men moving along the alley now, and Emile swiftly drew Aimée into the building. He closed the door and embraced his daughter. "Listen to me, dear Aimée. We cannot go together. Alone, each of us might make it. But you must understand that your life is in as much danger as mine, for my enemies fear that you can tell the whole story, the *true* story. This is what you must do—if you manage to escape. Go to the residence of Roy Vardeau. Do you remember him?"

"No . . . but I recall the name."

"He is part of this undercover rebellion against the Mexican occupation. Go to him and he'll do what he can to hide you, to see that you reach safety. He's one of us. Don't argue with me, just leave, here, through this building. When you reach the street, make sure no one sees you. I think they're concentrating on the alley now."

"Father," Aimée asked in alarm, "what will you do?"

"Remain where I am now. Perhaps they won't think to look in here. When I see my chance, I'll run for it. Should we escape, I'll try to contact you. Meanwhile, go to Monsieur Vardeau for help and do what he says."

Aimée held out her arms and embraced her father fervently, as if she might never see him again. All too soon he pushed her gently from his side.

"Trust me, Aimée, and don't worry about my welfare for now. If they capture me, I'll try to reason with them instead of putting up a fight. Don't forget, my dear one, that I'm an important man in Paris, a friend of the emperor, as they well know. Now go." He drew her close again, kissed her, and thrust her in the direction of the passage.

She stood still for a moment, trembling with fear and indecision as she heard the door close behind her. Then she stumbled through the darkness, listening for any sound that might tell her that they'd found her father.

She knew she was in a store, for she could just make out shelves and counters, even though it was too dark to see much except the shaded door at the front. All her senses alert now, she made her way quietly to the door and cautiously pulled the shade aside to look out on what seemed to be an empty street.

She unlocked the door, listened again in renewed

hope that her father had not been discovered, and then stepped quickly out into the deserted street.

She composed herself, straightening her hat and pausing to take a deep breath. Then she walked toward the busier avenue, willing her feet to keep an unhurried pace. She was at the corner when she heard the shooting. Her heart sank. She forgot all caution and ran down the avenue, along with other curious passersby, in the direction of the alley from which she had escaped only moments before.

When she arrived, a crowd was already collecting. "What is it?" she asked a man beside her. "What's happening?"

"They shot a traitor," he told her, "and for his sake it's just as well they killed him. Otherwise it would mean the guillotine for him."

"Oui," she said in a small voice. Too shocked to really comprehend the news, she knew only that she shouldn't linger here, that she should try to reach Roy Vardeau. But in all the excitement, her father hadn't told her where he lived. She would have to inquire, and that might be very dangerous.

Men were coming out of the alley now. A dozen or more, and they were moving about, looking carefully at people, stopping women. Aimée knew they were searching for her and she restrained a moan. There seemed to be no way to escape them. She knew how dangerous it would be to try to run for it. And if she stayed with the crowd, chances were she'd be recognized sooner or later. She turned and walked slowly away, knowing her only hope was in leaving the scene as casually as possible and praying her departure would go unnoticed. But with every step she took, she knew it would be only a matter of moments before she was stopped either by the secret police or the uniformed police.

She sensed someone moving closely behind her. She was certain she was about to be arrested. Instead, a voice whispered, "I am a friend, Aimée. Keep walking.

Move to the curb and step into that brougham near the corner. Do you understand?"

She nodded, afraid to speak, not knowing whether this was an attempt to help her to escape, or the means of getting her quietly into the closed carriage where she would be placed under arrest and taken to her doom. Since it was her only chance, and could be a genuine effort to help her, she had no choice but to obey the voice.

Feigning a casual manner, she approached the brougham, opened the door, and stepped in. But before she could close the door, a man followed her into the dark interior.

"Keep your head down," he warned. "If we're stopped or approached, play along with whatever I do. We have a chance."

There was such a crowd gathered, and so many carriages and other vehicles jamming the street, that the driver couldn't obey the man's command to move on.

Suddenly the man at her side bent over her, pulled her to him and fastened his mouth against hers. Aimée gasped and drew back, but the man pressed closer. A moment later the door was pulled open, and Aimée heard a soft chuckle from the intruder who assumed he saw only young lovers locked in a passionate embrace.

The door closed again, and finally the man released her. Thus far, she'd not had even a glimpse of him and now, in the gloomy interior, she could distinguish little more than his shadowy form.

"Merci, monsieur," she whispered. "I am most grateful."

"I think we're safe now," he said. "The driver is one of mine, and he'll try to get us away from here as soon as the congestion eases. You're all right, mademoiselle? Not injured in any way?"

"Not at all. But . . . who are you? Why are you helping me?"

"I'm one of your father's friends, Aimée." His voice softened as he added, "You know that he is dead?"

Still in shock from the evening's fateful events, Aimée stared at him blankly and then nodded.

"Do not grieve too much for him. He was a brave man. He died for what he believed in, and one day it will be proven he was not wrong. They'll say he was a traitor, but don't be deceived by that. He was a true patriot. . . ."

As his voice trailed off, she nodded again, pondering how far she might trust this man. Finally she spoke. "You've proven that you were my father's friend by helping me, but I must ask if you'll help me one more time."

"Whatever you wish."

"My father told me to go to . . . I cannot name him, not even to you. But then I must. How else can you help me? You see, monsieur . . . ."

"Did he tell you to go to Roy Vardeau?" he asked abruptly.

"Why, yes! Yes—to such a man."

"I am Roy Vardeau," he said quietly.

"Thank God." She sighed in relief. "I was afraid to go about asking where I might find you, and I didn't know whom to ask."

"It could have been fatal if you had."

"You're also in danger?" she asked.

"Not yet. They've never suspected me. I was compelled to pretend to be one of them, and when I heard what was happening—that your father's arrest had been ordered—I went along. They even knew where you and your father were. I could do nothing without revealing my true alliance, so I remained quiet and looked for an opportunity to help."

"The little man called Henri?" Aimée asked.

"Shot as he came out of the restaurant. They tried to question him, for he was only wounded. He refused to answer their questions so they shot him on the spot. But he provided the time needed for you and your father to get away. They'll be searching for you everywhere. And while they do, you can stay with me in my home. They don't suspect me and will never search there. When things quiet down, we'll determine what's to become of you."

"What is to become of me?" she murmured numbly. Then, recalling the conventions of good breeding, she asked, "How can I ever thank you, monsieur?"

"You already have," he said with a chuckle. "When we kissed to fool that gendarme, I was well repaid for what little I was able to do. You're a lovely young lady, my dear Aimée. Also a courageous one."

As the carriage lurched into motion, Aimée sat back and thought sadly of inoffensive little Henri who had given his life for her father—just as her father had provided for her possible escape, she now realized, at the sacrifice of his own life.

The carriage threaded its way through the heavy traffic towards a wide avenue lined with lavish shops. They were approaching one of the best residential parts of the city. And then where? she wondered.

Turning from the window to look at her companion, she said, "Monsieur, will I have to leave France?"

"It was agreed that if there was any trouble we were to do our best to see that you escaped. But that's easier said than done. If you're caught, you'll surely be imprisoned."

"Where can I go?" she asked in fresh alarm. " I have no money, no means of getting away safely. They certainly won't allow me to claim any part of my father's money."

"They'll have your head if you even apply for it. But could you relate what your father told you before he was killed?"

"He told me so little. Something about a Hapsburg being made emperor of Mexico. Archduke Maximilian."

"Maximilian was crowned emperor months ago," Vardeau said. "Your father predicted that Maximilian will fail and that France will lose many of her soldiers and, finally, all of Mexico as well."

"I lived with my father in Mexico when he was

ambassador," Aimée said, " and I agree that the Mexicans will not let themselves be conquered or ruled by a stranger. . . . But tell me, who is this Maximilian?"

"No time now," Roy Vardeau said. "We're almost at my apartment. You'll be safe there for a time because I live alone. And I took the precaution of dismissing my servants in the expectation that I might have to hide someone. In that respect I'm lucky," he added with a chuckle, "for I didn't anticipate a guest as lovely as you."

Aimée was warmed by the knowledge that this man was a friend of her late father, but she felt oddly disquieted by him nonetheless. She smiled wanly.

Chapter 2

The carriage stopped in front of a magnificent building on a fashionable boulevard. Vardeau got out and casually looked about before he signaled Aimée to step down from the carriage. He closed the door behind her, seized her elbow, and propelled her switftly across the walk into the deserted lobby of the building.

As they ascended the staircase leading to his apartment, Aimée had her first opportunity to note the appearance of the man who had befriended her. She was mildly surprised to see that he was so young—nowhere near her father's age as she had assumed. She judged him to be in his mid-twenties. He was tall, sturdy-looking and quite handsome, with a clean-shaven face, slightly wavy brown hair, and tawny eyes. He was well-dressed, too, obviously a gentleman.

As they reached the second floor landing and hurried down a short corridor, Vardeau produced a set of keys. He unlocked his door and they entered a drawing room that was furnished expensively. Aimée was trembling.

Too exhausted to pay attention to her surroundings, she dropped into a chair and tried to compose herself.

Vardeau glanced her way, removed his jacket, left the room for a moment and returned with two glasses of brandy.

"I'm sorry," Aimée said where he offered her a glass. "I don't care for brandy."

"Take it, sip it," he insisted. "It will help you to relax."

She obeyed him, grimacing as the powerful drink seared her throat. He sat down opposite her, his eyes taking her in with a frankness that was both flattering and unnerving. She flushed under his scrutiny and shifted uncomfortably, but his sudden smile reassured her.

"No doubt you're hungry," he said.

"I have little appetite, monsieur."

"You must have something. I'll send for supper to be served here in my apartment. It won't take long. You may use the time to wash if you like." Aimée watched his departure with relief, although she couldn't help noticing the self-confidence and strength of her rescuer's movements.

Shortly after Vardeau returned, two men arrived with hot food and chilled wine. They set up a table and then departed discreetly. Vardeau escorted her to the table and they sat down to a fine meal of beef, vegetables, savory sauces and small sweet cakes for dessert. The sumptuous repast accompanied by wine—on top of the brandy—did exactly what Vardeau said it would do. Aimée felt the weight of her sorrow and the grip of terror leave her, and she found herself relaxing in response to Vardeau's attentiveness.

"What will become of me?" she finally asked.

"I'm already working on a plan," he said, "but I won't tell you what I have in mind. That way, if you are apprehended you won't be able to destroy my friends by revealing what you know."

"Monsieur, I would never tell—"

"Do not say 'never,' *ma chérie*. They have ways to make you talk. Ways they enjoy and you will not . . . ."

She shuddered. "Then I'll ask no questions, monsieur. But please get me away from here."

"You have my promise. It's late, and tomorrow there will be much to do. I suggest you retire now. You may have the guest room. I'm sure you'll be quite comfortable."

He led her to a small but nicely furnished and comfortable-looking bedroom, unusual only in that the ceiling was mirrored.

"Alas," he said with a smile, "I don't have night clothing for a woman, but I shall take care of that tomorrow. Good night, Aimée."

He bent and kissed her lightly on the cheek. After he left, she closed the door and sat down to consider her predicament. She knew she was still in considerable danger; there would be very few places in Europe where she could hide safely, for Louis Napoleon Bonaparte's influence reached almost everywhere. Vardeau had something in mind but she had promised not to question him, and that meant she had placed her future completely in his hands. There was nothing she could do but trust him.

But as she sat there, her anger rose by degrees. During her lifetime she had been protected from all harm, from every frustration, and she certainly hadn't been prepared for what had happened in the space of a few hours by her years in a convent. But her anger wasn't caused by the danger confronting her, nor by the sudden change in her life; it was a rage aimed solely at those responsible for the death of her father and of Henri; at the emperor, who would not listen to wise advice but regarded it as treachery; at his aides and friends who were using him to fatten their own coffers at Mexico's expense. But her anger was suddenly blunted by the wave of sorrow that overcame her when she thought of her father who had sacrificed his life for her.

At last she rose wearily, disrobed down to her undergarments and climbed into bed where she lay for what seemed like hours before falling into a fitful sleep. But her sleep was haunted by terrifying dreams of disembodied faces, bloody bodies, and evil pursuers who would make her die a horrible death if they could only catch her. As she ran away in her dream, she struggled to the surface of wakefulness. She heard her own scream echoing in her ears and realized she was sitting up in bed. Moonlight streamed into the room, but she realized she was safe here.

She was so engrossed in her own thoughts that she almost screamed again when Roy Vardeau swept into her room and wrapped his arms around her. "You screamed. Are you all right?" he asked, apparently concerned.

"Yes, yes," she said uneasily, for even though his arms seemed so protective, were they not a little closer around her than necessary? And suddenly she was aware of how little she was wearing. She had never been this close to a man before. Nevertheless, she began to relax as he held her in his arms and rocked her gently. Then one hand began to stroke her long silken hair which cascaded over her shoulders halfway to her waist. Her heart was beating wildly. She tried to withdraw from his arms, but they only tightened around her. He tilted her head up to meet his and kissed her full on the lips. The first kiss between them had been to escape danger, but Aimée sensed that this kiss could only lead her into a new kind of peril.

Through her thin undergarments she could feel a heat radiating from his body as his hands now roamed over her satiny-smooth skin. She happened to glance upwards and, with a start, saw the mirror and the whole scene upside down. She realized that in his haste to come to her, he had thrown on only a dressing gown over his broad shoulders and it had fallen off, exposing his naked body. It had seemed stocky in clothing but now she saw that it was really a well-muscled body.

The sight fascinated her in spite of herself. But what fascinated her more was the sight of her own body. There had been no mirror in the convent, for they were the sin of vanity, but here she saw her own voluptuous body, and was aware that it must have tempted him just to look at her. After all, he was quite clearly a man, a virile young one at that.

"Don't be afraid," he murmured into her ear. "You will know pleasure."

Aimée resisted his advances and tried to pull the covers over her. He watched in disbelief for a second and then, without even really trying, he simply tore them away. She cowered on the far edge of the bed, trying to judge the distance to the door.

"You can't escape me," he said, when he realized what she intended. Then, he said, "Aimée, my dear, why do you pretend to be so innocent? . . ." His words trailed off as he thought, *"My God, she probably is! A convent. Years. A virgin! In Paris, no less!"* The idea seemed to stagger him, but even more, it excited him. He was determined to have her. "You can trust me," he said softly.

Aimée said, "Please leave."

"You jest," he said, admiring her heaving breasts, pearly-white in the moonlight, her long silken hair, and her lush body. "I could no more leave you alone than—"

"—Oh, please," she whimpered.

"My dear Aimée," he began, inching toward her. No more was said as he caught her in his arms, kissed her eyelids, blew warm breath into her ears, and nibbled on her earlobes. Aimée felt a curious warmth in her body, but hated herself for feeling these sensations and him for his insensitivity to her fragile state of mind caused by the death of her father only hours earlier. Now his hot lips traveled across her breasts, and almost like an observer she saw her nipples grow firm and hard and stand out. He took one between his lips and sucked on it. At first she felt nothing, but when his other hand started to explore the secrets between her legs, she clamped them together.

"No, no," she moaned, trying to push him away. But mere words were not enough, nor did she have the strength to resist his muscular body. Then she felt a hardness against her hips, and tried to wriggle away. It probed between her legs and she fought even harder. He gave her a broad smile and said, "If you relax, my sweet, it will not hurt. You might even enjoy it. . . ."

The first thrust was gentle, but it hurt her and she cried out. The second was stronger and took her by surprise, and she shrieked with pain. His hand covered her mouth and he hissed, "Quiet! Do you want my neighbors to know you are here!"

Her heart wilted. If she cried out and was "rescued," then he would surely turn her over to the police and she would be sent to prison—or even worse, the guillotine. To endure his assault might be painful, but at least she'd be safe for the present.

Vardeau's thrusts became stronger as he penetrated her secret chamber, and her struggle became even more frantic as her pain increased. It came in waves, but he was oblivious to her distress, for he seemed driven to possess her, to penetrate her, to make her his—and he did. Then he cried out with a moan that surprised her, and his whole body shook. Then he was still.

There was a wetness between her legs and, on top of her, the dead-weight of Vardeau. In disgust, she shoved him aside—and this time he did not resist, but simply rolled over. Then she looked up in the mirror and saw the pool of blood between her legs. She shrieked again, rousing Vardeau from his stupor.

"Be quiet! I warn you." But when his eyes followed hers and saw the blood, he gasped. "You were a virgin; it wasn't an act," he said in a hushed voice. Then that waggish grin appeared again as he said, "Well, I was the first—but I promise you, my fair Aimée, there will be more."

She winced at his words, but curiously enough she

was vacillating between pain and a strange sort of pleasure. She was confused, but more than that she was furious at Vardeau for taking advantage of her. "I trusted you to protect me," she accused him.

Wearily he looked at her, picked up his dressing gown and said, "Aimée, I am a man. Even though I tried to resist, the temptation was too great." As he prepared to leave, he added, "Remember, you are my guest—and at my mercy. If you want to live long enough to escape, I suggest that in the future when I visit you, you receive me gladly.",

"Gladly!" she sneered. "I'd rather die."

"If you refuse, you will," he reminded her arrogantly.

When she awoke the next morning, the apartment was silent. She suspected she was alone, for the time being. The memories of the night before flooded back, and when she tried to walk, it was a curious kind of gingerly treading, as if she'd been on a horse too long. She pulled a cover around her and went to inspect the apartment; it was empty, as she'd surmised, so she drew a bath and let her wounded, tired and dirty body relax in its luxuriousness. But her ears were alert to the slightest sound—perhaps a key in the lock. . . . Would Vardeau be the next person to come through the door, she wondered? Or the police? Would Vardeau betray her? If he did, probably he would be richly rewarded. But then he'd have to fear her accusations and be damned as well. On the other hand, she understood now the power of her womanhood and took some small comfort in the realization that even if he were to betray her, he would bide his time until his desire to possess her body had cooled. The thought of him forcing himself upon her again disgusted her, but at the same time it gave her a sense of power and superiority over him.

She was already dressed when he let himself back into the apartment. She was amazed to see his arms loaded with boxes, some gaily wrapped and bearing the names of the best shops in Paris. He placed them before her. As she opened them one by one, folding back the tissue paper slowly, she was astonished to discover costly lace lingerie, two daytime dresses that were perfect for strolling on the avenue—or for escaping—and the most appropriate accessories: a hat, gloves, stockings, even shoes. As she was to ascertain, everything fit perfectly. Vardeau had still more gifts to show her. Another box held soap, toilet water, perfume and powder—cosmetics calculated to make her look and feel ravishing. She was relieved to realize he meant for her to look well, for she had only the clothes on her back, and those were from her innocent convent days which already seemed a lifetime ago.

He insisted that she model her new clothes for him. She could tell from his wide grin of approval that he liked the first dress, a subdued gray poplin with violet braid trimming and a tiny velvet rosette of the same color on the pocket. It was demure but showed off her tiny waist and pale coloring. He had also bought a bonnet of lilac silk with matching braid. Then she changed into the other dress: a black silk, its overskirt edged with a narrow fringe. She had also noticed, under the dress, a traveling *paletot* of fine wool in a deep violet with a silk lining. The *paletot* pleased her most of all: A coat meant she soon would be leaving Vardeau's.

She smiled at the thought of leaving, but Vardeau interpreted it to mean she was pleased with his gifts. "For last night," he said, then added, "I'm not apologizing. And you must realize it will happen again. I do hope that this time you will be more cooperative when I come to visit you in the night." Last evening's experience had already taught her to beware a man's sexual parts. And glancing at him, Aimée saw that their next encounter could take place far sooner than she had expected. But apparently Vardeau had other duties to take care of, for he excused himself, and left.

Alone again, Aimée tried the door, but found it

locked from outside. It was foolish to try to escape in daylight, and with a sinking feeling, she realized she had no friends to help her even if she did escape Vardeau's apartment. So she decided it was best not to anger Vardeau any further and not to resist him, but merely to bide her time until he completed his escape plans for her—which she thought he might be doing at that very moment . . . .

He returned early that evening. Again there was dinner with wine. He seemed slightly tired. She did not pry into his affairs, and they ate in a strained atmosphere. Although she had eaten nothing all day, except some cheese and bread, Aimée merely picked at her food. But Vardeau was ravenous and ate heartily, barely glancing at her until he had pushed back his plate. She also noticed that the bottle of wine he had opened just recently was empty and that he was already beginning a second. He urged her to partake, but she simply pretended to sip from her glass.

After dinner she retired to her bedchamber. She worried because aside from a few amenities, Vardeau had not said a word about when or how he would get her out of the country. She dared not anger him by pressing him for answers. Now she dreaded the visit she knew would soon be coming. Indeed, only moments later she heard him push his chair back from the table and walk with heavy steps down the hall to her chamber.

She had put on a lace-trimmed silk nightgown with a plunging neckline that half-exposed her breasts. She felt quite uncomfortable in something so daring compared with the simple cotton convent clothing. But as she lounged in the bed and looked up into the mirror, she saw no simple school girl staring back at her but a fashionable woman of Paris, probably no different from the way the gay women strolling on the avenue would be dressed right now. She recalled her last ride through Paris with her father and it sent a pang of grief through her heart. She mourned for him and felt guilty because she'd had no opportunity to bury him with the honors he deserved. But she had no time to dwell on these thoughts. Barely knocking, Vardeau flung open the door and strode towards her.

Boldly, he began to strip off his clothes. At first, Aimée averted her eyes but then curiosity overcame her and she watched as he bared his muscular body to her. She was intrigued by his smooth skin, strong thighs and calves—and then gasped in horror as she got her first good look at the strange object that had penetrated her the night before.

Vardeau stood there, obviously proud of his virility, and said, "It is a marvelous instrument of pleasure, Aimée. You don't appreciate it yet, but I hope you will learn to. . . ." He approached her as if she was supposed to do something, but she didn't know what he expected. So she sat in the middle of the bed and looked at him blankly.

"Take it in your mouth," he commanded. She recoiled in horror at the thought. Perhaps remembering that she was more virgin than seductress, Vardeau didn't press the issue—this time—but instead, almost flinging himself on her, proceeded to kiss, caress and fondle every inch of her body. Slowly, not rushing or asking her to do anything in return, his hot lips explored up and down all the valleys and contours of her body until her cheeks were burning and she had a strange need that she never had felt before. She longed for him to do something, but she didn't know what. At last, when his mouth and flickering tongue dwelled on her most private place, she closed her eyes to the sight in the mirror and gave herself up to the thrilling twinges and tingling sensations that were shooting through her body. When his lips met hers again, Aimée kissed him back, her tongue meeting his. It was all so new and so strange, and she resented being forced, but Vardeau was a handsome, strong young man, and he honestly seemed to want to please her, too.

This time when he penetrated her, there was a moment of pain, but she felt a wetness down there that contrasted with the dryness of the night before. The girls at school had never dared discuss such an intimate matter as exactly what did go on when a man and woman were alone. Now she was finding out, and it was not entirely unpleasant.

"Move," urged Vardeau, his hips suspended over hers. She didn't know what he meant, so he grasped her hips and forced them to move in rhythm with his. Sore as she still was, she cooperated and sensed his mounting excitement. Soon—apparently forgetting she was even there—Vardeau began plunging in and out of her—his movements accompanied by animal-like grunts and groans that left Aimée praying that she could endure this torture until he was through with her. Again came that curious little cry and shuddering, and then Vardeau was still. The second night was over. But this time, Vardeau slept next to her, one hand on her breast. She lay awake for hours wondering what fate had in store for her.

When she finally awakened the next morning, Vardeau was gone. She bathed and wondered when he would return. The mantle clock ticked off noon and then each hour of the afternoon, but still she did not hear his key in the door. She grew hungry, and ate whatever leftovers she could find, but there was little, and obviously Vardeau took most of his meals out. She tried to read, but her mind kept wandering. She dared not even stare out the windows lest she be seen, so she simply paced the apartment from one end to the other for hours.

It was after nine when Vardeau finally came stumbling in, reeking of liquor and perfume. He was drunk, his eyes glazed, almost wild, and his movements clumsy. He grabbed her and kissed her roughly, his beard irritating her delicate skin. She tried to push him aside but he would not be put off so easily. Any vestige of acting like a gentleman was gone as he pushed her into the bedroom and virtually flung her onto the bed.

He stumbled out of his clothes and pressed his already hard member against her. She cried out as he tried to penetrate her immediately. She was tight and dry and frightened. He sucked at her breasts until they were sore—she was positive they would be black and blue in the morning—and his hips pummeled hers so hard, she could only lie there and pray that he would finish soon. But the liquor must have affected him for the abuse went on for what seemed like hours. "Please, have mercy, please," she implored at one point. "I hurt. I am in pain ." But he no more seemed to care about her feelings than if she'd been some cheap whore he'd bought in an alleyway. Anger welled up, then hate as he used her body until he collapsed, satiated. This time when she pushed him off, he slumped over to one side, snoring loudly.

Overcome with disgust and alarm, Aimée jumped out of bed and paced the drawing room, trying to decide what to do. This was the third night she had spent here, and he had done nothing to indicate that he was making plans for her to escape. How long could she endure being locked up here for his private pleasure—and what would happen to her if he tired of her?

She was pacing up and down when she saw, lying on a table, the leather case he always carried with him. He had been very secretive about it, but now she was certain he would sleep for many hours, so she decided to open it and see what she could learn. She sat in a chair near a candle and began to read the official-looking documents and letters she found inside.

As she read, rage overcame the apathy and hopelessness that had pervaded her soul for the past few days. Here was evidence—letters and instructions from the secret police—proving that her beloved father had been, indeed, betrayed by someone close to him—none other than Vardeau himself. The "trusted" friend Vardeau was the very traitor who had turned in her father. No wonder Vardeau was waiting for her. If she escaped the pistols of the police, she would be helpless and walk right into his clever trap. How she loathed the man!

Aimée knew that she would do anything, even kill him in order to be free. Surely, when he tired of her, he would turn her in—and probably claim a reward from Louis Napoleon for doing so.

She devised a plan. Working swiftly, she gathered up the most incriminating of these documents and put them in an envelope. She carefully replaced the rest of the papers in the case so Vardeau would not immediately suspect she had even read them, and then she hurried into her bedroom. Vardeau was still snoring in his drunken stupor, oblivious to the world. She dressed quietly, put on her coat, found the key, let herself out, and locked him in.

It was a dangerous plan. The streets of Paris were deserted at this time, and so she took a desperate walk and left the envelope in a safe place. Then she hurried back to the apartment, undressed and slept on the couch in the parlor. For the first night since she had become Vardeau's prey, she slept a little better. Now, at least, she had a plan.

A hand shaking her roughly awoke her in the morning. "Why are you sleeping here?" he demanded.

She was instantly clear-headed and determined to carry out her plan. "Sit down, Monsieur Vardeau," she said quite levelly.

"What—you ordering me around?" He laughed aloud, even though he looked quite terrible.

"Sit down," she said again, more sharply this time. "I have something to talk to you about."

Vardeau didn't seem to have much of a sense of humor or appreciate her self-confidence, until he saw her coat on a chair. "Have you been out?" he said in alarm, suddenly realizing that he had been asleep for hours.

"What have you done about getting me out of the country?" Aimée demanded, ignoring his question.

Vardeau became agitated, jumped up and reached toward his briefcase. As he rummaged through it, he realized important papers were missing. He seemed dazed.

"I asked you, what have you done about getting me out of the country?" Aimée repeated.

"What I could. It's a tricky business," Vardeau answered evasively, running a hand through his tousled hair.

"Tell me, Monsieur Vardeau—and tell me truthfully—how long do you intend to keep me prisoner here?"

"Until I tire of you," he answered candidly, "Besides, my fair damsel, the price you are paying for your freedom is not half so great as you pretend it to be. Poor young women are out on the streets of Paris every day and in a year they could not get the fine clothes and toiletries you received for one night's pleasure."

"Pleasure?" Aimée laughed in his face. "It may be pleasure for you, but it is repulsive to me—as you are. I read the papers in your case—and I know that you have no intention of getting me out of the country. So I went out for awhile"—she inclined her head toward her coat—"and now I have some assurance that it would be in your best interests, Monsieur Vardeau, to see that I leave this country safely—and very, very soon."

"Where have you been?" Vardeau asked uneasily.

"Your case, the missing papers. They have been delivered to someone who is instructed to expose you if I am not out of this country safely on the next available ship. Monsieur," Aimée said with a confidence that was sheer bravado, "you have twenty-four hours before those papers are turned over to certain interested parties."

"You devil!" he cried. Apparently he was going to strike her, but thought better of it. There had been some very incriminating papers in that case, and while her father had told her to seek him out, perhaps she did, indeed, know someone else. And obviously she had been out. And, as he searched the apartment, the papers were indeed gone.

"You have hidden them and are play-acting," he accused her in a final attempt to defy her demands.

"You can not find them. I have been out. They are gone. Why waste valuable time? In just hours they will be delivered to people who will be only too happy to shoot you down like a dog . . . ." she warned him ominously. He had no choice. Anguish crossed his handsome features.

He stood up resolutely and said, "I must leave. I have plans to make. But you must promise me that if I get you out of the country, those papers will be returned to me."

"They are in a sealed envelope, and I promise you I will tell you where they can be found. They will not be opened until the time is up. So I suggest that whatever you have to do, monsieur, you hurry. Remember," she said, "you are now in as grave danger as I am."

And as he prepared to leave she said firmly, "Oh, monsieur, I am hungry. I would appreciate it if you would arrange for my meals to be delivered here."

He grunted in sullen assent and then slammed the door on his way out. Aimée sat back and smiled grimly, feeling secure for the first time in days. He had no choice but to obey her. For the first time, she had the upper hand. This power, she vowed on the spot, was something she meant to keep—wherever she went, whatever she did, and whatever became of her.

Chapter 3

Vardeau did as she requested. Her meals were sent up, and it was almost twelve hours before he returned. All the while he was gone, Aimée's worry grew because she thought that she might have gone too far and that Vardeau would not return but instead would send the secret police for her. She was on the verge of gathering up what she could carry and departing when he at last appeared, moody and sullen. She sat quietly, waiting for him to begin. He held back. It was a brutal form of teasing that increased her fears.

"Monsieur Vardeau," she said finally, "time is passing swiftly. In a matter of a few hours, who knows what will happen when those papers are finally examined?"

"Tonight you will board a ship, bound for Mexico," he said curtly.

Her hopes soared. Escape! At last! But instead of betraying her elation, she said very severely, "I warn you that if this is a trick, you'll never live long enough to regret it. Do not play games with me."

"It is the truth," he said simply, sounding like a

beaten man. "The clipper *Republic* will sail at midnight with the tide. I've arranged passage for you."

"First-class passage," she said promptly.

He made an elaborate mock-bow and said, "How else would one expect a lady of your station to travel?" Did she detect a note of irony in his voice? But then he added ominously, "However, I warn you, my dear Mademoiselle Gaudin, that one day you shall pay for this treatment. I don't allow myself to be used this way."

It was all she could do to contain her laughter: To think that Vardeau considered himself to be the injured party when he had already betrayed her father and would have just as easily betrayed her after he had taken his pleasure. "You are getting off lightly," she shot back at him, giving vent to her indignation.

"I suggest you hurry, for we leave soon," he said calmly. The hint of arrogance behind his mock humility worried Aimée, but she had no time to dwell on the possibility that he was tricking her. Once again, she had no choice but to follow through. Behind her lay only treachery and death. Once on the ship, she would decide what to do next.

Promptly at eleven, the brougham that had brought her to Vardeau's apartment arrived to take her to the docks. Vardeau accompanied her in silence. She sighed in relief when she saw the *Republic* tied up. Passengers were embarking and there was much activity. The *Republic* was a sleek clipper, about 2500 tons, one of the first iron ships with wooden planking, and it was a large, three-masted rig obviously capable of great speed. Aimée had heard that a ship like this could cross the Atlantic in only twelve days, sometimes less if the weather was good and the winds were with them.

"Now," Vardeau said at last, "about the stolen papers . . ."

"Monsieur," she replied sweetly, "as the ship sails and I am safely aboard, I will shout down from the rail where you can reclaim them. Not before. Now I will go aboard and to my freedom. You may carry my possessions on board, or at least to the gangplank," she added briskly.

Inwardly her heart was pounding and her pulse was racing but freedom was only a few feet away. However, she trusted him so little, she could not breathe freely until the ship was at sea. Once on deck, she walked to the rail and waited for Vardeau to find a spot on the dock near her. Only a few feet of dank and evil-smelling water separated them. The gangplank was hauled in, the ropes untied, and as the ship began to move, Aimée shouted down at Vardeau, "You will find your precious papers in the sewer half a block from your residence. Look there, in the sewers of Paris, for what you seek!"

By the stiffening of his body she knew he had heard and was furious, but she was too far away by now and it was too dark to see the expression on his face. He stalked off in obvious anger. She smiled to herself in secret satisfaction at how well her bold but flimsy plan had served her. Then she sought out the purser to show her to the cabin Vardeau had reserved for her.

The purser was a middle-aged man with a harried air and a kind expression, and he searched the first-class list for her name. He shook his head and said, "Mademoiselle, there is no provision for a first-class cabin for you. . . ."

Aimée's heart sank because she realized she had thought of everything but money. She was penniless. Vardeau had tricked her. They could turn back the ship. "Oh, wait, mademoiselle," said the purser, "since your name is not on the first-class list, you must be in steerage. . . ."

Aimée realized Vardeau must have achieved some satisfaction from this small victory, but after what she had endured, she also knew she certainly could survive a few days in steerage. Or so she thought until she went below.

"Steerage" was a polite term for one large room amidships. Even though the *Republic* hadn't been at sea for half an hour, the room reeked of days of sweat, urine and filth. No fresh air ever touched these quarters. Aimée gagged at the stench alone, but searched with a will for a space to place her possessions. Soon a sweet-faced, auburn-haired girl of about seventeen, a year or two younger than Aimée, got up from the floor and moved her cheap suitcase to make room for Aimée.

"Thank you," Aimée said, smiling gratefully.

"Indentured girls can't be proud. We have to stick together," the girl replied simply.

"What do you mean, 'indentured'?"

"It means our passage has been paid by someone. I don't know who paid mine, but when we reach Mexico we have to work for two years to pay them back." She sensed Aimée's confusion and asked, "If you aren't indentured, what are you doing here?"

"But, I . . ." Aimée sat down on the floor with a thud. "Damn that man!" she cried out. "Damn him to hell and back."

"I know what you mean," the other girl answered calmly. "I was also betrayed. 'Come live with me,' he said. 'Come share my bed and you'll never want for anything.' But after a month of getting beaten and raped, I had a choice of being thrown out onto the streets—or being sent off to Mexico as a servant. At least I have a chance in Mexico. In two years . . ."

Aimée was in a daze and didn't hear another word the girl said. She could visualize Vardeau laughing at her because he had, in the end, betrayed her again. Two years. . . . But at least she had escaped with her life. What was two years if it meant her freedom? Then she realized the girl had fallen silent and was simply sitting there. "What is your name?" she asked. "Mine is Aimée."

"I'm Marie-Clarice Desmolay," the other girl said.

"You're a pretty child," Aimée said off-handedly.

34

"I'm almost seventeen but I'm no child. I've been raped nine times."

As her eyes grew accustomed to the dimness, Aimée noticed the circles of fatigue under Marie-Clarice's eyes and the hollows in her cheeks. There was a bruise over her left eye.

"Yes, that brings one out of childhood quickly enough," Aimée said, as much to herself as to her companion. "Do you know exactly what happens when we reach Mexico?"

"Yes. As soon as we dock, we will line up and there'll be men waiting to look us over and pick the women they want to take home to work for them."

Aimée could imagine what kind of men would be awaiting them. "It's better than walking the streets of Paris," Marie-Clarice said "and what else is there for girls like us?"

"I assure you I don't intend to become an indentured servant," Aimée declared.

Marie-Clarice frowned and asked, "But how will you manage to escape that fate? You *must* work off your passage; there is no other way."

"I will find a way," Aimée said with more assurance than she felt. She was tired. It had been a nerve-wracking, exhausting day—no, days, she reminded herself. Little more than a week ago she had been an innocent schoolgirl. It seemed to her that an eternity stood between those days and the present. And now this: a wooden floor for a bed, probably some kind of slop for food, and at the end of her journey, the horror of being chosen by a man who undoubtedly would treat her even more brutally than Vardeau had.

Somehow Aimée managed to sleep, using her bundle of clothes as a makeshift pillow and protecting it, with her body, from being stolen. Aimée had noticed how poorly dressed, even ragged, were the women consigned here. She could imagine what they would do if they discovered what finery she had hidden in her bundle. With so many bodies crammed into that one stifling room, she did not need a cover.

When she awoke, she fixed her hair and smoothed out her clothes as best she could. Then she made her way toward the deck for some fresh air. She instinctively knew that steerage passengers were supposed to stay below, but she felt she looked enough like a lady to take the liberty of going above. She had to escape that awful place, even for a few minutes. Boldly, she stepped out onto the deck. It was a clear, chilly morning and she filled her lungs with the fresh air. She was a bit nervous about being stopped by one of the crewmen who hastened around, but then she realized that in the fashionable clothes that Vardeau had bought for her, she surely appeared to be a first-class passenger, not some poor servant girl from steerage.

She grew even more encouraged as she paced the deck when a junior ship's officer saluted her with a cheery good morning. She replied with a warm smile. She was getting away with it! But her spirits sank when she realized that though she could walk the decks all she wanted, it would not get her a meal or a bed. First-class passengers not only had assigned cabins but also assigned tables in the dining room.

After about an hour of promenading on the deck, she grew tired, and it seemed futile to continue the charade. Soon she would have to return to steerage and to the fate that awaited her on a hot, Mexican dock. As she turned towards the steps, a swarthy, portly man of about fifty approached her. He seemed slightly ill, even though the seas were calm, but he removed his hat and bowed gallantly.

"*Buenos días,* señorita," he greeted her.

"*Buenos días,* señor," she replied, for she had learned Spanish when her father had been Ambassador to Mexico. "Are you ill?" she asked him, observing that his hands were shaking slightly.

"A touch of *mal de mer,*" he said. Then it registered that she had spoken to him in flawless Spanish without

the wooden inflection that many people have when
they are not speaking in their native tongue. He looked
at her French clothes and fair skin and said, "You're
not Mexican, are you?"

"I am French, señor, but I can speak Spanish."

"How delightful. May I ask you to share my table
at breakfast?" he asked.

Aimée hesitated. "I would like that very much,
señor, but—"

"—If you are worried that there will not be room at
the table, please don't be concerned. My niece was
supposed to have been traveling with me, but at the
last minute she decided to remain in France, so I have
two places reserved at the breakfast table. You shall
be my niece."

What luck! "In that case, I accept your invitation,"
Aimée said, grateful that she'd at least get one decent
meal before returning below decks.

He offered his arm and together they walked into
the main salon and were promptly seated. No one questioned her presence. Aimée ordered an enormous breakfast of eggs, ham, hot biscuits, fruits, honey, and coffee
—and proceeded to eat every bit of it. It had been days
since she'd last enjoyed her food and suddenly she was
ravenous. If her breakfast companion found her tremendous appetite astonishing, he kept his thoughts to
himself.

"I must introduce myself," her escort said when the
waiters were out of earshot. "I'm Nemecio Miranda."

"You may call me Aimée."

"A pretty name. Where is your cabin, if I may ask?"

"You may, but I won't tell you," she replied coyly,
affecting the manner of the society belles she had so
often observed when out with her father.

"You do not trust me!" he exclaimed. "Look at me,
my dear. I am old enough to be your father."

"*Si*, it's true, but even a grandfather has the power
to charm and the experience to seduce a young girl,"
she observed bluntly.

He laughed aloud and reached across the table to pat her hand. Aimée was amazed at the ease with which she had taken to the role of coquette.

The rest of the meal passed comfortably, even though Aimée was sure she sensed that the man was worried no matter how affable his manners or wide his smile. However, she was more concerned with her own future than with any worries he might have. She was pleasantly surprised when Señor Miranda asked if she would care to dine with him that evening. She graciously accepted and then departed, leaving him at the table. She was almost giddy with glee. The return to steerage dampened her spirits. She had managed to save some scraps and gave them to Marie-Clarice, who ate them greedily, as if she expected someone to reach over her shoulder and steal them away. The girls chatted for a while and then Aimée took a nap. She awoke feeling refreshed and more optimistic.

She changed into another dress from her bundle, trusting it to Marie-Clarice's care with the promise she would bring her more food.

Señor Miranda met her in the dining room at his table a few minutes after she had been seated there. He apologized for his lateness and then complimented her almost endlessly on her beautiful gown and her pretty face. But underneath the Latin gallantry, Aimée sensed his fatigue and uneasiness. As at breakfast, the conversation was light and easy, yet Aimée also sensed that he was on the verge of saying something important but was holding back.

Finally, he cleared his throat and spoke his mind. "Aimée, I am not trying to pry, but I suspect you may be in some sort of trouble, and I think I might be able to help you." In spite of her composure, Aimée's nerves were stretched to the breaking point. Did he suspect she was fleeing her country? However, he seemed to take no notice of her momentary panic. He went on, "You will no doubt think me a devious old man, but this morning I saw you returning to steerage after breakfast. And I also watched this evening to see if you would appear from there to meet me at dinner, which is why I was late. I wanted to be sure. . . ."

Aimée flushed in embarrassment, but looked him squarely in the eye and said, "Yes, I'm a passenger in steerage. A man I trusted tricked me by saying I had a first-class cabin. . . ."

Señor Miranda regarded her gravely. "I have also made a few discreet inquiries into the fate of girls who travel by steerage. And I have been told that they are handed over to men who use them as whores, or worse, as slaves if they tire of their favors. In Mexico, my dear, those two years are not an eternity, but a death sentence." He sighed deeply and shook his head of thick gray hair.

Aimée felt as if her fate suddenly lay in this man's hands. He sighed again and said, "Perhaps there's a way. I'm not sure. You must tell me more about yourself first."

"Señor," she said respectfully but warily—after all, she had been taken in by Vardeau's promises of aid, and she was not going to hand herself over blindly to any man again—"I know no more about you than you know about me."

"Aaaah, that's true. But there's no need to fear me. I'm an important man in Mexico. I have a large estate and I am very wealthy. My name is known everywhere."

"You have, no doubt, a wife and family?" Aimée pressed on.

"I had a wife. She died less than a year ago. I have a brother and a sister, nieces, and nephews, in-laws, but no family. My wife couldn't bear children." He paused, as if in memory, then went on proudly, "But I do have one of the most luxurious homes in all of Mexico."

"And how have you grown so wealthy?"

"Perhaps by luck," he shrugged, "or by perseverance. I'm what you might call a middle man. The fruits of

Mexico's production go through me and the money is paid in Europe. It is an honorable business. . . . But what of you? You're clearly a well-educated young woman, an aristocrat. How do you come to be on your way to Mexico in steerage?"

Aimée studied the man sitting opposite her. Even if she didn't trust him, what good would a wealthy Mexican gain from turning her over to the detested French authorities? Recklessly she decided to tell him the truth. "The French police seek me for having offended Louis Napoleon Bonaparte."

He lifted his thick eyebrows in amazement at how such a young thing could offend an emperor, but said nothing.

"That is, my father offended him," Aimée amended, "and they killed him. Now I am being sought because they think I might know too much." She paused to let this information sink in. If he thought she was valuable because she either knew something or sympathized with the Mexicans, he might not betray her. It was a desperate gamble but the thought of what misery lay concealed in steerage beneath this lavish dining room was enough to spur her on.

Miranda was serious. "You might know too much about what?" he asked. "Your answer is most important to me."

"My father was against the invasion of Mexico. He was also against imposing the puppet emperor, Maximilian."

"One could lose one's head for even voicing such an idea, least of all to the emperor himself," observed Miranda. "Your father must have been a man of great integrity and influence to have said so."

"He was ambassador to Mexico at one time," she added proudly. "I lived with him in Mexico City."

"Aahh, that explains why you speak our language so well." he exclaimed. Aimée could see many thoughts were running through his head as she waited for his next question. "Did you father commit any other 'crimes'?" probed Miranda.

"Yes, it was"—Aimée hesitated—"because he was discovered to be in touch with Juarez. He thought that Maximilian would do more harm than good, that in the end Mexico would rise up and throw the French out."

"*Si*, that is what I also think," Miranda said.

Aimée was relieved to be able to talk freely of her plight with someone who might help her. As Miranda paused—presumably to consider her situation—she detected a subtle change, calculating and satisfied, come over his face; it made her uneasy. When he finally spoke again his eyes were gleaming. "Señorita, he said, "I believe we can help each other."

Aimée was startled at the thought that she could help him. "How?" she asked.

"All you need to do is play a simple role for a very short time. Since my niece wasn't able to accompany me, I have more than adequate room for you in my suite."

"Señor," she began, a warning note in her voice.

"Please, I assure you I'm a gentlemen with the highest regard for a lady."

The devil you are, Aimée thought, but she nodded to encourage him to tell her more.

He poured himself a glass of wine, gulped it down and signaled the waiter for a fresh bottle—the third one that evening—before continuing. "You recall I said my niece wasn't able to return with me from France? She is my sole heir and I was looking forward to her return, not only because of my affection for her, but also because I felt that her presence would serve more or less as a slap in the faces of my greedy relatives, a reminder that they won't always be able to live on my largesse and rob me blind. But she refused to return, preferring to continue her studies in France."

"But what has all this to do with me?" Aimée asked.

"What I offer you, señorita, is the opportunity to

help me play a little trick on my relatives. If you'll pose as my niece for just a little while, I'll have the satisfaction of seeing my relatives make fools of themselves, trying to win your friendship and generosity and thinking their future secure. Perhaps it sounds heartless to play such a trick, but you'd consider it a small meanness if you knew the extent of their greed and devious ways. In return, I will send you anywhere you wish to start a new life—and with enough money to get settled comfortably. What do you think?"

Aimée saw that Señor Miranda was actually sweating. Beads of perspiration covered his brow. He was in some kind of difficulty, of that she was sure, and somehow this strange offer was connected with it. But there had to be a catch.

"But how can I do this, señor? Your relatives will surely be aware that I'm not your true niece?"

Her question seemed to give him hope that she might go along with his scheme, for he visibly relaxed. "They'll accept you if I say so. The last time they saw Angela she was two months old. Her father was French and took her to Paris when she was an infant. But he, too, is dead now. Her mother, my sister, died when Angela was born. So who is there to say that you are not Angela?"

The more Miranda talked ,the more reasonable the scheme sounded to Aimée. "Besides," he was saying, "you and my niece would fit the same general description: same age, same height, blue eyes . . . And I repeat, no one in Mexico has seen her since she was an infant. And she will never return. I assure you that your secret will be quite safe."

"But how can I pretend to be your niece when I know absolutely nothing about her or your family?" Aimée reasoned.

"My niece was a very special young lady. She took great pride in her Mexican heritage, and she wrote long letters to her relatives there. And they wrote back. She saved all these letters, also a detailed diary that will give you all the information you need. And I'll answer any other questions you may have."

"But I know nothing of your family," Aimée said doubtfully.

"There's time to learn," he reassured her. "I also have albums you can study. Angela had them and now they're in my suite. You'll know everything there is to know about a family you have never met in person. Anyway, all of her information came from their letters, too. So you see, it will be easy."

Easy it wouldn't be, but Aimée felt she could do it. "You'll send me to the United States?" she asked doggedly.

"*Sí,* I swear it," he answered fervently.

"Won't your relatives be suspicious if your 'niece' leaves?"

"My dear, these relatives of mine live with me only through my tolerance. I detest the lot of them. They greedily await my death. If I send you away, my sole heir, it means you are no longer in my favor. Of that, I can assure you, they will heartily approve."

"That is a very attractive offer," Aimée admitted. What did she have to lose? In the United States she would begin a new life. The thing that bothered her was the conviction that Miranda was holding something back from her, something very important. . . .

"Very well," she said at last. "I accept your offer."

"You won't regret it in the least my dear," Miranda assured her, a broad grin breaking out over his face. The waiters were standing at a discreet distance, for most of the other diners had already finished their meals and departed. When Miranda stood up, he was unsteady, due both to the wine and the rolling of the ship. He asked Aimée to accompany him to his room to give her a chance to see all the letters and albums.

She agreed, but said, "First I must go back and arrange that my things be cared for."

"My cabin is Suite B. I'll be waiting," he said.

Down in steerage, Aimée searched for Marie-Clarice and handed her the food she had wrapped in a napkin.

"I wondered what happened to you," the girl said between enormous bites of food. Aimée realized the girl was starving. "Oh, this is so very good. Thank you so much, mademoiselle."

"Please take care of my things," said Aimée, "and I will see that you have food. I will return as quickly as possible. If I don't return in a day, two at the most, please tell the captain I went to suite B."

"A man?" Marie-Clarice smiled knowingly.

"Yes, a man, but I'm not sure of him. So if I'm not back in two days, please tell the captain."

Aimée went back on deck a few minutes later without being stopped. It was marvelous, she thought, what proper clothing could do. She knocked on Miranda's door. He opened it immediately. The room reeked of brandy and she saw with alarm that Señor Miranda's face was contorted from the amount of alcohol he'd drunk.

She hesitated for a moment, but it was long enough for him to grab her wrist and pull her close. "Señor," she said, struggling to free herself, "let me go or I'll scream loud enough to wake the entire ship."

"Need I remind you that I can simply throw you back into steerage—or even turn you over to the authorities as a traitoress?" he leered. He covered her mouth with foul-tasting kisses.

She relaxed for a moment, pretending to return his passion—then wrenched free of him, and backed away quickly, ready to fight.

Miranda laughed. "What will you do now, Aimée? All I need to do is say I discovered you robbing my suite. No one will believe an indentured girl, much less a traitoress."

Aimée knew what he said was true, but she was angry to have been trapped like this. "Very well. But I warn you I won't give myself willingly."

In his drunken stupor he mumbled, "I like a woman

with spirit. But I suggest you at least pretend to go along because I'm your only chance to escape."

Aimée stood there, judging the distance to the entrance door and just how fast the drunken Miranda could probably move. When she thought she saw her chance she bolted for the exit. Oddly enough Miranda didn't move a muscle. But when she got to the door, it was locked. She turned and faced him like a cornered animal.

"You have no choice, Aimée. I am a man who needs a woman, but I will be gentle with you—and generous. Don't fight me."

His words brought back the image of Vardeau, sending a shiver of terror through her, and she cast her eyes desperately about the suite for another means of escape. If she could reach the door to the other cabin, she might be able to close it and lock him out. He was moving toward her now, but he seemed disconcerted by her wandering glance.

One arm reached out and grabbed at her dress, tearing the delicate silk bodice until one breast was exposed. Aimée cowered, trying to cover her nakedness. "Ah, beautiful," Miranda murmured. With his other hand he lashed out and ripped away the top of her dress as if it had been made of paper. One nail left a scratch that drew blood across her left breast. Now the brutal Miranda was tearing off her dress and fumbling simultaneously with the buttons on his pants. Aimée managed to wriggle away from him and run towards the door leading to the second cabin. Luck was with her. The door was open. She darted inside, turned the key and threw her weight against the door, waiting for the assault she knew would come soon.

What a quandary! Perhaps she was a fool for resisting his advances. Might it not have been easier, in the long run, to have suffered him for a few minutes in order to live like a lady aboard ship and later, in Mexico? Now surely she would be doomed to travel steerage class. As she looked in desperation around the dimly lit cabin, her eyes grew accustomed to the shadows and she finally was able to distinguish a bunk. She gasped with surprise to see that it was occupied. Someone lay beneath the covers, someone who was not aroused by the noise she had made when she ran in.

Aimée drew close, hoping this person might be able to help her. Aimeé found herself looking down on the serene face of a girl who could have been little more than nineteen. This was a very lovely girl with chestnut hair, a most attractive face . . . a very still face . . . too still. Aimée reached down and touched a cheek cold as marble.

Chapter 4

Aimée drew back with a little cry as she realized the girl was dead.

There was a lamp beside the berth, and Aimée used a match to light it. She pulled back the sheet and saw the naked body was bruised in several places and there were purple and red marks around the throat, for the girl had been strangled savagely. Quickly, Aimée covered her again. She walked weakly to a chair and almost fell into it.

Surely the dead girl was Miranda's niece. And just as surely she herself had just escaped a similar fate. The horror of this revelation jarred her senses, but she forced herself to keep thinking how she could use this new information. She realized she now had a weapon against Miranda. He was in no less a predicament than she was. Realizing she was half-naked, she took one of the dead girl's dresses. It fit perfectly. Composing herself, she went to the door between the two cabins, unlocked it, and stood in the doorway, calmly.

Miranda, bent over in a chair, his face buried in his

hands, rocked back and forth in misery. When he became aware of her presence he looked up and said pleadingly, "It was an accident. Believe me, it was an accident, dear Aimée. I did not mean to kill her. I was fought me . . . and threatened to tell everyone what kind of man I was. In anger I tried to silence her, but I went too far. Before I knew it she was dead."

"And so when you saw me you thought that I could pass as your niece? You *had* to do something, didn't you?"

"No one saw her come aboard," began Miranda, "for we arrived early. We went directly to our cabin, and then it happened. That was why I approached you this morning. I was very eager for your help, and I knew you could pass as my niece once I learned you could speak Spanish. Will you help?" he added almost pitifully. "I will pay well."

"Tell me your plan," she said, hoping that they could reach a compromise so she could remain in first class during the voyage and escape once they reached Mexico.

Eagerly he said, "It's simple. You'll be with me for the rest of the voyage. I will introduce you as Angela Fuchard, the only child of my dead sister. No one will question it. Like you, Angela lived in France all her life and attended convent school. When it was time for her to return home, I went to get her."

It did seem simple enough, Aimée admitted to herself. "And after we go to your hacienda, then what?" she asked, playing out her role to convince him that she intended to go along with his entire scheme, although now she was forming a scheme of her own.

"I will say that you wish to continue your schooling in the United States, and I'll send you there. I swear it," he vowed, sounding most serious.

"Even if I do agree to go along with your plan, how do you expect to explain the fact that there's a dead girl in your cabin?"

"I'll throw the body overboard—tonight," he re-solved.

"If you lay a hand on me," she warned, "I'll report you instantly. I'm in desperate straits myself, but not half so serious as yours."

"I'm a dead man unless you help me," he admitted. Aimée had bluffed him. He could have disposed of the body himself and kept her prisoner, but now that she knew his hideous secret he would be at her mercy as well.

"I will be your niece," announced Aimée.

He sat back in his chair and wiped the sweat off his brow. *"Gracias,* señorita. You won't be sorry, and I promise you you won't have to worry about yourself or your safety. I swear I won't harm you in any way. I need you," he added, almost pitifully.

"I wouldn't believe you before an altar of a thousand candles," Aimée shrugged off his promises. "But there is one way I can feel more secure."

"What is that?" he asked eagerly.

"If there was someone else traveling with us, a duenna, a chaperone. Then, and only then, if she slept in that room with me, would I not fear that you'd go back on your words."

"Nonsense!" he blustered. "Where can we find a chaperone?"

"There is a girl in steerage. I can bring her to you and tell the captain that I saw her while taking a walk and I think she might do as my personal maid. Either you go along—or. . . ." She let her threat trail off, but if she could bring Marie-Clarice up here, it would not only give her protection but an ally in escaping once they reached Mexico. Yes, it seemed like a perfect solution. Miranda agreed grudgingly.

"And you will pay her passage so she will no longer be sold as an indentured servant when we arrive," Aimée insisted.

"You drive a hard bargain," Miranda finally said, apparently deciding that for the time being Aimée

would have her way. He poured himself a giant tumbler
of rum and downed it in a gulp. Then he suggested they
wait until later that night, when Aimée could check
that the decks were clear so that he could throw
Angela's body overboard.

It nagged at Aimée's conscience that she had agreed
to be an accessory to this man's crime, but she realized
that after the suffering she had been through, this was
simply a tiny compromise, for it meant she could now
pose as Angela Fuchard. What good would the cabin
do a dead girl, anyway? But there was an uneasy silence
in the room for Aimée no more trusted this man than
she did Vardeau. Not wanting to be alone with him in
the cabin until it was late enough to dispose of the body
undetected, she suggested that they should stroll on
deck.

She and Miranda, arm in arm, walked the deck as
casually as they could that night. He nodded amiably
to the ship's officers and to the other passengers. He
was very good at fooling people, Aimée realized. Aimée
insisted they remain on deck as long as possible. Because it was growing stormy, they spent some time in
the lounge, a small room where some people were
gambling. Miranda downed several more brandies while
they sat there. Finally it was late enough. . . .

They returned to the cabin to the accompaniment of
a rising wind and the creaking of the ship. "Do you
wish me to have a look first?" Aimée asked.

"If you'd be so kind."

She stepped out onto the deck, leaving the cabin
door open. As she reached the railing and scanned the
deck for any sign of other passengers or crewmen,
Miranda blew out the lamp so no light would be seen
coming from their cabin. The wind whipped her hair
about, but there was not a soul in sight. She made a
small signal with her hand and a second later Miranda
emerged with the dead girl in his arms. He had only to
cross the few feet of deck and toss the body over the
railing. The wind and the rough sea covered up the

sound of the body slipping beneath the surface. She was gone without a trace.

Both of them hurried back to the cabin. Miranda downed some rum, raising the bottle to his lips in his haste. Some of the liquid splashed on his clothes, but he seemed not to notice. His hands were shaking and his eyes were bloodshot. "Don't think this hasn't disturbed me," he said to a watchful Aimée. "I loved Angela. I'd give my life if I could bring her back." As Miranda's speech began to slur, Aimée became apprehensive. "It was all done in a drunken passion," he said.

"It's time to find the girl who will stay with me," Aimée announced, even though the hour was so late. She dared not be alone with him while he was in such a drunken state.

"Bear with me a moment more," he pleaded, leaning forward and speaking earnestly. "I have an offer to make you. If you agree to stay with me after we return to Mexico, instead of going to the United States, I will make you my heir. In fact, I've already done so, assuming you'll impersonate my niece. The will I made is in my portfolio. You may see it. You may have a copy for yourself if you suspect I'll change my mind. The will is irrevocable. This is a provision I insisted upon in case my dear relatives rendered me incompetent or challenged the will. They're not above it. But you must promise me," he added anxiously, "that you'll never let them have any part of my money."

"No," Aimée insisted. "It's impossible if for no other reason than that I don't like or trust you. Don't ask me again."

His mood was changing. He did not like being challenged by a mere girl. "You are a foolish girl not to take advantage of a situation that would someday make you a very rich woman."

Aimée shook her head and started to rise from her chair. "I shall be a danger to you and one day you'll decide that the danger is too great. Or you'll get drunk and lose control of yourself."

He bent toward her and placed a hand on her knee, gripping it so tightly she feared it would be black and blue. "You could make me a very happy man, Aimée." His foul breath blasted her nose. "I would not demand your body too often. Otherwise, you'll be alone in a strange country with no money and nowhere to go. True, I'll give you some money, but it wouldn't last. You'd be better off with me."

"I know the United States. I speak English fluently. There are always opportunities in a country like the United States."

"You're wrong," he said flatly. "The United States is divided and a war has begun between the North and the South. Nothing is normal in a country where neighbor is fighting neighbor and brother his own brother. You'll find no opportunity anywhere you go, just war."

Aimée tried to free herself from his grasp. "I insist on bringing that girl from steerage here. That was our agreement."

"Agreement. Agreement. What is that? Look here, I'll show you how generous I am. Wait—you'll see."

He rose and made his way unsteadily to one of two brass-bound wooden trunks in his cabin. He took a key out, opened the lid, rummaged in the contents, and returned to stand before her with a heavy gold necklace in which a score of dazzling diamonds and wine-red rubies were mounted. It was clearly quite an extraordinary, and valuable, piece of jewelry. Aimée had never seen anything like it before, even on the richest ladies of Paris.

"Let me put it on," he said. "See yourself in it, Aimée." He stepped behind her and draped the necklace around her throat. The clasp was fastened and then his hands came down, slipping beneath the low neckline of the gown. His hot breath was rasping in her ear as he cupped each breast in his hands. He gripped them so hard it hurt, and she cried out. One hand came up and clamped her mouth. She tried to tear free but he was too strong and he tossed her onto the bed. She hit the wall and bounced off. She was in a daze, her head hurt, and she realized she might be killed just as his niece had been, for in his drunken state he didn't realize how strong he was. If she resisted again, she'd be dead.

Then she saw the rum bottle rolling on the floor with the rocking of the ship. One good rock and she'd be able to grab it. The storm was raging and the ship tilted violently. As Miranda lurched toward her she swooped up the bottle and swung it squarely at the top of his head. He went down without a sound. She was just beginning to feel safe when he sat up, stunned but still conscious.

"You ungrateful bitch," he cursed, struggling to his feet. "I'll give Angela company in those black depths before the night is over if you dare resist me again."

Aimée darted out the cabin door wildly. He was right behind her, so close she could smell his rum-soaked breath. Just as he was about to put his hands on her neck, the ship lurched violently in the rough seas. Thrown off balance, the drunken Miranda fell against the rail, made a vain grab at it, and then went over the side. Aimée ran to the rail, gripped it, and peered down into the roaring blackness, but there wasn't a sign of him."

She was about to shout for help but the howling winds and snapping sails would have drowned out her weak cry even if there had been someone on deck. The storm had sent the passengers into their cabins, and the crew to safer, dryer quarters. Aimée groped her way back into the cabin and sank heavily into a chair, numbed by the horror of what had just happened. She bent over and wept bitterly, not for Nemecio Miranda, whose death certainly seemed some sort of retribution for what he had done to his own niece and what he most certainly would have done to her. No, her tears were for her dead father and for her own desperate fight for survival. Would she ever find peace and safety?

A feeling of dullness and emptiness had melded into

calm by the time her tears dried. She sat wondering what to do next. If she revealed her identity when she reached Mexico, now controlled by France, she would certainly be sent back to Paris—in chains. And she knew the fate that awaited her there. It was impossible to leave the ship as Aimée Gaudin, daughter of Emile Gaudin, traitor.

She felt she had only one course of action: To elude the French and somehow reach the United States. There she would be safe. But she could accomplish this only by taking the identity of Angela Fuchard. . . .

Hadn't Miranda given her the dead girl's necklace? Didn't Angela's clothes and general description fit her? Hadn't she been seen and introduced to the other passengers as his niece? Why not continue the masquerade? Then the wooden trunk caught her attention. Hadn't he said something about papers, albums, a will? She steadied herself and began searching through the trunk.

Inside it she found documents, many bearing official-looking seals. But one, unsealed, was a copy of Miranda's will, and he had not lied to her about that. It was brief. It was clear. No one on earth could break it. And it named Angela Fuchard as his sole heir, bequeathing her everything he owned, earned and possessed in this world. But Angela was dead. And Aimée could take her place if Aimée Gaudin were to vanish forever and Angela Fuchard was reborn. Hadn't Nemecio said he'd give his life to have Angela live again . . . ? The irony brought a flitting smile to her lips.

It was her only chance. If Aimée Gaudin were to declare herself at the docks, she was doomed. Angela Fuchard would be welcome, perhaps not warmly, but at least not at gunpoint. The decision made, she looked about carefully. The cabin reeked of rum. The bottle she'd struck him with still rolled to and fro on the floor. Leaving everything as it was, she locked herself into the second cabin, where she rummaged among the clothes Angela had brought with her, and found an embroidered nightgown. She slipped into it, and then into the bed where the dead girl had lain, even though it gave her shivers. But she felt she had no choice if her desperate plan was to succeed. She settled herself down for the night so that when they came for her—if they did, if Nemecio was missed—it would appear as if she'd just been wakened from sleep.

But sleep simply wouldn't come. Finally, she lit the lamp and pulled the porthole shade shut. Then she began going through Angela's baggage. The girl may have been shy, as Miranda had told her, but she was not shy about spending money. Everything she possessed was of the finest quality. But what caught Aimée's interest were the packets of letters from the Miranda relatives and two large, leather-bound diaries that had belonged to Angela. Apparently while living in the strict convent, she had poured all her thoughts and feelings into these pages. They were filled with her tiny, clear handwriting beginning with the childish penmanship of a ten-year-old girl and ending with adult writing entered just days before this voyage. The diary revealed a lonely, cloistered young woman yearning for excitement and love.

Aimée skimmed the pages. During the long voyage she would have ample time to study it and absorb the details of the diary as well as the letters. By the time she landed, Aimée would know as much about her "family" as Angela herself.

Fatigue began to set in just before dawn, but although she was extremely tired, she was still unable to sleep for some time. As she lay in that bed she wondered if she would ever be able to forget the horror of seeing Miranda heartlessly throw the body of his own niece overboard—or the sight of him lunging for her, intent on having his way with her or killing her too—and slipping into the sea without a sound.

Finally she slept, but awoke with a start of fear. The instant her eyes opened she remembered the events of the night before. So far no one had come to look for Miranda. So it was up to her to create the alarm.

She chose a morning gown of Angela's and as with the dress the night before, it could have been made for her, the fit was so perfect. She unlocked the door of Angela's room and opened it slowly, as if half-expecting Miranda to be standing there waiting for her. The smell of rum in the close cabin was overwhelming. She held her breath, walked through the room and stepped out onto the sun-drenched deck. It was a beautiful day and the sea was calm again. She made her way to the salon and stood in the doorway, making a show of looking over the passengers already breakfasting.

The headwaiter approached and Aimée steeled herself for the scene she was about to play out. From this moment on she was Angela Fuchard. Aimée Gaudin had died along with Miranda.

"Good morning," she said pleasantly. "Have you seen my uncle this morning?"

"He is not here, señorita," the headwaiter said respectfully.

"Oh, dear," Aimée said, appearing slightly agitated. "He wasn't in his cabin, and I've looked everywhere on the decks. I supposed he would be waiting for me here."

"I'm sure he is strolling the decks and you simply didn't see him," the headwaiter said.

Pretending to go along, but feeling a genuine sense of alarm in that he would somehow know she was an impostor, Aimée tried to say lightly, "Well, perhaps he is just taking his morning constitutional. I'm sure he'll be here soon. I'll order and await him."

She was led to Miranda's table and ordered her breakfast. She kept glancing at the door, even though she knew he would not appear. She saw the headwaiter whispering to a ship's officer after half an hour had passed and she was still sitting there alone. He disappeared, and perhaps fifteen or twenty minutes later, another officer appeared and approached her table.

"It isn't like uncle to be late for breakfast," Aimée fretted.

The officer smiled politely and said, "Perhaps when the señorita has finished her breakfast, she would come to the captain's cabin. He'd like to discuss the matter with you."

"The matter?" she asked, feigning bewilderment. "What matter?"

"The disappearance of your uncle—"

"—Disappearance?" She rose quickly. "Do you think something has *happened* to him?"

"If the señorita wishes to see the captain now," the officer said, his face blank, "I will be happy to escort her to his cabin."

"Why, yes, of course," she quickly agreed.

The captain of the *Republic* had the bearing of a man who was in command of every situation, but he seemed just slightly at a loss with Aimée. So he dispensed with the amenities and began, "Please, señorita, tell me when you last saw your uncle? We know both of you dined together, but what happened after that? Where did you go? Where did he go?"

"To our suite. We strolled for a while, and then I went to sleep."

"And your uncle?" he probed gently.

"Ah," she reddened and acted as if she was holding something back out of shame.

"Señorita, we know he was drinking heavily. He drank in the salon and the cabin reeked of liquor. He must have been quite drunk. Tell me, we found a bottle on the floor. It was almost empty. Do you know when he opened it?"

"Why, yes, last night just before I went to bed. I remember because he cursed the cork for he had trouble removing it."

"That's all we need to know," said the captain decisively. "If he drank all that run last night in addition to what else we know he drank . . ."

"Have you found him?" Aimée broke in, playing the role of the concerned niece.

"I'm afraid not, señorita. Since there was a heavy

sea last night—and he probably stepped out for a breath of air—he probably fell," the captain hesitated, "overboard," he added at last. "We have searched the entire ship and he is nowhere to be found. There is no other place he could be. I am sorry, señorita, but—"

At this, Aimée burst into tears. It was as if the anxiety of playing the role, the tension, and everything that had happened to her came rushing out in a profusion of genuine tears.

The captain was a good man, but he obviously felt at a loss with this young lady weeping before him. So he continued talking. "I offer you my most sincere condolences, señorita. A wireless has been sent to your family so they will know and meet you at the dock."

She raised her tear-stained face and asked beseechingly, "But have you truly searched *everywhere?* If he did go overboard, can we not turn around and go back for him?"

"It is hours since he disappeared. We couldn't possibly find him, and if we did, he'd be dead by now anyway. There is nothing more we can do."

Aimée fled from the cabin without another word and ran all the way back to her cabin. There she sat down and continued to weep. But slowly, as her tears subsided, she realized she was safe. They had not questioned that she was Miranda's niece, and they had not been the least bit suspicious about the nature of his death. They drew the conclusion he'd been drunk and gone overboard. In a way, that was the truth. Only he'd fallen overboard because he'd lunged for her in his drunken lust and lost his footing.

A steward knocked at the door. He had come to her on the captain's behalf to see if there was anything he could do for her to ease her grief. As graciously as she could, Aimée told him to tell the captain that she appreciated his concern, but for the time being, preferred to be left alone.

She managed to get through the day remarkably well. Word quickly spread through the ship about what had happened to her uncle and a steady stream of respectful visitors came to express their regrets and to offer her company and assistance. The most difficult thing, Aimée soon discovered, was not in playing the role of the niece-in-mourning but of answering to her name. Angela Fuchard. She said the name aloud, over and over, and resolved that for her charade to succeed, she had to forget that there ever had been an Aimée Gaudin. From this moment on she *was* Angela Fuchard.

Another day passed. It was time to make her move. Besides, she remembered she had given Marie-Clarice the instructions to raise the alarm if she hadn't returned in two days at the latest. Even though Aimée doubted Marie-Clarice was bold enough, she decided to act first. She paid a visit to the captain. She knew it made a deep impression for one so young to be dressed head to toe in black.

"Captain, sir," she began respectfully. "I have a request which I hope you can grant me."

"If it's within my powers, I will be pleased to be of any assistance to you, my dear señorita," he said stoutly.

"It is this," began Aimée timidly. "I do not relish the thought of traveling alone, and it would be very helpful if I could have some company. I understand that you are carrying a number of passengers who will become indentured servants when they arrive in Mexico. Would it be possible for you to arrange for me to have one of these girls as my personal maid?"

"It's an unusual request, I must admit," the captain said slowly. "It's never been done before, but these are not ordinary circumstances. I don't see why you couldn't. But you realize that their passage must be paid?"

"I understand. Uncle," she made the sign of the cross when she mentioned his name and glanced heavenward "told me all about these girls—and what would happen to them when they reached Mexico. There was one girl, in fact, whom he had seen and thought might work for him."

"If you know her name, I'll have her sent to your cabin immediately, señorita," the captain decided. Obviously he hoped it worked out so he wouldn't have to feel responsible for a young woman traveling alone on a ship with so many men—both passengers and crewmen.

"It is Marie-Clarice," she said. "I do not know her last name."

"Fine. In a matter of minutes she will be with you. If you like her, then she is yours. And," he added, "since your uncle's passage was paid and he is no longer here to take advantage of it, by a small manipulation I could enter this girl as a first-class passenger in place of your uncle. I'm sure we'll have no trouble finding her, but if she doesn't please you, I'm sure one of the other girls will."

A half hour later, a ship's officer brought a wide-eyed Marie-Clarice to the cabin. Obviously ill-at-ease at being summoned, she still had sense enough not to show any sign of recognizing Aimée. Playing the role of Angela, Aimée studied the girl for a moment, then said to the ship's officer, "I like her appearance. Clean her up and she should do. But first let me talk to her alone for a few minutes to see if she has the qualities I am seeking. Then I will advise the captain of my decision."

It was a very reasonable request. The officer saluted and quietly withdrew to wait outside the door for her decision. The minute he was gone Aimée rose and embraced Marie-Clarice.

"I'm so glad to see you," she whispered into her ear. "Much has happened and even more will. Go along with me and then we will have time to talk freely."

They held a mock "interview" for a few minutes, and then Aimée motioned for Marie-Clarice to open the door and summon the officer. "She'll do," Aimée said casually. "Please thank the captain for me for seeing to the matter so quickly."

The officer saluted again and was gone. Now they could talk freely. Aimée told Marie-Clarice all that had happened since they had last met, except the details surrounding Miranda's death. Her experience since her father's betrayal had taught her not to be quite so trusting . . . of anyone. If Marie-Clarice proved to be a loyal friend, and if there was a good reason, then someday Aimée would tell her. For the time being, she told Marie-Clarice only as much as she needed to know.

"And it's a way out for both of us," she concluded. "If I land in Mexico as Aimée Gaudin, the French authorities will surely be on the lookout for me. And you, if you are lucky, will wind up the mistress of some Mexican. So let us play this masquerade long enough to see us both to safety. But it is only fair to warn you that this is dangerous. If you want to back out, do so now."

Marie-Clarice shook her head decisively. "I shall be frightened every single minute, but I'll be happy to be your maid and companion—and grateful for the opportunity to escape my fate. We must take advantage of this good fortune."

"Then it is agreed. Remember, I am Señorita Angela Fuchard. You must always bear that in mind. It won't be easy for either of us, but if we make just one slip, we are finished," Aimée warned her ominously.

"I'll be very, very careful," promised Marie-Clarice.

"Now," said Aimée in a very businesslike tone, "here is what we are going to do. During the rest of the voyage we'll dine together and you'll sleep in the small room. And together we'll study all the papers until, by the time we land, we'll know everything there is to know about Angela Fuchard."

"Oh, I'm so excited," exclaimed Marie-Clarice.

"Yes, but remember that when we land, Miranda's relatives may pretend to be happy to see us, but once they learn the contents of his will, they will be our enemies and take any opportunity to rid themselves of us." Aimée thought over her plan and spotted one flaw. "One indentured girl will be missing when they call the roster. Me! What can we do about that so they will not be suspicious?"

"Dear, Angela—and see I remember to use your name already," began Marie-Clarice, "you don't have a thing to worry about. They don't know exactly how many girls are aboard. Some were practically kidnapped and brought here, and you came aboard just before we sailed, not even long enough to have been noticed before you met Señor Miranda. I assure you that you need not worry about that or about me. I will be eternally grateful," Marie-Clarice said with a fervor that Aimée could not doubt.

"Good," Aimée said in relief. "Now let us begin our brand new life."

Chapter 5

The clipper *Republic* made a swift and uneventful journey and in twelve days was tied off the coast of Veracruz. Marie-Clarice, who had played her role beautifully, was now so apprehensive that Aimée feared she would give them away. She had never been out of France before and everything about this new land frightened her.

"Look," Marie-Clarice exclaimed, pointing toward the dock, "those huge, circling black birds are so ugly."

"Zopilotes—vultures," Aimée explained patiently. "They are birds of prey who keep the streets clean of anything dead. Don't be afraid of them; be thankful they do their job well."

"Are we to live in this city? Or one like it?" Marie-Clarice asked, looking in horror at the slovenly hovels and dirty streets that spilled down to the docks and which seemed to stretch before them as far as the eye could see.

"We are going to Mexico City," replied Aimée, "and

it's nothing like this. It is a long distance but the city is modern and not at all like this pigpen."

"I know so little about Mexico, Angela. Is it true that France owns it?" Marie-Clarice asked.

"Yes, but only by the points of its bayonets—and not for long. This is a country where revolution is seething just below the surface . . . but let us not talk more of such matters. We have much to do. Our journey has not ended, it has just begun," she said briskly, hoping to take Marie-Clarice's mind off what might happen. "We must learn to live among them as peacefully as possible. Now be courageous. And remember, once we reach Mexico City, our future should be bright . . . if we are clever."

Marie-Clarice embraced her and she could feel the girl's heart fluttering as if it were going to burst. Suddenly Aimée felt years older than Marie-Clarice, even though only two years separated them. So much had happened to her. She held Marie-Clarice for a moment then said softly, "When I left France, I vowed never to be afraid of anything again in my life, to take whatever opportunity might come my way. I had to grow up quickly—or die. You must learn to do the same."

"But you're well educated," protested Marie-Clarice.

"And you will learn from me," declared Aimée. "Besides, you are my servant girl, and it is your duty to keep silent and assist me. But watch me. See how to behave. You are smart, you will catch on quickly. Now, since you are my servant, you must act like one. From this moment on, our lives depend on carrying out our new identities. I am the Señorita Angela Fuchard and you are my personal maid."

"*Oui,* mademoiselle," Marie-Clarice replied quietly.

"But, my sweet Marie-Clarice, even though you must act like my servant, we will still be friends. And remember, that even though you didn't know me in Paris, we met on this trip when I bought you out of indenture. So if people try to question you, you know nothing more about me than I have told you."

Marie-Clarice nodded and then smiled gratefully. "I will not forget, Señorita Fuchard."

Inwardly Aimée breathed a sigh of relief that she had restored some confidence in the girl. Although Aimée wasn't half so self-assured as she appeared, Marie-Clarice seemed dangerously unnerved, and she didn't want to chance that the girl would give them away. Thank goodness she had no idea of the journey that lay before them. From Veracruz to Mexico City, it would be a long, grueling trip by carriage and train. Not only were the roads poor, but there was also the danger always of being held up by bandits. And being French, they would not fare well at their hands.

Aimée shut out these troublesome thoughts as a boat arrived to begin taking first-class passengers onshore. As she and Marie awaited their turn, they noticed that another boat had arrived and watched as a number of frightened-looking indentured girls were herded aboard like so much cattle.

As they approached the shore, they saw the hapless girls standing in a row while Mexican men circled them like vultures. Some leered, others boldly reached out to touch the girls. Aimée and Marie-Clarice couldn't help shuddering to think how close they had come to a fate such as that.

The driver of a carriage approached Aimée and gave her an elaborate bow before announcing he had been hired to take them to the train station. What he called a train station turned out to be a rickety-looking shanty. Stopped in front of it on the tracks were four dilapidated cars, which waited for them. The car they were put on contained a few Mexicans, and several French soldiers who sullenly turned their backs when their mild advances were ignored. The forty-five mile trip was agonizingly slow, and the car was stifling. Even more, the air was filled with soot and dirt from the wood-burning locomotive which chugged along.

At La Soledad they transferred to a large stagecoach which, happily, was in their sole possession all the way to Cordoba. The ride over the mountains was treacherous, with muddy roads and cliff-hanging turns along a highway so narrow it seemed impossible the wide coach would fit. There were drops so steep that Aimée turned her face away from the window while Marie-Clarice alternated between covering her eyes and blessing herself, keeping her head bent in fervent prayer.

There were two more stops and a change of coach, one at Orizaba, another at Puebla—before they finally rode, exhausted, into Mexico City. Here was civilization, at last. When their coach reached the wide avenue, they found it strewn with flowers and the sidewalks lined with Mexicans, dressed in their finery. Marie-Clarice's spirits finally brightened. She made a tiny motion with her head toward some brightly clad French soldiers.

"How handsome they are," she exclaimed. "Every one of them."

Aimée laughed. "It's their uniforms that enchant you. Beware," she said, then laughed, realizing she sounded like an old duenna herself. But even she had to admit the soldiers looked handsome in their baggy crimson trousers with white gaiters and turbans that trailed scarlet tassels. The *Pantalons Rouges*—the Foreign Legion—as they were called, were lined up behind the people to make sure they would behave. Mexican lancers were posted at strategic positions for the same purpose. Suddenly the driver of the coach was shouted at by the soldiers and commanded to pull to the curb. Only then did Aimée see the reason for all their grandeur. Down the avenue came a platoon of French soldiers, followed by another of Mexican lancers. The crowd began to shout and then they saw a gilded landau. It had a royal crest on it, and inside, in regal state, could be seen the Emperor Maximilian and Carlota, his empress.

As the coach passed, Aimée told Marie-Clarice as much as she knew about this Austrian who had been sent to Mexico as emperor.

"Isn't he handsome though?" said Marie-Clarice dreamily. "He looks like a blond god."

"True," conceeded Aimée, "and he's said to be a most charming and well-meaning man. But that's not enough to rule a country like Mexico. These people who cheer him today will throw him out as soon as they are able."

By now the procession had passed and their driver urged the horses into motion. They approached a large square, and as the coach drew to a halt, three women stood to one side, waiting expectantly.

"That must be them," Aimée said, forcing a bright smile. To Marie-Clarice she said out of the side of her mouth, "Hang onto your wits. This is the test. If we act natural, they will accept us and never suspect a thing."

The three ladies were standing besides a grand carriage, each of them dressed from head to toe in black. Two were young and the other, judging more by the style of her dress and the stoutness of her figure, was much older. It was difficult to see her because her bonnet was veiled. The black didn't surprise Aimée, since the captain of the *Republic* had already informed them for her of the tragedy.

Just before they got out, Aimée turned to Marie-Clarice and said, "Once more, what is my name?"

"Señorita Angela Fuchard," came the polite reply, with just the proper air of deference. Aimée gave her a nod of approval. Marie-Clarice got out first and then offered a hand of assistance to her mistress. As Aimée alit, the older woman immediately approached, though she semed uncertain which one was her niece. Her indecision was understandable since Marie-Clarice was wearing the fashionable clothes Vardeau had bought Aimée, and which she had passed on.

The woman raised her veil. Middle-aged, close to Nemecio's age, her dark brown eyes were large and deep-set. Her face was round, with incredibly smooth, golden skin. She might have been beautiful, except for her thin, tightly compressed lips. She spoke the name of her niece in a cultured voice and Aimée stepped forward. Then her features softened and she gave her niece a warm embrace.

The woman stepped back and said, "I am Antonia Santos. Your mother was my sister." And nodding toward Marie-Clarice, she asked, "Who is your friend?"

"My personal maid, Marie-Clarice Desmolay," Aimée said without ceremony. Marie-Clarice curtsied prettily.

Antonia Santos gave her a short nod and then said, "I welcome you both to Mexico, and so do my daughters."

The two girls stood slightly behind their mother. Aimée had never seen two sisters so beautiful and yet so strikingly different. One had oval features, green eyes and golden hair, while the other had her mother's deep brown eyes, round face and jet-black hair.

"Melania and Della Santos," Antonia gestured toward the slender blonde when she said the name, Melania, and toward the black-haired, golden-skinned one when she said, Della. Aimée embraced each of them briefly and expressed her delight at meeting them. Their smiles of welcome and greetings seemed warm and genuine. She judged them to be a year or two older than she was. Their costumes were of black silk, full-skirted and worn over large crinolines. They had matching, three-quarter-length coats with large open sleeves, trimmed down the outer seam with black braid. The collars were very narrow and edged with velvet ribbon. Their hats were small and round and each sported a single feather. Aimée noted that they weren't wearing veils like their mother.

While the introductions went on, Marie-Clarice directed the transfer of their baggage to the second carriage. When all was loaded, Antonia placed her arm around Aimée's waist and led her into its plush interior. Melania and Della entered after them, and Marie-Clarice last, sat up with the coachman.

"Angela, I hope you won't look down on us as the French do," her aunt began.

"Why, of course not," Aimée exclaimed. "I'm proud of my Mexican heritage."

"I'm afraid," Antonia said, "that the French think us provincial."

"Have they rejected you?" Aimée asked curiously.

"Not rejected, exactly," Antonia went on, this plainly a source of great concern to her, "but ignored. And, if they do talk to us, it is with great condescension."

Aimée smiled mischievously and said, "Wait until they address me and I answer in perfect French. I've spent my life speaking that language—along with our Spanish, of course."

"And they sent so few men, gentlemen that is," Della commented. "Only soldiers; they're so stiff. Or," she added meaningfully, "if they do take notice of us, it is because they only want one thing. And we ignore them."

"I've told the girls and I'll now tell you Angela," Antonia said. "It's dangerous to consort with the French military for another reason. We can never be sure how long the emperor will remain in power here. Benito Juárez is very active. It's said, in some quarters, that when he's adequately armed and ready, that he'll fight the French to the death."

"So it would be wise not to be thought to sympathize with the French," Della added.

"I'll remember, aunt," Aimée said seriously. She was well aware that they spoke the truth. "It's a frightening situation."

"Didn't Nemecio speak of it to you?" her aunt asked, referring to her brother for the first time.

"Yes," Aimée replied carefully, wondering what questions would come next.

"You'll soon meet another uncle. He's also a Miranda. His name is Lino, and he has a son named Renato who's your cousin," she went on.

"I'm looking forward to making their acquaintance,"

Aimée said politely, secretly hoping Nemecio's brother and nephew did not share his nature.

Della, who was seated opposite her cousin, leaned forward in her seat and said, her brown eyes alive with excitement, "Did you see Maximilian? Isn't he handsome?"

"Very," Aimée agreed, though secretly puzzled as to why there'd been no direct questions about Nemecio. She decided she'd be the one to mention him and see what kind of a reaction it got.

"I think the emperor is handsome," Melania went on. "Do you know, I think he looked my way when he passed," she added smugly.

"Hush," Antonia scolded. "He's a married man."

"But there are rumors that he doesn't let that stand in his way," Melania replied.

"I'm ashamed that one of my daughters would entertain such a thought," Antonia said quietly.

"I've had the same thought, Aimée," Della put in calmly. "I wouldn't object in the least to a rendezvous with him."

Antonia glowered at her daughters. "Uncle Nemecio wouldn't be so intolerant," Della said in an undertone Aimée doubted she was meant to understand—although she did, and only too well.

"My poor brother," Antonia sighed, and all conversation came to an awkward halt. "Such a horrible death. And such a noble man," she dabbed at the corner of her eye with a huge handkerchief.

Aimée saw Della and Melania exchange knowing glances. But if Antonia noticed, she gave no sign.

"My dear, Angela," Antonia shifted her position slightly. "We wish you to know you're welcome to remain with us as long as you desire."

"That is very kind of you, aunt," she replied. "In truth, I have nowhere else to go."

Antonia smiled benevolently. "Have no fear. We shall not turn you out."

Aimée expressed her thanks while thinking how

Antonia would feel when the truth about Nemecio's will was discovered. But right now she had to escape suspicion as an impostor.

Miranda had told her that his home was luxurious, but, when the carriage turned down a driveway paved with bricks and she finally saw the hacienda atop the hill before her, she drew in a sharp breath. It seemed enormous even seen from here, half a mile away. Behind the house was a thick forest, providing a perfect, lush background. The grounds included formal gardens, great sweeps of lawns and terraces. Not even during her travels with her father had she seen a home such as this one.

"I had no idea it was so grand a house," Aimée marveled. "Uncle Nemecio said it was large, but. . . ."

"He was never one to brag," Antonia said. "It is a very large house. We even have a ballroom we hope to use to lure some of the French aristocrats to visit us. And I assure you that not even Maximilian's palace is better furnished."

"I shall feel quite lost in it. In the convent," Aimée went on, playing her role, "the only furnishings in our rooms were a hard, narrow bed, a bureau and a chair. Not that I resented the austerity, for there are no better teachers in all of France than the sisters. . . ."

"From some of your letters, we doubted you were that happy there," Della exclaimed.

"When you've known little else but the convent you begin to doubt that there is anything else," Aimée said, realizing her mistake. "But from your letters to me— and I saved every one of them—I realized there were other things in the world. I envied you."

"Were you ever engaged in a romance with some handsome Frenchman?" Melania asked with great interest.

"In a convent?" Aimée almost laughed. "No, we were given little freedom." Aimée didn't have to pretend to be Angela when she sighed and said, "Oh, how

I longed for some romance and adventure. I'm sure both of you have been in love," she added in an envious, but flattering, tone.

Della evaded that subject but added, "Having you here isn't going to help." Aimée nodded her head at this flattery. Then Della went on, speculating, "But then you may. With the name Fuchard, and the word will get around that you lived in France all your life, people may be curious. They'll want to meet you."

"I don't understand," Aimée said blankly.

"You will, in time, dear cousin," Della said somewhat mysteriously. "But, for the time being, look at it this way, your being more French than Spanish will make the men gather 'round."

Just then the carriage pulled up before the wide stone steps leading to a pillared veranda that ran the length of the house. Over the arched entry was a wooden sign etched in gold. *Mi casa es su casa,* it read, and Aimée couldn't help smiling at the irony of those words, given her situation as Miranda's sole heir. Indeed, his house was now her house.

The windows were deeply recessed, giving evidence to the thick walls which assured coolness inside against the stultifying Mexican summer heat. Her glance shifted to the heavy front door composed of solid beams of wood studded with nailheads. Suddenly the door opened wide and two men stepped into the entryway. One bore a marked resemblance to Nemecio, and was close to his age. The other was young, of medium height, with curly black hair that almost covered his ears. His eyes were a dark brown, and even from the carriage Aimée could see they were heavily lashed, giving him a sensuous look. As his features softened in a wide smile of welcome, Aimée could well imagine the effect this young man had on the impressionable Marie-Clarice.

The older man stepped forward and helped his sister from the carriage. Antonia turned and said, "Angela, this is Lino Miranda. Nemecio's brother, your uncle."

Lino bowed, accepted Aimée's hand and kissed it gallantly. The young man was assisting his cousins from the carriage. Antonia motioned for him to approach. "And this, Angela, is your cousin, Renato, Lino's son."

Aimée extended her hand, saying, "It is a pleasure, Renato."

He acknowledged the introduction and soon they hurried into the house. Aimée had to admit that she thought her "cousin" was the handsomest gentleman she had ever seen. He offered her his arm as they entered.

"I hope your journey wasn't too difficult," he said.

"No, although it was tiring, and, of course, dirty. It is embarrassing to meet you in such a disheveled state," she replied with a blush.

"I hadn't noticed," he said in such a charming way that Aimée almost believed him. "We are most happy to have you here. And that you have arrived safely."

"I was afraid you and your family might not be so pleased to have me here," she said as lightly as she could, to test his reaction.

"In heaven's name, why not?" he asked in apparent puzzlement.

She gave a slight shrug. "I'm part French, and it might make things awkward for you, in view of the present political situation."

"I'm most pleased you have come, and I hope you'll stay with us. I believe your father would have wanted it," he replied.

"Do you really, Renato?" Aimée asked in surprise.

"Yes. He worshipped your mother and was so heartsick when she died that he simply couldn't remain here with his memories."

"I know little more than what Uncle Nemecio told me before his tragic accident," Aimée said simply.

"Of course," Renato said. "I forgot your father had no family in France."

"Did he resent me because my mother died in bearing me? I was so young when he died that I hardly remember him. . . ." Aimée's voice faltered, partly with the tension of playing this role, and partly with the sudden memory of her own father.

"Oh, no," quickly put in Renato. "Papa told me that when your father left, he gave the family assurance he would devote his life to raising you. When he died, he left a will stating he wished you raised in his beloved France."

"There was enough in his will for that, but no more than enough," put in the practical Antonia, who had been walking near them. "However, I've already told Angela we welcome her as one of us."

"Which she is," Renato said gallantly.

The coolness of the wide reception hall was refreshing after her arduous travels. The hall was in half shadows, which the heavy, dark, ornately carved Mexican furniture did nothing to relieve. However, beautifully designed and highly colored rugs were scattered about the polished stone floors and lent a cheery air to the place, as did a scattering of large, brightly colored woven baskets. An Indian blanket was spread across the back of a long bench. Another, more ornately designed, hung on the wall. Aimée had forgotten the Mexican's love of color, and now the childhood memories of the time she lived here with her father came flooding back.

She wanted most of all to take a bath and could hardly suppress a sigh of exasperation as Antonia insisted on first giving her a tour of the house. However, she almost forgot her discomfort as the wonders of the house slowly revealed themselves. There was primitive Mexican art in a brightly lit room and the next was filled with magnificent antiques and thick Persian rugs. Nemecio had chosen well from his European contacts and this house revealed his fine taste.

Aimée exclaimed aloud in admiration as they entered the ballroom, a huge salon draped in mauve satin, with crystal chandeliers hung from chains of gold and sparkling from a thousand facets. The wood floor was highly polished. Enormous mirrors covered the walls and were hung with crystal sconces. It had all come from France, Aimée knew, and was of the finest quality.

The dining room was more austere, with a long, highly polished, simple table. Around it were ornately carved armchairs with seats and backs of hand-tooled leather. There was also a music room and library on the first floor, and probably the kitchen and pantry as well, although Antonia did not condescend to show this to Aimée.

On the second floor were the bedroms. Each bedroom had its own parlor suite and looked out on a patio around which the house was built. From her window Aimée had a view of a glorious fountain and palms and exotic plants with brightly colored flowers whose names she did not know. It was gay and charming.

Aimée's room was done in a deep shade of rose, with bright pink accessories. It was not only very comfortable, but elegant, too, and she knew she would like it very much indeed here. "I hope you approve," Antonia said as Aimée's face lit up in pleasure at "her" room.

"It's wonderful," she exclaimed honestly. "The whole house is wonderful." The aunt and "niece" hugged.

"I hope you will be happy among us," Antonia said.

It seemed so warm and genuine that it took Aimée by surprise. She had really expected them to be a jealous, cold lot who'd greet her as so much excess baggage. Certainly Nemecio had led her to expect the worse, but she was beginning to wonder if she had been foolish to be guided by his words. And certainly Nemecio was hardly one to inspire warm family feelings. But, on the other hand, they may have regarded her as a simple girl, straight out of a convent. She would certainly pose no problems, and she had gathered that they thought she might even give them an advantage in attracting the French aristocracy to their house to meet her. On the other hand, as Nemecio had made quite clear to her, he had been the master here, and surely they had suffered from his moods and demands.

Lino knocked on the parlor door to her suite. "This evening," he said politely, "our lawyer is coming from the city . We're not at all sure whether my brother provided for you, my dear, but I assure you we'll not turn you out."

"Oh, thank you," Aimée said guilelessly, wondering how they'd react when they learned the truth.

"The lawyer was very vague yesterday when we called on him," Antonia said out loud, her tone registering dismay. "Not at all open. I couldn't help feeling there was something he wasn't telling us."

"My dear, Antonia," her brother began, "what could be wrong?"

"I don't know," she fretted, "but it's just a feeling I have. Pedro is usually so outgoing. Yesterday, he barely seemed to have the time to see me, and he certainly didn't volunteer any information even though he most certainly must be privy to the contents of Nemecio's will."

"Well, we'll find out in a few hours," said Lino confidently. "I think you're worried about nothing, my dear Antonia. Let us leave Angela so she can bathe and change before the lawyer arrives."

Chapter 6

The family was gathered in the library when Pedro Vicientis arrived. Each was seated in a huge leather chair; the chairs had been placed in a semi-circle around the desk that had been Nemecio's. Aimée watched their faces and saw the naked greed exposed as each one speculated on how much he or she would get.

Pedro Vicientis, the family lawyer, was a man of about Nemecio's age, with a trim black goatee and side whiskers. He was introduced to Aimée and regarded her politely, giving no clue to his inner thoughts. He inquired briefly into the family's health, then stepped behind the desk, opened his portfolio and took out the will.

There wasn't a sound in the room. He had a booming, mellifluous voice which commanded attention, and he wasted no time. "This is the will of Nemecio Miranda. I will be short, although I will read it in its entirety if you wish. He left everything to—" the hush that had fallen over the room was deafening as they leaned forward in their chairs "—his niece, Angela Fuchard."

A babble of voices greeted this terse announcement. Lino's voice rose over all as he said, "The fool left everything to this child. Every damn peso, everything, even the house and furniture?"

The lawyer nodded. Lino arose and pulled Aimée from her chair and shook her violently. "Did you have anything to do with this?"

"Papa, stop it," Renato objected, standing up.

Lino let her go but repeated, "Did you have anything to do with this?"

Señor Vicientis said quietly, "His will was made, as you can see from the date, before he ever sailed for Europe. These were his last wishes and they are irrevocable. Everything belongs to Angela."

His anger cooled, and Lino covered his face with his hands. "I'm sorry I lost my temper. Of course you're innocent of any wrongdoing."

Antonia had gasped, turned pale, and had just sat there dumbly. Now she said aloud, but more to herself than to the others, "It means that we are all at the mercy of this child."

"At my mercy?" Aimée asked innocently.

"It means," said Lino, "that we've been disinherited by Nemecio. He was the sole owner of everything here, and we expected that when he died, it would go to us."

"Now I understand what Uncle Nemecio meant," Aimée said, turning to face them all. "He told me right after we sailed that should anything happen to him, I wasn't to change the household to which I was going. I hadn't the faintest idea what he could have meant by that, but now I see that I am to leave everything as it is."

"How nice of him," Antonia commented tartly, obviously not relishing having this "child," as they called Aimée, as her financial support.

"How do we know he's dead, anyway?" Lino suddenly broke in.

Aimée related the story. "I suppose there's no doubt," Antonia shook her head.

"The captain said surely he was dead. I even asked him if we could turn around to go back to look for Uncle Nemecio," said Aimée in a tiny voice, "but he said it would be useless. But why," she asked, directing her question to Lino, "are you so upset?"

"Upset," he said, making an effort to control himself. Obviously hot tempers ran in the family. "I'm upset, Angela, because this house, this estate, all of our businesses and all of the money belongs to you. And we, his loving family, are left destitute and at your mercy."

It was all Aimée could do not to laugh as he referred to them as "his loving family," but she had resolved to play the role of the innocent. "You're not destitute by any means. Everything will go on just as before. Things ran very well that way, didn't they?"

"She's right, uncle," Della said, speaking for the first time, and obviously regarding her cousin in a new light. "We owned nothing when Nemecio was alive. Nothing has changed."

"Maybe," Lino said ominously. "It remains to be seen."

At this point Señor Vicientos gathered up his papers and said, "I think it is my duty to inform you that this document will be upheld in any court. I advise you to adjust to the state of affairs. Meanwhile, I have other pressing business and must bid you good-night."

To Aimée he added quietly, "If you have any questions or problems, please feel free to consult me. I was your uncle's lawyer—and his friend—and he has made provisions for me to be of any service you may need, if you so desire."

Apparently deciding to make the best of it, Lino attempted to smile and said to Aimée, "And please feel free to consult me as I have been running the estate for many years."

"I appreciate your kindness," Aimée said to both

men gratefully, "but I am tired from my long journey and wish to retire. Perhaps it would be better to discuss this among us in the morning."

As she prepared to leave the library, Lino put a hand on her arm and said, "Angela, please bear with us. This has been a terrible shock, one which we didn't take too well, as you saw for yourself. However, in the short time you have been here, we've become aware of your warmth and wish you to be part of our family, which you are."

"Oh thank you," Aimée said, and kissed her uncle, aunt, and cousins good night. She went to her bedroom where Marie-Clarice was anxiously awaiting her. "How did they take the bad news?" she asked immediately, as she helped Aimée undress.

"Better than I expected," admitted Aimée. But what secretly puzzled her was why they hadn't reacted more. The cousins had said almost nothing, and Renato hadn't even expressed any shock when he heard the will. Time would tell if they were truly as greedy and devious as Nemecio had described them to be.

The next week passed quietly. Most of the time Aimée was busy learning how to run the household and deal with the servants. By nightfall she was always too exhausted to spend any time chatting with Marie-Clarice, and so she didn't notice the change that had come over the girl. At first Marie-Clarice had been excited to be in this house, believing her troubles were over, but slowly, she became more apprehensive, and finally she insisted one night that they talk.

"What is it, Marie-Clarice, I'm exhausted," said Aimée. "Can't it wait?"

"No, now," whispered Marie-Clarice with an emphasis so out of character for her, that Aimée turned around to stare at her. She nodded in the affirmative, and was astonished when Marie-Clarice ran to the suite door and made sure it was locked.

"What is it?" demanded Aimée wearily.

"I'm sure they are going to discover we are impostors, and they'll turn us over to the French police and have us shot against a wall," said Marie-Clarice in one giant breath.

"That's ridiculous," scoffed Aimée, trying to remind herself that in many ways Marie-Clarice was still a child with a child's fears. "In the first place, there's no way they can discover I'm not Angela. Secondly, they simply don't go around just backing people up against a wall and shooting them."

"Oh, but they do!" a wide-eyed Marie-Clarice gasped. "They do. They told me in the kitchen that the French soldiers automatically shoot every *Juárista* they discover."

"We're not *Juáristas*. We're French," Aimée corrected her. "I'm in danger because I'm here under false pretenses. You're not. Besides, how can you give credence to mere gossip you hear in the kitchen?" she scoffed lightly.

"But it's true," insisted Marie-Clarice urgently. "I am with you and I help you. Therefore, I, too, am guilty. I will die with you, señorita. I will never abandon you. . . ."

Aimée was glad of the girl's loyalty, but disturbed by how readily she succumbed to gossip.

"I'm told," Marie-Clarice went on, "that the French don't even hold a trial. They just kill you," she ended dramatically.

"If that's so, I'm not aware of it. However, if you're that frightened, my real threat is you, not them. In your fear you may give something away that will get us both into serious trouble," Aimée told her sternly. "If you wish to leave, I'll make up a story, something that will make it imperative for you to go to the United States, and you can simply get away."

Marie-Clarice gave a despairing shrug and her voice took on a doleful tone. "They're shooting people there, too. They say, in the kitchen, there is a great war going on, far greater than even you suspected."

"You heard it from me first," Aimée reminded her. "If that war wasn't going on, you and I would have left immediately."

"The French soldiers—"

"—Marie-Clarice," Aimée said in a voice so stern it surprised even her, "there will be no more talk of this. We do far better by staying here and playing our roles —if you do not betray me."

"Oh, never," cried out Marie-Clarice, hugging Aimée as if she would rather die first. "But you must be careful," Marie-Clarice warned, "for the city is full of spies, and the servants tell me they are everywhere— they might even be among our own servants. Sometimes," she sighed deeply, "I think I would have been better off if I'd remained indentured and let them sell me off to someone. I might have been lucky. . . ."

"You are going to be very unlucky if you keep talking this way," warned Aimée. "We are in this together and we can only trust each other. So be quiet and remember that for now we are not in any trouble. If we *both* are careful, it will stay that way."

"I hope you're right, señorita," she said somberly, apparently deciding she'd said enough for the time being.

Aimée switched to lighter topics to brighten Marie-Clarice's mood. "I do like the uniform my aunt gave you. It's a maid's uniform, but of silk."

"I have five," Marie-Clarice exclaimed, brightening noticeably.

"Do you dance?" Aimée asked.

Marie-Clarice flushed and said, "I can, but I haven't done much. As a maid. . . ."

"I'll see that you attend a soirée, or even a formal ball," Aimée said quite sincerely but mainly to cheer her up.

"Could you, señorita?" Marie-Clarice asked hopefully, the dreamy smile on her face apparently mirroring her hope of attracting a handsome young man to romance her, or at least, dance with her.

"These beautiful uniforms," Marie-Clarice suddenly interjected conspiratorially. "I'm told in the kitchen that they are so unusually pretty because they used to belong to Nemecio's personal maid."

Aimée knew there was more to tell, so she played along, and prompted her, "Tell me, what else?"

"Well," began Marie-Clarice, obviously relishing her tidbit, "It is said that he always had a personal maid who slept in the suite next to his, which is grandly furnished. There were very many of them and they were always young and beautiful."

Aimée lowered her eyes as she nodded. "I'm beginning to understand. . . ."

"Oh, but there is more," an excited Marie-Clarice told her. "He abused them. Their bodies. Sometimes there were even permanent scars. When that happened, they were sent away."

"What gossip goes on in that kitchen," Aimée exclaimed, trying to feign disapproval, but secretly she remembered her encounter with Nemecio and thanked her lucky stars that she was still alive and well. Apparently, Nemecio's sexual desires had been fulfilled by abusing women, and he hadn't even had the decency to let his own niece alone.

"Don't you want me to learn all I can?" asked Marie-Clarice, interrupting her thoughts. "You said I was to keep my eyes and ears open."

Aimée nodded. "We're lucky that the other two men in this house don't share his nature."

"No, you're lucky," Marie-Clarice pointed out, "that you're alive if your supposed uncle was such an animal."

"I agree," Aimée said, but she wasn't about to tell her the true story of what had happened. "But just to be on the safe side, why don't you lock your door at night before you go to bed?" she suggested.

"I do. And you must also."

"Why didn't you tell me this before?"

"I tried, but you have been so tired, and we have had no time to talk together."

"Oh, by the way," added Aimée. "In the morning we will open some crates that arrived today. . . ."

"Oh, let us do it now, said Marie-Clarice. "I am not tired. You watch and I'll open them." Aimée had known this was what she would say, and she also knew what was in the boxes, which were in the parlor adjoining her suite. She heard Marie-Clarice open one and cry out in delight.

"Crates of beautiful clothes," Marie-Clarice announced with obvious pleasure. "They are filled with beautiful gowns, gloves, hats, stockings, lingerie, shoes, even combs and lacy scarves. There is everything a lady would want—and more—in those crates."

Marie-Clarice disappeared for a moment and came back holding up a pale blue gown. She laid it carefully on the bed, then brought in a gown of burgundy satin with touches of green. It seemed almost alive with color. She also brought in a gown that had Antonia's name written on it on a piece of paper. It was dark-blue satin almost completely covered with hand-sewn jet beads, thousands of them.

Aimée said, "You must choose a gown for yourself."

"Oh, no, señorita! I couldn't! Besides, it would cause suspicion and gossip among the other servants if I were to have such a fine dress. I am, after all, just a maid."

"You may hang the gown in my closet. Also select appropriate slippers, stockings, gloves, and a mantilla. Let them all remain here. That chest"—she pointed to the far corner of the bedroom— "is practically empty. Put your things there and no one will ever be the wiser. It may come in handy someday."

"Oh, señorita." With a cry of pleasure, Marie-Clarice ran to Aimée and embraced her, then stepped back. "Please forgive me, señorita, for taking such a liberty."

"We are friends, Marie-Clarice. And even though you must pretend to be just my maid, we are still friends, and it pleases me to see you so happy. And I promise you will get a chance to wear your finery."

"I can't choose one. They are all so beautiful," protested Marie-Clarice. So Aimée chose an ensemble for her —a green gown with a green and gray striped bodice and everything she needed to go with it, including shoes.

"In the morning, tell Della and Melania that I wish to see them."

"Señorita," Marie-Clarice said respectfully, "except for the dress with your aunt's name on it, your name is the only one on the trunks."

"Letting them choose a gown will make relations better. And it will have cost me nothing. Until tomorrow then," said Aimée.

The next morning Aimée and Marie-Clarice unpacked the crates. It was astonishing how much they held, carefully wrapped in clouds of tissue paper. The gowns and accessories were laid out onto the bed, then the chairs, the settee, a chaise-lounge, and eventually spilled over into the parlor.

Melania, the first one to enter the room, couldn't help voicing her enthusiasm at the sight of so many beautiful things.

"Uncle Nemecio took me shopping and bought me all of these things, but I wanted to share them with you and your sister," Aimée said graciously. "I want each of you to select a gown. And there are two gowns and some other personal things which Uncle Nemecio selected for your mother."

"I've never owned a Paris gown before," Melania exclaimed, her eyes greedily devouring the sea of color and design that lay everywhere. "How kind of you, and I'm so pleased we're the same size."

"So am I," said Aimée, as Melania ran from one magnificent gown to another, picking each one up, exclaiming over it, and then, no sooner holding it up in front of the mirror, discarding it as another one caught her eye and she ran to try that one on. Finally, she picked the pale blue dress which was the first one Marie-Clarice had unpacked.

"This one, may I have this one?" she asked, barely able to conceal her pleasure at possessing a real Paris gown.

"It's yours," said Aimée. "And choose the accessories to go with it."

"Oh, thank you, but I have silver slippers that will look just right with the silver braid that edges the sleeves."

Aimée thought that Melania had chosen well, for the pale blue dress would compliment her golden hair and the off-the-shoulder neckline would display her fair skin. There were other, less daring dresses with modified plunging decolletages, but Aimée suspected that her cousin was quite a flirt, and, clad in this gown, she would take full advantage of her natural assets.

Then Della came in, yawning, until she, too, spied the wonderful clothes that were displayed everywhere. She wasted no time in choosing the burgundy satin dress with the touch of green in it that made it shimmer even in the daylight. Melania and Della went off to their rooms to try on their dresses just as Antonia entered.

When Aimée told her there was a crate of things just for her, Antonia didn't even ask what they were but ran toward it without a word. Soon the mother and two daughters were strutting around in their gowns, twirling and turning and exclaiming to each other how wonderful they looked. Even Aimée couldn't help but marvel at how stunning they looked in their dresses. Then she excused herself and brought out two nightgowns and presented one to each cousin. They thanked her with warm embraces as their faces glowed with

Antonia also warmly embraced her niece and then held her at arm's length. "My dear, I cannot allow such pleasure.

gowns as these to hang in the closet. We shall give a ball honoring the return of our dear, dear Angela—at once. We'll make it the most fashionable affair in all of Mexico. It will be as good—or even better—than the balls the emperor gives. I am sure my dear brother, Nemecio, would have wanted us to honor you and acknowledge your return."

Della and Melania immediately cried out what a good idea it was and instantly began making plans. They left, chattering, passing Marie-Clarice as she entered.

Privately, Aimée reflected that it had never occurred to her dear aunt to honor her return, but rather it gave her an excuse to wear the new dresses and perhaps catch the eye of some rich and noble Frenchman or gain social standing.

To Marie-Clarice Aimée said, "See. Now I'm honored as the beloved relative returned. Even if they had any doubts, which I don't think they did, we are now accepted by them, and at the cost of three gowns and a few accessories, all paid for by Nemecio."

"You were right," admitted Marie-Clarice who had seen their faces as the women were leaving. "You are far wiser than I am in these matters. And I swear, señorita, I won't be afraid any longer. Besides, you would be foolish to run away from all this wealth."

"One day we may have to leave, but for the time being, we shall do nothing but enjoy our good fortune and thank God for it," said Aimée.

The ball was planned for the following Saturday, only a week away. Invitations were promptly sent out by messengers dressed in special style. And one invitation was even sent to the palace in the rather forlorn hope that the emperor might attend.

"She'll never let him come," predicted Antonia. "Carlota doesn't trust Maximilian. He's such a beautiful man and he could dally with any of the girls in his court. None would refuse him."

"I wouldn't," Della declared frankly.

"Nor I," Melania quickly added.

Antonia chided them. "What a thing to say! Both of

you should be ashamed of yourselves, especially speaking in such a way in front of dear Angela, who was raised and educated in a convent. She is most certainly not accustomed to such loose talk."

"Are you offended by our talk, Angela?" Melania asked.

Privately Aimée thought they would all be shocked by the loose talk in a convent school where girls can only whisper and wonder about such matters. Aloud she said, "Certainly not. I must agree that the emperor is such a handsome man it would be hard to deny him anything."

"You came from Europe," Della said with a sly wink. "You must have heard of Maximilian there. Do you think he might, well, be taken with one of us?"

"I do recall that some of his behavior at Franz-Josef's court was considered something of a scandal," admitted Aimée.

"We can hope, then," said Della happily, until she noted Antonia's stern features, and added, "that he will come to our grand ball."

"And we can pray," Melania said dreamily.

During the hectic days preceding the ball, Aimée rode around her estate. She was by no means an expert horsewoman, but she was determined to learn. Some day it might be a great advantage to know how to ride, considering her uncertain future.

She found a beautiful riding habit in Angela's wardrobe. The sleeves still had tissue stuffed into them. It was a princess dress of fawn-colored cloth, with a skirt of enormous width. It buttoned down the front and had pale pink cuffs and a collar of fine linen. The cravat was fawn-and-pink striped silk. The hat had a high crown, and narrow brim that dipped in front, with a twist of pink-and-fawn silk chiffon wound around the base of the crown ending in streamers that fell halfway down her back.

When Aimée had first tried on this outfit, she felt as regal as the Empress Carlota had looked riding by with Emperor Maximilian at her side. She wasn't aware of how handsome a picture she made riding sidesaddle with the wide skirt almost covering the beautiful horse she had chosen from the stable.

She had known Nemecio's estate was large, but just how extensive were his holdings was becoming apparent as she rode and rode and rode and still found herself on her own land. It amazed her to see that all the people she encountered worked for her. There were men who mowed grass, tended the gardens, kept up all the repairs on the patios and outbuildings; there were hostlers who cared for the animals, and men who kept the carriages, landaus and buggies in order. All the servants were Mexican, most of whom rarely spoke to her, although the men promptly doffed their straw hats and the women curtsied whenever she passed. Aimée realized that she was responsible for a virtual army of workers who depended on her for a living.

And she also learned that the estate was financed largely by foreign investments. Nemecio may have been a Mexican, but he didn't seem to trust the future of Mexico half as much as that of England and France, at least so far as his money went. From Europe came the bulk of his income.

By now Aimée also knew that Lino, Antonia, Della and Melania were anything but thrifty. Surprisingly, Renato seemed to be spending more than anyone; yet whatever he spent it on was a mystery. He was neat and well-dressed, but apparently he had bought nothing since her arrival. And yet, he had withdrawn considerable funds, according to the accounts. Aimée, who knew Marie-Clarice looked upon him with some fondness, wondered if Renato spent all of his money on women. He was handsome, and so it seemed most likely that he had a beautiful mistress or two hidden away.

Aimée was quickly learning that this was a greedy crew, and despite her dislike for the deceased Nemecio, she knew he had spoken the truth in this particular respect. But she wasn't about to make a fuss about their spending so freely, nor was she going to even complain. The estate could afford it, and for the time being, outwardly, at least, everyone was pleasant and gave the impression that this was a happy household.

Della and Melania were usually together and seldom sought her out. Renato was away most of the time, and never gave a clue as to his whereabouts during his disappearances. Lino was businesslike, overseeing the running of the estate and eager to answer Aimée's questions. She had to admit that he worked hard, and he was truly responsible for coordinating everyone. Still, she doubted his sincerity as he explained everything to her. As far as she could determine, Lino wasn't appropriating any money for himself beyond what had been agreed upon as his generous pay.

Aimée had expected more hostility than she encountered and she was pleased there was no trouble. But she intuitively felt they were waiting for the right opportunity to steal from "Angela," or to rid themselves of her. But since everything appeared normal, she also wondered if her experiences with Vardeau and Nemecio had made her too suspicious about people's motives. In any event, she was only waiting for the proper time to pass before she escaped to the United States. So long as France governed Mexico, she feared she might be tracked down. And so long as she lived with these people who obviously would be so much better off without her, she considered herself in danger. The peaceful life was simply on the surface; beneath simmered intrigue and plots.

The day of the ball, the house was filled with confusion. All employees who could be spared from their usual duties were put to work decorating the grounds and polishing and cleaning the house until everything sparkled. More than a hundred couples had been invited, and this alone required a huge space just to park the carriages.

By the time the carriages began to arrive, everything

was in readiness. Servants wearing white livery and gloves were ready to serve as waiters. The kitchen was overflowing with cooks and their helpers preparing sumptuous dishes that would soon be appearing on magnificent solid silver platters.

Antonia, Lino, Della, Melania and Renato were in the reception line to greet their guests, along with Aimée. The ball promised to be the merriest, grandest and most talked-about affair outside of the palace. It seemed that a never-ending stream of happy, gorgeously dressed guests arrived to meet Aimée and take advantage of the family's hospitality.

The air was heavy with the exquisite aroma of floral fragrances, and the rooms came alive with the profusion of brightly colored Paris gowns, embroidered shawls, mantillas, gloves and sparkling jewelry. The women were curious and gracious, the men polite and obviously appreciative of Aimée's beauty.

The tables were heavy with platters of rare foods, all cooked in French style with aromatic sauces. Wine flowed freely and so did the liquor of the cactus plant, which was too strong for the ladies, but was well savored by most of the men. At ten, Lino and Aimée led the grand march and danced the first dance. There were polkas and waltzes and then, out of respect for their Mexican guests, there was a resounding *habanero,* a native dance that required more energy and enthusiasm than a waltz.

Aimée was aware that Renato had excused himself after supper and didn't reappear until halfway through the ball. When he returned and presented himself to Aimée with a deep bow, and asked her to dance, she couldn't resist questioning his absence.

"You were gone for some time," said Aimée coyly. "Were you bored?"

"No, Angela," he said tensely, "I have headaches that come quite often and I must be by myself when that happens. I hope you will forgive my rudeness, but I could not help myself."

"Of course. It was kind of you to return," Aimée answered politely, wondering if this was the truth or simply a convenient excuse.

"I wouldn't have allowed the evening to end without dancing with you," he said gallantly and with a grin that made his preoccupied mood vanish into the air. As they stepped onto the dance floor Aimée noticed that Renato's usually well-groomed hair was a mass of unruly curls, as if windblown, but she kept this observation to herself.

"If you hadn't returned, I would have understood," said Aimée, looking around and seeing the faces of happy guests.

"Gracias," he answered. "I'm pleased you feel that way. Are you enjoying yourself?"

"It's a beautiful party. It was so kind of your aunt to honor me in such an extravagant manner."

"You deserve it. And, you've made a hit with our guests. All the men are talking about your beauty, and even the women have to admit you are charming and vivacious—and your gown is the most beautiful in the room . . . ." Renato suddenly broke off and stood transfixed. Aimée looked around to see what had surprised him so. And then he whispered in her ear, "Speaking of honors. See who has just entered the room?"

He casually resumed dancing, maneuvering her so she was able to view Emperor Maximilian and his staff entering the room. But the music stopped and everyone in the room stood aside to let him pass. The ladies curtsied and the gentlemen bowed.

Maximilian's manner, although regal, was gracious and every now and then he stopped to say a few words to a guest, whose face would flush with the honor of being singled out.

Finally he reached Aimée and paused, his eyes coolly studying first her face, then her beautiful dress, a pale yellow gown that she had wisely kept for herself. "My child, I welcome you to Mexico," said the Emperor in a low, modulated voice that sent a thrill through Aimée. "May I have my first dance with you?" he went on.

"I am honored, Your Majesty," Aimée answered, curtsying gracefully. Little did he know that some of the flush that appeared on her face wasn't maidenly modesty but genuine fear that somehow he would know who she was. Could he see through her facade as Angela Fuchard—and know that before him was the daughter of Emile Gaudin who had advocated his downfall?

However, the Emperor seemed happy, and he was an excellent dancer. Aimée noted that he held her closer than was customary. The hand against her back as he guided her about the dance floor moved almost imperceptibly, and the effect was to send a deeper thrill through her body than she had ever felt before, even when Vardeau had aroused her. And it was deliberate, she knew, for when she dared glance up at his face, there was the faintest smile around the corner of his mouth. Of course, to any bystanders, he was most discreet and attentive without being bold, but Aimée was certain she detected a hint of desire behind his blandly polite expression.

In fact, Aimée could barely force herself to look away from his compelling gaze, for never had she seen eyes as blue as his. And his mane of blond hair and beard had a golden glow under the lights of a thousand candles twinkling in the chandeliers. And this man whom she had every reason to detest and fear looked to her like a gilded god.

Aimée forced herself to look away and only then did she become aware that they were the only ones on the dance floor. She felt her face flame with color and heard him chuckle softly. He knew he had aroused her. He pressed her close to him for a second, and then danced her over to the side of the room and surrendered her again to Lino. Immediately other couples went onto the dance floor and the emperor promptly selected

Antonia, who was sitting next to Lino, as his next partner.

"What do you think of him, Angela?" Lino asked as they watched Antonia dance with the emperor. "As if I need ask! You're flushed and I can see your breath comes quicker."

"A handsome man is hard to ignore," she answered quickly, although it angered her that her feelings could be so easily read. "He is also a divine dancer."

Lino chuckled. "I won't deny either of those things. However, he's a weak man, a gullible man who's never done a worthwhile thing in his life. And he was selected to become emperor of Mexico because no one else was foolish enough to accept the post."

"Uncle Lino! What you are saying could be construed as treachery, as treason," Aimée whispered in his ear, hoping no one had overheard this unwise remark. She remembered what Marie-Clarice had told her about spies being everywhere. She didn't want a careless remark at so public an event to put her life in danger.

"I know that," Lino replied easily, "but you are one of the family and you can be trusted. Besides, I do not wish him ill. I hope he remains for a long, long time because he's brought some kind of prosperity to us. Oh, every *sou* he spends, every payday for the soldiers— all of that comes out of Mexican pockets—but we're fairly exempt from the worst of the taxes. He doesn't wish to offend the rich and the influential. Someday he may need us."

"Is it true that France is lining her pockets with money from Mexican taxes?" Aimée asked, knowing that such a naive question was expected of his niece, but she was also curious to hear more of his views. Would her father's views be confirmed?

"France is looting Mexico—and everyone knows it. Max keeps his throne with the threat of bayonets to anyone who opposes him. But the trouble isn't far off. Benito Juárez has never been totally defeated and he's a clever man, no doubt hatching his schemes right now. There's bound to be trouble in our country. But, then, there has always been trouble . . . ."

The conversation was abruptly halted as the emperor approached and asked Aimée for his last dance. "You do me great honor," he told her as she nodded her acceptance. And this time when his blue eyes gazed deeply into hers, she didn't look away.

"On the contrary, Your Highness, I am the one who is honored. I am sorry the empress could not attend tonight," she added politely.

"She's ill. Alas, quite ill. She attends few functions and social events lately. I'm deeply concerned about her health," said Maximilian, "though the doctors are hopeful."

"I shall pray for her, Your Highness," Aimée responded, almost mesmerized by him.

"I'll inform her of that," he said in an amused tone. Then, glancing around the room, he added, "I must say that this is the best ball I've attended since my reign began. In return, I shall give a ball at the palace. You shall be the first to be invited. Will you attend?"

Did she detect a note of concern in his voice? Aimée answered noncommitally, "A royal invitation is a command, Your Highness. Of course, I shall attend."

"Will that be your sole reason for coming?" At the same moment he asked that question, he gave her hand a quick, intimate squeeze, and she could feel that his palm was wet with perspiration. Aimée struggled to keep her expression as casual as his, yet the subtle movement of his hand on her back was arousing her in a way that left her quite uncomfortable. She was also silently praying that the other guests were not aware that anything more than polite conversation was going on.

"I will come, Your Majesty, because you've honored me and my family by coming to our ball tonight. It is a great honor indeed," Aimée replied formally. "And it is an even greater honor to be invited to the palace."

"Then we will dance again," he said. "Of course, the

other members of your family will also be invited. I'll set the date for a week from tonight, but I may have to change that. Sometimes I'm more busy than I like, there are other matters . . ." His words trailed off as if he was saying too much to a mere woman. Women, for him, were good for one thing. He went on lightly, however, "But I'll make an effort to hold the ball as promised. We need more happy occasions like this to keep people's minds off other, less pleasant matters. It brings us together. It teaches the French and the Mexican to understand one another."

"That's true, Your Highness," Aimée agreed. She and Maximilian had been speaking French. He had been delighted that she spoke "his" native tongue so fluently, but now she was wondering if she had not aroused his suspicions as to her true identity.

"Your aunt informs me your name is Angela Fuchard, that your father was French and that you were educated in French convents," he smiled. Obviously when he danced with Antonia he had asked about her. Aimée wasn't sure how pleased Antonia was since she had two eligible daughters, but it also made her uncomfortable that he had taken the trouble to inquire into her background.

Aimée smiled back pleasantly at her royal dancing partner. "That is true, Your Highness. I have only recently returned. I'm pleased to be with my family again, and I must say it was lonely growing up in France without them.

"I can well imagine, orphaned as you were. And I am sorry to hear about the tragedy which befell your uncle aboard ship."

"Thank you, Your Highness," she said, bowing her head as if remembering her uncle, although her thoughts were only of the man in front of her. Maximilian was perhaps fifteen or sixteen years older than she was, almost old enough to be her father. But the warmth in his eyes and the feeling of his hand pressing her close as they danced belied his paternal and sometimes condescending manner toward her. She suddenly thought of Vardeau. Was it possible he had informed on her, that Maximilian had come to the ball and singled her out merely to tease her before having her thrown into prison as a traitor? She couldn't help but wonder as she recalled her father's betrayal and the French government's quick and lethal action against him if the soldiers who accompanied the emperor would arrest her. She had no choice but to hope he had singled her out because she had caught his fancy and pray that her fears were groundless.

The ball lasted well into the morning hours. Aimée's new relatives were exhausted but exuberant, chattering happily about how the emperor had chosen to come to their ball and how he had mentioned his desire to have a ball of his own.

"You have no idea how important this is, socially," Antonia said, her dark eyes glowing with satisfaction, as she sat back in a chair, her shoes off and her dress loosened.

"I'm sure I made a hit with him," Della confided. "He dances so close."

"I've heard," Lino said sourly, "that he's a man who considers thirteen year olds as prime. The man isn't a monk. Be warned about that ."

"But his empress, doesn't she know?" asked Aimée naively.

"Of course she does," Antonia said. "But all royalty carries on like that. The empress has learned to keep her mouth shut and her eyes closed to what goes on."

"If she knows what is good for her," added Lino.

"He told me she's been ill," Aimée said.

"The gossip is that she hasn't been seen for weeks," Antonia said, "but perhaps she'll appear at the palace ball."

Melania caught Aimée's hand. "Please, cousin, may I wear one of your gowns for the ball? This one is beautiful, but the emperor has seen me in it—and you have so many."

"Of course," Aimée answered, but personally she was annoyed. These people weren't as evil as Nemecio had led her to believe, but they were self-centered and grasping at times—and pushy.

"What about me?" Della asked, pouting. "Both Melania and I have a few gowns, but they aren't from Paris . . . ."

"You may have another one also," Aimée said, "And whatever else you need to go with them."

"You are a dear!" Della exclaimed happily now that she knew she was going to get what she wanted.

"Thank you, Angela," Antonia said graciously, "for being so generous to my daughters. And to me also."

"I did nothing for you, aunt," Aimée protested.

"You helped my brother make the selection for the gowns he brought back for me," she replied serenely. She went over and gave Aimée a kiss on the brow.

Aimée gave an inward sigh, wondering guiltily if she was being too hard on them because of Nemecio's judgment. Certainly they had no reason to love him— or the fact she had been his sole heir. She decided that she had to form her own opinion of her bogus relatives. It was the only fair way, the only adult way, and Aimée was well aware that she had to grow up fast.

"I'm glad you came back," Antonia said, with apparent sincerity. "You've brought some life back to this old house and my old bones . . . . But now I'm tired, and I'm going to bed."

Antonia and her daughters left, and Aimée was about to leave when Lino signaled her to remain. He summoned a passing waiter and asked for wine. The glasses were filled with a fine Madeira, and he and Aimée sipped the sweet, heady drink slowly. They were alone. All the servants were now retired.

"Angela," began Lino, looking her directly in the eye, "I'm going to tell you about certain preparations I'd like to make, with your permission, of course. And it involves money, your money."

She looked at him quizzically wondering why he had

chosen this moment, after such a long night, to speak to her, but obviously he had his reasons. No one was around or likely to be around for a while, a fact which made her slightly nervous when she realized it.

"Listen carefully, Angela. I know what I'm talking about. Maximilian is in trouble, more trouble than I think even he's aware of. I get information from many sources, some from Paris and some from London, and I've just learned that Bonaparte isn't going to send any more soldiers to help Maximilian keep down the rebellion. Even worse—for Maximilian—he's going to reassign about half of the army elsewhere, and at a time when Juárez is only a few hundred miles away and working day and night to train and arm his peons. They are fierce fighters and they are certainly going to wrest Mexico back from the French invaders."

"You seem so sure of this, Uncle Lino," Aimée said quietly, absorbing every word. After all she'd learned in the past weeks, she understood very well that this might be serious trouble indeed.

"I am absolutely positive about this information, Angela. It comes from an impeccable source. And keep this in mind: We are all Mexican. While we prosper under Max's rule, others are suffering, millions of them, and this can't go on. When Juarez gains power, people like us are going to be accused of supporting the French Empire. The fact that we are Mexican will be forgotten as they try to punish everyone who gained from the French. They'll strip us of everything. Quite possibly they might even shoot us."

"Yes, I can believe that," agreed Aimée, realizing he was probably right, but wondering what he had in mind.

"So here is my plan," he said, leaning toward her, their heads almost touching. "I suggest that we begin slowly, so we will arouse no suspicion. We'll send gold to the United States, as much as possible, as quietly as possible. Do you see what I'm getting at?" he asked. He had spent many days with his niece, and he knew she had a quick mind. He also knew he needed her consent.

"I believe it is a fine precaution to take," agreed Aimée quickly. "But how can we send gold across the border without being suspected or discovered?"

"Renato has good relations with the rebels. They trust him, and they'll let him through the lines. There will be no trouble from them. And so far as the French are concerned, they have no way of discovering what we are doing."

"Then do it," Aimée said decisively.

"Of course, if by some chance, we're discovered, it will go very hard on us, Angela," he warned.

"It might go much harder if we do nothing but sit here," she said firmly. "I approve of your idea."

"Good. We shall test our method with a small sum at first. Of course, this mustn't appear on our books, but I will manipulate them in such a way that the tax collector will never even suspect."

"Do what you will, uncle. I trust you. I'll ask for an accounting from you now and then, but just let me know how things are progressing," Aimée said simply.

Lino patted her cheek. "You're very understanding. And you made quite a hit with the emperor. Watch out for him, especially with the political situation as delicate as it is. We're treading a thin line and can't risk alienating either side," he emphasized.

Lino seemed genuinely concerned, and he escorted her back to her room. Marie-Clarice, fully dressed, had fallen asleep waiting for Aimée. She woke up the instant she heard the door open. "You looked like a princess!" she exclaimed. "And I saw you dancing with the emperor. How thrilled you must have been, actually dancing with royalty."

"It was exciting," Aimée agreed, deciding not to alarm Marie-Clarice with her fears, "with more excitement to come. In a week's time, there'll be another ball at the palace."

Marie-Clarice gave Aimée a knowing smile. "In your honor, I'm sure. Am I not right, señorita?"

"What makes you say that?" Aimée asked.

Marie-Clarice shrugged. "The way he looked at you, the way he held you. He was having his thoughts about you, señorita, intimate thoughts. I could tell."

"Good gracious," Aimée pretended chagrin. "I hope no one else thought as you did. It's unfair to the emperor."

"He's a man, señorita," Marie-Clarice said, as if that explained everything.

"That's enough, Marie-Clarice. But I've made up my mind you should have some pleasure, too. You already have a gown and everything to go with it. I'll arrange some way for you to attend the palace ball. If the emperor can dance with a woman wanted by the government he represents, I'm certain no one would object if a member of the court dances with a pretty maid."

Marie-Clarice expressed her delight, then hurried to the dressing table and pulled out the chair so Aimée might sit while she took down the elaborate coiffure she had created for her mistress. Then she brushed out the long, silky hair until it shone.

By the time Marie-Clarice finally held out her nightdress, Aimée was so exhausted she could barely keep from falling asleep. She lost no time in getting into bed. But despite her weariness, she let her mind linger on the details of the evening. Perhaps Marie-Clarice was right about the emperor's interest in her, and she was worrying needlessly.

She felt her face flush with the memory of his hand moving ever so subtly on her back, then pressing her against him. She relived those sensations as if his hands were on her now, and her nagging worries disappeared as she gave her imagination free rein, wondering if it was possible that what had begun as her only means of escape from the French authorities had turned into a fairy tale—complete with an emperor whose attentions made her pulse pound and her whole body tingle in anticipation of a love affair. And, if others had noticed, she would be the talk of Mexico City at every breakfast table in town. But that might work to her advantage, for to be considered a favorite of the emperor would make her powerful. She only hoped she might use that power to escape before being discovered as a traitor and impostor.

At noon Aimée was having breakfast in bed. Still weary from the night before, she was disturbed by a light tap on the door of her sitting room, which Marie-Clarice went to answer. The sound of voices announced the arrival of Della and Melania. Even though she could hear Marie-Clarice protesting that her mistress was not even out of bed, they brushed past her right into Aimée's bedroom.

"You promised we could select another gown, Angela," Melania reminded her, without greeting or ceremony.

"Yes, you did," Della said loudly, walking in the direction of the closet.

"Marie-Clarice, open the door and let them choose," Aimée said, trying to disguise the disgust in her voice. She caught a glance from Marie-Clarice as the sisters practically shoved her out of the way in their haste to choose their dresses. Melania chose a violet gown.

"This one, Angela, may I have this one?" she asked.

Aimée couldn't help thinking that what Melania lacked in tact and subtlety she made up for in taste, for she had chosen the most beautiful gown. She nodded her assent.

"Thank you, cousin," Melania said over her shoulder as she ran to her room to try it on.

Della chose a black one, with a full ruffled skirt and a bodice covered with tiny crimson rosebuds of silk.

Marie-Clarice couldn't keep from crying out, "But señorita Angela, that would look stunning on you."

Della's hostile expression as she turned on Marie-Clarice hinted that she had chosen that dress for exactly that reason.

"In this country, servants do not speak to their mistresses in such a fashion," Della scolded Marie-Clarice. "Remember that."

Aimée said quietly, "Marie-Clarice is my servant, not yours, Della. You may have the gown but please don't either of you ask for another. You'll get no more."

Della opened her mouth to speak, apparently thought better of it, and stormed out of the room.

A few minutes later Melania reappeared and said, "My sister loses her temper easily, but you've been very generous, Angela. Mama is taking us shopping in the city, and you're welcome to come with us, if you wish."

"I'd be delighted," Aimée said, glad for a change of scene. "But first I must bathe and dress."

"In one hour we will leave, then," Melania said. "And thank you again for our gowns. Don't tell mama," she added confidentially, "but I'm going to do my best to seduce the emperor. It shouldn't be difficult with this gown, and if I succeed I'll owe it to you."

Aimée smiled. "I shant' tell your mother."

Marie-Clarice closed the door and couldn't keep from asking, "Why did you give them those gowns? They're so selfish and greedy, and they're jealous of you."

"I need their friendship, and those gowns keep me in their good graces," Aimée reminded her. "Besides, I have kept one dress for myself. Now hurry," she chided, "I have to bathe and get ready."

"I don't think it matters what they wear, anyway," said Marie-Clarice. "I think he'll have eyes only for you. And I hope he ignores Melania and her bad-tempered sister."

"She's very beautiful and so is Della. They have as much of a chance of attracting him as anyone."

"But they're so, so shallow," sputtered Marie-Clarice. "I doubt either one of them could please the emperor, at least more than once. They're too conscious of their beauty. And they lack charm."

"Would you please draw my bath?" Aimée asked sternly, but she couldn't help smiling. Marie-Clarice was right. Della and Melania were very beautiful, but that was all. And their French was atrocious.

The group traveled to town in a landau, for the weather was comfortably warm this early autumn. Each carried her little parasol and wore a splendid dress. Aimée knew long before now that this was a very socially-conscious family who flaunted their wealth as a sign of their importance. Perhaps this was a natural reaction in a country where they were snubbed by their French overlords, but Aimée knew also that their behavior was at least as much a matter of vanity as circumstance.

The landau bumped through the uneven streets on its way to a cluster of imposing stores. Antonia suddenly ordered the driver to pull over.

"What is it?" Aimée asked, worried because the stop had been so abrupt. She didn't see a shop worth exploring.

"They're doing it again," Antonia said soberly. "They are going to kill more."

Aimée followed the direction of Antonia's wide-eyed gaze and saw a squad of *Pantalons Rouges* march two men to an adobe wall. A officer stepped back and issued crisp commands which were answered by rifle-shots. Seconds later the bleeding bodies slumped to the ground, a sight so terrible that Aimée could not speak. More horrible still, the officer nonchalantly strolled over to each victim, put his pistol to their heads, and shot them again.

Aimée buried her face in her hands. "P-please send the landau on."

"Why are you so shocked?" Antonia asked.

"I did not know," Aimée managed to say.

"I thought you knew," Antonia said softly, almost apologetically. "But, of course, how could you? This was your first trip to the city since you arrived. Yes, it happens every day. Sometimes there are several executions in a single day. And in the open. They want everyone to see—and be warned that it could happen to them."

"But why? Why were those men shot?" Aimée asked.

"They are *Juáristas*—men who fight and spy for Juarez. Some time ago, Maximilian issued what is known as the Black Decree. This says that any Mexican captured in the fighting or even suspected of being a spy is automatically sentenced to death. There's no trial, just a wall."

"What a terrible thing," Aimée murmured, her mind dredging up memories of the shots she had heard in a Paris alley, the alley where her own father had been murdered just as cold-bloodedly as these *Juáristas*.

"You see," Della said, "even a handsome emperor can be cruel."

Chapter 7

"Did you notice," Della asked with great glee, "that the invitations from the palace were handwritten?"

Aimée looked puzzled. Her cousin went on grandly, "It means we are special. Usually the invitations are printed, but we have gotten hand-written ones."

"Not only that," Melania added, "but the ball is bound to be the most important social event in years."

"And I trust," added Antonia, "that you girls will behave as you're expected to. Remember that champagne is a wine with alcohol and it affects one's equilibrium if taken to excess. And remember, too, that young officers will one day return to France and quickly forget any impassioned promises they have made. It would not be well to fall in love with any of them."

"So long as the officers are handsome," Della said with a laugh, "I don't care. And, Angela, if this keeps up, you shall have to send to Parish for more gowns."

The women had gathered in the music room to compare gowns and hairdos before the royal dinner and dance at the palace. Ever since receiving the invitations, everyone had been lighthearted and there had not been one single argument or harsh word. Even Aimée found herself enjoying the serenity and gaiety so much that she had brushed aside Nemecio's warning about his relatives' deceit. No worse than he was, she thought, remembering the still, battered body of the real Angela Fuchard.

Antonia's gown was a black silk that mirrored the sheen of her jet-black hair. A black lace overskirt was looped around the skirt, the loops held up with pink roses. Her gloves and fan were also of black lace, embroidered with tiny pink roses.

"You look lovely, aunt," Aimée said.

Antonia beamed with pleasure. "It's the most beautiful gown I've had, except for the one I wore to our ball. You displayed excellent taste in your selection."

"What about me, cousin?" Melania asked. Hers was a pale lavender grosgrain, trimmed with three pinked flounces in a deeper shade of lavender. It had a lace overskirt that fell in graceful folds. The decolletage was so low that Aimée couldn't help wondering how it could possibly contain Melania's more than ample bosom.

Renato smirked and said, "I'd advise you not to bend over, Melania."

"What do you mean, Renato?" Melania asked, trying to appear innocent, but apparently quite aware of the spectacular effect that the plunging neckline created.

"Suppose I put it this way," said her cousin with a leer, "if you weren't my cousin I'd invite you to take a walk in the garden. For a dance, of course," he added laughing.

"You are vulgar, Renato," Melania said haughtily, though she turned and regarded her reflection approvingly in the huge drawing room mirror.

"Vulgar, yes," he admitted, "but truthful." Then he shifted his glance to Aimée. "I can't imagine you selecting anything so daring. Surely the convent wouldn't have approved of a gown that completely reveals your charms."

"It was so beautiful, Renato," Aimée said with a smile. She still found she liked Renato in a special way that was unlike her reactions to the rest of her relatives, and yet he remained a mystery. He was so unlike the rest of his family—indeed, his manner toward them might be described as tolerant—and there was also the matter of his unexplained expenses and absences.

Antonia let out an audible sigh, attracting Lino's attention. "What's wrong, Antonia?" he asked.

Her plump hands touched her waist. "I suppose it's this new corset. I didn't get a good fit and it pinches."

"It'd *have* to pinch for you to get into that gown," Melania retorted. "You eat too many sweets, Mama."

"Can't the seams be let out, aunt?" Aimée asked, trying to avoid one of their petty squabbles.

"I never thought of it," Antonia exclaimed.

Aimée stood up. "I'm going upstairs to finish dressing. I'll send Marie-Clarice to your room to look at it. She's clever as a seamstress."

"I'd be most grateful," Antonia exclaimed as best she could with the little breath she could get into her lungs.

Marie-Clarice found hidden seams in Antonia's gown to let out and thus ease her discomfort, even though she fussed with Aimée about performing tasks for such ungrateful people. Aimée shushed her by reminding her again that they must do whatever necessary to play their roles convincingly, to prevent suspicion. Marie-Clarice sighed in resignation but her feelings were eased when Aimée started talking about the ball, which Marie-Clarice was to attend with her mistress.

Aimée's gown was fashioned of nile green tulle. She had a fringe of curls across her brow and Marie-Clarice had drawn up her hair to form a crown from which thick curls hung to just below her shoulders. A coronet of zinnias encircled her head.

"It's most becoming," Aimée said as Marie-Clarice

finished her handiwork. "I hope the empress won't object to my coronet."

"I doubt it—since yours is only of flowers and hers will be of diamonds," said Marie-Clarice dryly.

"I do hope she makes an appearance," Aimée went on.

"So do I," Marie-Clarice said, "if only to see you, señorita. Now you are ready and I must go and prepare myself."

"Please hurry. The carriage will be coming for us any minute," Aimée reminded her.

Aimée put on the necklace of gold pendants which had been carefully locked up in a jewel box belonging to Angela. It was indeed a magnificent piece. Aimée then eased her hands into her white kid gloves and went downstairs to join the others who were waiting, impatient to go to the ball.

Everyone was gay and smiling and excited. They were going to use two carriages since there would be eight of them. Besides the family there would be Marie-Clarice and Antonia's maid, Teresa. The girls would be there to attend to their mistresses in between dances and would be allowed to dance the last *galop*, if they could find a partner. And for once, Antonia had no objections to Marie-Clarice's presence since she had wrought a miracle with her needle, enabling Antonia to wear a corset which fit her properly.

The coachmen were specially uniformed for the occasion. Each wore white linen trousers, a white cotton shirt covered with a three-colored poncho and a gigantic white sombrero.

Renato, after studying the coachmen's uniforms, was pleased. "Papa," he said to Lino, "I think they should use these uniforms all the time."

"What a marvelous idea," exclaimed Della.

The others agreed so enthusiastically that Aimée wondered what made this apparently trivial matter seem so important to them. The answer came quickly: such distinctive uniforms would make it known when one of the family was in Mexico City. It was a matter of self-esteem then, Aimée thought, mildly surprised that this would matter to the usually indifferent Renato.

The trip through a wooded area always generated a certain amount of apprehension. Bandits often were seen in this particular area. Guerilla fighters of Benito Juárez also could be a threat. A rich party like this was a great temptation, but the ride was uneventful and their timing was perfect: They arrived at the palace not too early and not too late. Antonia was a master at judging proper arrival and departure times. To arrive too early would have shown they were too eager to attend. To arrive too late would have risked the wrath of the emperor, who expected all of the guests to be gathered before he made his appearance. So it was a delicate matter, this question of when to arrive. Antonia may have been a social snob, but she knew instinctively the right thing to do, Aimée noticed. She would do well to learn some of her aunt's "tricks."

The palace's uniformed servants, wearing white gloves, helped them out of their carriages. Antonia and Lino led the way, Renato offered his arm to Aimée, and Melania and Della followed. Behind them, at a discreet distance, was Teresa in an elaborate servant's costume and Marie-Clarice in her new green gown, its decolletage every bit as revealing as Melania's. But while Marie-Clarice had tucked a large yellow rose between her breasts for partial concealment, Melania had put a beauty spot near her heart, calling further attention to her bountiful endowment. Aimée had expected Antonia to protest Marie-Clarice's gown, but apparently she didn't notice or pretended not to. Antonia was probably so busy hoping her Melania's blond beauty, so unusual in this country of dark-skinned, dark-haired people, would catch the emperor's eye that she probably didn't even notice Marie-Clarice. If gossip about the emperor was true, there was every chance that Melania would meet with great success.

They were ushered directly into the ballroom so

Aimée had only the briefest glimpse of the palace. But a half-open door leading into the drawing room showed it was decorated opulently, with furnishings from Vienna and Paris. Fine paintings hung on the wall, and elegant lamps gave just enough illumination to show off the rich trappings. Aimée wondered if Mexicans had ever seen anything like this before. She could imagine what a poor peon who probably owned a few pottery bowls would think, and had even a better idea of what Benito Juárez would think if he ever saw it.

The ballroom opened on three sides onto an enormous formal patio. It was an amazing setting. In the center of the patio, a huge fountain sprayed water high into the air, and then the water splashed down into a huge basin where nymphs seated on the edge caught the water. On all sides were lush tropical plants and bushes so laden with flowers that it seemed impossible for one bush to hold so many blooms. On a dais at one end of the room an orchestra, direct from Vienna, was already playing softly. The musicians were enchanting in their Hussar uniforms, and between the music and the aroma of the flowers, it was a heady atmosphere indeed.

At the far end of the ballroom was another, smaller dais. There, two large, tall-backed chairs, beautifully carved, gilded and upholstered in plush, sat under a draped crimson canopy. This was where the emperor and his empress would be seated during the festivities.

When they entered, the ballroom floor was filled with long tables. Dinner would be served here, then the guests would retire—the men to smoke and drink, the women to attend to their toilettes and be fussed over by their personal maids—and the floor would be cleared for the dancing to follow.

The *Pantalons Rouges* were everywhere about the room, conspicuous even in this opulent setting in their scarlet trousers and white tunics. There were also officers from the Mexican army—but their uniforms were drab in comparison with the *Pantalons Rouges* and the regular French army.

Aimée's gaze shifted to the tables, which were covered in heavy white damask tablecloths and set with silver and crystal that sparkled in the light from the overhead chandeliers and the hundreds of candles. The gold dishes gleamed on the tables, and servants were bustling everywhere.

There were to be more than four hundred guests, which meant the ballroom was well filled, but not over-crowded. Aimée had been told that Carlota hated great masses of people. For Aimée, it was an enjoyable experience to meet so many new people and to see the often suggestive looks of handsome young men, and some not-so-young men. Della and Melania were also greatly admired. Aimée realized she was genuinely beginning to enjoy her new life, even though she knew that it would all end abruptly when she escaped from Mexico—or when her true identity was revealed. But in the meantime, she reveled in the finery around her, the elegant manners of the fashionably dressed men and women, and the fine food and wine that was being served. The thunder of a heavy staff wielded by a uniformed guard announced the entrance of the emperor and empress. All motion and talk came to an immediate halt. It the past, Aimée had seen the pomp of royal functions while traveling with her diplomat father, but she had to admit that this almost outshone anything she'd ever seen anywhere.

As Maximilian and Carlota slowly and majestically entered the room, their subjects drew back in rows leaving a path to the thrones. They would stop and greet each guest with a smile or a nod of recognition. As they came abreast of Aimée, she curtsied but couldn't bring herself to avert her eyes from Maximilian's gaze. It was as if he had willed her to look at him—his blue eyes, his blond beard, parted in the middle, his compelling face and his truly regal bearing. Carlota seemed a mere shadow in comparison, and her pale, mask-like face betrayed no emotion or spark or liveliness. There was little doubt that she had been ill and was making an effort to make this appearance. Aimée had heard that at one time Carlota had attended balls frequently and had outdanced everyone present. But this was her first public appearance in a long time.

Maximilian's steady gaze met Aimée's, and he gave her a smile and moved on.

After they had passed, Della whispered, "Did you see his greeting to us? He even paused slightly, as if it pleased him that we had come."

"I noticed," Aimée said, trying to compose herself.

When the royal pair was seated, the guests took their places and the waiters sprang into action. There was silence after everybody was seated. Then Maximilian arose and bowed regally.

"We are honored by the presence of so many loyal subjects and we hope that this will be an evening for all to enjoy. I'm delighted to add that Her Royal Highness feels well enough this evening to join in the dancing, though I have implored her not to overtax her strength."

He said a few more words and then sat down. That was the signal for the waiters to bring on a steady flow of exquisite food. If Juárez's recruits could see this, they would drill longer hours and with more fervor than ever before to put an end to such ostentation. After all, the Mexicans were footing the bill, Aimée thought, as she ate and occasionally turned to chat with a French army officer on one side and a *Pantalons Rouges* colonel on her other side.

The dinner lasted for two-and-a-half-hours, after which the guests retired. When they returned, the orchestra began the evening's dance program with a quadrille, danced by Maximilian and Carlota. Then the royal pair was escorted by two officers to their thrones under the canopied dais, where they could sit and watch their subjects for the evening and join in, if they cared to.

The dancing began in earnest then, and Aimée took part in every dance until she finally had to plead fatigue to her admirers and rejoin Melania on the sidelines where she, too, was recovering from a wild dance she had had with an amorous and somewhat intoxicated major of the Foreign Legion. Aimée noted the beauty spot was still intact, but Melania was fussing with the decolletage which threatened to collapse under her heaving bosom.

Aimée indicated Maximilian and his empress. "Why aren't they dancing again?"

"Carlota used to. Maybe she still will, since she loves dancing, but Maximilian claims it tires him. He dances to be polite, and then in a half hour or so he will probably quietly excuse himself and go to bed."

"I suppose, as emperor, he can do what he likes, but I don't think he honors his guests by retiring so early," Della said sourly, coming over and joining the group.

"Maximilian doesn't give a damn what anyone thinks. Did you ever hear of a Hapsburg who did?" said Melania.

"I really don't know," Aimée tried to make light of it, but secretly she was surprised at how disappointed she felt that he might leave without dancing with her. Despite herself, she had been looking forward to seeing him again. Just the memory of his hand on her had been enough to make her tingle all over. And each night before she'd gone to bed she had lain awake for what seemed like hours fantasizing about being in his arms again.

"I danced with him once," Melania said with great pride. "At one of his first balls he did dance, for half a minute, with all the girls who lined up. There must have been more than a hundred of us. I was tenth in line—and last. He gave up after he danced with me and Della was seething with jealousy that he should not have danced with her."

"And his dancing!" She went on, oblivious to her sister's very pointed glares: "He was holding me so close and his hand kept moving about; sometimes it was even where it was not required to be and . . . Carlota spied this and when he saw her watching him, he ended his dancing right there. You might say I was the last girl to dance with him." Aimée listened with amusement to this retelling, since Melania seemed to have forgotten that Maximilian had danced with her not once, but twice, and only the week before. But politely she said to her cousin, "You were fortunate. Well, here comes a lieutenant with his eyes on me."

Aimée was swept up into the dancing crowd again, with few breaks. During one, there was a trumpet note from the orchestra, and Maximilian arose, bowed briefly to his guests, and bowed even more deeply to his empress, and then withdrew. Aimée's heart sank.

But it was now that Carlota arose to join in the dancing. Another trumpet blast sounded and a *galop* began. It grew faster and faster, encouraged by Carlota who seemed to have almost miraculously regained strength and energy. She was a wanton, wild dancer, Aimée noted with great surprise, and she urged on the orchestra with wild yells, usually for yet faster music.

Aimée was now tired and had withdrawn from the dance. Antonia, who had done little dancing, joined her, but Della and Melania remained joyously on the dance floor, constantly changing partners and flirting outrageously with the handsome young officers.

Fanning herself and puffing a little, Antonia asked, "Well, what do you think of our royalty, Angela?"

"They certainly do know how to enjoy themselves," Aimée answered. "It's a wonderful evening. Also an extravagant one, at least to my eyes," she added.

Antonia shrugged off this last comment as if what else could you expect from royalty when they entertain. As Aimée was sitting and catching her breath, a major approached, saluted, and bowed. Then he offered her his arm.

"I'm sorry, major," she said graciously, "but I'm resting at the moment. Perhaps the next dance?"

"Señorita, this is not an invitation to dance," he said stiffly. "Your presence is desired elsewhere."

Aimée raised one eyebrow in surprise. "Oh? May I ask by whom?"

"No, señorita, you may not," he answered blandly. "Please . . . come with me." There was something about his tone that made his request one not to argue with, even though Aimée felt flustered. It was a command, not an invitation. Aimée excused herself and accepted the major's arm. She was swiftly led away from the ballroom, but in a manner that did not seem to arouse any curiosity. As they reached a long hall outside the ballroom, Aimee said, "Major—"

"—There is no cause for alarm," he assured her politely.

She found herself ushered down a long corridor, up stairs and through a dark maze of halls that left her quite confused. She realized she was in the palace, but she had no idea where. Finally they approached a door and it opened, as if by itself. Right behind it was a lady-in-waiting who obviously had been expecting her imminent arrival. The major bowed as the door closed behind Aimée and she found herself in a dimly lit room. The middle-aged lady said nothing, but began to open the buttons on Aimée's gown.

"Stop! What are you doing?" Aimée protested, more shocked than indignant. "Why are you removing my gown?"

"Please, señorita, do as you're told," the woman answered in a hushed but urgent tone. "You'll find it a very pleasant experience. You will not be hurt. I must ask that you remove all of your clothing. In the next room, a bath has been drawn that is warm, perfumed and waiting your pleasure."

This was all so mysterious, but Aimée was intrigued. And she instinctively knew that the major was outside the door, and who else might be close by in case she resisted.

"A bath?" she asked incredulously. What a strange request. This was turning into a most extraordinary evening.

"*Si.* Please hurry," the woman almost begged her. "We cannot delay."

"I want to know what this is all about," began Aimée. But the woman simply ignored her and hurriedly kept undressing her until she was quite naked. But there was something about the woman's manner that indicated she found Aimée's questions almost amusing, as if Aimée should know why she was there in this strange, dark room having a bath while perhaps a few hundred feet away a royal ball was going on.

Aimée submitted. The woman said quietly, "Believe me, señorita, after this evening, you will be held in the highest regard, I repeat, the very highest regard."

Maximilian! Of course! He was coming for her and she was being prepared. Her heart skipped a beat with excitement—and fear. There was a timid knock at a door she hadn't noticed and another woman came in with an elaborate silver goblet. "Here, drink this," said the first woman, offering it to her. "It's very, very special wine and it will help you to relax."

Aimée sipped it and found it a warm, spicy drink that was sweet but with a subtle undertaste she could not identify. Its soothing warmth seemed to spread through her body and she stepped into the bath and for the first time since she was a baby, was sponged from head to toe—everywhere on her body—by another grown woman, who acted as dispassionately as if she were washing a fine plate of china. Then she was dried off, given a fine lace nightgown and ushered into yet another room.

Here was a huge bed. The silken coverlet was turned back to reveal silken sheets and a virtual mountain of silken pillows. The woman's flickering candle shed the only light in a room so dark there didn't seem to be any windows.

Aimée allowed herself to be led to the bed, and her mind was so sluggish, it was as if she were in a dream. Even her limbs seemed to belong to another woman. It was as if she floated somewhere above this fantastic scene. Aimée didn't even protest when the woman closed the heavy drapes around the bed and withdrew from the room. Aimée lay on silken sheets that seemed to caress her body, and all thoughts of what went on elsewhere seemed to drift away as she lay on this huge, goosedown filled mattress. The room was so silent she could only hear her fluttering heart.

She sensed rather than heard footsteps approach the bed. The curtain parted briefly and she knew she was no longer alone. She felt the warmth of his body and his skilled hands caressing every inch of her, although she could see nothing and could barely find the strength to move at all. She lay back and allowed these gentle hands to caress her everywhere without a murmur. She heard a sigh, and realized it had been her own.

Then a whiskered face and mouth closed over hers in a kiss so passionate she almost gasped for breath. His breath, too, came faster, as his lips now explored everywhere his hands had been only seconds before. Aimée felt sensations aroused in her that she had never dreamed possible. She wanted it to go on forever even though a tiny voice, from far, far away cried out that it was wrong for Maximilian to virtually command her into his bed, and to steal into it as a faceless stranger in the dark. But she was in such a stupor these thoughts were quickly forgotten, and she realized she'd been drugged. Her body was there, her cheeks were flushing from the warmth this man aroused in her, but she could no more respond than resist.

The nightgown was ripped off her body with such ease, Aimée suspected it had been made for this purpose. There was no brutality in this gesture, only haste now. It seemed as if he could hardly wait to consummate their pleasure.

He teased each nipple until it was hard and erect. He gently took it in his mouth and Aimée was amazed at how it excited her. She almost wanted him to make love to her. She felt an urgent need she had never felt before and yet he was teasing her, arousing her, and taking his time to kiss every inch of her body, even though she could feel an amazing hardness pressing against her. He must be huge, she thought, a ripple of fear passing through her body. But when his arms went around her and he lightly climbed on top of her, she felt first his hand and there was an audible squish in the room, she was so hot and wet. Then for the first time he made a sound, a giant, "Aaaah," and then she felt his organ pressing against her. But he did not thrust his way in. Gently, inch by inch, he burrowed into her most intimate chamber. And, to her amazement, it yielded to his great size. There was no pain, no discomfort, only a hunger that shocked her. She wanted him to take her. She found her hips moving in rhythm with his, their bodies meshed as if they were one in a harmony she had never known. It was natural, it was exciting and it felt so very good that she moaned in pleasure. He was an exquisite lover. He'd withdraw for a half second and then plunge in. She felt her hips rise up to greet his. He'd move rapidly and then in slow, almost circling strokes that must have touched every inch of her now dripping wet female organs.

She pulled his head down to her breast and he teased her nipples with his teeth and she felt this explosion building up inside of her. She felt as if she were going to burst from pure pleasure. She sighed and moaned and began writhing against him with a passion he matched stroke for stroke. Together they moved in unison until the silken sheets were dripping wet with their perspiration and the air was hot with their pantings. It was reaching an unbearable tension until all of a sudden Aimée felt a release spread through her body that was like a pleasure she had never known—and her body responded to his like that of a wild animal, bucking and arching and writhing under his now powerful thrusts. His moves became so fast, so rapid that it was like beating a tattoo on her hips, but she gasped in pleasure and tried to keep up with his urgent need to relieve himself. At last it came. She felt the gushing of a hot liquid inside her and it seemed to go on and on. She could feel convulsions from his throbbing manhood and a sigh escaped his lips that told her he, too, was as pleased as she was.

They lay there in each other's arms for a few minutes. Not a word had been spoken, but Aimée knew full well who her thrilling partner had been. But she knew she had experienced more pleasure with him in these few minutes than in her encounters with Vardeau. Oh, what a lover!

His hands continued to caress her even after sex. He was breathing hard and she could hear his heart pounding, and with one hand she boldly reached down and touched him there. God, it was still full and swollen and slippery wet. For the first time she appreciated what this organ could do for a woman. It wasn't a weapon in the hands of a lover, but an exquisite source of pleasure. Her breath still came in gasps and her chest heaved as she held him close. She never wanted to let him go.

He held her tightly for a second, clasping her head to his broad chest, and then there was a light kiss on her forehead before he let go. She heard the heavy fabric of the bed curtains move. He was gone. She was alone. It had all been dreamlike, and she felt as if she were in a trance. This couldn't have happened. Although she had never seen his face and could never swear with certainty that her lover had been the emperor, she knew without a doubt that it had been he who had visited her. Time stopped when he had been with her. If the world had ended at that moment she wouldn't have noticed. She sighed out loud and realized she had to get back to the ball before she was missed.

She got out of the huge bed and found the door leading to the bathroom. A fresh bath had been drawn and her clothes were carefully laid out for her. In a langorous stupor, Aimée tried to hurry and bathe, get dressed, and return, but this feeling that permeated her entire being was so relaxing, so pleasant, that she wanted to remain in this state forever.

Finally she dressed and noticed in the mirror that except for a few stray hairs, somehow her coronet had miraculously stayed in place, and she probably appeared to the casual onlooker the same as she did when she'd excused herself from the dance floor. She also realized that she'd been drugged. And she couldn't help wondering how much of her euphoric feeling was the result of the drug—and how much was the passion that Maximilian had aroused in her. In this almost trance-like state, but trying to appear as normal as possible, she opened the outer door. She was not surprised to find the major waiting outside the door as she reappeared. He bowed respectfully and offered her his arm as casually as if she'd only been gone a few seconds.

Without a word, they walked back through the maze of corridors and down the stairs, the major pointing out different rooms so Aimée now could have a glimpse of them. All of the elegant furnishing appeared to be a million miles away, but Aimée tried to concentrate so she would be able to report what she had seen, for she doubted that her cousins had ever seen the inside of the palace except for the most public rooms. Finally, the major returned her to the row of chairs where Antonia sat now with Lino at her side.

"Where have you been?" Lino asked curiously.

"Inspecting the palace," she replied quietly. "It was a privilege extended to me as a newcomer that I could not refuse."

"I should think not," Antonia said, with no attempt to hide her envy.

Aimée fought her way back to reality. It was easier now, for the gay music, the voices around her, and the people moving to the music didn't seem so far away now. But she was still floating in a world of her own and had to be careful not to give herself away. She told herself that she hardly looked as if she'd just been to bed with a man. In fact, she looked as if she'd just returned from a lengthy and rather boring tour of the palace with the major. Her remoteness might be attributed to the fact that her feet hurt and she was genuinely tired and wanted nothing more than to be left alone, to go to sleep.

"You must be in His Majesty's good graces," Lino commented with an approving nod. "That's good, my dear. Very good." He patted her hand. "Well, the evening is almost over, so I insist on the last dance with you, Angela, since Antonia doesn't feel up to it."

"I never said a thing of the kind," Antonia said tartly. "But go ahead."

Aimée breathed a sigh of relief. They seemed to have accepted her explanation that she had been given a tour of the palace. And soon they were all on their way home, exhausted from dancing and sated with food and drink, as each of them privately relived the highlights of their evening.

Aimée fell asleep the moment she lay down, for the drug had induced a soporific effect. Her dreams were filled with images of a golden, godlike man making love to her for hours. At one point she came to orgasm and woke up to find the sun streaming in through her window. It was late morning, judging by the humid air which even the thick walls could not keep out.

Instantly the events of the night before came rushing back to her. She didn't feel resentment or anger over what had happened for her passion had matched his. But what galled her and made her clench her little fists was the fact he had been so *certain* she would comply. But then again, had he ever been refused? The idea of refusing him brought a slight smile to her face. But she had been used. She realized she should have felt honored for having been singled out from all the other women, and in a curious way she was, but not entirely. What would have happened, she mused, if he had not had her drugged?

Obviously he wanted her badly enough not to take any chances. And if she had refused, she felt certain his retribution would have been brutal and swift—and not only on her but the entire Miranda family. Then she realized she was ravenous. She had hardly eaten at the banquet the night before, and so she got up, dressed and went down to breakfast.

During the day she half-expected someone to mention her absence from the ballroom. No one did. Aimée assumed that no one did because it would have been a breach of etiquette. But Aimée knew her cousins well enough to know that they'd never let mere manners stand in their way when the subject was the seduction of Maximilian. No, they must have believed what she had said about being given a tour of the palace. But she could well imagine their reactions if Melania and Della ever learned the truth. All of her good works would be forgotten for they woud loathe her forever for having gotten what they had plotted so long and hard for.

She mulled over her own feelings. She should have been angry at him, she scolded herself, but then the memory of his gentle caresses—and her passionate responses—would make her breath come quicker and her cheeks flush, and she knew she was not angry. Nor was she humiliated at having been taken like a common servant by any landowner. No, she had to admit she had given herself freely in order to guard her safety, she rationalized.

Of course the subject of the ball and Maximilian were brought up frequently for the next few days, not least by Marie-Clarice.

"I danced with officers," she said one morning as Aimée was getting dressed. "They didn't ask who I was. But if they had I would have lied. It was wonderful, Angela. You see, I have never called you anything but Angela. I am so grateful you gave me one of your gowns. I received many, many compliments," she added gaily, prattling on.

"I'm sure you did." Aimée added, "I'm very pleased that you had a good time."

"Isn't the emperor magnificent? But where did he go? He left early, while the empress danced until we nearly dropped."

"I suppose he went to bed. I was told he often retires early for these affairs bore him," said Aimée easily.

"Well, anyway, señorita, it was the most wonderful evening of my life." Marie-Clarice's voice trailed off, as if hesitant to bring up the subject, but she must have decided to get on with it for she said, "But sometimes I worry. Do you think one day they will find out?"

"So long as we are careful," Aimée said wearily. "I see no way they could become suspicious. Everything is going so well, in fact, I'm beginning to think we will get away with it, forever if we like."

"It would be nice," said Marie-Clarice wistfully, probably thinking of some handsome soldier. "Do you like Mexico?"

"I'm not sure. But so long as you're rich and in favor with the court, it is a wonderful life," said Aimée honestly. "However there's another side to Mexico that you've never seen. I know it from the time I was here with my father. Its people are oppressed, hunted down if they don't obey every little rule. They live in conditions that make ordinary poverty on the streets of Paris seem like a life of luxury. The way we live, yes, I like Mexico. But I can never forget those others, the peons who are starving, who live in another Mexico that is more real than this one."

"I know what being poor is like," Marie-Clarice said solemnly.

"We shall not talk of it again. The people in this house have chosen to be blind to the way the other half lives, and there is always a chance we may say something that could create doubt in the minds of those around us."

Marie-Clarice carefully laid out Aimée's riding outfit. "Do you trust them?" she asked, her eyes revealing she was almost desperate to be reassured.

Aimée thought about it for a moment. "I don't know That's what bothers me. I remember how Nemecio criticized them, saying they were only waiting for him to die so they could lay hands on the estate and his money. If that's true, then they might secretly regard me in the same way, as someone to be rid of...."

"I don't trust Renato. He danced with me last night," said Marie-Clarice, "and flirted with me and held me too close. I liked it, but I don't trust him. There's something about him, a secret ..."

Aimée sat down to draw on her riding boots. It was curious the way Marie-Clarice often expressed her own doubts. "What is it about him that you don't trust?" she probed.

"I think he wants but one thing from a girl. But that isn't what bothers me so much as the feeling that he's hiding something, something important under the pretense of being a gay cavalier," Marie-Clarice summed up. Apparently Renato had gone no further than holding her too close, thought Aimée, quietly amused at her indignation. After all, Marie-Clarice had been taken by Renato's good looks from the moment she had first seen him. Apparently nothing more had happened or she was certain that Marie-Clarice would either breathlessly announce it or blush at the mention of his name.

Aimée found that she was the only one who had gone downstairs for breakfast. At the stable a horse was saddled and waiting for her. She was surprised to see that Renato was there, too, preparing for a morning ride.

"Would you like some company?" he asked.

"I'd be delighted, Renato. I'm not a good enough rider to enjoy riding alone."

"Then I'll be there to catch you if you fall," he said gallantly, a grin lighting up his dark good looks as he swung easily into his saddle.

They walked their horses toward a riding trail that went through the forest behind the estate. When they reached the woods, the trail widened so they could ride by side.

"What do you think of our aristocracy?" Renato asked lightly. Surprised at the directness of the question, Aimée hedged her answer.

"They seem to be nice people. I don't think they mean to harm anyone," she said evasively.

"You haven't heard of Maximilian's Black Decree then?" said Renato.

"I've heard it's very cruel and unforgiving of anyone who violates the laws he has set down. Yet he's done a great deal of good in some ways," she added cautiously.

"Perhaps," he said, then was silent for a minute. "But I'm inclined to favor the peons who've never known anything but poverty and hunger," he went on earnestly.

She gave him a sharp glance. "That means you are in favor of Juárez?"

"Not exactly," he said, equally as evasively. "He threatens our way of life, too, but I understand what he's after."

"And what is that?" Aimée wanted to know.

"Freedom for the masses. Freedom for the peon to keep at least one row of corn that he has raised. Things weren't good before the French came, of course, but they are worse now. We had hoped the United States would invoke the Monroe Doctrine, which warns all foreign nations to stay out of this hemisphere."

"They did nothing?" asked Aimée, realizing how little she knew of world affairs.

"Their President, Abraham Lincoln, could have, but he felt that the French would bring about their own downfall without any intervention from him," explained Renato.

"Will they, Renato?" Aimée asked quietly.

"In time . . . yes," he answered.

"You seem very well versed in politics, I must say," she complimented him.

Renato gave a humorless laugh. "Whatever my family may be, I'm not completely the fool, Angela. How do you feel about Juárez?" he asked curiously.

"I know so little about him. . .."

"His goals then? What he represents?"

"I know little of that either, Renato," she said impatiently, uncomfortable with this line of questioning. "And I don't think any of us should discuss politics too openly. It might be dangerous."

"Life is dangerous," he said philosophically. "But you're right. If we gossip about this, some day we're liable to say more than we mean to, and we will end up with our backs against a wall."

"Then we shall talk of other matters. . . . I think some of the terraces need attention. Some of the plants seem to be dying. Will you see to it?" She was silently wondering when he'd get to the point. He always seemed to go out of his way to avoid her and she suspected that today he had just as deliberately chosen this morning ride, when they would be alone, as an excuse to talk with her.

They rode in silence for a while. Renato hesitated then began, "Tell me, Angela, did Uncle Nemecio really fall overboard or did he . . . jump?"

"Renato, what a horrible thing to say!" She reined in her horse and Renato stopped as well. She was shocked by his words and wondered if it was possible that he suspected the truth. "It was an accident. Everybody said so," she said.

"Yet no one saw him fall," Renato pointed out.

"He was very drunk. I'm sorry to say it, but that night he'd been drinking much too much. He drank so much that he dropped the rum bottle on the cabin floor and apparently never even tried—or wasn't able —to pick it up during the storm. Besides, the sea was rough and the ship was pitching so badly that he must have lost his balance. It couldn't have been difficult to lose his balance, drunk as he must have been," she went on, feeling somewhat defensive.

"I don't miss him," Renato said bluntly. "He was as much an emperor on this estate as Max is over all of Mexico. But Uncle Nemecio was far more cruel. He liked to taunt us with the threat of disowning us. He said he'd make paupers of us. He said we were leeches, and perhaps he was right since now we live off your bounty. But we take care of the estate and all that is connected with it, and we have no time to work elsewhere for our own personal success. We think we did well for him, just as we're doing well for you now."

This was the longest single speech Renato had ever made to her, and now Aimée thought she understood his point—that she needed them as much as they needed her, for the time being, at least. "How it was with him here, I don't know," said Aimée slowly. "But I quite agree that without you and your father I could never run the estate or the business of making the money to support it."

"I'm grateful that you said that. I. . . ." His words trailed off. He had been about to say something more when he stopped and cocked his head. "Did you hear anything?" he whispered.

"Nothing," Aimée whispered back, looking around apprehensively.

"I heard a rustling sound in the brush," and even as he was saying it, Renato reached under his riding jacket and produced a pistol.

Aimée was shocked that he was armed and about to say something, when she saw Renato point the gun at the bush and a man step out. He was certainly not a bandit. In fact, he gave no evidence of even being armed. He was sixtyish, with thick gray hair and a troubled-looking face that was deeply lined from too many years in the sunlight.

"Señor," he held up both hands to show he was unarmed, "one moment, please."

"I know him," Renato said, dismounting and moving toward the man. "Stay here, and I'll find out what he wants."

Aimée sat on her horse while Renato spoke to the man who waved his arms excitedly as he spoke and was clearly frightened about something, although not of Renato. Then Renato spoke. The man bowed several times, retreated a few steps and then turned and dashed back into the brush and disappeared. Renato returned to his horse.

"A poor man who lost everything to the French soldiers," he said by way of explanation. "So I gave him a few pesos."

Aimée had seen no money passed, and the man had been terrified. Why had he approached Renato? What could Renato do for him—or what did he have to tell him? So she asked as casually as she could, "He didn't appear to mean any harm, but could he have been running away from the French? Could he be a Juárez spy?"

"Him?" Renato scoffed. "I think not. I also think we'd best get back. It will soon be time for dinner," he said, turning his horse's head back the way they'd come and neatly changing the subject. On the way back they trotted their horses and there was no more conversation, even though Aimée was positive she had seen something she was not meant to see. If that man was a Juárez spy and he had come to Renato, that meant Renato might be engaged in some dangerous business. Aimée was glad they had this chance to talk together, but she was as puzzled as ever about Renato. To her, this handsome cousin remained an enigma.

Dinner was already on the table when they returned home. Aimée and Renato apologized for their lateness and hurried upstairs to change from their riding clothes.

"What kept you?" Antonia asked as they joined their family at the table.

"We had a fine ride," Renato said. "We had much to talk about."

Melania pursed her lips for a moment. "Could it have been a guessing game about who the emperor sought out to bed with him while the ball was going on?"

Aimée paled and prayed no one had noticed. Her heart began to pound. How could Melania have known? How could anyone have known? It had all taken place in the strictest secrecy. And it was only later, when she had returned, that she realized what a short period of time she had actually been missing from the ball.

"You sound resentful that it wasn't you," Renato said with a chuckle. "Certainly you did your best to entice him with that gown. Don't think I didn't notice that beauty spot. Did any of your partners try to remove it?" he leered.

"Mind your own business," Melania shot back at him.

"May I ask this one question, dear cousin?" Renato went on. "How do *you* know the emperor beds with someone each night? Other than his empress, of course."

"It's said he does," Melania replied. "It's said that's why he retires early from state social occasions, so he can bed the woman he's chosen."

Almost about to faint, Aimée now was able to compose herself. Melania had been guessing, and her question had been based on gossip not suspicion.

"Gossip," sneered Renato, adding, "Perhaps if my cousin was less obvious she might have caught the emperor's interest. When will women learn that the more mysterious they are, the more desirable they are? A man loves mystery. Don't flaunt your charms so openly, Melania. The same goes for you, too, Della," he said bluntly.

"And what about Marie-Clarice?" Melania asked scornfully. "Her decolletage was the same as mine."

"Perhaps," admitted Renato, "but she partly concealed hers with a large flower."

Della, never one to pass up a good argument, now made her stand with her sister. "Unless you've changed, my dear Renato," she said, her voice dripping sarcasm, "nothing would have pleased you more than to have removed that maid's flower."

"If I'd had the opportunity to be alone with her, yes, you are right," he agreed lightly. "She's a pleasant companion. Gay and—"

"Stop it!" ordered Antonia sternly. "Here comes your papa. He might not approve of you even dancing with Marie-Clarice, a mere maid, at an important social event."

Renato's smile mocked Antonia. "I doubt he noticed, and I don't really care if he did. She told me I'm jo-lee," he said, taunting his mother and mocking Marie-Clarice's French accent. "I like her French accent. She was jo-lee too."

Lino drew out his chair, sat down and looked at his son. "What kind of language is that?"

"The language of love, father," Renato replied. "Surely you wouldn't deprive me of that."

"If you're like me, you need it," his father remarked with a sly grin.

"Like Uncle Nemecio?" Melania asked caustically.

"He's dead," Lino said softly, but gruffly. "Let him rest in peace. My son is not like my dead brother. Nor am I," Lino went on.

"True. To me, love is beautiful, but just now, I've talked enough of it," Renato said, his patience suddenly at an end. "Sometimes my dear cousins sicken me. This is one of those times. Please excuse me."

Renato stood up so suddenly his chair fell back with a loud clatter. Antonia opened her mouth to protest, but a glance at Renato's flushed and angry face stopped her.

The remainder of the meal was eaten in comparative

silence. Aimée's effort to form a fair appraisal of her bogus relatives was hampered by Renato's behavior. Now she didn't know what to think. But she was sure that something urgent was smouldering beneath the surface of this family, and she found the thought most unsettling. How right her suspicion would prove to be!

Chapter 8

Aimée was spending the morning in the library going over Lino's bookkeeping. For once in her life she was grateful that she had had a gift for figures when she had attended the convent school. If she hadn't she never would have learned, for the nuns were busy teaching their young charges the social graces so they could assume their positions in life as upper class ladies of leisure. The idea of them burdening their minds with columns of figures was ludicrous. But since Aimée had shown a natural talent in this area, they had taught her well.

The books revealed that the estate was showing a good profit from bank interest both in Mexico and abroad, and from their middleman trading business. Their European investments, which provided a very nice income indeed, assured the family further financial security. Aimée found she was a very wealthy woman. And she realized with a shock that she was going over the books as if it really mattered to her, so immersed had she become in her role as Angela Fuchard. And yet she was obsessed with the idea that she would be identified at some ball or some casual social event that she might attend. She'd found herself carefully scrutinizing the faces around her at the ball, but to her relief she hadn't seen even one that looked vaguely familiar. It wasn't really that surprising. She had led a cloistered life, divided between the convent and her infrequent visits with her father. Her childhood years had been spent traveling with her father, but there was very little resemblance left between that pretty child and her appearance as a young woman now.

Her greatest advantage had been the letters the real Angela Fuchard had saved. Aimée had read each one until she had practically memorized them and was totally familiar with the subjects. It wauld have been impossible to have succeeded in her masquerade if she hadn't had these letters. No one apparently seemed to doubt that she was the real Angela, and yet she never felt secure. She frequently thought of escaping to the United States, but she was realistic enough to face the fact that once she got there she would not have the faintest idea of where to go or what to do. Money wasn't the issue. She had easy access to Nemecio's assets. But in the United States, she'd be friendless and always in danger of being questioned about her identity.

Aimée also recalled, somewhat vaguely to be sure, that there was an agreement between the United States and France to extradite criminals back to their own country. Aimée dreaded this possibility most. If she was caught, she would be on the next boat back to Paris.

Yes, it was safer and wiser to stay where she was. It was silly to be anxious when she could stay here and enjoy all this wealth. It was ironic that the very government her father had died opposing was probably the one that would keep her alive and safe for the time being.

And safe she felt. After Maximilian's secret visit, she

felt sure he would offer his protection. She wondered, though, if there would be other such visits. After her experiences with Vardeau and Nemecio, being loved by this gentle, understanding man was the difference between heaven and hell. For once Aimée knew what it was like to feel alive as a woman, to thrill to a man's caresses, to respond with passion to his very kisses, and to ache for the feeling of his manhood buried deep inside her. And she realized that she wouldn't hesitate to be with him again—and not only because she thought it would give her some power or assure her safety.

But in some way she still felt cheated. He had been her lover, and unlike the brutality of Vardeau and Nemecio, he had truly tried to please her, to arouse her so that when he entered her she was ready and willing and frantic with desire. Now, was he going to forget her? Aimée yearned to be intimate with him in a way that made her lie in bed at night and feel a wetness between her legs when she thought of him. It was a feeling so strong and irresistible that she almost hated him for arousing it in her. After all, he was the enemy, she kept reminding herself. If he knew her true identity, he would have her stood up against a wall and shot on the spot. The figures in front of her blurred as Aimée realized she had been lost in another daydream about Maximilian. If only she could get her feelings about him straightened out in her own mind. If only she could hate him . . . or love him. Now at least, she realized what really went on between men and women, and she also realized she wanted it to happen to her again as soon as possible.

Finally she closed the books, placed them back in the desk drawer and rested her head against the high-backed leather chair. Her musings were interrupted by a maid who timidly knocked on the door and entered the room as if she was expecting to be shot on sight herself. "Señorita," she began respectfully, eyes downcast, "there is a gentleman who wishes to see you."

"Who is he?" Aimée asked, her composure shattered by the news, although she took great care to maintain an outward composure. Why was a man calling on her? A soldier?

"I don't know, señorita," she apologized, "but he is an *Americano*. He wishes very much to speak with you."

"Very well," Aimée said, sparked by curiosity and realizing that sooner or later she would probably have to meet him, so why postpone it? Besides, when she heard he was an American, she relaxed because she didn't know any, so what could she possibly have to fear from him? "Please bring him in," she instructed the girl, who was virtually trembling.

"He's just outside the door, señorita," the maid said uncertainly. Then, lowering her voice, "He's very bold. I couldn't make him wait in the entryway. Very bold, this *Americano*," she said disapprovingly.

Aimée smiled to reassure the maid that she didn't blame her for the brash American. Obviously the girl expected to be punished. "Well let him in," said Aimée, trying to appear as relaxed and confident as she could. She had become quite adept at the art of deception as a matter of survival. But now she had a feeling that this American's visit could only mean trouble.

The maid had no sooner withdrawn than the American boldly entered, striding directly toward her desk, arm outstretched to shake hands. Aimée remained seated, regarding the tall, slender, dark-haired man who stood before her and smiled down at her. There was something about him that made her sit up even straighter. Not a word had been spoken, and yet an electricity flowed between them and Aimée's heart was pumping wildly. She cautioned herself to remain as calm as she could.

The man gave a slight bow of the head as he spoke, "Señorita Angela Fuchard, my name is Alex Mooreland. I'm a newspaper reporter with the *New York Globe*."

A reporter! Aimée's heart lurched. "You're quite brazen" was her cool response to him.

His gray eyes didn't flicker as they studied Aimée with more than necessary interest. "I couldn't risk your not seeing me," he said coolly.

"You're also impudent," she shot back, unflinching from his penetrating gaze.

"It's necessary in my profession, señorita, though I do apologize for it," he said quietly.

"At least you have the graciousness to admit it. I've heard that *Americanos* are very forward, even to the point of rudeness," Aimée said blandly as if his very existence was of no more interest to her than the untouched cup of chocolate the maid had brought in earlier.

"I don't wish to be rude, señorita, please believe me," he said earnestly, speaking in atrocious Spanish. "But I must admit I am a very determined man."

"Indeed you are. And your knowledge of Spanish leaves much to be desired," she said pointedly, trying to get the upper hand and so she said, "Speak English, please."

"Splendid!" he replied, switching to his native tongue. "What other languages do you speak?"

"French, German and Italian. I was educated in France and have been in Mexico but a short time." She could have bitten her tongue for volunteering any information about herself to this man.

"I know. You're an heiress," he stated flatly. But there was an amused look in his eyes that infuriated Aimée. She wished to be rid of him.

"Does your newspaper want to do a story on me?" she asked, deciding that it was time they came to the point of his visit.

"Not you, señorita, Emperor Maximilian."

"If that's the case, why didn't you go to the palace? Why come to see me?" asked Aimée, her heart pounding. What had brought him to her, of all people, when there were so many others who knew Maximilian?

"I've already tried to arrange an interview with him, without success. I must have it," he said with an urgency that took her by surprise.

"I can't help you. I'm sorry, but the emperor would no more see me than he would see you," she said, as if the matter were closed.

"I'm not so sure," he said quietly but pointedly.

Aimée felt color suffuse her face. "What do you mean by that?" she demanded.

"I understand he favored you above all the others at the ball he gave recently," Mooreland had the boldness to say to her face.

Aimée stood up, making no attempt to conceal her anger. "What are you implying, Mr. Mooreland?"

"He . . .danced with you. Also, he attended a ball here and danced with you twice."

"Who gave you this information?" Aimée and Alex were now practically head to head in this confrontation and Aimée was determined not to back down an inch.

"Señorita Fuchard, it is common knowledge," he said smoothly.

"You are very presumptuous to come into my house uninvited and to say such things," Aimée countered.

"I'm desperate, señorita. I've been sent all the way here by my newspaper to report on the political climate in Mexico City and all of Mexico. It's very important for me to get that interview," he said, a hint of desperation in his voice. For the first time, Aimée saw that his brashness was an act, that he was truly grasping at any possibility he could find in order to contact the emperor.

Aimée was most anxious for him to leave, but she was also aware of how persistent he was. If she sent him away, he would simply haunt her until she told him what she could. It was better, even safer, to deal with him now, and be rid of him. With a sigh she sat down and said, "I can not excuse your boldness, but I believe the more that's known about Emperor Maximilian and Mexico, the better it will be for my country. It isn't easy to understand my people, Mr. Mooreland. I will try to help you."

"Then you will arrange the interview?" he said, excitement lighting up his features.

"I'll have to see what I can do. I can't promise anything," she said honestly. "No matter whether an emperor danced with me at a ball or not, it doesn't mean he will do something he doesn't want to do. You have a President whom you elect and who must be responsive to his people or he will not be reelected. An emperor is different. He does not need the approval of his people, and he certainly doesn't have to do what a mere subject requests," she said.

"Look, I need this job," he blurted out. "I'll be forever in your debt if you can help me to arrange to speak with Maximilian."

"Be patient," Aimée warned, sympathetic now that his brashness had proved to be sheer bravado and that he was being so honest with her. "You must convince me first that you mean no harm to Mexico."

"I swear to you. . . ."

"Will you make our emperor look like a fool?" she persisted. "Will you say that Mexico is a land of revolutions and ignorant peons?"

Mooreland sat down on a chair, and edged it closer to her desk. "I write facts, señorita. Just facts. I write what I learn, and I'm just looking to report the way things are."

"Even if it hurts those you write about?"

"Even if it hurts. But I promise you I'll be fair. I think Mexico is a country with a great future. What I'll write on that subject will help, not harm, your country."

"You have come to me for information. You know

141

my family and I are members of the aristocracy and that we do favor Maximilian. Will you favor us?"

"If you deserve to be favored," he answered, his gray eyes seeming to evaluate Aimée in a way that she found most disconcerting. She knew she could easily order him thrown out of the house and never allowed back on her property, but there was something compelling about him that made her almost enjoy this verbal sparring match in which they were engaged. "That is about as vague a statement as I've ever heard," she snapped, trying to make him less sure of whether she would truly help him at all. But he seemed to ignore the fact that she could throw him out. He wasn't about to be put off.

"I am trying to be as fair as I can," he said.

"Do you know of the Black Decree?"

"Who doesn't? It's a cruel, barbarous law, but I don't think it was Maximilian's doing." He paused and shook his head. "If you're trying to interview me, you're doing a good job."

Aimée acknowledged his compliment with a nod of her head, but her brain was working furiously. Finally she made up her mind. "Wait here. I'm going to change my clothes and we will go to the palace," she told him. It was a daring plan, and it might expose her to trouble, but she thought it might work. . . .

In her bedroom with Marie-Clarice fussing over her hair, Aimée decided she rather liked Alex. There was something about him that fascinated her. Too bad he was not only an American but a newspaperman. Another part of her mind told her to be careful, for he might discover her secret.

"He's very handsome," said Marie-Clarice. "I saw him when he came in."

"Is that all you see when you look at a man?" Aimée snapped, and then regretted it. She forgot that Marie-Clarice was in many ways just an impressionable young woman.

"All I meant was that he wasn't ugly," Marie-Clarice backed down. "And his being an American might prove very helpful one day," she pointed out.

"I've already thought of that," agreed Aimée. "It's the main reason I want to help him. He wants to interview Maximilian."

"Mon Dieu! These Americans. What nerve!"

"I rather like that about him. . . ." Aimée said, her thoughts drifting to Alex. As soon as she was ready, she hurried downstairs to find the reporter standing at the foot of the stairs. She had given Marie-Clarice instructions.

"You were quick," he said.

"Yes. I'll ride with you in your carriage, but I've arranged for my carriage to follow us so you won't have to drive me back."

He took her elbow as they descended the veranda stairs. As he handed her into the carriage, Aimée decided she liked the firmness of his hold on her arm, and his easy manner toward her. She realized that besides Renato, and her encounters with Maximilian, she'd led a rather sheltered life in Mexico, too.

They were silent for the first few minutes. Finally Aimée could no longer restrain her curiosity over the extent of his knowledge about her. She felt an urgency to find out what he knew that she didn't stop to question. "What do you know of me, señor?" she asked bluntly.

He looked at her with surprise and answered slowly, "I know that you are rich, that your family is among the wealthiest in all of Mexico. That you seem to favor Maximilian. And Juárez does not like your kind, if you'll excuse me for being so bold as to say so."

"You know Juárez? Have you talked to him?" What he knew about her suddenly seemed unimportant. Juárez was, after all, the man her father had been in touch with and whom he had seen as the next leader of Mexico. She was very anxious to learn more about this mysterious man whom everybody talked about, she was careful not to appear too interested.

"He's very easy to approach," began Alex. "He's an intelligent, very capable man—although I have to admit that he certainly doesn't look like the leader of a revolution. I would have guessed that he was a bookkeeper."

Aimée laughed lightly. "And what have you heard about Maximilian?"

"If you tell him what I tell you, he'll never see me, but I'll trust you, Miss Fuchard. I've heard he's a rather quiet man who dotes on uniforms, is dependent on his empress and to put it indelicately, no good-looking young girl is safe in his presence."

"Men have been executed for saying such things about an emperor," she told him, half-teasing, half-truthfully.

"I know. Even when it's true. Tell me, do you feel safe around him?"

There was a curiously personal tone to this question which Aimée brushed off by saying lightly, "What a thing to ask!"

"I mean it," he persisted. "You're everything a man like Maximilian would desire. In fact, that any man would desire . . ." His words trailed off. Even his boldness failed him but Aimée realized that he, too, found her intriguing. She flushed and looked away. Her heart was pounding, but this time she had not taken a drugged drink. In fact, she was quite wide-awake and sober.

Misinterpreting her looking away to mean that she was upset at his innuendo, Mooreland hastened to apologize, saying, "Forgive me. I am in the habit of saying what I think—and it sometimes gets me into trouble. Please don't let it influence you into changing your mind about me."

Aimée saw that as much as he was attracted to her, he didn't dare risk offending her and thus losing his one opportunity to meet with the emperor.

Not receiving any answer from Aimée, Mooreland continued: "I really appreciate your help. Would you like to hear what he tells me? Before I write the story? Perhaps you will be able to explain anything you object to or that possibly I misunderstood."

She was on the verge of turning down his offer, but suddenly she knew she wanted to see him again and he had just given her the perfect excuse. "That might be very wise," she agreed. "Thank you for offering me the opportunity to learn what you are writing."

"You asked me earlier what I knew about Maximilian. Let me tell you what I've heard of him, Miss Fuchard. I must admit that I rather like him. I think he's a fool for allowing himself to be talked into coming here because it's inevitable that he will be expelled from the country when the forces behind the revolution are ready to oppose him openly. However, I've heard of nothing that he's actually done that is unfair. In fact, he doesn't seem to have done much of anything at all. The military rules Mexico. Maximilian is just a figurehead," he concluded.

Aimée found what he said fascinating but said nothing. After a few more minutes' silence, he began to tell her about himself, his experiences as a young Northern officer during the War between the States, about his home in Vermont, and his widowed mother. Before she knew it they were at the palace gates.

They approached the sentries, two *Zouaves*.

"I wish to see the emperor," Aimée said simply.

"She wishes to see the emperor," one *Zouave* laughed, nudging the other one with his elbow. "Did you hear that?"

"Nobody sees the emperor without an appointment," the other guard said. "Do you have an appointment?"

Aimée had to admit that she didn't, and suddenly she felt very unsure of herself, but she decided to brazen it out. "If you send word to the emperor that Señorita Angela Fuchard is here, you will find that I'm welcome," she said in her sternest voice. "And if you don't do as I ask, you'll both be sent on active duty and not paid to lounge around pretending to guard the palace. Now, one of you go in and announce me," she ordered grandly.

Their smiles faded at the tone of authority she used so easily, and one of them walked stiffly inside. When he returned a few moments later, he saluted, bowed and addressed her respectfully. "Señorita, His Highness will see you now. A secretary is waiting to escort you to him."

"Thank you," she said graciously, and to Alex, she said, "You'd better wait here." Inside, a different secretary led her to double brass doors that were gleaming with the Hapsburg coat of arms. He opened one of the doors for her and she entered alone.

Maximilian sat at the far end of the room at his desk writing in a heavy, leather-bound volume. He rose as she approached, took her hand, and raised her from a deep curtsy.

"My dear Señorita Fuchard, how nice of you to call on me. My day is so much brighter just gazing on your face."

Aimée was disconcerted by his polite but impersonal manner, especially after what had passed between the two of them. But then he was royalty and she could hardly expect him to welcome her with open arms and smother her with kisses as if he were some common suitor. He was the emperor, she reminded herself, and he had simply used her—once—for his pleasure.

"Now," he said, sitting down and urging she sit on a chair near his desk, "what can I do to be of service to you?"

"Your Highness," began Aimée, eyes downcast, for she was very uncertain now that she was facing Maximilian of the wisdom of so openly approaching him, "There is a reporter outside. He is from the *New York Globe*. He approached me to write a report on what is happening in Mexico. But since I have been in the country such a short time, and since what he writes will be printed in the United States, I thought it better to seek advice from Your Highness about what to do."

"I see," Maximilian clasped his long, slender hands together, and rested his chin on them. "It is important that he get a favorable view of Mexico, is it not?"

Aimée promptly agreed.

"And it is true that you have only recently arrived and are hardly well informed on the state of the nation. While I, as emperor . . ."

Maximilian had walked right into her trap. "Oooh," she said excitedly, "you should talk to him. How clever! And the words from an emperor will be very impressive and he will let the United States know what you are doing for our people. What a fine idea!"

"Yes. And he is from an important newspaper. I should see him."

"His name is Alex Mooreland, Your Highness," said Aimée.

"Have him sent in, my dear. I'll grant him all the time he needs. I am grateful that he came to someone who had the wisdom not to speak for all of my kingdom. This could be of great benefit to me."

"Thank you, Your Highness," Aimée said gratefully. "If I've been of some slight service . . ."

"In more than one way, my dear," he said, and this time there was ample meaning behind the statement.

She smiled shyly as she recognized his admission of the intimacy they had shared. He took her hand again, bowed and kissed it. "You've given me great satisfaction. I trust we'll soon meet again. . . ."

When she left Maximilian, she hurried to the palace door to find Alex. He was standing outside, looking with great interest at the carriage Aimée had ordered to follow them so she might use it to return home.

"I've never seen anything quite like the outfit your coachman wears. Surely it's unusual, isn't it?"

"I don't know," she said. "You're to see the emperor at once. He'll be pleased to see you, but be gentle with him, please."

"You certainly arranged that quickly. Thank you, señorita," said Alex. "I'll call on you as soon as my article is finished."

"I look forward to reading it, Mr. Mooreland. *Adios.*"

She walked toward her carriage, smiling. Alex was right. The livery of the coachman was unusual. The white linen trousers, the starched shirt, the colorful poncho over it, and the enormous sombrero seemed extreme in a city where many of the aristocracy emulated European customs. This had been Renato's idea, she recalled, and the rest of his family had been taken in by it as a sign of ostentation rather than a statement of belief. She admired him for his slyness in expressing his sympathy for the Mexican cause, but she hoped his beliefs would not bring him trouble.

The coachman remained on the seat, and did not offer to help her into the carriage, but she was too excited to notice. Seeing Alex again had stirred up a desire for him so strong that she was exhilarated with the pure thrill of honestly wanting a man. True, Maximilian had aroused her, but that was a combination of his power, his beauty, the drugged potion, and her desperate need to guarantee her personal safety. With Alex, it was different. She liked him for no other reason besides the urgent attraction he aroused in her just by being close to her. Aimée was honest enough with herself to realize that she wanted to go to bed with Alex . . . soon.

Preoccupied by these thoughts of a man she had just met, she was well out of the city and on a rutted road before she became aware of the distance they had traveled—and the pounding of fast-running horses behind the carriage. When the driver looked back to see who was following them, Aimée realized she had never seen him before. The huge sombrero had hidden his face when she entered the carriage, and now she was with a man who was definitely not her coachman or even one of her servants.

He reined the horses to a halt and started to get up from his seat when more horsemen darted out from the forest and surrounded the carriage.

"Madre de Dios," said the coachman in a prayerlike tone under his breath.

Fear seized Aimée, too, as she realized they were all French soldiers. Was it possible they had come for her? Did they know her true identity? She felt faint with terror. The driver, who was an elderly man, she now saw, raised his hands and stood beside the carriage. A lieutenant dismounted and arrogantly approached the carriage. As he came up to the driver he slapped him so hard in the face that his whole head snapped back. The man cried out in pain. Then the lieutenant put one foot on the step of the carriage and stared suspiciously at Aimée.

"Is this your coachman?" he demanded suddenly.

Surprised by his question about her driver, Aimée steeled herself and very quietly said, "No. I never saw him before."

"Who are you trying to fool, señorita?" the officer sneered. "You're under arrest." With that he climbed into the carriage beside her and shouted an order to the guards to take the driver prisoner, too. They tied his hands behind him, tied a rope around his neck and attached the other end of the rope to a saddle. The elderly man was dragged along, crying in protest, but no one raised a hand to help him. As the horse moved faster the man fell to his knees, and then was dragged along by his neck, his body zigzagging on the rocky dirt road like a ragdoll's.

"Will you explain your actions?" Aimée said with measured control. She had long ago learned her lesson about being intimidated; an air of authority might save her neck.

"Don't play tricks with me," the lieutenant said with disgust. "You're a spy. I know the man driving your coach. He is a *Juárista*."

"Lieutenant, I told you I never saw him before and I came direct from the palace——"

"——Be still," he cut her off impatiently. "General Romay will know how to handle you."

"He'll know how to handle you as well, lieutenant," she shot back undaunted by his approach, now that she realized they had been after the driver and not her. "I'll be silent until I meet the general, except to say that what you're doing to that poor man is brutal. He could die before he reaches the city."

"He'll die there anyway," shrugged the lieutenant indifferently. "I advise you to be silent."

Inwardly Aimée was shaking. Careful investigation might reveal her identity, even if they didn't know who she was now. Being accused of spying for Juárez was a serious charge, of course, but there was no way that they could find her guilty. But any arousal of suspicion might provoke a full-scale investigation, and this she dared not risk.

The coach turned and passed under the archway of what must have been a prison. The lieutenant helped her down and held her elbow securely as he led her to the entrance of the grim, brown-painted adobe building with heavy doors and narrow slits for windows. Inside, he left her with two huge soldiers and instructed them to guard her well. Frightened, she wondered how she could get word to the emperor. He would rescue her surely, if he learned of her dire predicament. But since the French executed people the minute they caught them, it might be too late. It didn't matter whether Angela Fuchard, sympathizer of Juárez, was backed up against a wall or Aimée Gaudin, the traitoress, was backed up against a wall. In a few minutes, she might be dead. . . .

*   *   *

The lieutenant returned a short time later and signaled her to follow him. She found herself in a large office where a man sat behind an untidy desk. He regarded her casually at first, then his eyes studied every curve, lingering finally on the swell of her bosom.

"They're making the young ones far more beautiful these days," he said casually to the lieutenant. Then he turned back to Aimée and his features became stern. "You, señorita, will give me your name, your father's name, and your address. Then you'll tell me how it came about that a spy we have sought for some time happened to be engaged in driving your coach."

"I'll make no statement of any kind," she said defiantly, "until you notify His Highness, Emperor Maximilian, that Angela Fuchard is in your custody."

"That's the same crazy story she told me," the lieutenant said to his general.

She gave him a frosty glance, but the lieutenant merely laughed and shook his head. In French, Aimée presented him with a terse idea of what she thought of him. He sobered quickly.

The general wagged his head. "Señorita speaks French very well indeed—and in a forceful manner."

"I was raised in France, in a convent," she said. "I arrived in Mexico City only a few weeks ago and I know nothing of this Juárez or any of his spies. I can only say that I never saw my driver before. But in that outfit and that silly sombrero, it was impossible to see who he was—and who pays attention to servants anyway?" she went on grandly. "That is all I have to say. It would be very wise of you, general, to send word to Maximilian, as I've suggested."

"Whether you know Maximilian or not, if you are proven to be a Juárez spy, you'll still end up against a wall."

"If Maximilian doesn't recognize me, you may put me up against a wall—but please do as I ask—or risk your own future," she said boldly.

The general instructed the lieutenant: "Send a messenger at once. Report to me the minute he returns."

The lieutenant saluted and strolled away, obviously assuming she was stalling for time. The general looked at Aimée and said more amicably, "It wouldn't surprise me if you did know emperor. He likes pretty girls."

"Sir, if you're insinuating—" Aimée sputtered.

"I insinuate nothing," he said smoothly. Then, impatiently he added, "I have important business to attend to. Please sit quietly in that corner and say nothing and make no attempt to escape. If you do not agree, I shall be compelled to have you locked in a cell, which I can assure you might be a most unpleasant experience, for who knows what my soldiers might do to a girl as pretty as you are when no one is looking. So it's your choice."

"I'll sit and be quiet," she said coldly.

"A wise decision," he commented before shouting an order. A soldier promptly appeared, stood at attention and saluted.

"Bring in the old man."

While all this was going on, Aimée sat watching as if she were a thousand miles away. She couldn't believe it was happening. Where was Alex? Was he all right? She hadn't had time to think about him, but now she did— and she couldn't help wondering whether she'd led him into a trap or he'd led her into a trap and betrayed her. Her anxiety grew, even though she struggled to appear composed on the surface. Her hands were ice-cold and yet tiny beads of perspiration began to break out on her brow. It was quite stuffy in this room and her heart was pounding wildly. She realized that no mention of Alex had been made and decided it would be wiser not to inquire after him. If she did, it might arouse suspicion about the *Americano,* and if he had betrayed her, then there was no need to ask about him. She would find out soon enough. But the anxiety and tension was giving her an enormous headache. She also realized that she cared very much about Alex. Looking back over what she had done, she realized it was sheer foolishness to approach the palace in person on behalf of a total stranger. It had exposed her and her family—and had come to this . . . Despite her attempt at composure, she wrung her hands in anguish.

She had been so engrossed in her own thoughts that she hardly paid attention as they dragged the old man before the general. He was bloody and bruised from the brutal way he had been dragged into town. His stolen uniform was torn and filthy. In a quavering voice, he declared he was a poor farmer who had been paid by the lady's coachman to drive the carriage back and not let her know there had been a substitution. The regular family driver, he reported, was in the throes of passion over some lusty girl whose favors he had sought for some time, and this had been his chance to take advantage of the opportunity.

"You're a peon?" the general asked harshly.

"Sí, señor. A poor peon who knows nothing of what goes on these days. I raise a crop and sell it for just enough money to support my family. I am a poor man. I know nothing," he whined.

The general gave an abrupt laugh and said, "Then let me refresh your memory. You are Manuel Valdez from Cordoba. You have been a soldier in the army of Benito Juárez—an officer by the way. We know who you are and we are not fooled by your story that you are a poor peon. In fact, I don't think you've ever hoed a row of corn in your life. Come closer to the desk," he commanded. To the lieutenant, "Untie his hands. I want to see them, palms up."

The old man gave a sigh that showed he was beaten. The general gave a cursory inspection and said sarcastically, "Soft hands are not those of a peon. You are Valdez—and you are a dead man if you don't tell me where the rest of your group hides."

"I am a peon," he insisted. "I know nothing of such things, general."

This time the general struck the man a blow that sent him staggering to his knees. Aimée half rose to protest, but realized there was nothing she could do to stop this torture, and to complain would be to align herself with this Mexican. She had to control herself and sit there as if this whole scene meant nothing to her. She tried to calm herself by thinking of Alex, of his eyes, his steady hands and strong body. Anything to distract her from the horror of what was happening before her very eyes. She realized that the old man was trying to bluff his way out, but it wasn't working. Nothing could save him now anyway.

The general came around to the front of his desk and delivered a few well-placed kicks with his hard leather, pointed boots. The old man writhed in agony on the floor at his feet, clutching his groin. The blow to his face had opened up a long wound that bled freely, but the old man admitted to nothing.

"I'll ask you one more time, old man, and if you talk, you miserable dog, perhaps I'll spare your life," the general taunted him. "All right now, the others, where are they?"

Despite his obvious pain, the old man maintained, "I'm a poor peon who knows nothing. . . . Please, general, you must believe me. . . ."

One more kick and the old man was barely conscious. The general gave orders in a low voice which Aimée could not hear and the soldiers dragged the old man away.

The general came over to Aimée, bowed and said, "You will come with me, señorita. I have something to show you."

Obediently she followed him out of his office, down a long corridor and finally through a door that led into a large, empty courtyard. They stood there in silence for a moment. Then a six-man squad of soldiers with rifles took up a position facing a wall. Even from this distance Aimée could see the wall was pockmarked with bullets and splattered with brown spots that could only have been the dried blood of Mexican martyrs.

The old man was marched before the soldiers and half dragged in front of the wall. Aimée knew what was going to happen and wanted to close her eyes, to look away from the ugly scene, but she knew she could not. The general was watching her closely to see if she cared about this man or his cause.

As the rifles were raised, the old man shot one arm up into the air and shouted with his dying breath, "Viva, Mexico! Viva, Juárez! Goddamn Maxi . . ." The rifles had cracked and the man's body was hurled roughly back against the wall, then his bullet-riddled body slumped to the ground. The body was still. However, the officer who had given the orders casually walked over and put another bullet through the old man's temple.

"That," said the general gesturing toward the body, "is how we handle traitors. Now if you wish to change your story, señorita. . . ." Obviously he had hoped to frighten her into admitting something, but Aimée didn't flinch.

"I have told you the truth. I am Señorita Angela Fuchard and I own an estate to the north. The emperor was a guest in my home and he'll confirm what I've said. I regard him as a friend. I warn you that he holds me in the highest esteem and will not appreciate how you have treated me."

The general studied her silently for a moment. Aimée hoped her bravado would convince him at least to wait for the messenger before he put her in front of the wall. Finally he said, "I am beginning to believe you. No girl in her right mind would be so bold as to pretend to be a friend of the emperor's if it weren't true. If I'm wrong about you, I beg your pardon, señorita. If I'm right, you'll wish that you never thought up that story. For not everyone dies so quickly and easily before a firing squad. . . ."

Soldiers were now dragging the body away, leaving a trail of fresh blood on the dirt. Aimée turned away, brought her hands to her face and wept despite herself. She half-stumbled as the general escorted her back to his office. However, when they arrived there, an equerry of the emperor was waiting for them and began issuing commands that made even the general cringe.

The general turned immediately and bowed before Aimée. "Señorita, I am abjectly sorry for having suspected a person such as yourself. I beg your pardon, but hope that you will remember that your story was quite incredible, and that the driver was a spy after all, there are spies all around us, and they would try to assassinate the emperor himself if they could get close to him. It is a difficult job we have here, our small force, in this large and rebellious country. We have to be ruthless. Again, I am most humbly sorry."

"Please, just let me go," Aimée said numbly, "and have some one drive me home in my carriage." She wanted to tell the general that his "necessary" brutality repelled her, but she was too overcome with fear and horror to utter a word. The memory of that poor man's execution would remain with her forever! She needed to escape as quickly as possible from this horrible place.

Aimée marched out, and as she passed the red-faced lieutenant, she gave him an angry glance. A soldier ran past her to the carriage, opened the door, and got into the driver's seat.

Once the carriage was in motion, Aimée leaned back and closed her eyes. As much as she tried to relax and forget what she had witnessed, her mind's eye kept replaying the old man defiantly shouting "Viva, Juárez" as he died in a hail of bullets. But as the carriage neared the estate, a coldness settled over her. She realized with a start that the soldiers had known that the old man was not her regular driver. Someone had betrayed him.

She wondered if the regular driver had been arrested and tortured. That was possible, but what would he know? Someone else had betrayed the old man, but who? Or was this entire plot aimed at placing her under suspicion?

Aimée shuddered. This did not bode well for her future. . . .

Chapter 9

When Aimée had bathed and changed her clothes, she summoned the entire family to meet in the library. They were mystified by her request, but sat there waiting for what she had to say. No servants were present.

Aimée related all the events of the day, and as she did she watched their faces. She had been so obsessed, up to now, with preventing them from discovering her charade, and concerning herself with their greed, that she hadn't any idea of how vulnerable they were. Now that she knew them, she could see easily that Lino was frantic with anxiety and the others were with fear.

"You are saying that our coachman gave up his uniform and his place on the carriage to a Juárista?" asked Lino, absolutely stunned at this piece of information. Had he been forced? Who knew?

"That is precisely what happened," Aimée said coolly. "Now you well know that the uniforms of our coachmen are such that their faces cannot be seen. Up until now, who really cared? But now this has happened and I am very, very worried," she said; her fear was reflected in the faces of the family around her.

"*I'm* worried," said Lino, "because this means we may have been harboring a Juárez spy. That in itself is enough to bring the French military here to search and to suspect us of being *Juáristas*."

"True," Aimée acknowledged his point, "but that isn't what bothers me most. The point is that the French soldiers not only knew the route the coach was to take, so there was an ambush set up, but there was no chance to escape. It was foolproof. Someone knew about the driver. Someone informed on us. Someone in this household is a spy ... for the French."

Silence greeted this announcement. Antonia, who usually had no qualms about expressing her thoughts on every matter, was sitting there ashen-faced, her lips tightly pursed. Della and Melania sat there stupified, each one probably engrossed in thinking how it could affect their chances of catching a husband. Up until now, even Renato was quiet, except for his pacing back and forth, back and forth until Aimée wanted to order him to sit down. She held her tongue.

"We are in great trouble," began Lino slowly, speaking for the family. "Great trouble. There are two forces and we are caught in the middle between the French who see us as Mexicans, and the Mexicans patriots who see us as consorting with the French. We are in considerable peril no matter what we do. But somehow we must find out who these spies are and be rid of them."

Antonia agreed, adding, "The emperor trusts us. We mustn't allow anything—or anyone—to jeopardize that trust."

"Why did you even consent to see this reporter?" Della asked accusingly, as if Aimée had brought this whole affair down on the family by seeing Alex.

"I already told you," Aimée said with some exasperation, "He practically forced his way in here. He'd still be here if I hadn't consented to try to get him an interview with the emperor. He is a most insistent and determined *Americano*."

"What did you say his name was?" Renato asked.

"Alex Mooreland. He works for the *New York Globe*."

"What reason did he give for wanting to interview the emperor?" asked Lino.

"It's part of his work—and it would be a great coup for him to speak directly to the emperor," said Aimée. She realized she had said more than she meant to about Alex. After all, why should she, an heiress, care about a lowly American newspaper reporter?

"Why did he come to *you*, Angela?" Melania asked, her expression indecipherable, but her innuendo quite clear.

Equally as blandly, Aimée replied: "He had no luck trying to gain entry to the palace, so he did some investigating and learned about the two recent balls—and that the emperor had favored me with his company on the dance floor. Perhaps he thought the charms of a woman might help, who knows?" she shrugged. "Mr. Mooreland also learned I was an heiress and assumed my sympathies would lie with the emperor, so he tried to impress upon me the importance of a favorable press report about the emperor in the leading newspaper of the United States."

"He should do well, this Alex Mooreland," mused Lino aloud. "Certainly he was quite effective in convincing you that his interview would be beneficial to Mexico."

"I hope you made a wise decision," Antonia said coolly.

"She did," Lino stepped in, preventing any further comment. "She made a good decision if for no other reason than we've learned that we have both a spy and a traitor here. Besides, I am very pleased that a New York City newspaper has sent a reporter all the way here. I'm sure the publicity will serve us well."

"I agree, uncle," said Aimée. "I think that this re-

porter could enhance the image of Maximilian throughout the world. He could write of the conditions in Mexico and might even say that Maximilian was good for
the country, regardless of having French rule imposed
on us."

Melania's tone had a mocking quality as she added,
"Your reporter might even reveal that Empress Carlota
has returned to France."

"I didn't know that!" exclaimed Aimée, and she
could have bitten her tongue. She wondered how
Melania knew that, but she didn't want to appear too
interested in Maximilian. She was afraid that the family
already suspected she might be involved with him since
he had so readily agreed to see her.

"It's not generally known," Lino said. "But Carlota
had been very unhappy here. She's most despondent
and was reported to have spent most of her time weeping and accusing Maxmilian of unforgivable escapades,
adultery in particular. Her doctors felt she wasn't adjusting to life in Mexico and finally decided that a trip
home might make her feel better."

"Maximilian leaned heavily on Carlota for advice,"
said Renato. "He needs her. Without her, he's a weak
man."

"Renato, what a thing to say," Antonia chided him.
"He is strong and powerful. He rules Mexico, doesn't
he?"

"No, he doesn't," Renato said firmly. "He rules
Mexico City and a few other cities, but Juárez rules the
rest of Mexico. And he is growing in power all the time,
just as Maximilian's power weakens every day."

"I doubt Maximilian is even remotely aware of what
is really going on," Aimée said. "Rulers like Maximilian
don't live in the same world we do."

Lino and Renato nodded in agreement. "Those
around him keep the truth from him," went on Aimée,
recalling that Maximilian had been unaware of Alex's
attempts to see him. "Yet I believe that if he knew the
real conditions he might try to do something to help.

The saddest part is that he believes himself to be a just ruler adored by every Mexican."

"What a joke that is," sneered Renato. "But people like us tolerate him and let him think we love him so our standing will not diminish—or our income. Let's be honest about the fact that we are only pretending to support him because it's good for us."

"Let's have supper," said Della with a yawn brought on by boredom. "I'm hungry."

It was past their dinner hour. Antonia suggested that serious conversation be suspended at the dinner table where servants might overhear what they had to say. Aimée quickly agreed. It bothered Aimée that Melania seemed to know so much. It also bothered her that the more she knew of Melania, the more she questioned what was going on behind that honeyed tone and her role as peacemaker following Della's frequent outbursts. Della was short-tempered, which made her easy to read; Aimée was beginning to have serious doubts about Melania. . . .

Aimée excused herself immediately after dinner, pleading fatigue. She really was exhausted. She fell asleep but kept waking up because she thought she heard stealthy footsteps. She would listen intently, hear nothing more, and then drift back to sleep. It dawned on her that fitful sleep and the feeling of being spied upon was a warning, a premonition of disaster soon to come. . . .

She rose early the next morning and dressed carefully, hopeful that Alex might pay her the visit he had promised. She asked Marie-Clarice to pay particular attention to her hair.

"I'll make thick braids on the sides behind your ears and let curls fall from the crown on your head, señorita. We will show your brow, for there's not a frown mark on it—a sign you do not worry. . . ." When Aimée didn't respond, Marie-Clarice quickly apologized and said, "A bad joke, señorita, a bad joke."

"Yes," agreed Aimée. "I *am* beginning to worry, though I mustn't allow it to show."

"If that newspaper reporter hadn't come here, you wouldn't have had such a terrible experience."

"It's good he came. It revealed a spy in the house."

"I can't figure out who it is," said Marie-Clarice with perfect seriousness, as if she should have known. Then she went on to say, "I brought your breakfast upstairs today. It's in the sitting room, waiting for you."

"I'm too upset to eat," Aimée said, realizing how much she wanted to see Alex again. No word had come from him or about him since the day before. And he didn't know the secret of her identity, as she had feared, for the general never questioned that she was Angela Fuchard. No, those fears about him had been exaggerated. Now, her fears were about herself and the strong, urgent need she felt for this man she hardly knew.

"Please eat something," urged Marie-Clarice, sensing that her mistress was drifting into a world of private thoughts. "You ate so little last night."

"Do you wonder?" said Aimée.

"No, but this is another day. I'll lay out your clothes while you eat."

Aimée started to pick at her food and then, to her surprise, discovered she was ravenous and devoured the eggs, bacon, fruit, warm bread and wonderful hot chocolate of Mexico that Marie-Clarice had brought for her. She chose a lavender-and-mauve day dress of fine cotton. The full skirt, worn over a crinoline, billowed out and was double—tiered and showed her tiny waist.

The sound of a horse's hooves pounding along the driveway made Marie-Clarice run to the window and peer out. "Oh, señorita, it is Mr. Mooreland," she exclaimed.

"We mustn't keep him waiting," smiled Aimée as she left her room. Alex was already standing at the foot of the stairs as she descended. His gray eyes regarded her with warmth. She started to smile in greeting but quickly lowered her eyes lest he read the extent of her pleasure at seeing him again.

"Good morning, Mr. Mooreland." She extended her hand, American-style, to shake his. He took it and held it briefly between both of his, just as Lino emerged from the drawing room.

"You look beautiful, Miss Angela," Alex said.

"Thank you, Mr. Mooreland. I didn't expect you would call so early," she said noncommittally.

"I couldn't wait." Alex began to talk in English, which Angela knew Lino barely understood, but he was so intent on his message that he probably wouldn't have been able to express himself in Spanish. "Señorita, I wish to express my regrets for what you were subjected to on your return yesterday. Your safety was in great peril on my behalf," he said.

"It was terrifying, but not your fault. Now, we will speak no more of it," she dismissed the matter.

"I have ordered coffee in the drawing room," Lino told them. "We shall talk. Just the three of us. I've informed the others that we wish to be alone."

With Aimée interpreting, when needed, the three of them sipped coffee and exchanged small talk. Then there was an awkward silence and finally Lino cleared his throat and came to the point: "Señor, what kind of story are you going to write about Mexico?"

"It's hard to say. There are so many factions. Mexico is a very complex country and with a very complex—and delicate—political situation right now," said Mooreland.

"Come now, Mr. Mooreland, either you praise Maximilian or condemn him. Which will it be?"

"I can also praise or condemn Juárez," Alex countered. "These are two very different men, with very different visions and hopes, but they're both good and sincere men who believe in what they are doing. It is a very difficult position to try to represent them both fairly."

"So what are you going to write?" persisted Lino.

"I will write the facts, but the article will be a favorable one so far as Maximilian himself is concerned."

"The emperor will be grateful," Lino said soberly. "I suppose you will be remaining in Mexico for a while."

"Why do you ask?" Alex's tone was deceptively casual.

Lino smiled. "Don't play games with me, señor. I'm aware of the Monroe Doctrine. I'm also aware that your government completely disapproves of Emperor Maximilian and of his role as monarch here."

Alex returned the smile. "I think you mean to say the role Maximilian attempts to play here. You're right, but when I say the article will be favorable I speak the truth. A reporter must report the facts as he sees them. Then let the American people judge for themselves."

"Since you live in a democracy, I believe I could predict the conclusion they will draw," Lino said sardonically.

"I believe you could, and so could I. Many Americans have come from countries where they knew oppression. However, Maximilian is not a tyrant."

Lino stood up and offered his hand. "I'll leave you two to get better acquainted. It was a pleasure to talk with you, señor. If I can be of service with your article, please feel free to call on me."

"Thank you, Señor Miranda," Alex clasped the outstretched hand. "And while I'm truly grateful for your offer, I realize the delicate situation you're in and don't wish to involve you in it any further."

Lino spoke sincerely when he said, "I think your paper sent its most astute reporter. I wish you luck. Now I must get to work. Please excuse me," and Lino was gone, leaving the two of them alone together.

"I'm sure you also have things to attend to, but I hope you won't send me away immediately."

Aimée smiled and shook her head, both pleased

and embarrassed under the steady scrutiny of his gray eyes. "I was wondering if you'd care to ride?" she asked.

"I'd be delighted, though not too far. My horse has already had a good run today and is tired."

"We'll let him rest. I'll have him rubbed down, fed and watered, and you shall have a fresh one. However, I must change into my riding habit. I shan't be long," she promised, going upstairs again.

Marie-Clarice helped Aimée change, asking countless questions about Alex Mooreland which Aimée impatiently brushed aside.

"Surely you're not going to pretend you aren't interested in him," Marie-Clarice said as she helped Aimée draw on her boots.

"I'm pretending nothing and I'm telling you nothing." Aimée took the riding crop which Marie-Clarice had extended to her, then relented and gave her a light embrace. "When I return, we'll talk," she promised.

Alex and Aimée walked slowly down the path to the stables. They talked only of the beauty of the surroundings. Mexicans were busy at work on the grounds, though none looked up as they passed. Both Aimée and Alex were careful to say nothing that might interest a spy, either from Juárez or from France.

Once on the trail through the forest, they maneuvered their horses so they might ride close enough to carry on a conversation.

"I feel I should warn you," Alex began.

She shot him a startled glance. "Warn me? Of what? What does that mean?"

"Mexico will soon be in a state of turmoil, with Juárez on the march. He's recruited quite an army and he's intent on driving Maximilian and the French out of the country."

"Is he strong enough for that?"

"Easily. Poor Max. He doesn't even know it, but the military does."

Just then they passed by a glen that Renato had shown to Aimée. It was a peaceful spot that was well hidden from the trail. Aimée had come here herself for some solitude, for time to think. She indicated that they guide their horses off the trail in that direction. "We can talk safely here, Mr. Mooreland," she informed him.

He looked about and nodded his approval. They dismounted, let the horses graze and Aimée sat down on the broad trunk of an old fallen cyprus tree. Alex joined her, sitting so close that his thigh brushed hers. Aimée drew in her breath. Just brushing against him had sent an electrifying thrill through her body. She yearned to reach out and touch his handsome face. . . .

When he was settled, he went on intently about the rebel army as if he had felt nothing from that contact. Aimée listened, trying to concentrate on his words.

"I've interviewed people who know Juárez well and they're all of the same opinion: He cannot be stopped. His army may be ragtag, but they'll be fighting for their country. The French soldiers fight only for their salaries, and that in itself can make a difference. Also, the Mexicans are experts at guerilla warfare, and the French know only their regimented drill attacks. With a Mexican victory, you, and people like you, will be in a very difficult situation.

"To the *Juáristas,* the French occupation represents oppression by the rich. They're convinced your kind not only helped the French to get here but that you actually want them to remain. For that reason, true or not, they may take it into their heads to eliminate the wealthy. I'm not saying that it will happen this way, but it very well might."

She turned her head to look directly at him. "Is this why you are warning me, Mr. Mooreland?"

His answer was to grasp her by the shoulders and say, "You're so young, young and beautiful. It is a dangerous combination in times like this."

"Gracias, señor, but I am not afraid."

Alex let her go and sat back, observing her coolly. "I'd like to know one thing. How do you wield such influence over Maximilian?" All warmth had left his voice.

"I'm afraid I don't understand. . . ."

"I couldn't get near him. And I saw many others turned away by those guards in the same offensive way they tried to turn us back. But you gave your name and the gates opened. *Voila!*"

She looked at him through narrowed eyes, realizing what he was getting at, and she could feel her anger rising.

"Maximilian has a reputation for bedding down beautiful women," he said quietly, with an edge in his voice. "Especially young, beautiful women."

Aimée stood up abruptly, feeling almost faint with anger and disappointment. "I think we should go back now," she murmured.

He rose to his feet and stood towering over her, his handsome face devoid of expression. "Any woman in Mexico would lie down for him gladly and consider it an honor. Don't you?"

She slapped him, hard, across the face and backed away. "Because I do not wish to be embarrassed before my family, you may ride back with me, but you'll not remain. I don't wish to see you again, señor."

She managed to take half a dozen steps, but he didn't move and she didn't want to leave him. She wanted to explain to him, to have him understand everything about her. What he suspected was true . . . but she was unable to admit it because the risk was far too great.

Then he seized her and turned her around, bringing his lips to hers in a kiss whose open-mouth ferocity stunned her at first into submission and then into passionate return. Then as they sank to the ground, she pushed herself away with an effort that required all her strength. "No! No, Alex. Not from you . . . please."

He seemed startled at the intensity in her voice. "You want me as much as I want you," he exclaimed.

"Yes," she admitted, "but not now, not here, not this

way, Alex. I can't tell you why now, but I promise I will someday, but you'll break my heart if you don't stop. I must not let myself . . ."

He released her and she scrambled to her feet. Her eyes were filled with sadness as she told him, "There are matters I must tell you someday, but please understand that I can't now. . . ."

"A day will come when I'll have you—and you'll be happy that I do. I don't give a damn what your reasons are"—his eye flashed—"These matters you speak of—"

"—Alex, listen to me now," Aimée begged miserably, afraid she would lose him. "Will you please hear out what I have to say?"

He shook his head slowly. "What is this awful thing you're so afraid to tell me? If it's that you're Maximilian's whore," he said as if the very word left a bitter taste in his mouth, "it's hardly a secret. The whole world knows."

"No, Alex, not that," said a pale and shaken Aimée. "There are—" and then she stopped herself. Desperate as she might be not to lose Alex she did not yet feel she could trust him with her true secret, her real identity. She chewed her lip, struggling between the tuggings of her heart and the wisdom she had learned so violently about trusting men who offered her help.

"Keep your damn secret, whatever it is," spat out Alex, fists clenched tightly. "I can't see anything you may have been involved in that could be so important. Unless. . . ." He stopped and Aimée could see that his mind was suddenly churning with possibilities—and perhaps he would discover her secret.

"What? What are you thinking?" she asked now, frantic with fear that once she had aroused his suspicions that he would stop at nothing to discover what she considered a secret more important than the fact she was sleeping with Maximilian. His reporter's instincts were aroused and that made her terribly, terribly afraid.

"Is this secret of yours concerned with Juárez?" he

asked, his tone softening. "Are you in his service as a spy? Is this the reason you don't trust anyone, for fear someone might make a careless slip. . . ."

"It has nothing to do with Maximilian or Juárez. It's a personal thing. Please be patient," begged Aimée. It was dangerous for her if he asked too many questions. She might slip and tell him more than she planned. Indeed she realized she already had. She didn't need him checking into the past of Angela Fuchard.

He regarded her for a long moment and then shrugged and they walked toward their horses. When he reached to help her mount, she shied away.

"Do you distrust me that much?" His eyes flashed with anger.

She only stared back at him and shook her head miserably. She'd been right, she thought as they rode back silently along the trail toward the house. She could easily have had this man. But she thought of Vardeau, Miranda, and yes, even Maximilian, and how they had used her. This helped her to keep her head. And it angered her that Alex thought he could first use her influence to get to Maximilian and then use her body.

But Aimée realized that Vardeau and Miranda had taken her against her will, and that Maximilian had drugged her, but even when she was in full possession of her senses, she wanted Alex; she wanted him desperately. But she had to be on her guard for she dared not fall in love with him. She already understood his attitude with respect to her forced alliance with the emperor—and she wasn't any man's slut, she told herself. No, even though she cared, she mustn't let herself be used again. And to reveal her secret to him was to further endanger her safety. There was no easy answer: to have Alex and tell all—or to risk losing the only man she had ever truly cared about.

When he rode away after escorting her to the house, she watched his back, stiff with anger, and she felt ill. But her instincts told her she had been right to resist the temptation of telling him the truth, no matter how sharp the pain she felt as she saw him ride away—and probably out of her life forever.

Later that morning she found Lino in the drawing room. She sat down opposite him. Obviously he had something on his mind.

"You and Señor Mooreland had quite a ride," he commented laconically. "You were gone for some time."

"We talked about the article he's going to write," she said. "That's all."

Lino seemed quite enthusiastic about the story he believed Alex would submit. "I've talked to other reporters," he told her, "and they treated me like a leper. Because we have a few dollars more than most people, they see us as oppressors of all mankind, exploiters of the poor."

"He'll write it as he sees it," Aimée said briskly, not wanting to be reminded of her encounter with Alex. "There are even more serious matters to discuss, Uncle Lino. The coachman who drove me to the city and who turned the carriage over to the spy who was shot . . . do you know if he is still here? I'd like to question him."

"He's disappeared."

Aimée sighed. "I wanted to find out if he had any idea who might have informed on him and Valdez. How could the military have set an ambush without information from one of their own spies?"

"You are right, my dear, and I wish I had the answer to that question, too," answered Lino solemnly. "I want no trouble with the French soldiers. They often shoot first and then ask questions. The only thing that will save us is the power of the throne. Fortunately, we haven't caused the displeasure of the emperor, although I'm afraid that if we were in serious trouble, the military would supercede anything he might do—or, again, it might be too late by the time he found out."

"It's best for us to be cautious," Aimée agreed.

Two hours later, Renato came riding frantically toward the house, whipping and spurring his horse, as if his life depended on it. The poor, driven animal was foaming at the mouth. Renato was already shouting as he reined up in front of the house. Aimée and Marie-Clarice ran outside to find out what was going on. Lino had already reached Renato, heard the news first, and excitedly reported: "There's a detail of *Pantalons Rouges* coming. Renato thinks they're headed here to see if there are any more spies on the estate. Things might get very difficult," he said, in a state of visible agitation at the thought of the French on the property.

"They're vicious," added Renato. "We must be very careful about what we say."

"No matter what they do, we cannot interfere," Lino warned ominously. "Let them have their way. It is far wiser to let them pick up a few peons for spying than to resist them."

Only minutes later the *Pantalons Rouges* came galloping into view. One sergeant and ten men rode up to the mansion, and lined up with rifles free and ready for action. The sergeant, a beefy, red-faced man, approached the veranda where Renato, Lino and Aimée stood. Marie-Clarice had hastily and fearfully departed. Antonia, Della and Melania remained locked in their rooms for the *Pantalons Rouges* were not above using what attractive women they encountered in some most unattractive ways. . . .

"Good afternoon," the sergeant said crisply. "Does anyone here speak French?"

"I am Señorita Angela Fuchard, monsieur," Aimée said in French. "How may we serve you?"

"I should have recognized you," he said, a sly grin spreading across his broad face. "I was at the prison when you were brought in with that spy we shot. Mademoiselle, we must have your help. We have reason to believe there may be other spies here besides the one who escaped."

"You refer to the coachman who drove us to the city and then turned the carriage over?"

"Yes. We'll cause as little trouble as possible. I'd advise you to remain in the house until we're finished."

"It is very warm inside. We wish to remain on the veranda." Aimée informed him pleasantly, as if this were a normal conversation.

He shrugged indifferently. "But do not interfere if you hear a commotion," he warned. The three of them nodded in agreement, and watched as the sergeant returned to his horse and the patrol started searching the grounds where the Mexicans worked. Aimée sat down in one of the veranda rockers. Only her quick rocking betrayed her inner anxiety over what might happen.

Lino and Renato paced up and down. "If they find anyone, there will be the devil to pay," Renato said.

"They won't accuse us," Lino said confidently. "We're too well connected."

"Uncle, those men don't much care who you are. Take the seargeant's advice and don't interfere."

"Perhaps you're right," Lino said. Then he walked over and clasped Renato on the shoulder. "Son, perhaps we should go inside and warn the women. We don't want their screaming or weeping to attract any attention to them at all."

Renato obeyed and returned promptly to resume his watch on the veranda. They waited another few minutes and then they heard shouting. A Mexican came running up the path with two soldiers on horseback close behind him and gaining fast. He threw a glance over his shoulder, saw their sabres held high in the air and stopped, his hands high above his head.

The first sabre slash severed his arm, the next one decapitated him. The body fell and even though headless, wriggled on the ground in a horrifying manner. The soldiers turned and left it there as if it were just another piece of trash on the ground.

Renato gasped and turned his face from the scene. Lino softly cursed them. Aimée hadn't looked up from the moment she saw the Mexican was doomed.

Soon the patrol returned. Tied to the last horse were

two Mexicans. Their hands were secured behind their backs and they were forced to stumble along behind the horse. Both were dazed by fear. The patrol stopped. The sergeant rode up to the veranda, saluted and said, "You see, we were correct," with great pride. "There were spies for Juárez among your peons. They'll be given a fair trial and shot later today."

"The one whose body is beside the path," blurted out Aimée. "Did he confess?"

"He ran as soon as he thought he had a chance. Of course he was a *Juárista* or he wouldn't have run. I leave the disposal of the body to you. Good afternoon, mademoiselle, messieurs," said the sergeant as casually as if he had thanked them for some tea.

The patrol rode off. One of the prisoners fell before they reached the main road, but they simply ignored him and rode along, dragging his body behind them.

Lino let out a huge sigh of relief. "They could have made more trouble here than that. Damn it, Renato, I let you have charge of the hiring of the employees. How does it happen that you hired so many spies?" he accused his son angrily, as if somehow Renato had brought all of this down on the family.

"Father, they are no more spies than we are. That stupid sergeant couldn't question anyone and get proper answers. He only took along those two men because it makes him look good."

"Do you mean they might not have been spies?" asked Aimée, her eyes wide open in horror at the thought.

"My sweet, innocent cousin," Renato said, "I told you before, every last one of our employees is a spy in his heart, at least. We are lucky they took only two."

"And killed only one, I suppose," said Aimée, aghast. "Uncle, will you please see that the poor man is given a decent burial? And if he has a family, I wish to give them enough money so they can live decently."

"The military might regard that as showing too much sympathy for the enemy," warned Renato.

"Let them," Aimée said enraged. "We'll be safe enough if that's the worse we do against the edicts of our dear emperor."

She was thinking back to the night when she and her father had run from the police. When they shot him down in cold blood, she had had no option but to run to Vardeau for safety. The thought of that now made her blood boil. After what she had seen, Aimée was beginning to wonder if she couldn't love Juárez as much as any of the Mexicans. . . .

Chapter 10

Scarcely an hour had passed before Renato saw a cloud of dust announcing that more visitors, in force, were on their way to the house. He ran to tell the others. Still shaken from the earlier acts of brutality, they waited apprehensively for their uninvited visitors.

"It doesn't look good," said Lino, shaking his head.

"I agree," said Aimée. "The prisoners they took may have been forced to 'betray' us to save their own necks. I can imagine the methods they use to make people confess."

"This visit can only mean worse trouble," Renato said as he paced up and down.

"But how can they think we're guilty of any crime? We didn't know there were *Juáristas* working for us." Lino complained bitterly.

"The French don't need reasons," Renato replied quietly. "And they don't need proof."

Aimée shaded her eyes. It was late afternoon, and in the rays of the setting sun she saw in the distance a moving object that shimmered like a gold leaf.

"Look!" she exclaimed excitedly. "It's not the *Pantalon Rouges*. It is the Royal Guard and I think that's the emperor's gold coach coming here."

"What in the world?" exclaimed Lino, his spirits lifting. He shaded his eyes with his hands to see better. "You're right, Angela. It is the royal coach."

"Surely there's nothing else like it in all of Mexico," said Aimée. "That coach was used by Franz-Josef in Austria. I wonder what Emperor Maximilian wants with us?"

"Go call the women down," Lino addressed his son. "The more women here, the better. If he comes to berate us for the spies, he'll be far more lenient in the presence of ladies."

The procession swept into the driveway and came thundering up to the veranda where the entire family had gathered. No one spoke. No one was capable of speaking for there was too much fear that they had been betrayed—or that if they spoke their own fear would give them away.

The coach door opened and Maximilian stepped out. Instantly the men bowed and the ladies curtsied as he strode toward the veranda steps. He was dressed in the uniform of an admiral and looked every inch the royal person. He took Aimée's hand and, with a warm glance, kissed the back of it.

"I came here to deliver my deepest apologies," said Maximilian, "for I have learned that a patrol of the Foreign Legion came here looking for spies. It was an insult to you fine, loyal subjects, and I deeply regret it."

"But your Majesty, no apology is necessary for they did find spies," Lino hastened to say.

"My dear Señor Miranda, spies are everywhere. Every lowborn Mexican is a spy, or at least in favor of Juárez. However, no raid should have been carried out on these premises, for I assure you that this house is under my royal protection."

He hesitated—uncharacteristic for him, noted

Aimée—and then went on to say, "I am embarrassed by this unpleasant incident and would like to make it up to you by asking Señorita Angela to ride with me to my castle at Chapultepec. I've just finished renovating it and I believe it to be the equal to anything in Europe. I'd very much like the opinion of someone not connected in any way with my household or my soldiers. I believe Señorita Angela can best fill that role, so I beg of you, Señorita, to come with me and judge the castle. I hope you'll return to your family with enthusiastic comments about it."

The family had just barely absorbed the fact that they were not about to be shot as traitors, and now this. Even Aimée was in shock at the emperor's request. Was this the real reason he had come to call on them in person? She almost suspected the death of the so-called spy had been an excuse to see her—but why did an emperor need an excuse?

"Your Highness," answered Aimée demurely, "I am greatly flattered. Perhaps you'd also like my cousins to enjoy this honor," she added, not wanting to be alone with him—and also knowing that when she returned she'd have to face the envy of Melania and Della.

"No, no. It is you I have chosen. You were in National Palace and you made some gracious comments about it, though there was some helpful criticism too," he lied smoothly. "This isn't a command, of course. But I would instead consider it a great personal favor."

While the entire family stared at her with envy and amazement, Aimée replied, "Of course, Your Highness. I shall need but a moment to prepare myself."

She curtsied and went inside to her room with Marie-Clarice following closely. The powder she applied to her cheeks was meant to hide the flush she saw. She felt anger at being sought out thus by Maximilian, but she was compelled to play her role and not let even Marie-Clarice suspect her true feelings about Maximilian.

"Ask him if I may go, too, señorita, please," Marie-Clarice pleaded.

Aimée spoke sternly. "One does not make requests of royalty. Besides, I may be gone for a day or two. I think I can take care of myself."

"I suspect you will," Marie-Clarice said dismally. "And return, perhaps, worse for wear—if you know what I mean."

"I know very well what you mean," she snapped angrily.

"I only meant that it's a strenuous job inspecting an entire castle," Marie-Clarice tried to say with a straight face, but a hint of a sly smile played over her features.

"What you meant has no significance," Aimée told her. "This is a royal command. After what has happened here today, I think it would be far wiser to obey than to challenge the authority of Maximilian or have him withdraw his protection from this entire family no matter what I personally think or feel for him."

Marie-Clarice flushed at this rebuke and said, "I know, señorita. Forgive me. It is just that I feel uneasy away from you."

Aimée softened her tone as she said, "Marie-Clarice, you have looked after me well and have been a loyal friend. I am sorry to have been so short-tempered with you. So much has happened, and just as I thought things were quieting down . . . I know it will be lonely here for you. All I ask is that you try to be patient for a little while longer."

"I just hope he treats you well, our emperor," said Marie-Clarice earnestly.

Aimée felt her color heighten. "I'm sure he will. Please don't worry. I'll be fine," she said, although she wasn't half so certain as she sounded.

"And what about that American reporter? What should I do if he pays a call?" Marie-Clarice asked.

"I doubt that he will," Aimée answered quietly, remembering how she had told Alex she never wanted to see him again.

"I'll think of something to tell him to explain your absence," Maire-Clarice volunteered. "Don't worry."

"I don't think I'll have time to worry about him," Aimée said, adjusting her hat.

The family was waiting for her at the foot of the stairs. "His Highness has returned to his carriage," Lino informed her. "Angela, please speak well of us to him," he almost begged.

"I shall, uncle," she promised, pretending not to notice the knowing looks on the faces of Melania, Della and their mother. Lino was far more concerned with the welfare of his entire family than the petty jealousies among the women. Renato gave her a brief smile and a nod, as if he understood and appreciated what she was doing for them. Renato was no fool. She thanked him with a grateful glance.

She could feel their eyes on her back as a guard in a colorful uniform escorted her to the coach. She took the seat beside the emperor, who favored her traveling clothes with a smile of approval. He gave a brief nod to the guard and the cortège was immediately on its way.

Maximilian took Aimée's hand and held it gently. "It's my wish that you make suggestions about the decor of the castle. A woman's ideas are always helpful."

"I'm honored, Your Highness," Aimée said in a small voice. Maximilian was stroking her hand, very gently.

"I shall be most grateful for your assistance. Would it be possible for you to become one of my empress's ladies-in-waiting?" he asked, then said, "No, what am I talking about? You are far too young. Perhaps your aunt would consider joining the royal family. Ah," he made a casual gesture with one hand, "The empress sailed for Vienna last week. I'm afraid she's quite ill. The doctors here know so little about her particular condition. In Vienna there are far more experienced and wiser doctors who will be able to help her. Let us hope that she will soon be healthy and return, ready once again to share my throne."

"I pray she'll make a swift recovery," Aimée said dutifully, wondering why he was making such banal comments. Perhaps, she realized, their every word was overheard and even the emperor did not feel safe from prying ears.

"It is very lonely for me. I'm a man who dislikes being alone. Perhaps you'll ease my loneliness by coming to visit me on occasion?" he asked.

"Your Highness has only to command . . ."

"My dear, I will never command you." He moved much closer, tilting her chin back and kissing her gently as he drew her into his arms. Even the most careful listener would have heard only silence in the royal coach. At first Aimée responded woodenly, and then she reminded herself that it would be far wiser to return his kisses with a passion that matched his own. It shocked her, as she wound her arms around his neck and pressed her body close to his, how easily she could carry out such an intimacy and appear so aroused—and feel nothing, except pity, for poor Maximilian.

Finally he released her and sat back and smiled. "You have been on my mind for too long. I had to see you," he said in a voice so low, it could not possibly have been overheard. "I think of no one but you."

"Thank you, Your Highness." Aimée blushed.

"I'm a gentle person. I try to be kind, and I say that in all humility. I honor my friends and make certain that their loyalty is never forgotten," he said, assuming a rather paternal air toward her, almost as if he were trying to reassure her. "You must understand that I love Carlota. She is an unusual person, well suited to be empress, and a sensuous woman as well. Do I embarrass you, my dear, by speaking so frankly?" he asked. Aimée had been listening open-mouthed in amazement at what he was saying to her. He was hardly treating her like somebody he bedded for pleasure; he was treating her with respect.

"No, I am not embarrassed, but flattered, Your Highness, by your openness and honesty," she replied truthfully.

"Ah, very well said. Now tell me what those hotheaded legionnaires did," he commanded her.

"They said they came searching for spies and I'm afraid they found some," admitted Aimée, adding immediately, "Of course, we were not aware that they were not faithful subjects of yours."

"Of course you weren't. A family like yours would have nothing to do with the *Juáristas*. I'd advise you to replace them with workers who are selected more carefully, my dear."

"Of course, Your Majesty. We will be most careful indeed," said Aimée earnestly.

"I think you should know that the men we captured confessed to spying for Juárez and they were shot."

"If they were spying, what you did is not my affair."

"Well said," he congratulated her. "My dear, we are going to get along very well. And I thank you again for sending that reporter. I'm sure he'll write a most favorable story about my reign," he said with satisfaction.

"He as much as told me he would, Your Excellency."

"Good! Tell him for me that he is welcome any time and that I give my consent for him to speak to anyone in my court whenever he desires."

"Your Excellency is most kind," said Aimée dutifully, but she was thinking that probably she would never see Alex again, a thought which cost her a pang of regret.

They reached the castle just before sunset and Aimée gasped at the magnificence of it. The castle had been built on a portion of a mountain surrounded by gigantic cypress trees, said to have been planted by Montezuma, king of the Aztecs. The coach rolled down an avenue of towering eucalyptus trees and began the climb to the castle between wide sweeps of lawn and formal gardens. Aimée couldn't help marveling at finding herself in such an exquisite setting. It was like a fairyland.

A liveried servant sprang forward to open the coach door the minute it stopped. First he helped Aimée out, and then the emperor. It seemed that they climbed an endless expanse of marble steps before they reached a great door which swung open as if on cue. Servants were everywhere, bowing and murmuring welcome.

Maximilian led Aimée into the main drawing room and spoke with one of the servants for a moment. Shortly, a bottle of fine Madeira in a sparkling crystal decanter was carried in on an exquisite tray bearing also two crystal glasses edged in gold. Everything in sight was magnificent almost beyond description. What appeared to be ordinary, perhaps a doorstopper, on closer inspection proved to be a brass sculpture of ingenious design. Here was evidence of the finest taste and best art that money could buy.

"To you," Maximilian raised his glass and they drank a toast. "I wish you to inspect my castle thoroughly, but now I am sure you are tired from your long journey and wish to bathe and dress for dinner. We shall inspect the castle tomorrow in the daylight when we are both fresh, if that plan is agreeable to you," he said. Maximilian had a charming way of seeming to cater to her whims at the same time he determined the way things would be. It was most winning, and yet Aimée now felt confident that she could be just as charming a partner to him.

"I think that's a splendid idea," she agreed instantly. "And I so would like to bathe for the dirt from traveling makes my skin feel so coarse. . . ."

"Of course, my dear, instantly." Maximilian issued some orders and Aimée was escorted to a grand room where her bags had been taken earlier. Two maids were waiting to assist her. She had an hour to herself to rest before a servant knocked and announced that her presence was requested in the drawing room.

There was more to drink before dinner. Maximilian was seated on a very low settee, and when she sat down beside him, their bodies touched. She refilled their glasses and proposed a toast to him and thanked him for his hospitality. When the glasses were empty this time, he set them on the table and drew her close, putting her arms around his neck. She looked into his blue eyes and saw they were already glazed with desire. His mouth covered hers with a kiss that grew in passion until their bodies were hot with desire. He moaned softly as his lips moved from her mouth to her cheeks, nibbled on her delicate earlobes, moved along her neck, and finally reached her bosom where he buried his head. He held her so tightly that Aimée thought she would burst from lack of air. She realized there was an urgency in his embraces that went beyond sexual desire. It was as if he simply needed to hold and be held, to be reassured, almost the way a young child will cling to its mother. Finally he raised his head and looked directly in her eyes. With one hand he cupped and caressed a breast and he asked her: "Have you ever been in bed when someone you couldn't see came to you and made passionate love to you?"

"Once, Your Highness," she said, suddenly recognizing that this was all a game, one that he not only enjoyed but needed. In truth, he had no real power, so he exercised what little power he had in this harmless and rather pathetic game—the seduction of women on command in supposed anonymity. By assuming a fatherly attitude and then becoming the lover, he made himself feel like a king.

Before their game could progress any further, a servant announced supper. Max cursed him under his breath but arose, took Aimée's hand and held it as they made their way to the dining room. Maximilian had brought his own chef in his entourage from Vienna. And tonight, to start, he had prepared a meal of refreshing fruits arranged on gold plates: there were beautifully carved pieces of avocado, papaya garnished with lime, pineapples, and nopak, a fruit that resembled watermelon in taste, cut into the shapes of little animals.

There was also vanilla-flavored sapote, pomegranates, guavas and passion fruit.

Servants were everywhere; one stood at all times behind each of their chairs to ensure that their glasses were full. Empty plates were instantly whisked away, and any special requests fulfilled on command. They had little time for intimate conversation.

Aimée sat at one end of a long table and Maximilian at the other end. They were too far away to hold an intimate conversation for they couldn't hear one another unless they half-shouted. It was a rather stiff and formal way to dine, especially when there were only two people at a table that could easily have seated twenty, but Aimée surmised that when you are emperor there are certain trappings that you are trapped by.

Aimée's glass was never allowed to remain even half empty, and it seemed that with every course a fresh wine was served that she had to taste in order to toast Maximilian. By the end of the meal she was virtually giddy from all the alcohol.

They had coffee and brandy in the library. They sat on a small couch, the windows wide open to let in the air. They made polite small talk but Maximilian grew restless and suggested they begin the inspection of the castle at once, despite the darkness. What little of it Aimée had seen already was the ultimate in luxury, and she sincerely doubted her ability to walk a straight line, let alone to journey through an entire castle by candlelight.

However, the inspection began—and ended—with the emperor's bedroom. At first they chatted lightly. He told her the castle was named Miramar West and was similar to a castle he and Carlota had in Europe. They had spent many hours there, he recalled almost wistfully. Like this one, it had two separate wings—the Alcazar Wing which was the royal residence, and the West Wing, which housed the palace guard.

Then Maximilian turned his attention to Aimée. They began lovemaking in a leisurely way, exploring each other's bodies—this time by candlelight—and slowly arousing each other until they could restrain their passion no longer and made furious love for a few minutes. Then, curiously, Maximilian withdrew without climaxing, leaving Aimée gasping and fearful she had offended him somehow. "Oh, no," he laughed. "I want to make it last and last. I want to make love to you all night until the sun rises. I want to please you as no other man has pleased you before."

Aimée realized his words were sincere and that she indeed aroused a passion in him that gave him great pleasure. She, in turn, was astonished at how much physical pleasure he could arouse in her. But Aimée secretly wished she could be in this magnificent palace, in this oversized bed with Alex and that he would spend hours exploring her body and making love to her. Throughout the long night that followed, Aimée played her role with Maximilian to perfection because she imagined he was Alex.

Maximilian resumed his movements and Aimée realized that while Vardeau had used her and tried to please her only in the beginning, Maximilian was truly a considerate lover who knew how to read her responses, how to tease her to higher and higher planes of passion till she was crying out, panting like an animal and clawing at his back with her fingernails to feel him penetrate her yet deeper and deeper. It almost amused her now to think that she had been so afraid of his great size during their first encounter in the dark. As if possessed, she succumbed to this golden man's tongue, hands and organ while he played her body like some rare and exquisite instrument. Now she knew how a man's organ could bring out feelings in her she hadn't even suspected she possessed.

But later, as he grew more tired, she discovered Maximilian was not only a wonderful lover but a fine and patient teacher. "You please me greatly," he sighed, lying back. "But there is something you could do to arouse me again. And I promise you that the second

time it will feel even more magnificent, my dear Aimée."
He guided her head, very gently, to where he wanted it.
When Aimée realized what he wanted her to do for
him, she thought it repulsive. She could almost hear
Alex's voice as he had cried out, "You're the emperor's
whore!" And if he could see this, he would certainly be
disgusted. But then another voice inside her defiantly
said, "Perhaps that is true, but would Alex call me a
whore if I were doing this for him?" Concentrating all
her energy on her task, Aimée, fumbling at first, but
then sensing how to read his reactions, aroused Maximilian again.

This time they made love with an intensity that left
even Maximilian gasping. He wrapped her legs around
his neck and plunged into her body like a wild stallion,
his nostrils flaring and his hands pinioning her buttocks
so she could barely move—and despite herself, she experienced ecstacy. Too, she marveled at her ability to
respond to his every move intuitively, to match him
stroke for stroke as if their bodies had been made to
play with each other.

As they lay there in each other's arms, Aimée felt
a smug sense of satisfaction. The last time, Max had
taken her quickly and urgently in the dark. This time
she had learned how to please him and realized that
now she had a measure of control over him. He needed
her. He fell asleep with his mouth against her breasts.
She lay there watching him until finally sleep came to
her in a golden glow.

When she awoke next morning, she was surprised to
see that Max had gone. She gave a huge stretch and
yawn and was surprised again to discover how well she
felt even though she knew she couldn't have had more
than a few hours sleep. Instead of draining her, their
lovemaking all through the night seemed to have un-
leashed an energy that made her positively glow—and
want to get on with the inspection of the castle. Her
clothes had been laid out in her dressing room and so
she readied herself and then began the tour without him.

Even though she'd had an idea of how lavish the castle was, by daylight and in her new frame of mind, Aimée was agog at the wonderful things she saw. Room after room was decorated wth ornate furniture, acres of rare tapestries, screens of exquisite beauty, and finally she found a full-length formal portrait of Maximilian himself. He was posed in an ermine robe and had such a regal bearing that she stood mute realizing that she knew this man in such an intimate way. A pity, she thought, that though he had the regal bearing of a lion, he was a mere puppet attached to strings controlled by his family. He had been doomed from the start. But she quickly pushed the pity out of her mind as she thought of the poor Mexicans working out their brief lives to scramble in the dirt so they could pay taxes to his government. All of this grandeur had been paid for with their sweat and blood, and if they could see his castle, it would only hasten his doom.

She was still standing there studying his portrait when he found her. He wore a gold dressing gown and his shining blond beard was carefully combed and parted in the middle. He was also in a despondent mood as he ushered her into the dining room.

They were alone this morning in a room that was almost cozy, but he was reluctant to speak his mind. Finally he did speak, and she was amazed to learn that his thoughts echoed her own as she'd stood before his portrait. He was very melancholy over the fact that he knew his rule was not a success and that his aides kept much from him. He was not a stupid man, even if he was a weak one, and he realized that the cheering Mexicans he saw had bayonets pointed at their backs. And that he really didn't understand the Mexican people. Aimée was truly amazed at how aware he was of his delicate situation and yet how powerless he was to change it.

"Your Majesty, I wish I could help you, but I haven't been in Mexico long enough to know its people either— or what you could do to win them over. I must confess that I still feel as much a stranger as you do. I even find it hard to understand my own family."

He nodded and rose to fetch more bacon and biscuits from the steam table in the small dining room. "I can understand that. They're such strange people, these Mexicans. They refuse to look me in the eye. I've sent for peons a number of times, just to talk to them, but they'll say nothing to me. I cannot reach them, my dear. I can't understand them, but I tried."

Then he went on in a somewhat more bitter tone. "The problem is that behind this whole senseless business is that man Juárez. I've been told he's an understanding man, a zealous patriot, a revolutionary hero. Now if *he* could come to talk to me, I'd be glad to receive him and listen to what he has to say. Maybe we could negotiate and put an end to all of this violence."

It was a lovely idea, Aimée thought, but impossible. "If you don't mind my saying so," Aimée began hesitantly, "You might soften the Black Decree. So many natives are executed—"

"It wasn't my idea," he broke in, a frown creasing his brow. "The orders came from France. I'm not French. Sometimes I think I comprehend their attitudes far less than I do those of the Mexicans. That decree was written by the military. I *had* to sign it. If I hadn't it would have been an indication of weakness, and there might have been a French military coup which would have been far worse for the Mexican peon than he could ever guess. This way the French are kept in some kind of check; otherwise they'd declare military rule and even you would not be safe, my dear," he added sadly.

But there was more on Maximilian's mind, much more, as Aimée was to discover as he unburdened himself to her. Despite all the luxury, she decided, being emperor was more than royal processions and luxurious castles. There were genuine problems, and in Maximilians' situation, at least, no power to solve them.

"It costs a great deal to run this country. The threat of open rebellion requires many soldiers. That's most expensive . . . though ten thousand soldiers left just recently. I regard my present army as insufficient, but Louis Napoleon Bonaparte will not listen—or doesn't care. All he wants is more and more money. He's sent me only a company of troops to serve as my personal guard." Maximilian reached abruptly for her hand. "Enough of that," he said.

"Before you leave I shall introduce you to the officer in charge of my guard and give him orders that you're to be admitted here or at the palace in the city at any time of the day or night. I trust that you'll come to visit me often. Very often. . . . Last night was most enjoyable," Maximilian said. For the first time, his grimly set features relaxed and a warm smile appeared.

"You've but to send word," Aimée said. She placed her hand over his. "I only wish I could do more for you," she added, knowing that she meant it, that he was neither unconcerned nor heartless as a ruler. Both he and the Mexicans were the victims of the French.

"Now I *am* gratified," he told her, a smile lighting up his handsome countenance for the second time. "It's become a fine day because of you. Shall we go to work and inspect the castle now? Or do you think that may be too much of an adventure? There are always other times. . . ." And it was quite obvious that he was looking forward to these other times, so Aimée took her cue.

"I think, Your Highness, that I would prefer another time, if you don't mind. I'm rather tired this morning, but very, very happy," she said, gazing deeply into his eyes.

He reached into his pocket to take out a purple, velvet-covered jewelry box, which he presented to Aimée. She opened it to find a fabulous brooch made of diamonds and rubies that glittered in the sunlight with such intensity that it took her breath away. "Oh, Your Majesty," she gasped. "It's so beautiful!"

"Wear it discreetly my dear, and never wear it to the palace—but keep it as a reminder of me," he told her.

She kissed him full on the lips, her tongue exploring his open mouth, as he had taught her. She felt his arms tighten around her in response. "I shall be most discreet in wearing it," she vowed. She knew that if Carlota returned and saw her wearing it, it would end any possibility of seeing Maximilian again, and it would probably be the end of her as well.

"Good," said Maximilian releasing her. "I'm pleased. Now, if you're ready, we'll go into the gardens where the Royal Guard has been assembled for our inspection. You may be assured that they'll never challenge you from reaching my side, day or night."

The heat of the day was oppressive as they walked outside. It was like being hit with a blast of furnace heat so drying that the green gardens and trees had to be watered constantly. No matter how hot Aimée found it, there were two lines of soldiers standing stiffly at attention as they entered the garden, and the soldiers were in full-dress uniform. In front of the lines stood two captains and before them stood a tall, beautifully uniformed colonel.

Maximilian faced the guards. "It is my wish that Señorita Fuchard, who stands now by my side, be considered a privileged person. She is not to be challenged, but is to be brought to me at any time she wishes to call, no matter what time of day or night."

The colonel, who wore a black velvet uniform with braid and aiguilettes and a gold-braided *kepi* approached stiffly to stand before Aimée and Maximilian. As he drew his sword and presented it with a formal salute, Aimée almost gasped out loud.

"This," said Maximilian turning to address her, "is Colonel Vardeau, just arrived from Paris. Go to him if there's ever trouble."

"Thank you, Your Highness," Aimée managed to say, a trifle unsteadily, his words an eerie echo of those of her father's—and she had hardly forgotten how dependable Vardeau had been then. It was a nightmare, an absolute nightmare. Of all people to be dispatched to Mexico, why did it have to be Vardeau—and just as she had begun to feel secure here? In the brief silence that followed Aimée expected Vardeau to accuse her of being a traitoress, but if he recognized her, he gave absolutely no indication that he'd ever even seen her before. Aimée was stunned by his entirely impersonal manner, every inch the soldier and the commander, the man lost inside the uniform. True, his eyes scanned her, but coldly and with no more than formal interest.

On the way back to the castle, Maximilian gave further voice to his dissatisfaction. "It's a shame I must keep so many soldiers around me. Everywhere I go, the route must be cleared of any possible chance of ambush. Do you know what the Mexicans sometimes call me? *A lavavava.* Do you know what that means?" he demanded.

"No, Your Highness," she replied vaguely, her mind still in a turmoil after coming face to face with Vardeau.

"It means 'featherhead,' " he stormed, and his vehemence wrested her away from her own private worries.

"Your Excellency," she replied, trying very hard to suppress a smile, "every ruler, no matter where, is always called by such names. It's one more penalty you pay for your exalted position. Such names are given in envy and jealousy rather than for their truthfulness."

"You're the most comforting and sensible young lady I've ever known," Maximilian said, mollified by her tactful answer. "Now we must prepare to go back. You'll tell your people that you slept in Carlota's private bedroom and you were assisted by some of her ladies-in-waiting."

"Thank you, Your Highness. I appreciate your thoughtfulness," Aimée spoke with sincerity, but she knew that no matter what she claimed Melania and Della would exchange knowing and jealous looks.

When they reached the castle, Maximilian apparently received some kind of bad news from a courier who was waiting for him. He rode back with her in the royal coach, enveloped in a shroud of silence for which Aimée was almost grateful.

Here she sat in plush luxury while her heart beat madly with fear, as it had in passion the night before. She was positive Vardeau had recognized her. How could he not have recognized her? And yet he had given no sign, even to her, that he did. She felt as if fate had played some sordid trick on her to bring Vardeau here and imperil the alliance with Maximilian she had so carefully nurtured. If she was exposed, even Maximilian's intervention probably couldn't save her from being shot on the spot as a traitoress or being shipped back to Paris.

She tried to reassure herself that she knew some very damaging information about Vardeau. She even considered seeing him privately and trying to blackmail him into silence. But on reflection she realized she could not bargain with a man as treacherous as Vardeau. There was nothing she could do, she concluded, except pray that he would think her resemblance to a certain Aimée Gaudin nothing more than a coincidence. It was a forlorn hope, but it was all she had.

Chapter 11

Aimée returned early one afternoon from a trip to Mexico City to find Alex seated on the veranda with Melania. She ran from the carriage and up the stairs, extending both hands toward him.

"I'm so happy to see you again," she said, unable to contain her rush of pleasure.

"I'm glad to hear that," he said, but his gray eyes were troubled. "I wondered if you'd like to go for a ride?"

"I can change in just a few minutes," she answered, subdued and worried by the smugness of the smile on Melania's pretty oval face.

Aimée gave orders for the horses to be saddled, then hurried into the house to change. Marie-Clarice was waiting in her room with the riding habit already laid out.

"You listen in on everything, don't you?" Aimée observed.

"It's a good thing I do. Melania has been whispering to him for quite some time. I couldn't hear what she

195

said, but you can be sure that it has to do with you—and it isn't nice."

"Then he must know I spent that night at the castle. Oh, damn! Marie-Clarice, why does Melania have to hate me so?"

"She's jealous. She can't stand the fact that Maximilian chose you and not her. She blames you for it."

"Well, I'll try to handle it the best I can. Hurry now. I want as much time with Alex as possible."

She was downstairs in less than fifteen minutes and she and Alex walked in silence toward the stables. Two Arabians—magnificent animals that Maximilian had sent as a gift—were saddled and ready. If Alex noticed these horses, he said nothing about them. He was so solemn as to be almost dour.

He didn't try to talk as they rode the trail into the forest and finally entered the lovely green dell presided over by that ancient cypress.

They dismounted, still in awkward silence, and he walked over to the cypress and sat down with his back against the trunk.

Aimée sat beside him. She studied his set face for a moment. "You don't seem glad to see me, so why have you come?" she asked at last. Obviously there was some other service or favor he wanted to ask, since it appeared that he wasn't personally the least bit pleased to see her again.

"Things are not going well," he said, ignoring her question.

"What things? What's happened?"

"Juárez is no more than sixty or seventy miles away, at the head of a huge army that's well equipped. The French know it and refuse to be worried—they don't really know the extent of the rebel forces. The French and the Belgian troops sent here fight well under ordinary conditions, but they've never had to contend with enemies who don't appear in straight lines like tenpins, but who shoot from behind any tree or rock. They don't know how to handle raiding parties that appear in the middle of the night shooting and setting fire to everything that might be of assistance to the enemy—and then vanish in the darkness. These tactics don't sound very effective, but if the same scene is played out every night, many times each night, and many French soldiers die. . . . The soldiers know, and those who are closest to the rebels are so scared that they are on the verge of deserting."

"Will the rebels get here?" Aimée asked, realizing that this must have been the news the courier had been carrying for Maximilian and was the reason he had been so withdrawn on their trip back.

"There's no doubt the rebels will get here. The only question is how soon will they get here. I don't believe there's much time. To make it worse, even Maximilian doesn't realize just how close they are. His aides keep this from him because they are afraid he might offer to surrender."

"It might be well if he did," said Aimée. "Alex, I want the rebels to win. This is their land. They have a right to it and the French should get out. They should never have come here in the first place. It's all been a dreadful mistake. There was a time when all of this could have been averted."

She stopped short. Aimée had been on the verge of revealing to Alex that her father had fought against the invasion and had died for his beliefs, but if she slipped into that she'd be compelled to tell him her whole story. She felt far from ready to trust him with her true identity—yet.

"You seem to have some mighty firm convictions about this," he said, observing her closely.

"It's the way I feel. I can't help it," said Aimée, realizing that the intensity in her voice had given away just how involved she was.

"Well, no matter how you feel," shrugged Alex, "the inevitable is going to happen, and soon. The French aren't even taking prisoners anymore. They just shoot every rebel they see or capture. The Mexicans are going to do the same thing and they swear they'll have their revenge. They haven't forgotten the Black Decree—and they blame Maximilian for that—and how many of their valuable men died as martyrs for their cause."

"Would their revenge extend to people like me? Is that what you came here to tell me?" she asked in surprise. If he came here to warn her, not ask a favor, then it meant that he must care for her.

"I think they'll put you in the same class with the French. You've toadied up to Maximilian too often," he said, trying not to reveal his feelings.

"Alex, remember, I've only been here a short time."

He shot her a strange glance that implied he knew more than he was saying. "Yes, I know," was all he said.

"What do you suggest we do?"

"There's only one thing you can do—run. And if I were you I wouldn't wait very long."

"How can we do that? How can we get out of the country?"

"You have a great deal of money. Money talks very loudly in a poor country. I doubt the rebels would rather have you when they could have your gold. I can't advise you how to escape, but I came back to warn you to begin making plans."

She looked away from him, more affected by his admission than by the news he brought.

"Listen to me," he went on urgently, "Louis Napoleon is getting sick of what's going on here. He no longer makes any profit out of his Mexican empire. In fact, it's costing him a lot of money. Tax collections have broken down and the whole country is in open rebellion, except here in Mexico City where they don't dare rebel. He's actually ordering some troops out of the country, and certainly isn't sending anymore. Get out while you can. . . ."

"And what about you . . . ?"

He hesitated, then said, "I've got a job to do."

"Yes, I know. But I feel something's wrong, that there's something you're not telling me." His hesitation and his refusal to meet her eyes gave her hope and she went on recklessly, "Did you come here only because you felt you owed it to me to warn me after the help I've given you?"

"Don't you agree it was?" he said in clipped tones.

"Alex, tell me the truth. Whatever it is, tell me."

He turned abruptly and faced her, and she heard anger and hurt in his voice as he spat out, "You're a whore!"

"Alex!"

"You've been sleeping with Maximilian. All this time you've been his mistress. When he beckons, you go to him—probably taking your clothes off as you run to him."

Aimée was shocked into silence by his hostility.

"How many more times will you go to him? Does he reward you in any other ways besides presenting you with this fine pair of Arabians? They're very valuable, my dear, and I'm sure His Majesty didn't give them to you out of the goodness of his heart. More like the heat of his passion. And quite likely yours matches his."

"Do you know of any way to defy his command?" she asked weakly.

"Command, hell," he spat. "You went willingly. You could have stood up to him and refused the old whore-master. In fact, I think you're in love with him."

Aimée bent her head and fought to keep the tears back. How could she tell him that she felt no love for Maximilian, that he had aroused her passion but that it was loveless, that she'd been left feeling empty and yearning for Alex the whole time she had lain with Maximilian? He wouldn't believe that unless she revealed everything, but with Vardeau now in the country, to reveal herself even to Alex was more dangerous than ever before.

"I see you have nothing to say," he said scornfully.

"You may leave now," she murmured, knowing she was powerless to change his mind.

"How dare you try to order me around, you whore! I'll leave when I'm damned good and ready to leave," Alex said vehemently. "I keep wondering why I don't tear your clothes off right now and take my own satisfaction with you. I want to. I always have, but I don't play second fiddle to anyone, not even an emperor. Especially one who'll bed any girl. Do you think you're the only one?"

"I said you may leave now. Please go away," she stammered, her voice choking on her held-back tears.

"Maybe what you should do is talk him into getting out, too, so he can go back to Vienna and take you with him. Carlota won't mind. Last I heard she doesn't even know what's going on. Why not take her place?"

"Damn you, Alex," she cried in frustration.

"You're about as low as they come, my dear. And I thought I wasn't worthy of you! But you're only the whore of an emperor who has a dozen ready to serve him whenever he beckons. Oh, I'll go. I'd better, before I forget myself and take you as my whore, too."

He rose angrily to mount his horse and, without looking back, rode off. Aimée remained there in the quietness of the glen. She was beyond tears. They'd do no good. The knowledge that Alex really did care for her brought her no relief, for she had no way of making him understand. She wished desperately that she could stay away from Maximilian, but that would be an impossibility. He'd send for her soon and she'd go. She'd go to him because she could do nothing else. Her own position was far too precarious to risk his anger, or risk being exposed for what she was. Colonel Vardeau could do that very well, especially if he learned she was no longer favored by the emperor.

Aimée realized that she had no choice but to make plans to leave the country. She could not go back to France. The United States was her only hope, although she now knew that she would have to make her way without Alex's help.

She considered her problems but knew they were too much for solution in her present, agitated state of mind. She rounded up her horse and rode back to the house. Alex's carriage was gone. There wasn't even a trace of dust to reveal his departure. Obviously he hadn't wasted a moment in leaving.

Aimée entered the house and was immediately confronted with Melania, who turned from the foot of the stairway and smiled in sweet-faced concern. "You look upset, Angela! Nothing is wrong with your friend, I trust. . . ." When Aimée didn't answer, she went on, a challenging look in her catgreen eyes and said, "I rather like your precious Alex. And he's a *very* good listener—"

Without thinking, Aimée slapped her face as hard as she could and saw Melania's expression change from surprise to open hatred as she reeled back against the wall, Aimée's hand-print bright-red on Melania's fair skin.

Just then Lino called to Aimèe from the drawing room. She whirled and stalked off without another word to Melania.

"You seem upset," Lino said mildly, as she entered.

"I was. . . . What did you wish to talk to me about, uncle," she said briskly.

"As you know, Nemecio's death left us to handle a large and once very lucrative import-export business. Even though Mexico has been in a state of turmoil for years, the business has continued to flourish . . . until recently."

"What happened?" asked Aimèe quietly, all her thoughts now bearing down on what Lino obviously had to tell her.

"The revolution. It didn't really show up at first that we weren't making the money we used to because old debts were paid, but every day I see our income plummeting. And the value of the peso goes down every day too. To add to our troubles, the French have been using the ships to sail their troops back and less of our goods have been coming in and out of Mexico."

"How bad is it?" Aimèe asked, but from the troubled look on Lino's face and the seriousness with which he addressed her, she knew that he wouldn't have told her unless it was a desperate situation indeed.

"We're not broke. It would take a long time before we ran out of money, but. . . ." Further conversation on that subject was interrupted by the sound of Antonia, Melania and Della chattering as they came down the stairs. It ceased once they entered the room, sought out chairs and arranged their skirts. Apparently, Melania had recovered her spirits quickly after their confrontation and she now seemed composed and happy, as if nothing had happened.

"Angela," began Antonia brightly, "Did Maximilian mention anything about another palace ball soon?"

"At a time like this?" replied Aimée incredulously. "The way things are today?" Didn't they realize just how precarious a situation they were in, wondered Aimée, or were their whole lives centered around themselves?

"I don't see what difference that makes," Antonia said petulantly, as if this whole war was an excuse to deprive her of her pleasures. "Carlota will return and when she does there should certainly be some state function to welcome her back."

Aimée could hardly believe her ears. Were they truly that ignorant that they thought Carlota would come back, that Maximilian would stay in power, or that they could even keep their heads? "Aunt," Aimée said firmly, "it's quite likely that Carlota will never return. And it's even more likely that within a few weeks Maximilian won't be emperor, either. Don't you know that there's a war going on? Can't you realize that the French are going to be defeated? The *Juáristas* will soon be in control and Mexico will be free."

Instead of being pleased to hear that Mexico would

be free, Antonia turned petulantly to her brother and said, "Lino, this can't be true—or we should have heard about it."

"You've heard about it for weeks," he said dryly. "The trouble is that you weren't listening. Everything Angela just told you is true. Only too true," he mused.

"Well, then," said Antonia, as if it were as simple as that, "we'd best begin cultivating Juárez."

Lino laughed humorlessly. "For your age, you're certainly naive, Antonia. When the *Juárista* army finally arrives, it may very well take away everything we own—and us as well."

"We should be making plans to get out of here," said Della.

"Well, I simply don't believe it," said Melania. "Not a word of it. There are French soldiers everywhere. Angela is just trying to scare us."

"For what purpose?" Aimée asked, curious at how her cousin could so twist the truth for her own purposes.

"So we'll go and you can have the attention of the emperor all to yourself."

"Melania," chided Lino, "that's very unfair. And in my opinion it is a great advantage to us that Angela is so friendly with the emperor."

"It's not only unfair, but it's the most absurd statement I've ever heard," Aimée interrupted. She decided her patience was at an end with her family and it was about time they came out of their fantasy world and faced the grim reality of their predicament. "I'm going to tell you something else that may frighten you enough to take this whole matter seriously: It's suspected that we're harboring *Juárista* spies on this estate. And after that ambush on my way back from the city, we know we also harbor someone who informs the French of this. That puts us in trouble with both sides."

"We can't determine the political views of all of our employees," Lino protested.

"Quite true," agreed Aimée, "but we can try to

determine who tells the French about these spies who hide here."

"I think you made up the entire incident of the ambush," Melania said. "Either that or you're exaggerating. I simply don't believe a word of it," she said, her arms crossed over her chest and her chin held high.

Aimée ignored that insult, although it struck her that Melania was being unusually irrational about this matter. Jealousy didn't seem to be an adequate explanation for her strange behavior, for Aimée knew that Melania was much more intelligent than she pretended to be. Melania worried Aimée, and for more reasons than one, but there was nothing specific she could put her finger on to figure out how Melania could be trying to undermine her. Surely the rest of the family believed that she'd been ambushed, and hadn't Maximilian himself ridden out to the estate to apologize?

"Angela," Lino interrupted her thoughts, "who can we possibly suspect? We've certainly tried to maintain a neutral stand between Maximilian and Juárez. I thought we were succeeding."

"Obviously we're not," Aimée pointed out dryly. "And I'm worried that Renato's feelings about Juárez might be strong enough to be discovered. Where is he, by the way?"

"In the city," Antonia said. "He often has business there."

"He spends too much time away from the estate and our business," Lino complained bitterly. "Angela may be right. But even so, we can't fault him too much. We're Mexicans, and I've always believed the French never had any business here. But, who then is informing on the *Juáristas?* Renato isn't likely to be on both sides."

"The servants hate us," put in Della. "Any one of them would be happy to see us with our backs against a wall. And they snoop and know everything that goes on. I've seen some of them looking through letters and papers in the library."

"Who? Why didn't you do something about it?" Melania turned on her sister.

"Do you think I want a knife in my back or poison in my food? I'm sure you've seen this, too, and never mentioned it yourself," she shot back hotly.

"Stop it," Lino said sharply. "We have enough troubles now without you two carrying on so. Angela, as head of this household, do you have any suggestions?"

"She can have only one," Melania said, her innocent tone belied by a malicious gleam in her eyes. "She'll continue to cultivate Maximilian's favors. And in a way that will favor us all."

Aimée abruptly stood up, glad that Melania's viciousness was at least out in the open and that she could respond directly. "I think that's about enough of that kind of talk. And I'd like to remind you that if this matter goes too far, this property can easily be disposed of and we will all go our separate ways."

"Angela, you wouldn't!" cried out Antonia in horror at the thought of losing the house and being on her own. "Nemecio wouldn't have wanted that," she tried to bluff her way out.

"Nemecio couldn't have guessed that a rebellion would tear this family apart and place all of us in such jeopardy," Aimée told them without hesitation. "I may decide to do this. In the meantime, as Uncle Lino said, we should stop this bickering and use our efforts to our advantage, not to divide ourselves. Like trying to find out who is betraying the family to the French."

She left them and went to her rooms to change from her riding habit into an afternoon dress. "Will you really give up this place?" Marie-Clarice asked when she entered her suite.

"You don't miss much, do you?" Aimée retorted, realizing she was still so annoyed at the whole family that she had taken her temper out on poor Marie-Clarice.

"You did advise me to keep my ears open," Marie-Clarice reminded her meekly.

"I'm sorry. I've no reason to be angry with you," apologized Aimée. "And I did ask you to keep your ears open. I just know that so much more is going on than I know of, but there's nothing I can do personally to learn what it is. You're right, I'm angry because I feel so helpless, but not at you."

"Are you angry at the family . . . or because of the reporter?" ventured Marie-Clarice, again showing her uncanny ability to mirror Aimée's most private thoughts.

"What do you know of that?" demanded Aimée.

"I saw him ride back alone and he acted like a man ready to find a gun and shoot someone or get into a fight."

"He's jealous of Maximilian," Aimée said curtly.

"Just like a man, but it could be worse for you—and all of us—if it was Maximilian who was jealous of that reporter."

"Don't you think I know that? So does Alex, but he is so stubborn and hot-headed that he only sees what he wants to see so far as I'm concerned. I don't want to talk about him anymore. I don't even want to see him again," said Aimée, almost defiantly.

Marie-Clarice was not deceived. "By tomorrow you'll be praying that he comes back," she predicted.

Aimée sighed, knowing she was right. "Please, let's change the subject. Have you learned any more about our wayward cousin, Renato?"

"How can I learn about him when he's hardly ever here? I can only say I like him, and I'll never believe he has betrayed the family."

"I think he's betraying the French and that's even more dangerous. They would shoot him. Next time I'm with him, there's going to be some frank talk. But he's no child, and I'm sure he's aware of the risk he's taking. I just don't like the fact that he may be risking my neck, too."

* * *

Later in the week, Renato and Aimée did ride out along their favorite trail to the glen. There they relaxed and Renato gave her a rueful smile. "You engineered me into this ride," he said. "There's something on your mind, isn't there?"

"Are you working for Juárez?" she asked point-blank, having decided that was the only way she might get an honest answer from him.

"If working for him means being paid by him or being offered some important post when all this is over, then the answer to your question is 'no.' I do not work for him."

"You know exactly what I mean, Renato," said Aimée, not accepting this evasion as an answer. "Be honest with me, don't be like the rest of the family. All they live for is to get richer and richer and remain in favor with Maximilian."

"I hate the French," Renato said softly, almost dreamily. "They came here and defeated our army— which, at the time, wasn't even strong enough to resist a band of military school cadets. They imposed their will on us, taxed us to death, killed our people and desecrated our country. I'm a Mexican and proud of it. I do what I can to see that the French are thrown out."

"Were you responsible for that fiasco when the carriage was stopped and a driver I never saw before was taken away as a spy?"

"No. I don't know who was responsible," he admitted. "I wouldn't have involved you in a dangerous situation like that."

"My association with Maximilian has nothing to do with any personal feelings—although I admit I can't dislike the man, even if he represents all that is bad about this French invasion of Mexico."

"He's not to blame. Not entirely. And your friendship with him means a great deal to us. If there's trouble, it might even save our heads."

"I'll do what I can for all of us," promised Aimée.

"Thank you for calling me a friend of Maximilian and not something else," she added sadly, suddenly remembering Alex's words the last time she had been with him in this exact same place.

"The American reporter?" guessed Renato.

"We had words about it, yes," admitted Aimée.

"Doesn't he realize you can't help what goes on? If Maximilian sends for you, that's a command that must be obeyed. You simply don't refuse an emperor."

"You know that, and I know that, but he doesn't," Aimée shook her head sadly. "Renato, I love him, but I've lost him and there is nothing I can do about it."

"It will work out. He's hot-headed, no doubt, but he'll cool off when he thinks about it."

Aimée shrugged, feeling that Renato's optimism was ill-placed. "One more thing," she said, determined to talk no more of Alex, "you're in a position to know, or at least guess the answer: Are we going to have to make a run for it when the rebels come?"

"We'll be gone long before then, I hope. Yes, we won't be treated gently if they get their hands on us. They know about our 'friendship' with Maximilian and don't look kindly on it."

"If we insist on leaving now, the family's either going to panic or refuse to go—or to make trouble. I think we should say no more about it until we're sure we should leave."

Renato helped her up. "For a member of our illustrious family, you're far wiser than we deserve. You've gone far beyond my expectations of you as the head of this family. Uncle Nemecio, for all of his faults, knew what he was doing when he left everything in your hands."

"Thank you, Renato," she said gratefully. She was also relieved that there was at least one family member in whom she could confide. The rest treated her warmly but there was a way in which they held back that still made her feel like an intruder in their family clique.

They mounted and as they prepared to ride out,

Renato said, "I'll race you back to the house." It was an earnest race, but Aimée was soon left far behind. She caught up to Renato at the stables, where he was gloating over his victory. As they walked back to the house from the stables Aimée silently reflected that her own troubles were far more serious than Renato's or his family's. She had all their troubles plus her own. She was wanted in France for treason. And right here in Mexico City was a man who had reason to hate her—and who was in a position to denounce her at any time. If he did, the military would seize her and Maximilian's influence would be worthless.

But Aimée couldn't help wondering why Vardeau hadn't already exposed her. He must have had a reason to keep his silence and she dared not even contemplate what that might be. She could denounce him in turn, of course, if he did expose her, but that wouldn't lessen her guilt in the eyes of the French. And she thoughtlessly had thrown the only evidence she possessed against him into a sewer in Paris.

Chapter 12

The next few days proved uneventful. Aimée saw little of her cousins or aunt, who had chosen to confine themselves to a small sitting room on the second floor. There they spent hours working on their needlepoints. Aimée was too restless to sit still for so many hours and do such fine handiwork. She spent much time worrying about Alex's safety because she suspected that he had set out for the region where the fighting was going on. Fortunately, she hadn't heard from Maximilian, and she had no desire to go to the palace to play a game of make-believe—especially now that she was aware of how much this liason had hurt and alienated Alex. She yearned for the safety and contentment of nestling in Alex's arms, although she now felt that she could never have him.

So Aimée confined herself to her suite and attempted to concentrate on reading. When she became restless, she would go for a walk. Once she met Lino and also Renato, but when she attempted to talk to them, they excused themselves on the pretense of pressing duties.

She did see the family in the dining room during meals, but the women's conversation centered on needle-point and the ball they kept pretending they would soon attend. Sometimes they complained that the servants had become lax and that the gardens were being neglected. The men kept silent, if they appeared.

When the meal was over, they would excuse themselves and go to their rooms. There was nothing for Aimée to do. Upstairs, Marie-Clarice was unable to explain why the family was suddenly being so aloof and secretive. Their personal servants either avoided Marie-Clarice or acted as if there was no change in the family's routine.

But Aimée knew they existed in an aura of false tranquility and that every day the rebels must be drawing closer.

Everything changed one morning when Aimée went down to breakfast and found no one at the table. It was obvious they hadn't eaten, for their settings were still there, the silverware untouched. Puzzled, Aimée made a brief search of the house and found no one. Finally, in the kitchen, she found the servants as well as Marie-Clarice, but no one could—or would—enlighten her as to the whereabouts of her family. She managed to hide her growing concern and simply asked Marie-Clarice to come back to her room to help her try on a dress they'd been fixing.

As soon as they were alone in Aimée's suite, Marie-Clarice told her that the entire family had gone away very early that morning. "They went in the big carriage and they didn't seem to be in a hurry, but it was before seven o'clock in the morning," she said.

"I wonder what that means?" Aimée was frankly puzzled. "It's not usual for them to go off together. In fact, they usually don't even know where anyone else is."

"They were dressed up as if they were going to the city," put in Marie-Clarice. "And they didn't talk much.

But for this family to even be awake at that hour is very strange, very strange."

"Anything out of the ordinary worries me," admitted Aimée. "If they were going somewhere they should have told me. I'm not only supposed to be a member of this family, but I finance it—"

"Oh, by the way," interrupted Marie-Clarice, suddenly remembering something. "They didn't all go. Renato was missing. In fact, he didn't even come home last night."

"That's not unusual behavior for him," noted Aimée with a wry smile. "But have you found out where he is when he disappears like that?"

"Not where, but I know why," said Marie-Clarice mysteriously. "Or I think I do. I think he works for Juárez. I think he helps to move spies and assassins in and out of Mexico City. And he is helping to prepare the way for Juárez' army. When they come they'll find things made easier for them. . . . I think we should get out of here as soon as we can," she ended.

"We can't, not now," said Aimée in misery. "Have you actually seen Renato with some of these *Juáristas?*"

"I keep my eyes open. I saw him return one day last week and there were two strangers with him. Whoever they were, I never saw them again. I think they must have left by way of the forest. Renato got them out of the city somehow, I'm sure of it. And I think Melania knows about it, because I've seen her watching him. But she hides so he doesn't know she's watching him."

"I don't like it," announced Aimée nervously, wondering what all of this could mean.

"That's not the least of it," went on Marie-Clarice. "The family has been holding meetings behind locked doors, usually when both you and Renato are out."

"Why didn't you tell me?" demanded Aimée. "How long has this been going on behind my back?"

Marie-Clarice shrugged and said, "I don't know. I only found out accidentally and there was nothing to tell you. I didn't know anything and no matter how hard I have listened, I have heard nothing."

"But at least I should have known they were having these meetings even if you couldn't tell me what was going on," Aimée rebuked her. Then realizing it made no sense to offend her one ally, she started thinking aloud: "Nemecio was right then. He said they were never to be trusted, and I kept that in mind when I arrived. But they seemed so sweet. I was lulled into believing that they weren't as bad as Nemecio had said. I was wrong to trust them."

"From what you told me about Nemecio, he wasn't any better, maybe even worse than they were," Marie-Clarice sympathized.

"Perhaps that was a factor in my letting my guard down," said Aimée. "They seemed almost like saints in comparison to him. I'm sorry. But Antonia and Lino were good to me, in their own way, and so was Renato."

"If they ever find out who you really are, I don't think you'd find them quite so sweet and cooperative," warned Marie-Clarice. "I still think we ought to leave while we're still able to."

"It's occured to me, but it's not safe to leave yet. But when we do, I assure you we will take the fastest road to the United States."

"I can't wait," Marie-Clarice said earnestly. "Life here has been good, but it's too uncertain for me, especially as this war gets closer and closer."

"Yes, it's liable to overtake us any day now. But for the moment we make no move," decided Aimée. "And we keep our suspicions to ourselves. It is safer that way."

"Whatever you say, but, please, don't wait too long," pleaded Marie-Clarice.

"I don't intend to. And keep an eye out. You've done well, so far, and what you can learn is the only protection we have against them, if they are plotting against us."

Aimée was restless and thought about going for a

ride, but she was reluctant to ride alone. With *Juáristas* all around the area, it could prove very dangerous. So she contented herself with a brief examination of the books Lino kept so meticulously. As always, they seemed to be in order. They also assured her that even with trade falling off, the family was still in sound financial condition. There were no mysterious or unaccounted-for withdrawals, so far as she could determine. And even the sums Lino had told her he had planned to transfer had been well hidden.

It was late morning when the carriage appeared in the drive, accompanied by four of his royal guards in their resplendent uniforms. Aimée went out to greet the uniformed officer who occupied the back seat of the carriage.

When he stepped down, Aimée's heart began to pound with fear. It was Colonel Vardeau.

He paused at the foot of the veranda stairs and gravely saluted her. There was absolutely no trace of recognition in his eyes of her true identity.

"Señorita," he began crisply but respectfully, "I've been sent to escort you to the summer palace. His Highness is in need of your advice and asks that he be forgiven for not notifying you sooner."

"Thank you, colonel," she said formally. "I'll be with you at once. May I have someone bring you a drink?"

"Brandy," he said. "And thank you, Señorita Fuchard."

She hurried upstairs to pack a small traveling case, having no idea how long Maximilian would be in need of her services but grimly aware that it would no doubt be at least overnight.

"Don't tell them where I've gone," she instructed Marie-Clarice. "If they don't have the courtesy to notify me when they make plans, I certainly can let them wonder where I have been."

"When will you be back?" Marie-Clarice wanted to know.

"You know very well that I don't know. It all depends on him."

"Do you like the emperor?" Marie-Clarice asked, looking at her speculatively.

"I believe he's in the wrong place at the wrong time. He doesn't have the ability to be a powerful leader, and I think in the end it will prove a disastrous combination. But there are things about him to be admired, and I don't think he's a bad person. . . . What did you do with my hairbrush?"

"You put it in the little bag already. You're beginning to be nervous, Aimée," said Marie-Clarice quietly.

"I'm not really nervous. I'm just plain scared to death," she admitted, her fears flitting across her face in a way that Marie-Clarice found painful to watch.

She hugged Aimée and said, "Please, don't worry. You'll be all right. We both will." For once it was Marie-Clarice comforting Aimée.

"I—I know," stammered Aimée, "but it's the man who Maximilian sent to get me who frightens me. It's Vardeau."

"Vardeau!" echoed Marie-Clarice incredulously. "Do you mean the man who raped you and then put you on the ship as an indentured servant?"

"Yes. He is the one."

"But how can you go with him? Perhaps he isn't even taking you to the emperor."

"I doubt he would disobey a royal order, and besides, he shows me no signs that he recognizes me as Aimée Gaudin."

"You haven't changed that much," Marie-Clarice shook her head doubtfully. "How can he not recognize you?"

"I don't know. Perhaps there is a radical change. Perhaps he doesn't connect the frightened girl he once met on a dark Paris street with a self-assured young Mexican woman who is an heiress and the mistress of the emperor himself. Surely that would make you think twice, too. Don't you agree? And, besides, I am in favor with the emperor and if he does recognize me he may be afraid to voice his accusations and risk the wrath of Maximilian."

"Our bags will be packed," said Marie-Clarice decisively. "And I'll be sure the two Arabian horses are rested and ready to leave at a moment's notice. Hurry back ... if you can."

Aimée returned to find the colonel relaxing on the veranda. He stood up when she appeared and ceremoniously handed her into the carriage. She found his gallantry charming and confusing. She even began to wonder if there could be some mistake—on her part— and that this was not the same Vardeau she had known. How could one man change so radically?

"Señorita is very lovely today," he said.

"Thank you, colonel. Are you from Paris?"

"Oh, yes. I was born there. Have you been there?" he asked very casually.

"I attended a convent about fifty miles outside of Paris. In fact, I was brought up in France."

He smiled. "I wondered how you were so sophisticated and elegant—and spoke French so fluently—in comparison to the other Mexican women I've met, if you'll pardon me for being so bold as to say so."

"No, I don't object. But I am Mexican, and I, too, find Mexican women provincial, and if that makes me sound like a snob, perhaps I am, but the truth is the truth."

"I wish we could all be so frank," he said. "There's no doubt it is one of the qualities that's put you in the emperor's favor. He respects your judgment. He told me the summer palace wouldn't be as lovely as it is if it weren't for you and the advice you gave him."

She acknowledged this compliment with a smile, even though fear and doubt were boiling within her. What did he mean by all this? Was he teasing her? Playing an elaborate game of cat-and-mouse? Yet he seemed so sincere, she reminded herself. Yes, another part of her piped up, but this was the man who'd undressed her, taunted her, assaulted her and virtually held her prisoner in his house for his pleasure. How could he have forgotten her so quickly—even if she had changed so much since he'd last seen her?

"The emperor," went on Vardeau, "is very disappointed in Mexican women. But then, who can compare with the French, eh? Or someone, even a Mexican, raised in France?"

"You're very diplomatic, colonel. I know what you mean, but in my family there are two lovely girls, as sophisticated as I. Or nearly so."

"I haven't yet met them, so I can't judge. But offhand I'd say that you're being quite generous with them."

"May I ask what you think of the revolution and of Benito Juárez?" she asked evenly, wanting to test his reaction after his betrayal of her father's cause.

"Oh, I could talk of that all day. Do you believe we're winning?"

She shook her head. "No, colonel, in all candor, I don't. I can't see how the French can possibly hang onto a country that hates them, especially when they are so far away from home."

"On the chance of committing treason, I have to admit that I agree with you," he said smoothly.

"Do you think Maximilian would agree that the war is lost?"

"Maximilian is a strange man in all practical affairs. I've no doubt that he's positive the French will win. That in an emergency, Louis Napoleon will send enough troops to force the Mexicans into submission."

"Will Louis Napoleon do that, colonel? You may speak freely. I don't talk of such matters with Maximilian."

"There'll be no more troops. No more of anything. I had that on good authority before I was ordered here to command the emperor's royal guard. As for you telling Maximilian what I've been saying, he wouldn't hear you. He grows utterly deaf when something he doesn't wish to hear comes up in converastion."

"Thank you, colonel. I will in no manner try to disillusion the emperor," Aimée said quietly. Ah, so Vardeau had been transferred here knowing he was defending a hopeless cause. Very interesting. It might account for his reluctance to commit himself—or to expose her.

Two of the guards who had been riding well ahead of the carriage signaled with their arms raised high and the procession came to a halt. Orders were given and half of the accompanying guards spread out to ride through the brush and nearby forest. However, they soon returned to report that it had been a false alarm and that no rebels had been encountered.

"We have to be most careful," Vardeau explained. "I've issued orders that no chances are to be taken. Juárez, I have heard, is a wily rascal and teaches his men well. I don't wish to alarm you but we are being careful because not only can they ride like shadows through forests that have no paths, but they are now armed with bombs—presumably to be hurled at His Majesty. It is a difficult and painstaking job we have here," he sighed, revealing his own worries.

"I had no idea the rebels were so close. . . ."

"No one does, except we who are responsible for the emperor's safety. I wouldn't give a sou for his life if he ventured out of the palace alone."

She turned their conversation to Paris. Their talk became more animated when they both discovered how much they loved that city. More and more she found herself being lulled into believing that Vardeau had accepted her as Angela Fuchard, an entirely different woman from the Aimée Gaudin he had sent packing as an indentured servant. And he seemed too frank, too open, to be harboring any doubts about her identity.

As they drove up in front of the summer palace, Maximilian appeared to greet her. His appearance was so immediate, it left no doubt that he had been awaiting her arrival anxiously. He helped her down from the carriage himself, and she kissed him chastely on the cheek.

"Your colonel of the guard is a very wise man," she said. "And most capable, I am sure."

Vardeau saluted smartly. "I'm grateful, señorita. Your Majesty!" He saluted again, did a military about-face, and marched off.

Maximilian took Aimée's elbow. "Thank you for coming. We who rule are alone too much. It is a solitary life, though few would believe that, surrounded as I am by all this pomp and ceremony."

"I'm happy to be here, Sire," she said, adding coyly, "I hope I can be of service to you." She had to force herself into the role of his mistress, but it was coming more easily each time, she admitted to herself.

Maximilian gave a loud, appreciative laugh at her offer. "Rest assured you can be of service, my dear. But I really do wish your opinion on a new suite I've planned especially for Carlota. I sent for the furnishings, but you'll know best how to place them to their advantage. We shall go into that . . . say in the morning?"

"Of course, Your Highness. In the morning." His plans for the future, she thought sadly, only confirmed Vardeau's observations that he didn't want to face reality. The emperor was both misled and deluded into believing his kingdom really could be defended.

Once again they dined elaborately: silver platters of sliced, red beef; squabs resting on yellow rice, and ham in a savory sauce that only a French chef could have concocted. There was a delicate fish course with a mustard sauce that caused the tongue to tingle. For dessert there were petits fours and cups of steaming coffee.

Maximilian was lighthearted throughout the meal, teasing her into comparing French cuisine with Mexican food. When she was finally forced to admit her dislike of the Mexican diet, he good-naturedly pointed out how difficult it was to assimilate new customs—and even for her, a native-born Mexican, being raised in France made her a stranger in her own land.

Aimée relaxed and enjoyed all of it, banishing from her mind thoughts of why her entire family had mysteriously disappeared that morning on some secret errand. She also gave no further thought to Colonel Vardeau, and she defiantly put thoughts of Alex out of her mind. If she was going to be the emperor's mistress, she might as well enjoy it while she could. . . .

They played chess for a while, and Aimée let Maximilian win. She had a difficult time losing—and thought it most impolitic to win—but obviously Maximilian spent more time observing even her modest decolletage and lovely form than his own game plan. They talked little now, and there was no more mention of the room being prepared for Carlota's supposed return. When she retired to his bedroom, she found a silk nightgown spread on the bed and nestling on top of it was a glittering bracelet of gold and diamonds. She caught her breath and thought with guilt about Alex's angry outburst. But she resolutely pushed these thoughts away. What did Alex have to offer her besides his anger? If nothing else, she decided she would use the emperor's generous gifts to buy her way out of the country if somehow she failed to have time to get money from Nemecio's estate. And in a country where a life wasn't worth a peso, these precious jewels could buy her freedom.

With these thoughts in mind, Aimée dutifully bathed and prepared herself for Maximilian's appearance. When he came into the room she was waiting on the bed, a sensuous woman with her hair cascading over her shoulders, the silk gown clinging to her voluptuous figure, thus revealing what it concealed.

With a sigh of happiness, Maximilian approach the bed. This time Aimée took the initiative, teasing and romping with him until his desire was so strong, he could no longer resist and he made no effort to be the gentle lover. In bed, he compensated—no, over-compensated—for his impotent position as an emperor. He was a ferocious lover that night, seemingly unable to satiate himself. Aimée was shocked at the way he held her wrists above her head and used her body in a way that left her feeling sore and dry. But now she, too, was cunning in the arts of love, and made sure that no matter what her private thoughts, Maximilian believed that she enjoyed every moment of his lovemaking.

She moaned and groaned and responded to his caresses with a passion that seemed to match his. She aroused him yet again, even though she yearned for the release of sleep, and this time she made love to him, climbing on top of him and pretending he was her favorite Arabian. He loved it, and she controlled the movement of her hips so as to tease him, to arouse him, and finally to have him climax in a cry of pleasure that even the royal guard discreetly stationed outside the door must have heard. She smiled in the dark. She had done her job well. . . .

Breakfast was as gay as supper had been the night before, but it was tinged with a bit of sadness on Maximilian's part.

"I must return to the city palace, even though I loathe the thought of leaving you, my dear," he told her. "There are formal court proceedings which will not wait, and my generals and I must plan our campaign to drive Juárez and his people out of Mexico once and for all. I've been thinking about this campaign for a long time, and now we must act."

"I hope Your Majesty will leave the fighting to the generals," Aimée said quietly, thinking sadly that it was far too late for Maximilian to begin his campaign. He had no soldiers to lead into his futile battle.

"My dear child, how can I do that? I'm the leader here. I'm the emperor. In the history of my family no Hapsburg has ever shirked fighting for what we believe in. No, I shall go forth at the head of my troops and rout the *Juáristas* out of the country," he announced with much confidence. "Then I will devote myself to finding ways to improve life in this miserable country."

"I'm sure Your Highness will find ways to improve the food as well," Aimée said, carrying over their private joke of the night before.

He laughed loudly in appreciation. But it was clear she was soon to be dismissed. He was restless. A message discreetly brought in to him—it was most unusual for them to be interrupted by state business—made him even more restless.

Aimée, anxious to attend to the problems she had left behind, addressed him cautiously. "Your Highness, can I be so impertinent as to request that you send me home now?"

He looked across the table as he crumpled the message into a ball. "You read my mind, dear Angela. Yes, I have urgent business in the city. Things are not going well. I'll have Colonel Vardeau assign men to escort you home for it is necessary that he go with me. . . ."

Going home, Aimée was alone in the carriage and had time to think. Maximilian's boast about leading a victorious army to defeat Juárez was an illusion, and ego aside, he must surely have realized he was doomed. She felt momentary pity for Maximilian. More and more, Aimée believed the Mexican armies were on the verge of victory. There was too much tension around the palace. Even the Royal Guard at the summer castle was anxious; it was surely an ominous sign.

Then her thoughts moved on to Nemecio's strange family. Here, too, she was puzzled. She was afraid that Renato was implicated too deeply and dangerously with the rebels. And even though Lino had been solicitous, she couldn't help but distrust him. And so far as Melania and Della went, she never trusted them to begin with.

She felt that matters were forcing her to make some decisions and take some action soon. She realized she could no longer delay, for not only her safety but her very life was in peril. The problem was that there was

223

no one she felt she could turn to for help, not a single person she could trust. In bitter frustration, she realized the only plans she could make right now were to instruct Marie-Clarice to be ready to escape whenever they though they had an opportunity. The flimsiness of this "plan" bothered her but she could not devise an alternative.

As the carriage came to a stop before the mansion, Antonia came hurrying toward her. "Where have you been?" she demanded angrily. Then she noticed the Royal Guards. "As if I have to ask. You're a naughty girl, Angela. We've been beside ourselves with worry about what might have happened to you or where you might have disappeared to."

Aimée dismissed the guardsmen and went into the house with Antonia. The family was assembled in the drawing room.

"She was at the palace," Antonia explained. "The Royal Guard accompanied her back. Angela, it was cruel of you not to leave word."

"You left me alone when you all vanished yesterday morning," she reminded Antonia curtly.

"We didn't wish to disturb you," Lino explained smoothly, too smoothly. "We went to Cholula to visit an elderly relative. We always dread such visits and we decided not to inflict it on you."

"How kind," she murmured. Then, *"All* of you were there? Even Renato?"

"Of course. All of us, as you were just told."

Aimée sensed that Lino suspected she knew better; he looked at her too steadily, as if he wanted her to know he was lying. "Well," she shrugged, "I forgive you as you'll assuredly forgive me. Maximilian sent for me quite unexpectedly."

"To help decorate the summer palace, no doubt?" Della asked with open sarcasm.

Aimée was about to express some rather pointed sarcasm of her own, but she had a better idea: To provoke the weak side of her dear, dear cousins. "Well, he wanted help in preparing a room for Carlota's return—"

"—Carlota's return," exclaimed Della, cutting off her answer.

Melania came to her feet. "That's wonderful. There'll surely be a reception to welcome her back, maybe even another ball. Oh, Angela, can you make certain that we are invited?"

"It will be even more important than the last ball," Della went on, undoubtedly planning her wardrobe.

Antonia and her daughters suddenly lost interest in Aimée as they hurried to their rooms to begin planning for the ball that would never be. At least that would keep their minds off plotting against Aimée, she thought with much satisfaction. Renato pursed his lips and stalked off, silent as ever. Lino sat back and gave Aimée a weak smile before claiming he had to see to the books.

Aimée went up to her room and was not surprised to find Marie-Clarice practically standing behind the door, a thousand questions springing to her lips. But first she listened to the news Marie-Clarice had for her.

"They all returned right after dark, all except for Renato. He didn't come home until very late. They looked for you and then shouted for me. I told them I had no idea where you'd gone. I told them that I was just a servant and that you did not confide in me as to your whereabouts." A smug smile of satisfaction crossed Marie-Clarice's face, for she had indeed played the role of the dumb French servant-girl well. The family didn't realize she understood most of what was said around her.

But there was more on her mind. "There's something *very* strange about their absence. I've no idea what it means or what they really did but I'm sure we'll find out before long. It is clear to me that it's almost time for us to move on. . . . I've packed some things and we can leave in ten minute, if we have to," Marie-Clarice assured Aimée.

"Good. Don't act nervous if you can help it or give away our plan. However, I am sure this family is on the verge of taking some rather drastic steps themselves. And I think some of their plans may concern us, though not in a nice way. But I don't want them to realize we're not quite as stupid as they think we are."

Marie-Clarice was helping to put up Aimée's hair when they heard the sound of a vehicle approaching on the driveway. Marie-Clarice ran to the window to have a look.

"It's a troop of soldiers," she exclaimed. "Some of them are going behind the house, I think. They seem to be surrounding the house. What in the world can this mean?"

"Trouble," Aimée answered tersely. "I'm positive it has to do with the family's mysterious behavior these past two days. Marie-Clarice, if they've come for me, try to reach the emperor and tell him what has happened. Perhaps it won't be necessary, but be ready."

Antonia was soon summoning Aimée from downstairs. "Angela, there are soldiers here. They ask for you."

Chapter 13

"They're *Pantalons Rouges*," Marie-Clarice whispered as she turned away from the window.

There were sounds of armed men running up the stairs and down the corridor. Three of them burst into the room, followed by a very dapper captain who eyed both Aimée and Marie-Clarice insolently.

"Which of you is Angela Fuchard?" he demanded.

"Why do you ask for me, captain?" Aimée asked, inching forward.

"Seize her," the captain ordered blandly. Two soldiers sprang to pin her arms behind her back.

"I'm entitled to know what this is all about," Aimée sputtered indignantly.

"You're entitled to nothing," the captain said coolly, "except a volley of bullets. Where's your clothes closet?"

Without waiting for an answer, he pulled open the closet door and began searching for something, throwing whatever he put his hands on—her beautiful Parisian gowns—on the floor as if they were garbage. Marie-

Clarice moved in front of him. "You will be more careful—"

Her answer was an abrupt slap across the face, so forceful that it sent her reeling across the room. Although dazed from the blow, she didn't back down. "You . . . pig!" she spat in disgust.

A third soldier seized her and held her; he was amused by her futile attempts to free herself.

Meanwhile the captain who had been burrowing into Aimée's closet finally held up her riding habit triumphantly. "We have what we want," he announced. "Take her away."

"What of this spitfire?" the soldier asked, holding a struggling Marie-Clarice.

"Slap her backside and let her go," the captain said with a laugh.

Marie-Clarice screamed as the flat of a rifle butt slammed against her sturdy buttocks. By then they had half dragged Aimée down the corridor and the stairs. Other soldiers had commandeered the family carriage and Aimée was rudely shoved into the backseat and sent sprawling on the floor of the carriage.

He heard Lino arguing with the captain. "We have a right to know why you're taking my niece away. I warn you, we're friends of the court."

"You're sly, conniving Mexicans who bow before the emperor and look for a chance to stab him in the back. Get out of my way," the captain said impatiently and rather ominously. Lino apparently decided it was wise to step aside, for Aimée heard no further protest as she sat down on one of the seats. The last view she had was of Antonia and her daughters standing on the veranda watching the soldiers take Aimée away. Then the family returned to the mansion and closed the door.

The captain had climbed into the carriage with Aimée and now he said to her, "I'll give you a bit of advice, señorita. You're in grave trouble and the wisest thing you can do is to tell the truth. It may save your life."

Aimée remained silent. The captain grasped her wrist

so hard her fingers began to turn white. It hurt but Aimée gave no indication of the pain she was feeling. "When I speak," snarled the captain, "I expect to be answered, especially by traitors such as you."

Aimée bit her lip. She couldn't very well answer. This arrest might have something to do with the *Juáristas* or it might mean that Vardeau had finally exposed her as a traitoress to France. The captain's use of the word "traitor" sent cold waves of horror surging through her. If possible, she turned a shade paler.

"Admit you are a *Juárista* or I'll break your pretty arm," the captain warned, giving it a sharp turn that sent waves of pain shooting through her body.

Aimée almost gave an audible sigh of relief. If they suspected Angela of being a *Juárista,* Maximilian could set them straight on that. She relaxed.

"You may let go of my wrist," she requested calmly.

"Answer me," demanded the captain, shouting now.

"Answer what?" she shot back. "You've put no direct question to me."

"The riding habit. Is it yours?" He relaxed his hold and Aimée flexed her hand as the circulation returned.

"Yes. Of course it is," she admitted boldly. "But I must tell you, captain, that I am thoroughly mystified as to why you are so interested in my riding habit."

"You'll be told presently," he informed her, apparently pleased with himself that she had admitted the outfit belonged to her. "General Romay has informed me that you were arrested once before for spying activities."

"So the general is after me again. I'd have thought that the first time would have taught him a lesson about persecuting me."

"Let me ask you this—and I expect an answer— where were you yesterday?" the captain asked.

Aimée's confidence was beginning to return—and with it a certain amount of defiance. She could account for her whereabouts on the day before with ease, and with an answer that would leave no question as to where her loyalties lay. But before she answered, she decided to learn all she could.

"Am I to be questioned by General Romay?" she asked.

"You may be assured of it," he smugly answered.

"Then I'll reserve any statement I have to make for his ears alone, captain. No offense to you, of course, for I realize your reputation will be enhanced if you can bring in a prisoner who has already confessed to whatever crimes I am charged with, but I will not make a statement to you except in the presence of General Romay."

The captain studied her for a minute and seemed to realize that he would not be able to convince her to talk willingly, and despite his use of force on her wrist, he was obviously reluctant to carry out any further violence. So he shrugged his shoulders and promised her, "When you're convicted I'll be happy to provide you with a blindfold before the guns are pointed at you."

"A silly promise," she retorted, feeling more confident than ever. "But under the circumstances I will forgive you."

Her arrogant attitude confused him and he flushed at her continued defiance of his authority. He slapped her. Then they fell silent during the remainder of the ride to the city. She was led into the same prison where she had been detained before and was promptly taken into the general's office. He was waiting and, she thought, probably gloating over her capture. To have ordered her arrest again, especially after the first incident, he must have thought he had some extremely strong evidence to present against her. But no matter what it was, she had an alibi as perfect—or even more so—as the first time.

"Sit down!" he said curtly, dispensing with any attempt at polite formalities.

She lowered herself gracefully onto the straight-backed, narrow wooden chair before his desk. "Are you once again about to risk your epaulets by having me arrested?" she said suddenly, catching him off guard at her boldness.

"This time it will be different," he said, his eyes gleaming with confidence. "Not even the emperor himself can get you out of the trouble you've gotten yourself into. I shall ask you one question: Have you been hiding spies and finding ways to get them out of the city and back behind the Juárez lines?"

"I have not!" Aimée said in a loud, clear voice.

"We shall see. Captain, have them bring in the three prisoners. But wait. You have the riding habit?"

"Yes, general. They were most reluctant to let me take it," he volunteered—as if two women could have stopped an entire regiment of *Pantalons Rouges,* Aimée thought contemptuously.

"Señorita," the general addressed her, "will you put on the riding habit." It was not a request, it was a command.

"Tell me why I should," she demanded.

"You'll put it on or I'll have my men strip you and force you into it. I mean what I say, señorita. I do not make idle threats. And my men might find it a very enjoyable assignment. . . ."

"Not even you would dare undress me in front of your men," Aimée stood her ground. "However, if there is a place where I can change in private . . ."

"Show her to the side office," Romay ordered. "And be sure the door is closed," he added, almost reluctantly.

Aimée gathered up her riding habit, stepped into the office, and quickly changed. When she returned to the desk, the general rose and handed her a square piece of black lace.

"Put this on."

"What in the world is this?" she asked, handling it. "A veil?"

"A piece of fancy cloth that may look frivolous to you now, señorita, but it will very likely get you a place against the wall. I'm very sorry you didn't learn a lesson when I made you watch that old fool of a spy as he was shot before your eyes."

"You're utterly mistaken by whatever you're trying to prove," Aimée protested, then shrugged and said, "But I'll wear the veil. Now, let's end this ridiculous charade quickly."

A nod from the general sent the captain out of the room for a few minutes. During his absence, the general taunted his prisoner: "This time the emperor will not be interested. He won't dare."

"We'll see," Aimée answered stiffly. "But if I were you, I'd notify him at once that you're holding me prisoner."

"I obey no commands from you," he grinned, eyeing her boldly in the riding habit and obviously finding the sight rather appealing.

Just then three cowering Mexicans were herded into the room. Their arms were bent around stakes that held them securely—and painfully—behind their backs. The general led Aimée before them.

"Is this the woman who helped you and promised you safe passage to Juárez?" he asked.

"We don't know what you're talking about," one of the men said.

A blow in the face from a rifle butt felled him, and he lay still.

"You!" General Romay moved to the second man, hoping he had learned a lesson from what he had just seen happen to the first man. "Is this the woman?"

The man gave Aimée a glance with haunted and frightened eyes and said in a tiny voice, *"Sí.* It is the woman."

"I'm glad you had some sense," the general said with grim satisfaction. The first man lay bleeding on the floor.

The third man gave a loud shout and tried to reach the general. What he intended to accomplish with his arms bound in such a way was not clear, but he never had a chance. He was struck on the head with a rifle buttt so hard that Aimée heard bone crack and give way as he shouted, "We did not see her face. None of us saw her face."

The general regarded the body at his feet with disgust. The two injured men were dragged away by the soldiers. The one still standing was prodded out of the room at bayonet point. The general sat down and folded his hands across his paunch.

"Now what do you have to say, señorita?"

"Why should I say anything? You heard the man. They didn't see the face of whoever wore my riding habit. And had they seen the face, it would not have been mine."

"You're a cool one. But no matter what you say I will not believe you. I know you're going to say you were at home with your relatives. Don't try to deny that. You believe that they'll give me proof that you couldn't have been the woman in the veil. Well, my sly one, I shall put a quick end to that silly hope."

He shouted. Lino and Renato were ushered into the office. They stared open-mouthed at Aimée in the riding habit.

The general said, "Was this woman at home yesterday afternoon and early evening? It's vital to her interests that you answer truthfully.

Lino looked at Aimée. She said, "Tell him, Uncle Lino. He thinks I'm trying to use you to explain where I was yesterday. Tell him the truth."

"We . . . I . . . don't know where she was," stammered Lino. "My family and I were not at home. We spent the day in Cholula and returned in the evening."

"So she lies," the general said with apparent satisfaction, rubbing his hands together.

"I told no falsehoods, general," Aimée said. "You never gave me a chance to admit that I was not with my family all day. It is true. But before we go any further. I demand an explanation. What is my crime? How am I implicated by my riding habit, the veil? And what did you want to learn from those three, unfortunate men?"

"She told us, when we returned, that she had been with the emperor at his summer palace at Chapultepec," Lino put in when Romay remained silent.

"All day and all night," Renato added.

"Now will you tell me?" Aimée asked again.

"The emperor isn't involved in this yet," the general said uneasily. "I will tell you nothing."

"We've sent word to Maximilian, general," Lino said. "We believe he'd wish to know if Señorita Angela was in trouble. She is . . . a favorite of his."

"Then listen to this," the general said menacingly. "This happened when three important *Juáristas* escaped from prison. They were found not far from your estate. They informed us, under pressure," the general admitted, "that they'd been visited and offered help by a woman in a riding habit, a riding habit which they described in great detail. They said she was veiled, but even a veil cannot hide a figure, well, like yours, señorita."

"Why, thank you, general," Aimée answered with a faint smile.

"We didn't believe them until one of the soldiers discovered the veil you're wearing, tangled in the branches of a small bush. You were alone at home—we determined that before we arrested you. We knew you had such a riding habit and it's unlikely there's another one like it in all of Mexico. That gave us cause to order your arrest. And you'll be brought to trial, señorita. Very soon," he promised ominously. Aimée had heard enough about French justice to know whether or not she'd be found guilty.

"I can't wait for the trial to begin, general, for I shall make a fool out of you. You're taking advantage of a coincidence that has nothing to do with me. You'd like revenge for the time I caused your censure for making the same kind of stupid mistake."

There was a commotion outside and then utter silence.

The door was pushed open by Colonel Vardeau. He strode into the room and saluted. The captain came to attention. General Romay rose slowly and bowed.

Maximilian walked into the office. He went directly to Aimée and kissed her chastely on the forehead.

"My dear child, I humble myself because of what these blundering fools have done to you. Are you hurt?" he asked solicitously.

"No, Your Highness."

Satisfied that she was unharmed, he turned to Romay and gave him a disdainful look. "General, while it is none of your business, for the sake of your so-called investigation, the Señorita Fuchard was with me on the day you accuse her of being elsewhere. I'm not familiar with the precise details of your accusation, but it's a mistake, sir. The last one you'll make. You're relieved of this command, and by evening you're to report to the troop of Mexican Lancers you will lead into battle tomorrow—against a *Juárista* army only twenty miles away. And you will lead them to victory, or do not trouble yourself to return. You'd be far wiser to die gloriously on the field of battle for your country, or even by your own bullet if need be, then to return home defeated. Come, Angela, your carriage is outside and you will be escorted home safely at once," he commanded, leading her outside. She walked out with Maximilian's arm around her waist.

"Thank you," she said softly. "It was getting most uncomfortable in there. . . ."

"What was it all about, my dear?" Maximilian asked.

"I really don't know. Not for sure. But it seems someone wore my riding habit and a veil—the one I'm holding—and this person apparently visited three spies, or whatever they were, to lend them aid. When they were caught, they implicated a woman in a riding habit. The general sent his men for me, after he made inquiries and learned I had such a habit. I was mortified and thoroughly frightened, but, thanks to you, it's all over now."

Lino and Renato had been following at a discreet distance. Aimée turned and called to them.

"Renato, will you please fetch my gown. It's in the small room next to the general's office."

"Of course." Renato hurried back while Lino waited for him.

"Could it be one of the girls who lives with you?" Maximilian asked.

"They were away, sir," she replied, although she couldn't help asking herself the same question. "But I do know there have been spies among our servants. Perhaps one of them visited my rooms during my absence and took the riding habit to disguise herself—or to shift the blame to me."

"Of course, of course, that must be what happened," he comforted her. "Think no more of it. It's all over and I assure you it won't happen again."

"Those three men," she asked hesitantly. "Can't something be done for them?"

"I'm afraid it's too late for that. Besides, they were spies for Juárez. I would have ordered them shot anyway, for accusing you," he said as he brought her hand to his lips.

If she hadn't known better, she might have taken his gallant remark as a callous disregard for human life. However, he was far from being the ogre some Mexicans thought him to be. Even so, he was royalty and assumed a God-given right that would one day probably spell the doom of all monarchies. If nothing else, her experiences in Mexico had given her the chance to see her father's beliefs vindicated.

The carriage was waiting and she was joined by Lino and Renato. Maximilian and his Royal Guard, headed by Vardeau, had already departed.

"Well," she asked bluntly, "who do you think is responsible for wearing my clothing and placing me in such danger?" She made it clear that this time she was not going to be brushed aside by some smooth but evasive answer.

Renato remained silent, deep in thought.

"I hate to say this, Angela," Lino began, "but have you considered that personal servant of yours? She's a mighty independent and headstrong person. I've tasted the lash of her tongue more than once."

"No," Renato said earnestly. "I don't believe that. Marie-Clarice does speak her mind, but she has nothing to do with helping *Juáristas*."

"We have to consider everyone," Lino defended himself.

"That," Aimée said pointedly, "is quite true. I don't intend to let this matter drop without trying to find out who was guilty. If only they'd let those three men live. With proper questioning, they might have helped find the answer."

"Angela," Renato said, "the French are shooting everybody they even suspect of being a *Juárista*. And I'll tell you why: Juárez is getting closer and closer. Some of his army is no more than twenty or thirty miles from Mexico City. They outnumber the French troops by more than twenty to one, and the French know it."

"How does it happen that you know it?" his father asked sternly.

"Because I get around. I've helped some of the *Juáristas*—with a few pesos and some advice," admitted Renato.

"You'd best be careful," Lino said. "In fact, I'd stay far away from anyone committed to Juárez. It's unhealthy to even talk about him these days."

While they talked, a sinister idea had begun to form in Aimée's mind. She didn't altogether believe that a servant or a stranger had borrowed her riding habit. But Melania or Della could have done it to implicate her with the *Juáristas*. What's more, they could have told the French where the three Mexicans might be found. The rest of the family would swear that they had been elsewhere, and Aimée would appear to be guilty since she would have no alibi for her whereabouts. They simply hadn't known that Maximilian would send for her. Even though Aimée knew Renato hadn't been with his family, she didn't entirely trust him, either. Her experiences since leaving France had definitely taught her the danger of trusting anyone, particularly a man.

The idea that her own family would try to have her shot as a spy gave her a chill. But if they had tried and failed, surely they would not give up so easily. Their next attempt might be successful. Deciding that her only way to survive, for the moment, was to act innocent, Aimée decided to give no indication that she suspected her family of betraying her. But she did ask: "Tell me, Uncle Lino, what will happen when Juárez takes over Mexico City and the French leave?"

"I don't know, Angela. I want Mexico to be rid of the French. I want the killing to stop, and to be able to enjoy some peace for the rest of my life, but Juárez has still to prove himself. Nobody knows what he'll do. Does he know what he will do once he has a taste of power?" A wise observation, decided Aimée. When they had heard Nemecio was dead, they had assumed the estate was theirs. Losing their power to a niece they never knew must have been a terrible blow both to their pocketbooks and their inflated egos.

"Juárez is a simple man," said Renato quietly. "He doesn't like people with a great deal of money, nor those who give great soirées and balls. He's in favor of taking the wealth of Mexico and dividing it among everyone, especially among the peons."

"That would destroy Mexico," Lino said sharply.

"Perhaps, what's left of it," admitted Renato. "But Juárez is going to win, and when he does he can do what he likes. I don't think he's going to like us, with our history of bowing to Maximilian and . . ." he glanced at Aimée, "other favors."

"What do you think we should do?" Aimée asked.

"Turn everything possible into gold," Lino answered promptly, "and take it with us when we escape—preferably, to the United States."

"We don't have passports or visas," Renato pointed out.

"We can swim the river if need be. There are many ways of getting over the border. That's what I'd do, and not delay too long about it. How much time do you think we have, Renato?"

"Not much. Perhaps two weeks. It's hard to say. A great deal will depend on the next big battle. If the French are beaten. . . ." He shrugged.

They grew silent after that, each with his own thoughts and none of them optimistic. When the carriage rolled into the driveway of the mansion, everyone came out to greet them. Aimée was hugged and kissed by Antonia, Della and Melania in turn and she did her best not to reveal her true feelings at this display of pretended affection. If what she suspected was true, they were glorious hypocrites, but this was no time to let them suspect she might be onto them.

"We were so worried," Antonia said. "The way those insufferable soldiers acted. . . . I hope Juárez kills them all."

"Not much of a chance of that," Renato said. "They'll get out if there's any stronger possibility of defeat. Angela was in serious trouble, but Maximilian appeared and settled the whole thing."

"He sent General Romay to what will surely be his death, leading Mexican Lancers into battle," Lino said. "Juárez doesn't spare any of them, I'm told."

Marie-Clarice, hovering in the background, signaled Aimée and when they entered the house Aimée begged to be excused. Renato had handed her dress to Marie-Clarice and Aimée followed her upstairs.

"What happened?" Marie-Clarice asked after she had closed and locked the door. "Are we in more danger?"

"I'm not sure," Aimée answered, and she proceeded to recount the details of her arrest. "I tried to figure out what it all meant," she said while Marie-Clarice busied herself with hanging up the just-discarded riding habit.

Marie-Clarice picked up the veil, studied it carefully and said, "You don't have anything like this, Aimée. It's not yours."

"I know. I don't even own a veil," Aimée shrugged. Marie-Clarice held up something that Aimée could not see from where she stood and said, "You don't own one of these either."

Aimée moved toward her. "What is it?"

"A strand of hair. Blond hair. Very blond. About the same color as Melania's, if you ask me," she answered dryly. Both Aimée and Marie-Clarice were well aware that there were no other blonds for miles.

Aimée studied the hair and shook her head. "It's flimsy evidence, but not too far from what I'd been thinking. Marie-Clarice, we will say nothing of this, not one word."

"I had a feeling this was their work. Now you have to watch out for them, as well as Vardeau."

"I don't know what Vardeau will do," Aimée said. "He'll do the one thing that's good for him, and if he does recognize me, obviously it's not in his best interests to say so . . . now," she said shivering with apprehension.

"We shall earnestly pray," Marie-Clarice said. "Do you expect the reporter to come back? He must have information that will help us plan the best escape route."

"I can't say. There's no way of knowing. He's probably been at the battlefields and he must know just how close the danger is. The family is getting very nervous too. Lino talks about running away with all the gold we can."

"That *he* can accumulate, you mean. If he gets his hands on it you'll never see him again," Marie-Clarice predicted.

"I can believe that. What puzzled me was that Nemecio had been so vehement about calling them thieves that I kept looking for any slip on their part, like altering the books or siphoning off money from the bank accounts. But none of that has gone on. All they had to do to get their hands on the money was to turn me over to the French and then everything would belong to them legally."

"Let them find their own way to safety—or let them fall into Juárez's hands."

"No, we can't do that. Be patient and don't show any sign of animosity toward them. Just keep your ears open."

"My specialty," Marie-Clarice said with a smile.

Chapter 14

She walked slowly, her head held high, as she made her way to where the carriage waited. When she'd first seen it approach and recognized its sole occupant as Alex, her spirits had soared with hope and relief. But the memory of their last encounter and the knowledge that she had visited the emperor again sobered her quickly.

When she reached the carriage she raised her eyes to his coldly, expecting more insults. But there was no anger in his manner, only weariness and concern.

"Will you let me talk to you for a few minutes? It's of the greatest importance," he said urgently.

"If you'll behave like a gentleman and not fly into a rage," she answered.

"You have my word. It won't make any difference anyway what I do—or you do. Everything is finished. It's over, Angela."

She flushed at his use of her first name and tried to concentrate on the rest of what he was saying.

"I just couldn't go away and leave you to the

mercy of the French or the Mexicans. In victory or defeat, one side can be as bad as the other."

She climbed into the carriage but sat far away from him, painfully aware of his presence—and longing to take him in her arms.

"May I drive somewhere? A quiet place where we can talk?" he asked.

"Of course. They're all gawking at us from their windows," she said, almost thankfully.

"Yes, I noticed the curtains move. Are you all right?"

"Yes, quite all right."

He drove back up the road leading to the mansion and then onto the main road which ran through the forest. She was thinking how wonderful it would be to be alone with him in the pretty, secluded glen. She could think of nothing else but embracing him, kissing him passionately and lying down next to him, the leaves serving as their bed. She would offer him no resistance. If she could just have him once! These were her private thoughts. Actually, she sat there, tense, listening to every word he said. But what he said removed all thoughts of passion from her mind.

"I came back because you deserve to be warned," he began.

Deserve, she thought bitterly. She listened as he said, "Right now Maximilian is with his troops at a place called Querétaro, a town and an abbey in the mountains. He has about five thousand men—or he did have. There won't be many left alive. The rebels have the town surrounded and no reinforcements could get through even if they reach him. Maximilian sent messengers to Mexico City, begging for help, but none of them made it through the rebel lines. They were all caught and hanged and the bodies displayed where Maximilian could see them."

"Then everything is lost?" Aimée said.

"Juárez has enough cannons in the hills to blow everything in that town to pieces," said Alex simply. "And there are at least forty thousand Mexicans ready to encircle Maximilian. The bombardment goes on day and night."

"Will they kill Maximilian?" she asked.

"Without question, whether in battle or in front of a firing squad. They have to kill him. He symbolizes everything that they have fought so hard against."

"He doesn't deserve such an end," she said quietly, tears starting to flow from her eyes.

"He means that much to you?" Alex missed nothing.

"I wasn't in love with him, if that's what you think— as you probably do. But he is a kind man, and whatever acts of violence were committed in his name were done largely without his knowledge or consent."

Alex listened but he said nothing when she finished speaking.

Finally Aimée asked, "Is that why you came back? To be the one to tell me everything was lost and that Maximilian would surely die?"

"Yes, but I came to warn you that you can't afford to lose much time," he said brusquely. Then he shook his head impatiently and said in a low, angry tone. "Damn it! I came back because I couldn't stay away. I hated you for what you did to me. But this is no time for hatred. I came back to help you get away. When the time comes I'll be here—or at the glen, if things get too bad. I'll be in Mexico City and I'll know exactly when it's time to make this move. Be ready."

She looked at him with wonder, a tentative but disbelieving smile touching her lips as she reached out for his hands.

He seized her in a tight embrace and his lips hungrily founds hers. One hand moved to her breast, closing roughly over it and kneading it through the thin fabric of her dress. She suddenly felt weak with desire, her breath came hotly and she felt her cheeks flush with desire. She felt her whole body straining against his, hungry for his loving. Abruptly, to her dismay, he let go of her, but it was only to leap out of the carriage and pull her into his waiting arms. Then he carried her deep into the forest and found a grassy knoll, where sunlight filtered through the leaves and cast a soft light.

He put her down and quickly shed his clothes. Then he bent over her once again, his powerful shoulders smooth and bare as he hastened to remove her clothes. The first touch of flesh upon flesh was electric, generating sparks that made both Alex and Aimée gasp. Never had Aimée been so aroused, so hot, so willing and so wet to receive a man—and never had she wanted a man as desperately as she wanted Alex Mooreland. Their mutual passion made them cling urgently to each other, each new caress sending waves of warmth and excitement surging through their bodies. This was not Maximilian's patient and calculated lovemaking. Alex's aggressive urgency brought an unthinking responsiveness to Aimée's lovemaking that left her shocked with its intensity.

His mouth upon her breast was rough, almost hurting, as if he did expect to find milk waiting in those rounded globes. Never before had she so wanted to nurture a man, to have their lovemaking go on for hours and hours.

She held his head against her chest and ran her fingers through his thick hair, caressing his earlobes and the smooth skin of his shoulders and back. She kissed his fingers, and then she reached down and brought his head back up to her hungry lips. The world around them ceased to exist as Alex and Aimée joined together in the ultimate intimacy, their bodies frantically moving together as if they could not get enough of each other. The leaves were an unyielding mattress but Aimée felt no pain as Alex's hips pressed against hers. Higher and higher their passion soared until even the sunlight was transformed for Aimée into a glorious glow that came from inside, that came from being wonderfully loved—and well loved—by the man whom she had waited so long to possess.

And Alex, too, seemed possessed. His heavy breathing and final cry sent a wave of pleasure through Aimée as she felt his manhood convulsing in her and releasing a gush of warmth that she wanted to retain. Aimée was nearly unconscious with fulfillment and bliss. When it was over, they neither could nor wanted to move. A peacefulness, a security that had eluded her for so long was hers at last. She reveled in the beauty of that feeling and of his arms still wrapped around her. Never had Aimée been so happy—or so satisfied.

Slowly she opened her eyes and the world was as it had been only minutes before: Birds sang and the leaves waved lightly in the breeze. Everything was the same—except Aimée—and the grass that had been crushed by the weight of their bodies. The glory of this consummation left her with a smile on her face, a glow that she didn't think any peril could erase.

And Alex's smile was as contented as hers. They looked into each other's eyes and simply loved each other. They needed no words to express their feelings.

At last he murmured, "What a damn fool a man can be. To think I almost lost you because of that one moment when you couldn't help yourself. I don't even hate Maximilian for what he did to you. I came back because I couldn't help myself. I couldn't resist you. I love you, Angela, and I don't even consider what happened between you and Maximilian as important as our love. And now that I've had you, I know what I would have missed. Forgive me, my darling, for the way I acted the last time I was with you," he pleaded, his eyes filled with love.

She touched his lips with a forefinger. "It is as you say—nothing else matters."

"Nothing," he repeated, holding her tightly.

However, Aimée was uneasy to learn that he thought she had been with Maximilian only once. This was the time to tell him everything, she decided, rather than risk his wrath at another, less opportune time. She drew away from him, though not far enough away to break the embrace. "There is something I must tell you, Alex."

"It won't matter, whatever it is," he answered

dreamily, reaching out to smooth her tousled hair. "I made one mistake but I'll not make another."

She took a deep breath and began. "Alex, I'm not Angela Fuchard. And that's only part of what I have to tell you."

"What difference does a name make? You're the woman I love," he answered, still caressing her arms and face.

"I'm Aimée Gaudin. I am French. My father was once Ambassador to Mexico and, for a brief time, to Washington. My father fought against the occupation of Mexico and he was murdered for it. . . ."

The reporter in Alex responded to this barrage of information and he sat up straight listening, his head cocked to one side. Aimée proceeded to tell him the entire story of how her father had been betrayed, and how she had gone to Vardeau for help—and exactly how he had "helped" her. Then she recounted the days on the ship, meeting Nemecio and what had happened and how she had come to assume the role of Angela Fuchard. Then all that had happened in Mexico: Her bogus relatives and how they resented her.

Alex listened with a sympathetic ear, as if realizing now the extent of the fear she had lived with ever since she had set foot in Mexico. And of how badly she had been used. He held her protectively in his arms and wiped away her tears when she was through. "You must have thought you had been betrayed again after your arrests," he said thoughtfully. "Did your greedy family have anything to do with that?"

Aimée smiled ruefully. "Yes. My dear family arranged those things so I would be conveniently removed from the scene. This time they went off to establish the alibi that they were far away—and innocent of any wrongdoing or involvement. Three *Juáristas* were arrested by the French and made to talk. They swore someone in my riding habit had come to their rescue. So I was once more arrested."

His shook his head in anger. "You'll do well to leave

them behind as soon as possible. Be prepared to leave tomorrow, two days at most."

Aimée was gratified with his response, but there was still more to tell Alex. Better that he should know all, she decided grimly and plunged ahead: "Don't you wish to know how I escaped that accusation? The French were ready to put me up against a wall, but the family made one mistake. They didn't know that I too would be elsewhere that day . . ." She took a deep breath. Here came the tricky part. "Maximilian had sent for me. I—I spent the night at his summer castle," she stammered.

In a way she was not surprised when Alex drew back and looked at her with shock and disgust. His hand dropped away from her arm. His back stiffened and his eyes flashed in a way that made Aimée's heart sink. "Are you telling me that you slept with him again?" he said in such an awful, cold voice that Aimée could have died with misery.

"This would be the third time," she said in a tiny, frightened voice. "Am I a fool for telling you this? Perhaps, but it was better that you know all now. I didn't want you to find out about this at some later time and think I tried to deceive you. Now you know—and you can leave me, if you wish. The choice is yours. But the first time I slept with Maximilian was at a ball he and Carlota gave. I was taken, secretly, to an upstairs room in the palace and given a drug, and then Maximilian came to me in the dark."

"Damn you!" he said in a tight voice. "I could forgive that one time because you couldn't help it. But three times . . . Three times you let him have his way with you. And you hardly resisted when I had my way with you, too. Why? Because you could gain my protection now that your darling Maximilian can no longer help himself, least of all protect you? I called you a whore, and I thought that to be a dreadful thing afterwards, but I was right. Oh, I was right. I had my doubts but you have just dispelled them." Alex was standing up now, his face red with rage, and he threw her clothes at her as if suddenly her nakedness disgusted him.

Aimée was speechless and simply started to dress. But Alex was not through. He had more to say, and with each sentence, Aimée died a little bit more. "I think you'd get into bed with anybody who could help you. You use your body to get your way. Of course, he did present you with those two valuable horses. Was that for the first time or for the second time?" he demanded, his jealousy growing so far out of control Aimée was afraid he might even strike her.

"I love you, Alex—" she implored. "I couldn't help myself."

He laughed in her face. "As you no doubt told Maximilian you loved him. Get up. If it wasn't so far back I'd make you walk home, but I can't do that to you. The French soldiers are looking for any sort of excitement they can find, and I couldn't leave even you in their hands."

He stalked back to the carriage, climbed into it and waved Aimée into the back. The passion, the romance, the love of only minutes before had disappeared in a wave of hatred. She huddled against the side of the carriage and covered her face with both hands and wept silently. Alex used a whip on the horses as if they couldn't move fast enough for him to be rid of his passenger.

At the house he brought the carriage to an abrupt halt, waited only long enough for her to climb down and then without a word or a backward glance drove off at the same mad speed. Aimée had dried her tears. She didn't want the family to gloat over this public humiliation and rejection by Alex. She walked proudly into the house and was relieved to find that no one was about. Not even Marie-Clarice was waiting for her in her room. With the door to her suite closed, Aimée threw herself across her bed and wept as if her heart would break. Indeed, she suspected she wept because it already was broken.

Damn him, she thought angrily. It was his jaunty independence that had drawn her to him from the moment he almost forced his way into her house. But it was that same quality that made him blind to her true situation and how delicate it was. A man like that probably could never understand why she felt compelled to submit to Maximilian—and to act as if she were pleased at his seeking her out. No, Alex would never bow down to anyone, and he could not forgive anyone else—even the woman he loved—for doing so, either.

Half an hour later Marie-Clarice entered the bedroom to find Aimée composed and dressed for supper.

"Your wonderful Uncle Lino wishes to talk to you," she said sweetly, although her expression said she privately thought he was anything but wonderful. "At once. The family has been holding a meeting in the library for the past few hours. They're up to something, Aimée, but I couldn't find out what. The library is one place where eavesdropping is simply impossible," she added in exasperation.

"Never mind," said Aimée, her mind on other matters.

"Is Alex coming back for us? Honestly, I didn't think he'd come back at all," Marie-Clarice prattled on, seemingly oblivious to the grim look that crossed Aimée's face when she mentioned Alex's name.

"He's not coming back, ever," she said dully. "Whatever we do now, we must depend only on each other. No one else. And, please—" her voice cracked—"don't ask me any more questions."

One look at her face and Marie-Clarice suddenly understood. "You're no genius at handling men, Aimée, if you'll forgive my saying so," she said blandly.

"I couldn't agree with you more. Are we now packed and ready to leave at any moment?"

"Is it as bad as that?" Marie-Clarice sighed. "Don't worry, we'll be ready."

Aimée's numbness gave way to cold calculation as she went downstairs to face Lino. She couldn't afford to let him know what she knew, or what her plans were.

"I'm told your reporter friend came back for a visit," he said amiably.

"Yes, uncle."

"You don't seem very happy about it."

"You wished to see me," she reminded him, changing the subject. "Is it important?"

"You have no idea. Did Señor Mooreland bring any information?"

"He said Maximilian and his soldiers are trapped, cut off from reinforcements and there's no hope for them. They are doomed," she told him curtly.

"That's what I heard also," he said, shaking his head gravely. "We can't waste any more time." Lino opened the cover on his heavy gold pocket watch. "If we hurry we can still get there before closing. I've already ordered a carriage for us."

"Where are we going?"

"To the bank. We must clear out the account and take away as much as we can carry in gold bullion. Then we'll come back here, pack what we can, and leave before morning. We must try to escape as soon as possible or we'll be at the mercy of both the retreating French and the victorious Mexicans—and this time you won't have Maximilian to protect you from their wrath."

"I agree. There's no time to waste, Uncle Lino," said Aimée briskly.

"It will take your signature to release the money and convert it to gold. But at least we'll have something when this is over. If we don't get what we can now, there won't be another chance. They'll take everything we own, if they don't kill us."

"Will the others come with us?"

"No, we don't want to make a parade out of this.

They'll stay here and prepare to leave. Renato is seeing to carriages and supplies and the women are packing."

"Where are we going?" Aimée asked curiously. "What plans have you made?"

"To Veracruz. There we'll try to get aboard a ship. It doesn't matter where it is going, as long as it takes us away from Mexico. We'll have the gold to pay well so I don't expect any trouble buying our passages."

"I'll be ready to leave in ten minutes," she assured him.

"I'll be waiting. Hurry!"

Aimée ran upstairs to her rooms, where she closed the door so she and Marie-Clarice could talk privately without being overheard.

"Everything is falling apart. It looks like we'll have to leave by tomorrow, at the latest. We'll be safe enough, with any kind of luck. Say nothing to the others. I think they're making their own plans and I doubt they'll include us. I'm going to the city with Lino to close out the bank account, if it's not too late for that. When I get back we'll make our own plans."

"I'm scared," admitted Marie-Clarice. "I'm scared of the French. I'm scared of the Mexicans. And I wouldn't put it past these people who live with us to leave us for dead. Please, don't stay away too long."

Lino had the carriage waiting. He gave some final, whispered orders to Antonia, who nodded tearfully. Lino drove the horses, using a whip at times. They were within a mile of the city when a patrol of *Pantalons Rouges* blocked their way. A sergeant approached and sternly demanded identification, though his manner softened when he recognized Aimée.

"You're the señorita who visits the palace often?" he asked.

"Yes, sergeant," she answered respectfully. "We're going there now, on business."

He wrote something on a slip of paper. "You'll need this on your way back. It's a pass. The city is surrounded because there are traitors trying to flee. Some we are especially on the lookout for. I'm sorry we had to delay you."

After they were on their way once more, Lino wiped the sweat off his brow. "I didn't realize the city was blockaded. Thank God you were with me. It pays to know the emperor, all right," he said as he took the pass from Aimée and pocketed it.

They talked little as they approached the city which usually was bustling with activity. Now the streets were deserted and the silence ominous. Patrols were everywhere, but no Mexicans were to be seen. At the bank Lino conducted the proceedings and presently brought Aimée several imposing looking documents to sign. Then Lino was handed sacks of gold, which he placed inside several straw baskets. They were very heavy and it was difficult not to stagger as he carried them out to the carriage.

In the carriage, he covered the baskets with a blanket and told Aimée, "Do you know that the banker demanded ten percent to exchange our money for gold? Ten percent," he sputtered angrily, seeming to forget that the banker could have charged anything he wanted since Lino was in no position to bargain. "After all the business we've given him—and it's been our money that has kept that bank going," Lino went on. "But when times are bad, there is no such thing as friendship if someone can make a peso," he added sullenly.

There was great truth in his words, Aimée decided, realizing the carriage was carrying a small fortune in gold. "It doesn't matter. We have enough," she said, trying to calm him.

"You're right," he admitted. "Well, that much is accomplished. Now we'll be ready when the time comes. The route to Veracruz is in French hands and will continue to be. They're trying to evacuate all the important people they can. It's safer than trying to get through Mexican lines."

"Where will we go? Paris? London?"

"It doesn't matter. With the money we now have it

doesn't matter at all. As soon as we're settled we'll invest in some profitable business with it. With your consent, of course. After all, this is your gold."

"I trust you to care for it, Uncle Lino," Aimée said, unnerved by the aura of fear that hung over the city. "We'd best try to return now. Things happen too fast these days."

"I agree, but first you'll have to visit the lawyer's office and make arrangements for the mansion. In the event it isn't confiscated, you should retain possession of it. We shall let out word that we're only going away for a short visit. You'll have to tell the lawyer so he can safeguard it during our absence."

"Very well," she agreed.

Lino drove her there, but when they arrived he stayed in the carriage. "Aren't you going to come in too, Uncle Lino?" she asked, a wave of apprehension sweeping over her.

"Impossible, Angela, not with all this gold hidden in this carriage. I must stay with it."

She saw the sense to what he said but she had an eerie premonition that his reluctance to accompany her meant deception. But she felt she had no choice but to trust him and to try and complete her business with the lawyer as quickly as possible.

Aimée promised she'd return quickly, but no matter how rushed she felt it took time for all the documents to be prepared and signed and witnessed. It was at least half an hour later when Aimée went outside to find the carriage gone.

She looked in every direction for the carriage, wondering if a patrol had come along and arrested Lino or confiscated the gold. There were no signs as to what had happened. Then she kicked the dirt in angry frustration. What an idiot she had been! She should have known better. It was obvious that Lino had planned to drop her off at the lawyer's and probably had driven away the second she was out of sight. This way the family had all of the money and might escape whenever they wished—*without her, but with her gold!* And she was left to the mercy of whichever side found her first.

It was late afternoon now. Aimée realized with growing despondency that she had neither money nor any means of returning to the estate. She only hoped that Marie-Clarice would have the good sense not to try to interfere with the hastily departing family. She could not stop them, and they might even kill her if she tried. Marie-Clarice would realize that Aimée had been betrayed again when she saw Lino returning alone.

Aimée trudged through the deserted streets back to the bank, praying she wouldn't encounter any patrols. At the bank, she sought out the very men who had always been so friendly toward her before.

"There's been a misunderstanding," Aimée explained. "Uncle Lino seems to have driven off alone and I suspect he was forced to do so by some circumstances I am unaware of. Perhaps all of that gold. . . ."

"My dear Señorita Fuchard," the banker said. "Of course Lino would hesitate to allow his carriage and himself to be searched. That's what's going on here all the time. No one is safe. The French are arresting every Mexican they suspect of even small violations, and the Mexicans are waiting for Juárez. It's very dangerous to be on the streets right now. I suggest that you get out of the city and go home."

"But I can't," Aimée said, trying to make him understand her plight. "I have no carriage. I have no money. Señor Gomez," she said, appealing to him personally, "is it possible for me to borrow enough so that I can return home?"

Gomez chuckled. "You, one of the richest women in the city asking for a small loan. Ah, yes, times have changed indeed. But, you see, your account has been closed and I have no authority to lend money without security," he said as formally as if he had never seen Aimée before.

"I don't even have any jewelry to offer you," Aimée said sadly. "What am I to do?"

His face lit up with a hopeful smile. "You know, of course, that you can't drive along the roads of the city without a pass. If Lino doesn't have it. . . ."

With a sinking feeling in her stomach Aimée remembered Lino taking the pass away from her. It had been no accident she now realized. "He has the pass," Aimée said resignedly.

"Then you can't get back even if you do find a carriage," the banker informed her. "They arrest everyone who tries to leave without a military pass." He gave a great sigh as if the matter was now resolved.

"Then I must find a place to spend the night," declared Aimée.

"I wish I could help you, señorita. Do you think," he added, a hint of slyness in his voice as if he had maneuvered her into a corner, "that you might get a pass? I'm aware that you're well known at the palace."

"I could try," she said hopefully, "but what good will it do me without a carriage?"

His eyes narrowed speculatively as he looked at her. "Tell me, how much do you admire Maximilian?" he asked slowly, as if her answer was very, very important.

"How much? I like him. He's an honest man who's been misled by the French and by the military, but he's neither cruel nor vicious," she said simply and honestly.

"You are Mexican, señorita. Do you prefer Maximilian? Or would you like to see the French booted out?" he asked, again probing for where her loyalties lay.

"As you say, señor, I am Mexican. I don't think the French belong here. They should all go home. They have bled the country dry already. They deserve to be thrown out."

"Then you would help a Mexican rather than a Frenchman?" he asked, obviously driving at something.

"Of course," she answered. It seemed to Aimée that the whole world had become one vast snakepit of intrigue and that she was always caught in the middle.

"I'm going to trust you because I have no other

choice," the banker began, lowering his voice to a conspiratorial whisper. "My life, the life of others, even your own, will depend on how you handle this delicate situation. Do not agree to what I ask if you're afraid to see it through to the end, whatever that may be," he added, somewhat ominously.

Aimée thought she should at least listen to his proposal. "Señor, please tell me what it is that you wish of me," she said in a businesslike manner.

"Here, in the bank, hidden away in an old basement vault that no one knows about, are three ladies. They are fine women whose husbands worked for Juárez. The husbands were arrested and shot. Now the French are searching for their widows. They will be shot on sight if they are discovered. What I ask of you is this: Can you get them safely out of here, through the blockade, and to your estate? Perhaps you can arrange for their escape from there?"

"You should have mentioned this to my uncle, señor," Aimée protested mildly at having such a responsibility thrust on her shoulders. How could she help them when it seemed she couldn't even help herself?

"I considered speaking to Lino, but he is a sly one. I don't trust him, if you will forgive me for saying so."

"You're very likely right about not trusting him. I'm willing to try to get the ladies out of the city, but there's the question of the pass. Let me think a moment. Perhaps . . ." Aimée thought . . . "if I can get a pass that will include three ladies I could say they're my aunt and my two cousins."

"That might work, señorita," said the banker.

"Do you have a carriage I can use so I can go to the palace and try to get the pass? I can't afford to waste a moment," she reminded him. After all he was a man, too, and she had seen that speculative look in his eyes, despite his problems, and had no intention of giving herself to him so she might obtain a carriage. No, Aimée had been given far more than the use of a carriage for her services.

The next moment the banker was shouting for a carriage, his own, to be brought around. "If you help these women you'll become a national heroine. They are very important, you understand. The French would take great glee in killing them. They are a reminder to other Mexicans of their martyred husbands, who gave money and assistance to Juárez when all of this first began."

"Expect me back within the hour," she told him. "With Maximilian gone, I may not succeed, but I intend to try my best."

"God be with you, señorita," he said fervently. "I'll have the women ready to depart when you return."

Aimée went right out to where the carriage was waiting and drove to the palace. She was stopped at the gate but the guards recognized her and let her through. Aimée was relieved to see the royal guard had not accompanied Maximilian into battle.

"Is Colonel Vardeau here?" she asked.

"*Oui, mademoiselle.* He's in charge of the palace in the emperor's absence."

"Please take me to him. It's very urgent," she said.

A soldier was assigned to accompany her. She left the carriage at the gate and walked into the building where Vardeau's office was located. He was seated behind a desk at work but the moment he saw her he promptly rose and bowed.

"Señorita, I'm honored."

"Thank you, colonel. How is Maximilian? Have you heard any news?" she asked.

"He's fine, in full command of his armies. We shall be victorious in the end. You'll see," he answered reassuringly. From his manner she judged they both knew he was lying, although she appreciated his reasons for doing so.

"He didn't take you with him?" she said questioningly.

"He was concerned for the palace and wished it to be well guarded. Unfortunately, my men and I were ordered to stay out of the fighting."

"I'm glad, colonel. I sincerely wish no harm to come to you," she said graciously, the lie coming easily to her lips since she needed his help, here and now, so desperately.

"And I'm gratified to hear that, señorita. Is there something I can do for you?"

Aimée almost shook her head in disbelief at his offer. She could hardly believe this was the man who had betrayed her and raped her—and now he was offering her his assistance.

"There's been an unfortunate misunderstanding, colonel. I came to Mexico City with my uncle, my aunt and my two cousins. We were stopped and given a pass, but my uncle has it in his possession and he's gone back alone. He thought we wished to remain in the city longer and that he would come back for us tomorrow, but we have decided it would be far wiser to go home tonight. I've been able to find another carriage to take us home, but without the pass we'll surely be stopped and quite likely arrested. Is it possible for you to give me a pass for myself and these three other ladies?"

"Why certainly, señorita," he agreed immediately. "The emperor would have ordered me to do so if he were here." Vardeau opened a drawer, took out a piece of paper and promptly filled it in. Then he handed it to Aimée.

"This will ensure your passage and a safe journey, señorita. I'm happy to have been of service."

"And I'm grateful, colonel," Aimée murmured, thinking he had no idea how sincere this statement was.

He nodded and rose, an act of dismissal with which Aimée was only too happy to comply. "If there's any news I'll call on you in person, señorita. And should the emperor issue any orders concerning you, rest assured I'll obey them."

She thanked him again, relieved that the exchange of such oppressively polite civilities was at an end. Clutching the precious pass, she returned to the carriage and drove away from the gates. The young man the banker had sent for the carriage was waiting for her return. When she stepped down, he drove the carriage behind the bank. Then she went inside to the banker's private office.

"I have it," she announced. "A pass for four women."

"Thank God," he said fervently. "There would have been no chance of getting them out of the city if you hadn't helped. The good Lord must have sent you, Señorita Angela. You're aware of the risk you're taking in trying to drive them through the blockade?"

"Quite aware, señor," she answered briskly.

"Then you'll find the carriage at the door with the women inside. I wish you all the luck in the world. You may be assured that all of Mexico will be most grateful."

She nodded. He opened a drawer and removed a small canvas sack. "Gold," he said. "I know your uncle has a small fortune with him, but perhaps . . . well, I know Lino."

"As do I," she said grimly, accepting the sack and giving him an appreciative smile. "Thank you."

"The ladies have all the gold they need. Don't worry about them. This is just for you."

"*Gracias,* Señor Gomez. I shall do my best."

She left the bank and approached the carriage as serenely as if there were no war, no trouble, no danger. She got into the driver's seat and took the reins. In back, she sensed the presence of the three frightened women, whose silence she could only construe as pure terror.

"It's all arranged," Aimée said softly, but loudly enough for them to hear. "I'm sure we'll be quite safe."

She drove slowly along the street, reached the road on the route to the estate and proceeded along it. When night was near, Aimée stopped to hang a lantern under the carriage. A carriage traveling without one might be suspect. Nervous soldiers on the alert for escapees would be only too happy to shoot first and ask questions later, if anyone was alive to be questioned.

A patrol barred their path at approximately the same spot where Aimée and Lino had been stopped on their way into the city. The soldiers, holding torches, surrounded the carriage.

Aimée produced the pass. "It's from the emperor's royal guard," she said. "I'm Señorita Fuchard and the ladies are my aunt and my cousins, as the pass states."

The officer in charge read the pass, then silently handed it back to Aimée and saluted. He gestured and the soldiers moved away and Aimée soon left the blockade behind. As they proceeded along the dark road she could hear the soft prayers of the women in back.

"You see," she said, "we're safe now. When we reach my home we'll discuss way of getting you to the Juárez lines. It shouldn't be too difficult. Juárez's troops aren't too far away, and once you reach them, you'll be quite safe."

"Gracias," one woman said. "We're most grateful."

"And happy," exclaimed another. "We thought we had nothing to look forward to except arrest and execution."

The trio, relieved of their greatest anxiety, now began to talk among themselves while Aimée kept the carriage moving at a steady but restrained pace. There might be other patrols and she didn't want to give any indication of haste.

The lamplight in the mansion never looked more welcome, although Aimée wondered nervously what she'd find there. She pulled up before the door. Marie-Clarice had drawn back a curtain to peer out and when she recognized Aimée she'd quickly opened the door and hurried out to meet her.

"What's happened?" she asked excitedly. "Where have you been?" She peeked into the carriage and said, "Who are they?"

"Guests," Aimée said coolly. "They'll stay the night and be gone as soon as we can provide means for them to travel."

"Spies?" she asked suspiciously.

"No, Marie-Clarice. They are the widows of important Mexican patriots."

"Oh, I see. I shall prepare as fine a meal as I can with what's left."

Inside, the three women removed the scarves covering their heads and faces. Aimée recognized them instantly.

"Why, you were at the ball we gave. I remember your faces, though not your names. But perhaps it's better that you don't tell me, señoras. If there's trouble. . . ."

"I am Yolanda," the oldest of the women replied. "That is enough for you to know. "You've exposed yourself to enough danger as it is."

"Marie-Clarice will show you to your rooms. No doubt you'll want to freshen up before dinner. If any of my clothes fit you, please feel free to help yourselves."

Marie-Clarice came down after a few minutes, anxious to tell her what had happened during her absence. "The family is gone, every one of them—with everything of value they could pack into the carriages. Before they left they dismissed all of the servants and sent them off. We're alone and I consider myself lucky they didn't kidnap me—or worse," she said with a shiver.

"How did you avoid that?" Aimée asked.

"As soon as I suspected what they were up to—and how could I help it when I heard them searching your room—I pretended I noticed nothing and said I wanted to go riding. They were glad to be rid of me and I stayed away, just at the edge of the woods until they cleared out. They carried out pillowcases filled with jewelry and silver and everything of value. . . . So we have this big house to ourselves along with three guests, almost no food and French soldiers everywhere," she sighed.

"Tomorrow our guests will leave. I came back alone because Lino left me stranded in the city, without the gold or a pass to return. He took it all and ran. We were right to suspect them of being clever thieves. Nemecio was right," said Aimée sadly.

"What are we going to do now?" the ever-practical Marie-Clarice wanted to know.

"Well, I have some money. Enough to get by for a while. After we get the women off, we'll begin our journey to the United States. We won't arrive there wealthy, but if we preserve our lives, that's all that really matters."

Chapter 15

The countryside appeared to be deserted and there was an eerie silence. Nothing moved on the main road above the mansion, and the house seemed desolate without the servants. However, there were still horses to be fed and watered, and Marie-Clarice took care of them. Blankets and saddles were readied, and the two Arabians were put in stalls close to the stable exit. It was hard work in the heat.

Aimée had given the three women horses and supplies and they had set out for the *Juárista* camp early that morning. Alone now, Aimée and Marie-Clarice were cut off from all sources of information about the battle in progress, although they were aware that they'd seen no French troops passing by as they so often had in the past.

"This silence is oppressive," Marie-Clarice announced grimly. "If the fighting has stopped that means it's all over for Maximilian and the French. What if the Mexican soldiers come and discover we're both French?"

"I wish Alex were here," Aimée blurted out, giving in to her tension. "I depended on him for advice."

"I take it, from the tone of your voice, that he will not be back," Marie-Clarice said.

"I'm afraid not. We've got to make our plans alone. And it will probably be even more difficult for us than for Yolanda and her friends. Those three women have every chance of reaching the Mexican lines. They've been well advised on that," she said forlornly.

They had no sooner returned to the house to pack up what provisions they could find when they heard a carriage approach. They raced to one of the upstairs windows to watch and saw that there was only one man in the carriage. Aimée's hopes began to soar.

"It must be Alex," she said.

Her elation turned to a gasp of dismay when the man who emerged from the carriage turned out to be Vardeau, no longer in the spiffy uniform of a colonel but dressed in civilian clothes. He looked just as he had when Aimée had first met him that night long ago in Paris.

She was too shocked to put on a brave front for Marie-Clarice anymore. "I'm afraid. I always found it hard to believe he didn't recognize me, and something tells me this is a bad sign, his coming here alone and out out uniform."

"He's a dangerous man," Marie-Clarice reminded her.

"I know that, but there's little we can do now. I want you to stay upstairs. Don't make a sound. It's possible he doesn't know you are here. I'll handle him the best I can."

"Two of us could handle him better," Marie-Clarice said staunchly.

"He's a big, strong man and we'd never have a chance, even the two of us together. It's better if he thinks just I'm here. If we fought him, he'd kill us. Don't forget he is a soldier and is not only trained to fight, but won't think twice about it, even if we are women. He's also a traitor and not to be trusted."

Vardeau was walking toward the veranda now, and Aimée motioned Marie-Clarice into the bedroom. Then she walked down the stairs and found Vardeau had entered unannounced.

"Good afternoon, señorita," he said with a bow, as he met her at the foot of the stairs. "I have sad news."

She paused, one step above him. "Is it Maximilian?"

"He's dead. They stood him up against a wall and a firing squad executed him in plain view of his officers," Vardeau told her bluntly.

Aimée closed her eyes. It was not unexpected news, but it certainly wasn't welcome news. Maximilian may have been an inept leader, a weak man, even an enemy of Mexico, but he didn't deserve a violent end like that. Aimée led Vardeau into the drawing room where she sat down and quietly wept.

"They say he died bravely," Vardeau went on.

"I'm sure he did. Thank you for coming to tell me this. I've been worried about him."

"The war is over now," he said. "There's only a very small garrison left in Mexico City. The palace has been abandoned. In another day or two the Mexican forces will occupy the city and it will all be over, for good."

"Then I'm afraid we'll have to move on," she said. "You especially."

"Yes, I intend to. How would you like to go to the United States?" he asked.

"I . . . what do you mean?"

"With me—Mademoiselle Aimée Gaudin."

Her eyes hardened. "So you knew! All along you knew."

"Of course," he said with a satisfied air. "But when we met at the summer palace you were no more surprised than I was. I'd say that chance brought us together and we can't fight this kind of fate. We can only seize it and hope it lasts."

"And you're suggesting that I go to the United States with you?" she said sarcastically.

"Why not?" he shrugged off the intended insult. "You'd have a difficult time getting through the lines. I can do it because I know the ways of troops."

"Monsieur Vardeau, I'd far rather let the Mexicans capture me and stand me before one of their firing squads. Please don't insult me again with such a suggestion."

"They'll shoot you, Aimée. There isn't a chance you'll go free. You, my dear, were Maximilian's mistress. How do you think a Mexican tribunal will feel about that?"

"I'd rather take my chances with a tribunal than go with you. Thank you for coming here with the sad news, but please leave now and save your own skin. You're in no less danger than I am, since you were the colonel of Maximilian's royal guards," she reminded him.

"Aimée, please use your head. Yes, I admit that I'm as vulnerable as you are, but that's no reason why we can't try to escape together."

"I don't understand why you didn't run with the rest of them. There are ships at Veracruz, surely you knew that. You belong in France, not here nor in the United States," she said in bewilderment.

"Aimée, I was sent here as a punishment. It was discovered I knew more about the Mexican revolt than I should have, but they were afraid to try me because of the publicity. If I go back this time, they're likely to put me in prison. After this fiasco, they'll have no reason to hide anything. I can't go back," he admitted.

"Then make your own way, and don't count on me," she said defiantly.

"What I intend to do," he went on smoothly, ignoring her order to leave, "is help myself to all that gold that you withdrew from the bank only a few days ago. It will be a comfort in my old age—as you will comfort me now. Do you understand, Aimée? I shall have the gold—and I shall have you."

She shook her head. "The gold is long gone. My dear family made off with it. They didn't leave a peso. They didn't leave a jewel or anything else of value that they could carry with them. You've come to the wrong place. I have no more than you have."

"But they *did* leave something for me . . . I've not forgotten the episode in Paris and I don't intend to let you go so easily this time. Remember, I can always turn you in as Maximilian's mistress."

"Quite true. On the other hand, to explain how you knew this for sure would be to reveal your position on Maximilian's staff."

"I wouldn't expect to be treated kindly by the Mexicans but I can always deny your story, and they're more likely to believe me than you. After all, they're soldiers and I was a soldier."

"I'd still prefer to take my chances with them."

"Oh, come now, I'm not as bad as that," Vardeau said, changing his tactic. "Besides, why discriminate against me? You were, after all, Maximilian's mistress. The mistress of the lion, that's what the household staff used to call you. If you could tolerate such a mollycoddle, surely you should be glad to have a real man for a change."

"You are wrong. This discussion is finished," she said, rising from her chair. "If you won't leave, I shall."

He stood as if to leave, but he whirled and caught her in his strong arms, pinning her arms helplessly at her sides. He bent down and kissed her with a brutal passion that bruised her lips. She struggled but couldn't loosen his powerful grip on her. Her efforts only seemed to amuse him, as he picked her up, flung her over one shoulder and marched up the stairs to her bedroom, while she kicked at him and pounded on his back. He didn't seem to notice her resistance. If anything, it made him more eager to have her. "Fight all you like my dear Aimée. We're alone here—you admitted yourself that your family had abandoned you. No one will come to your aid, so you might as well resign yourself to our reunion," he taunted her.

He carried her out of the drawing room, up the stairs, and into the parlor of her suite, which was the room nearest the top of the stairs. Aimée suddenly ceased struggling, remembering with alarm that Marie-Clarice was hiding in the bedroom. But when Vardeau kicked the bedroom door open, Aimée almost fainted with relief: Marie-Clarice was nowhere in sight. She must have fled into another part of the house upon hearing the commotion. She hoped Marie-Clarice would have the good sense to remain hidden.

Vardeau desposited her roughly on the bed. He stood there for a minute looking down at her, a wide smirk on his face. "You may fight if you like, but nothing can stop me."

He bent over to remove his shoes. Then he slipped out of his trousers and approached the bed. "Will you remove your clothes or shall I? No? I'll do it then. . . ."

With one savage pull Vardeau tore the bodice off Aimée's dress, exposing her breasts. She clutched at the fragments of her garment and tried to move away, but he caught her by the legs and yanked her like a ragdoll to the edge of the bed. Then he tore away her skirt, ripping it right up the middle as easily as Maximilian had torn away her nightgown. She lay there naked before him, trembling and yet defiant. How dare he try to take her against her will!

He practically threw his powerful body atop hers, pinning her to the bed. His desire for her was practically out of control. He was like a wild animal, pawing at her, not caring whether he pleased her or hurt her. She was simply an instrument of his pleasure. He ignored her cry of pain as he plunged into her. If anything, her pain excited him even more. "I could kill you," he hissed, a dangerous edge to his voice. "Fight me and I'll wring your pretty neck."

Aimée knew that he almost hoped she would fight him—and she had no doubts that he meant what he said. But she also had no reason to doubt that after he had finished with her, he could kill her anyway, just to complete his revenge.

After he had used her this way for a while, he suddenly withdrew and ordered: "Turn over." Aimée shuddered at the thought of what was to come. When she didn't move quickly enough for Vardeau, he flipped her over. She lay there, her head buried in the pillow, and she felt his hands probing and separating her two rounded globes. Then again he plunged into her and this time she could not hold back a scream of anguish.

"Enjoy it, Aimée. Pretend that I'm Maximilian," he laughed.

The idea of this savage animal thinking he was anything like Maximilian, her suave lover, was an abomination. Aimée closed her eyes and simply hoped she would be able to endure the pain a little while longer. But out of the corner of her eye she detected a movement. Vardeau was too busy to notice Marie-Clarice creeping stealthily toward the bed, a huge revolver clutched in both her hands, her eyes wide open with fear, her face white as a ghost's, but her aim steady.

Standing right behind him, the gun at his head, she said firmly, without a quaver, "That's enough of that. Prepare to die, Vardeau."

He looked at her and saw the gun and said, "What the devil?"

"It's too bad," Marie-Clarice said, "for a man to die with neither his shoes nor his pants on."

Vardeau climbed off the bed, very slowly, his hands up, and said scoffingly, "You haven't the nerve to shoot. Put that pistol down or I'll break your pretty neck and Aimée's, too."

Realizing Vardeau might try to grab her as a hostage or even a shield to hold in front of Marie-Clarice, Aimée bolted out of the bed to a far corner of the room behind Marie-Clarice and watched the grisly scene unfold.

"Come toward me," challenged Marie-Clarice, "just take one single step—and find out if I'll shoot."

Vardeau hesitated, but he saw the gun waver for a split second. So he took that single step to get the gun away from her. But Marie-Clarice steadied the gun again, aiming it directly at him. He took another step. Aimee saw in horror that with one more step he could take the gun away. Just as he moved toward her, Marie-Clarice fired.

Vardeau was like a doll himself, hurled back against the wall, a gaping hole in his right shoulder from the huge bullet. Blood was everywhere and the wound was bleeding profusely. Aimée was convinced he was going to bleed to death on the spot. He seemed stunned, almost as if he didn't know where he was, but his eyes watched the gun—which was still aimed at him. Except this time Marie-Clarice's aim was lower, pointed at a much more vital region than his arm.

"I think you'd better go, Monsieur," Marie-Clarice said evenly, pointing toward the door. Vardeau staggered a few steps, one arm hanging limp and useless at his side, the other arm clutching the wound to staunch the flow of blood. He sidled past Marie-Clarice, his eyes on where the pistol was pointed. She stepped aside for him to pass. When he reached the door, Marie-Clarice fired again. She had aimed high with no intention of shooting Vardeau, but his back was turned and he didn't know that. He cried out and ran down the corridor, never even looking back in his haste to escape.

When he reached the stairs he gave a fleeting glance over his shoulder and saw Marie-Clarice standing in the middle of the hall, the revolver still in her hand. He stumbled when he saw that, crashing into a wall, but then he managed to get down the stairs and out the front door.

Aimée and Marie-Clarice watched from the window as he managed to get into the carriage, obviously in great pain, and ride off as fast as he could.

When Marie-Clarice finally put down the pistol, her hands began to shake, her face was even whiter than before and she began to weep hysterically. Aimée went to her side, knelt and wrapped an arm around her shoulder.

Thank you, my dear friend. Thank you," she said softly. "You were very brave. That man would have killed me if you hadn't been here."

Marie-Clarice looked up, trying to calm herself. Her tear-stained face was drawn as she said, "I . . . I heard him downstairs. I went to get the gun, just in case. But when he took you into the bedroom I knew I had no choice. I . . . I didn't know if I could kill him. I guess I meant to, Aimée, but it was the first time I've ever fired a gun in my life."

"You didn't kill him," Aimée told her. "Not that he didn't deserve it—or that he wouldn't have killed us— but what you did saved both our lives. You're very brave."

Marie-Clarice's eyes brimmed with fresh tears, but instead of weeping more she suddenly began to laugh. "H—he didn't have any pants on. He ran away without his pants on—and no shoes."

"He'll have more trouble explaining that than the bullet in his shoulder," Aimée said, joining in her laughter. "It wasn't funny at the time, but now that I think back to the whole scene—you, standing there with this great big gun in your hand, and Vardeau, shoeless and pantless trying to bluff you out of it. And then the way he ran away as fast as he could. . . ."

"I don't think he'll come back here," Marie-Clarice announced firmly. "If he does, there are more guns and he knows I'll shoot. At least I think I will," she added soberly.

"I don't think he'll be back, either," agreed Aimée. She didn't want to frighten Marie-Clarice, but if Vardeau did live, their next encounter would not be so pleasant. He would be intent on having his revenge on Aimée and Marie-Clarice.

"I think that we deserve a drink of brandy," said Marie-Clarice. "At least they didn't take that with them when they left. And it's a fine brandy," she pronounced.

She brought the brandy and two snifter glasses and poured two huge drinks. She held her glass up high for a toast and said proudly, "To me! I didn't lose my nerve. But," she added, holding out her glass, "see how my hand shakes."

"You didn't shake when you held him off—and that's what counts," pointed out Aimée, taking a sip. Marie-Clarice's answer was to lean back and not sip but drain at least half the contents of the glass. Aimée watched in amazement.

"He knew who you were all along, didn't he?" asked Marie-Clarice, her eyes slightly glazed.

"Yes, he did. But he didn't dare even admit it to me because he was in trouble with the French himself, and he knew that Maximilian and I were so close that to reveal me would not be to his advantage."

"It's a good thing you were in Maximilian's favor." Marie-Clarice was beginning to slur her words. Aimée smiled, thinking her brave friend deserved a good drunk, and just hoped she would cope with the headache she'd have in the morning. Her thoughts were wandering. What if Vardeau actually made it back to Mexico City and told the French troops they were still at the house? The thought horrified her. But Vardeau would do it, even if it was just for revenge.

"I should have killed him," Marie-Clarice said drunkenly, her courage growing greater in retrospect.

Aimée began to wish she had too. She could just imagine the retreating French troops, humiliated by defeat, seizing any opportunity to carry back loot— and maybe take advantage of two French women. And if they came back to the house and didn't find Aimée and Marie-Clarice, they would surely be on the lookout for them. With rising desperation, Aimée concluded there was no way they could safely start their journey now for the United States.

Marie-Clarice said, "We must get out of this house as soon as we can."

"I know a place where we can hide for a while," Aimee told her. "There's a glen deep in the forest and there's a cave there. It's impossible to find unless you know it's there because there's no trace of it from the trail. Alex and I went there. Renato showed me where it was. The weather is warm enough so we can camp out—and it isn't far from here," Aimée said, realizing Marie-Clarice was in no condition to be of help.

"But if Alex should come and we're not here—"

"He won't. It's finished between us, and I can't blame him. The glen is our only hope," Aimée said with determinantion. "There's nowhere else we can hide. Let's go. We'll hide out there until we think it's safe enough to risk trying to get to the United States."

Aimée was thankful that Marie-Clarice had packed clothing and food and that the horses were ready. It was all she could do to get her unsteady friend on the horse and lead them onto the forest trail. "Don't forget to bring the brandy," Marie-Clarice said just as they were about to ride away from the house that had been their home ever since they'd arrived in Mexico City. Aimée went back into the house and brought out the brandy. She was surprised at how easily she could turn her back on this house. But then, she reminded herself, it wasn't hers to begin with. Aimée had the little bag of gold the banker had given her, too, but she knew there was only enough to bribe a few people.

"I don't like the idea of being poor again," Marie-Clarice said, as they trotted off. Marie-Clarice had been in no condition to help very much, but she had taken the pistol with her and another huge gun she had found somewhere. "Just in case," she had grinned.

By the time they reached the glen, Marie-Clarice was riding straight in her saddle. She marveled at the beauty of the spot and at how well it was concealed. They let the horses loose to graze on the grass and began to unpack what they had brought with them for living in a cave.

Marie-Clarice had provided well for them when she'd packed: enough food for quite a while, plenty of blankets so sleeping on the ground would be no great hardship, and some cards and a book or two so they could while away the long hours. As well equipped as they were, it was an inglorious end to what had been a life of great luxury.

They rested for a while and as the cool of the evening set in, they began to talk.

"If the Mexicans arrest Vardeau, he's going to tell them a great deal about you," Marie-Clarice said.

"And not all lies," agreed Aimée, "although it was a better life, while it lasted, than if we had been indentured. I just hope we can get out alive."

"Oh, please don't say that," implored Marie-Clarice. "I like to think we can get away without any danger."

"Perhaps we can, even without Alex. We have to try to make it on our own. But we'll have to stay here for awhile, until things have calmed down and the French are gone. Then all we have to worry about are the Mexicans."

"Do you think they'll look for us?" Marie-Clarice asked.

"I don't even know if anyone will come. We just must be very careful. Vardeau is a vindictive man, and he'd be very happy to see me humiliated."

"If that's what you call it," shuddered Marie-Clarice. "But, I really don't mind being here. It's nice."

Everything was under control, but the pack animals they had brought here to carry the provisions were getting restless and Aimée was afraid that if someone came looking for them they'd betray their presence.

"We'll have to lead them back," Aimée said, "turn them loose. And we'd best do it right now before Vardeau or any of the French return."

"Should we leave the Arabians here?" Marie-Clarice asked.

Aimée thought about this for a minute and said, "No, we'd better ride them, so that way if we are seen we have a chance to escape."

They rode back on the trail and headed toward the mansion, their ears alert for any sounds other than those of the forest. But they heard nothing and soon reached the fringe of the forest, about a quarter of a mile from the house. With a slap on the rump, they sent the beasts trotting toward the house.

There was no activity around the house and Aimée began to hope first that Vardeau had bled to death in the carriage. Or that he had been captured. Or that he decided against returning for revenge because he thought it more expedient to run for his life. But Aimée knew Vardeau better than that: He would rather have his revenge, even if it killed him.

"Maybe we should run for it now?" Marie-Clarice suggested, hoping that no one would be looking for them.

"I don't think so. We haven't given them enough time. They may be searching for us. I have a feeling they will come here looking for us and they may already be watching the roads. It isn't worth it. We have too much to lose," Aimée said cautiously.

"Then let's wait here and watch, Aimée. No one can see us and we can disappear back into the forest the minute we see anyone," Marie-Clarice said.

"All right. We'll watch for a while," agreed Aimée. "But we still haven't finished setting up our camp."

Just then Marie-Clarice saw a cloud of dust. "They're coming," she said, almost calmly. "By the size of the dust cloud, plenty of them are coming. Come on, let's get out of here."

This time it was Aimée who said, "Not yet. We're safe unless they begin fanning out to search. And I don't think they're interested in that. All they want is what they think they'll find in the mansion."

"And what they think they'll find isn't there anymore."

There were about a dozen of them. Vardeau, they noted, was not with them, and Marie-Clarice hoped out loud that he was dead. The soldiers pulled up in front of the mansion, whooping in delight at such an undefended find. They dismounted and rushed inside.

Aimée and Marie-Clarice heard windows breaking and shouts. Then some of the soldiers emerged from the house carrying their loot and loaded it onto their saddles. Two of them rode off to the stables, giving Aiméee a moment of anxiety because the stables were in a direct line with their hiding place.

However, the men spent little time in the stables since there was nothing of value to plunder there. Soon they rode back to the mansion and joined the others. A few minutes later all but one of the soldiers were back on their horses. That's when Marie-Clarice's sharp eyes noted the first wisps of smoke and fingers of flames rising from the stables and then the house. "They're probably burning it because they didn't find what they wanted," declared Marie-Clarice. "I hope they don't begin searching for us now."

"It will soon be too dark," decided Aimée. "But tomorrow we'll have to keep our ears open and be ready to ride if we hear anything. For now, they are of no worry to us."

When the final looter emerged, the troops rode off. Aimée and Marie-Clarice sat and watched the mansion burn.

"If the family ever returns, they're going to be mighty disappointed," predicted Marie-Clarice, as flames engulfed the house.

"Serves them right," said Aimée, thinking how easily they could have included her in their escape plans and at least let her leave the country alive. But no, they had run, saving only their own skins, without a thought for her or Marie-Clarice.

"Oh, look!" Marie-Clarice pointed. "Now there are

flames coming from your bedroom window. All those beautiful clothes. . . ."

"Thank God we weren't there," breathed Aimée fervently.

"I wish Vardeau had been," replied Marie-Clarice with equal intensity. "I wish he was trapped in that burning house with no way out."

Aimée sighed. "I don't want to stay and watch the final destruction. It didn't belong to me, but it's such a shame that it had to end like this."

She took one last look as she mounted the Arabian. The mansion was already so engulfed in flames as to be barely visible. The clouds of black smoke and sparks rose into the darkening sky. Aimée abruptly wheeled her horse and followed Marie-Clarice back down the trail to their hiding place.

Chapter 16

It was two days later. Aimée was sitting quietly in the glen, partly rolled up in a blanket against the early morning chill. Marie-Clarice was intent on her sewing.

Aimée asked, "What are you doing with that turban sewing it hour after hour, day after day?"

"I like it." Marie-Clarice glanced at her. "I look well in a turban. Besides, it's something to do to keep busy."

"I'm sorry," Aimée apologized. "Of course you look well in it, and you never were one to just sit still. This waiting is getting on my nerves and I'm just irritable. Forgive me for taking it out on you."

Marie-Clarice set aside the turban. "I've been thinking of something else to do. I think we're both getting restless and feeling trapped here. Since the French have already done their damage, how dangerous can it be to take a walk back to the mansion and look around. There might be something we can use there, and it would be a good chance to get away from here for a little while."

Aimée looked at her doubtfully, then decided she was right. They felt like prisoners just sitting there hour after hour. And what danger could there be there now?

They left the security of their grassy glen and walked along the forest trail, proceeding slowly and listening every few steps of the way. At the clearing they took refuge behind the thick brush. From here they had a clear view. The destruction was complete. All that remained of the wonderful house were five chimneys, which stood like silent skeletons presiding over the death of the house.

"Damn the soldiers!" Marie-Clarice said angrily.

They stepped into the open area, peered about and then ran to the blackened remains of the stables. They poked about in the rubble and were soon joined by the two pack horses who had evidently preferred to stay in familiar territory instead of wandering off. But Aimée and Marie-Clarice were disappointed to find that nothing of any value to them was left in the ashes. Marie-Clarice pumped some fresh water into the animal trough to use for bathing themselves, first. Then they went up to the main house—or what was left of it.

They were able to find the pantry area. There were perhaps a dozen jars of vegetables which had somehow survived the fury of the fire. They found some half-burned draperies which they used to wrap up the jars so they could carry them away.

They were ambling along the path back to the stables when Aimée spotted the cloud of dust.

They ran until they reached the cover of the brush. There they stopped, held back by curiosity to see who the riders were. It turned out to be a pack of men in ill-fitting uniforms and bandoleers of cartridges that crossed over their shoulders.

"Mexican trops," said Aimée thoughtfully. "They could have been just riding by—or they could have been sent here."

The soldiers dismounted. One of them noticed the two pack horses around the watering trough. He dipped a hand into the trough. They could not see the expression on his face but Aimée knew that by the fact that the water was still cold from the well, he could tell that someone had been there very recently. Aloud she said, "He knows someone must be close by. We've got to go back. Let's be as quiet as we can, but hurry," she whispered urgently.

They reached the glen safely, but their efforts left them both panting and filled with fresh concern for their safety.

"They were sent here. It was no accident," decided Aimée. "I don't know who sent them, but it's possible that Vardeau was captured and told the troops we were there. Since he was wounded he may not have made it back to his troops in the city. If he was captured, he surely informed on us, on *me*, that is."

"I shall curse myself to my dying day that I didn't aim better and kill that man," Marie-Clarice said bitterly. "If I'd killed him we wouldn't be in this mess."

"I'm afraid we'd be in trouble anyway," Aimée reassured the girl. "Too many people know about me and . . . about Maximilian. The Mexicans executed him and I don't doubt that they'll destroy every reminder of him."

"Then we'd best begin thinking about getting out soon," Marie-Clarice said.

Aimée signaled her to be quiet. Intuitition warned her that there were people nearby. Soon they could hear movements in the underbrush, then voices speaking in Spanish. The two women clung together in terror, barely daring to breathe for fear they would give away their location. They prayed that they would not be found in their well-hidden glen. Aimée also prayed that the Arabians grazing nearby would make no sound. At one point the tramping of feet against decayed twigs and branches seemed no more than a few yards away.

But finally the footsteps grew fainter and seemed to move off in the direction of the estate. They remained silent until long after the patrol had left. When they felt safe, they relaxed and Aimée prepared a cold supper while Marie-Clarice decided it was a fine time to sample the brandy she had brought. They sat and shivered that night, because they thought it much wiser not to light a fire in case the men returned.

Aimée was awakened by a voice calling her name. She sat up instantly. Marie-Clarice also had been awakened. They were startled and confused. Then Aimée heard her name called again, and this time she recognized the voice.

"Alex!" she called out eagerly. "Alex, we're in the glen."

She heard his footsteps racing toward her and then he burst into the glen. By now she was standing and would have rushed into his arms had she not remembered all too well their last encounter. He approached her slowly, his expression guarded. Marie-Clarice watched it all with an expression of surprise—and hope.

"The French are searching for you," he said simply. "And the Mexicans are searching for you, too. I wanted to come and warn you, but it was too dangerous. They knew I'd visited you and that we were . . . friends. I'm sure I would have been followed and thus led them right to you."

"The French and the Mexicans have already been here," said Aimée. "The French burned the mansion. The Mexicans looked for us but we were lucky and they did not find us."

"Tell him about Vardeau," prodded Marie-Clarice. "Tell him what happened."

"Remember that I told you I thought Vardeau knew my true identity? Well, I was right. He did. But he pretended not to recognize me because he was afraid of Maximilian. He came to tell me Maximilian was dead and . . ." Aimée flushed.

"I shot him," Marie-Clarice filled the pause with her proud announcement.

"Good for you," Alex said, his smile fading to a look

of concern as he turned to Aimée. "He's under arrest right now. He told the Mexicans you had shot him. I slipped away to try to find you. When I saw the ruins I thought I'd come too late."

"We escaped just before the French arrived," Aimée explained, searching his face for any sign of his true feelings toward her.

"I didn't want to surprise you here in the glen because I knew one of you had a gun—and wasn't afraid to use it," he said, half smiling and half serious. "I didn't want to be shot." Then he took a deep breath and said, "Not by the girl I'm in love with—and always was—even if I acted like a fool."

"Alex—" Aimée walked slowly toward him, her arms outstretched. But he wasted no time and ran and swooped her up in his arms and kissed her with a passion that embarrassed the usually unflappable Marie-Clarice. She wisely made her way into the cave to prepare some breakfast and let the lovers have their reunion in more privacy.

"Oh, Alex!" Aimée exclaimed. "I was so afraid I'd hurt you too much for you to be able to forgive..."

"Let's not dwell on it," he told her. "It bothers me to have been so blind. I love you. I do. I always have. If you regarded Maximilian with love—"

"No," she cried out. "It wasn't love. He could have had any woman, but it was me he commanded and I went to him because—what else could I do? If I had refused, he could have made it very unpleasant for me and my family. Or he could have been a beast, but he wasn't. Oh, I didn't love him the way I love you. But I did have feelings for him."

He kissed her again, brushed her shining, light brown hair back over her temple. "Forgive *me* for being such a fool. I was wrong to blame you for being involved in a situation over which you had no control. I couldn't understand the fear that drove you. I was hurt and jealous when I found out you'd seen Maximilian again."

Just then Marie-Clarice walked out and said, "This

is a fine place for a lovers' reunion, but may I remind
you that we are still in danger?"

"We'll go soon, but I have one more thing to tell
Aimée," Alex said. With a serious face he began, "Maximilian and his armies were trapped at Querétaro. They
never had a chance. There was a short time when Maximilian himself could have escaped. He had the chance—
but he refused to go. He said his place was with his
soldiers and no amount of persuasion could make him
change his mind. Perhaps he hoped reinforcements
would come, who knows, but they never did. In Mexico City," Alex continued, "all the Frenchmen were more
inclined to save their own necks than to risk their lives
to save his. So Maximilian surrendered rather than let
his men be killed.

"They held him until Juárez decided his fate. He was
to be executed before a firing squad. They say he died
with more courage than any of his generals would have
shown."

"I'm sorry he's dead, Alex. But in a way his courageous end proved he had the heart of a lion and was
not the mollycoddle some people thought him to be."

"He certainly wasn't that," agreed Alex. "The Mexicans are busy destroying what remains of his rule. This
man Vardeau was captured. They found him in a French
military hospital with a bullet wound that had caused
such a loss of blood that he was unable to escape with
the rest of the royal guard."

Marie-Clarice grinned, proud at what small part she
had played in his capture. "I should have killed him,"
she said fiercely.

"He came for us," Aimée went on, "and Marie-
Clarice wounded him. We think he sent the French
soldiers to find us. Perhaps he even told them to burn
down the house."

"He's a danger to you, even in custody, Aimée."
Alex paused, hesitating over the new name. "I'm going
to take you and Marie-Clarice to the United States.
But there are some things I must know before we begin

this journey. It's a long journey and all of it is through Mexican-controlled territory. But first I must know—and you must tell me the truth—were you actively involved in helping Mexican spies?"

"In a way, I suppose so. Yes. Yes. Just before we fled I helped three important Mexican widows escape from Mexico City. I'm not sorry I did that."

"You shouldn't be under the circumstances," he said. "Mexico won this war and should be grateful to anyone who offered help."

"But how will they treat me as Maximilian's mistress? I know I've been called that and I'm not insulted because it was the truth. One can't be insulted by the truth." She broke off and looked at him searchingly, suddenly more concerned with his reaction than with how the Mexicans might judge her.

"Tell me how *you* feel, Alex?" she begged when he remained silent.

"You want the truth and you shall have it," he said after an uncharacteristic pause for a candid person with a quick tongue.

She nodded. Even Marie-Clarice, who had been pretending to keep busy, forgot what she was doing as she waited for his response.

"When I first saw you I felt that you were the woman I'd been looking for all of my life. To me you were an innocent Mexican girl, brought up in a traditionally strict manner. You seemed to be so sweet and young and perfect, too perfect I suppose. When I discovered that you were far more worldly wise—and you admitted seeing Maximilian—my illusions were shattered so badly I lost my perspective. I had no right to make those assumptions about you in the first place. And what I didn't keep in mind is that in time of war the stresses are more intense because life is cheap and brutality commonplace. Maximilian ruled Mexico. He wanted you. Unless you decided to run away, you had no choice but to go to him. I realize that now. And now I realize that you couldn't have run back to Paris even if you had wanted to."

"I wanted so desperately for you to understand," Aimée admitted. "But I simply couldn't confide in you. I didn't dare. And even if I had, there was always the fear that you, too, might use me as the others had and that once you were finished with me, you'd betray me, too. And later I was afraid I'd lose you if you discovered the truth." She shook her head sadly.

"It's over now," Alex said. "Finished."

They both realized there was little time to waste on words and so they embraced, kissing and hugging and holding onto each other as if to make up for all the time they had spent apart.

"Well I'm glad that's all over with," Marie-Clarice muttered more to herself. At least these two headstrong people seemed to have gotten together. When the lovers finally released each other, Marie-Clarice pointed out to Alex: "You know her father was involved with Juárez. Maybe they would be more lenient with her, since he died defending their cause, and she helped those widows to safety."

"It may help or it may not," said Alex. "The real problem is that the Mexicans believe Aimée is Mexican and it is considered treason for her to have been Maximilian's mistress."

"How can I prove to them I'm French?" Aimée asked. "Or do I want to? I may be beyond help if they catch me in the passion of their victory. They may shoot me before listening to a word I say."

"It's so difficult. We have to get you out of the country without their knowledge. We'll have to travel very carefully, by night, if possible—and avoid contact with anyone."

"I'll gather up what we can carry and get the horses ready," announced Marie-Clarice.

"My horse is tied up in the forest," Alex said. "I thought I'd do better riding on horseback than trying to get here in a carriage. It was the right choice. So we'd better move on now as quickly as possible. I've got maps and I know where some of the army blockades are set up."

"Before we begin, I want to ask you something," said Aimée. "If we are caught, how will it affect you—helping someone who is considered a traitor to escape?"

"I can always tell them I'm doing it to get an exclusive story about you and Maximilian," Alex improvised to dispel her fear. "They may not like what I'm doing, but they probably won't say anything. Juárez is a fair man, and I've done a lot of favors for him. You might say, he owes me this one."

"That may be true, but he probably doesn't owe *you* enough to prevent me from being condemned as a traitor," Aimée said sadly.

"That's why I want you to get out of Mexico as soon as you can. Now!" insisted Alex, pulling her to her feet. "If we leave quickly while the country still is in turmoil, our chances may be better than we think."

They rode out of the forest single file and came upon a plain that seemed to stretch to infinity. They had no choice but to cross it openly. To circumvent it would take extra days they could not afford to waste. Luck was with them and no one appeared to challenge their passage.

For the next few hours the apprehensive trio rode through countryside and small villages, and were able to relax only when they saw that people were too busy celebrating their victory to pay attention to travelers. No one thought them unusual, for there were many people who had been uprooted by the recent rebellion.

Riding alongside Aimée, Alex said, "We're nearly past the most dangerous part. The Mexicans may know you left the estate and be on the lookout in this area, but the further away we get, the less likely it is that they will want to follow you."

"I hope you're right," Aimée said. "But when those Mexicans found the cold water in the trough yesterday, they probably assumed we were still hiding somewhere in the area. I hope they search around the house again instead of looking for us on the road."

"Don't worry," Alex reassured her. "We'll be going through some fairly large towns before the day is over. They may be too busy celebrating to stop every single traveler they see. And it's better to ride through these towns. We really can't avoid it. Besides, in the next town I can trade in these horses for a carriage. We'll not only be less conspicuous but more comfortable."

Aimée was grateful for his consideration. She had spent much time horseback riding since her arrival, but never had she spent so many hours at one time in the saddle. Her bottom was beginning to be very sore. Marie-Clarice rode without complaining—or talking. Probably she was nervous but was acting very calm indeed, Aimée thought proudly.

By mid-afternoon they had reached the outskirts of the large town Alex had mentioned. The entire town was celebrating Mexico's victory, and the people on the streets were in a highly festive mood, augmented by generous libations of fiery tequila. A religious parade was being organized. They saw the townspeople readying the statue of a saint to be carried through the streets.

"I'm hungry," announced Marie-Clarice, seeing a sidewalk cafe.

"You're right. We should stop and rest and eat," agreed Alex. "I think we can go over to the cafe for some food. We may be strangers but this is a fiesta and we won't be conspicuous. Are you willing to take the risk?"

"I'll take the risk," said Marie-Clarice. Aimée agreed because she felt that if she didn't get off her horse she'd never be able to sit down again.

So they rode boldly up to the hitchrack in front of the cafe, tied their horses and approached one of the tables. Gaily dressed and happy people swirled all around them on the street. Marie-Clarice was soundly kissed by a young man who was caught up in the spirit of the festivities. Roving bands of musicians were playing lively music, and people were already starting to dance in the streets.

Observing the joyous mayhem around them, Alex said, "While the fiesta goes on, I'll trade the horses for a carriage. It shouldn't be too difficult to find a buyer for some valuable Arabians."

"Please don't be away too long," begged Aimée. "I'll be nervous."

"You're quite safe here, I'm sure. I'll be as quick as I can," he promised, giving her a kiss on the tip of her nose.

Even though he saw no reason to worry, Aimée became tense the moment he was out of sight ."I've got a bad feeling. I just don't like it," she whispered to Marie-Clarice who was sitting beside her watching all the young men. "They must have some ways of knowing that we're traveling and certainly they're watching for us. If anything happens, and there's a chance for you to escape, run, Marie-Clarice, run," she urged her. "If we're caught, I'll swear to them that you're an indentured servant and that not only do you simply work for me but that I never confide in you."

Marie-Clarice drew herself up haughtily. "I'm not leaving you, Aimée. Not under any circumstances."

Aimée smiled and nodded. "Thank you. I appreciate your loyalty. And I'd also like to say that the turban was worth all the hours of work you put into it. You look very beautiful in it."

"It's protection from the heat," she said, smiling mysteriously. "I didn't think of that when I started it. But if you say it looks pretty, then I'm glad."

Half an hour went by and Aimée grew more and more anxious despite herself. She felt too conspicuous sitting there and yet she didn't dare move because this was where Alex had left her. But where was he? He should have returned by now, she thought, struggling to keep her emotions from showing. She tried to smile, to look happy and gay like those around her, but each minute her anxiety grew greater.

Was it possible the livery stable was far away? Or that everyone was out celebrating? What had happened to Alex, she wondered. If they couldn't get the carriage, then she wanted to be on her way again as soon as possible.

There was a sudden commotion at one end of the street and the crowd moved aside to allow a patrol of eight soldiers and an officer to pass through.

Aimée paled. She had a wild urge to get up and run, but she knew that would give her away—or arouse suspicion—so she controlled herself and sat exactly where she was. The patrol approached, and Aimée prayed that it would keep on going past her. But her heart sank when the officer signaled and the entire patrol stopped only a few feet short of the restaurant.

The officer dismounted, removed his gauntlets and marched directly toward their table. Aimée sat motionless, frozen with fear as he came to stand before her.

He bowed and saluted. "Señorita, you will please come with me."

Aimée sighed in resignation. It was a command not a request but Marie-Clarice apparently decided to brazen it out. "Why? We're only sitting here—"

"You will come, please. Both of you," he cut her off curtly.

Aimée put a restraining hand on Marie-Clarice's arm and nodded that she should go with the officer. She wanted no trouble here. She didn't want to give anyone a chance to shoot first or to say that she had acted suspiciously or resisted the order. Then she saw the patrol had a carriage waiting for her.

As they walked with the officer, Aimée said, "We might as well go with them. What can two women do . . . ?"

"You're right," Marie-Clarice answered, catching on that Aimée didn't want them to realize there were three of them. Perhaps this would give Alex a chance to escape. They were led to the carriage. Once they were seated inside, they were quickly surrounded by the soldiers on horseback and driven away. As she looked out into the crowd, Aimée gasped in surprise.

Astride his own favorite horse was Renato, tipping his hat in greeting and giving her an enigmatic smile. Then he wheeled his mount and rode off in the opposite direction.

Chapter 17

The journey back to Mexico City was long and arduous and there were no stops except for quick meals of rice and beans. The patrol dropped some members and picked up others along the way, although the lieutenant in charge stayed with them throughout the entire trip.

There was little conversation between Marie-Clarice and Aimée and any of the members of the patrol. They were told nothing and questions were answered only with gruff orders to wait and see. Alex wasn't even mentioned, so Aimée simply hoped that he had escaped unnoticed. And while she longed to have him with her, she realized how dangerous it would have been for him to have been implicated in trying to help her escape.

The carriage at last rolled down the streets of Mexico City and took them to Maximilian's palace, now occupied by Mexican troops. There were soldiers everywhere, their faces drawn and tired after their victory and sweating with the summer heat and humidity.

"At least there's no jail in the palace," Aimée said

as they were led along a corridor. "Perhaps we won't be locked up."

"That's not much comfort," Marie-Clarice said glumly. "They have walls here, don't they?" The implication was clear: they might not live long enough to need a cell. Aimée tried to keep her courage up, but she was secretly afraid Marie-Clarice was right. It was over.

They were left in a large room from which most of the furniture had been stripped. Looted was probably more like it, thought Aimée, remembering the magnificence of the place as it had been while Maximilian reigned. They sat on two plain, wooden, hard-backed chairs for at least an hour, afraid to talk for fear they might be overheard—or that they might reveal their own fears.

Finally Aimée broke the silence. "I wonder," she whispered, "what kind of a court we'll have to face."

"What difference does it make?" Marie-Clarice grumbled.

"It might. A military court is a fast and rough procedure without much regard to civil law."

The question they had both been thinking was now voiced by Marie-Clarice. "Do you think they'll execute us?" she asked in a tiny voice, tight with tension.

"We can pray—" began Aimée.

"In these circumstances, I don't trust the power of prayer too much. But, just to be sure, I'm going to keep praying," admitted Marie-Clarice.

Just then a door opened and a uniformed major strode into the room, followed by four soldiers who took up position at the open dor. The major apprached the desk which was still in the room. He didn't sit down but addressed them tersely.

"Señoritas, this will be brief. I ask that you identify yourselves."

Aimée gave a sigh of resignation before answering and said, "I have been known as Angela Fuchard, a Mexican, but my real name is Aimée Gaudin. I am French."

"Gracias," said the major to her, and then looking at Marie-Clarice. "And you?"

Marie-Clarice simply gave her name and her French nationality.

Aimée interceded before he could ask another question and said, "This girl is my personal maid. Whatever I'm accused of, she has nothing to do with it. I ask that she be allowed her freedom."

"All in good time, señorita," he waved away her request. "In the morning we shall conduct a hearing. It will be informal. We have no time for long trials." At this news Aimée's heart sank. She knew all too well that the Mexicans would well remember the short, "informal" trials of the French. "I'm sorry," the major went on, "but for tonight you'll have to be locked up. We've turned the bedrooms upstairs into a makeshift prison, so you can't be too uncomfortable, but I advise you that it would be most foolish to try to escape. That is all for now."

Aimée and Marie-Clarice were led through the ballroom where Aimée had once danced with Maximilian and so many other important French officials. That all seemed so long ago now, almost as if it had been another life. There were blank spots on the walls where imposing, gilded framed pictures and valuable tapestries had been torn away. The palace was only a shadow of its former self. As they were led upstairs, Aimée thought how ironic it would be if she were to be imprisoned in the very room where Maximilian had first made love to her.

It was with great relief that Aimée saw they were to be kept in another room, and that they were not alone. Three other women, all Mexican, were being held there as well. They had already appropriated the one bed and the floor alongside it, using the fine bed linen and blankets to protect themselves from the cool night air. But all those fine things, Aimée saw upon closer inspection, were now dirty, wrinkled and worn.

Aimée and Marie-Clarice sat down in two armless

chairs which were leaning against the far wall. One of the Mexican women got off the bed and approached them. She was dumpy and slovenly; her hair was tangled and matted with filth. Her eyes were dull and bloodshot, perhaps from weeping, and her clothes were those of a peasant.

"What are you two aristocrats in here for?" she demanded, a challenge in her voice. Ordinarily, thought Aimée, a woman like this would never have dared to address her in such a tone, but wartime made such strange companions, she realized.

"We don't know why we are here," Aimée told the woman politely. "No one told us why they are keeping us."

"That's not good," the woman said with a knowing leer. "If they don't know what you did, they usually shoot you on the spot on general principle. They must have a special reason for keeping you alive."

"We've done nothing to deserve a firing squad," Marie-Clarice said hotly. "We're not afraid."

"That is the best lie I've heard yet," the woman commented tartly, turning to her friends on the bed. They all laughed. The woman added sarcastically, "You don't speak very good Spanish. You're both French, which is not very good for you, is it?"

"Yes," Aimée said. "We are French, but we did nothing to harm the Mexican cause."

"They'll think of something, you can be sure of that," the woman taunted them. When she smiled, Aimée saw her rotted teeth and shuddered. The woman went on to say: "All three of us are going to be tried in the morning. And we know what's going to happen. We helped the French. We took their money and we slept with them. If we hadn't, we would have starved. But to the Mexicans, that alone is enough to earn us a place against the wall. . . ."

"I wouldn't give up hope so quickly," Aimée said.

The woman laughed disdainfully. "You mean *you* wouldn't give up hope. Well, we've been here longer than you have and we've seen how the Mexican justice works. They've taken four women out of this room since we've been here. And not one of them has returned. And we heard the shots. Does that answer your question?"

Marie-Clarice lowered her head and began to cry softly. Aimée put an arm around her. "We still have reason to hope," she told her. "Especially you."

"I'd like to believe it, Aimée, but I can't. Renato turned us in, and the things he can say against us aren't going to buy us any mercy with a Mexican court. We can't depend on Alex. And even if he did show up, I don't think there's any way that he could save us now."

"I think Alex isn't far away, but I doubt he's abandoned us. If he'd stayed they'd have arrested him too, and he wouldn't be able to help us at all if he'd allowed himself to be taken with us. And it would have been foolish for him to have tried to rescue us from all those soldiers."

"I wish I could feel as optimistic as you do," Marie-Clarice said. "Oh, what's going to happen to us?" She put her head in her hands and rocked her whole body in misery. Aimée searched for words to say to comfort her friend, but none came. So she decided the best thing to do was to simply face reality, as grim as that appeared to be.

"Let's just get through the night. And we'll see what happens in the morning," she said stoutly, hoping her courage would inspire Marie-Clarice a little.

"But if they shoot a Mexican woman because she slept with a French soldier, what are they going to do to us?" moaned Marie-Clarice miserably.

"I know what you're thinking. If that's their fate, what kind of revenge will they take on the woman who slept with the emperor?"

"Whatever you tell them, I'll back you up," promised Marie-Clarice, regaining a bit of her former spirit.

"Thank you, my dear Marie-Clarice." Aimée hugged

her and held her close. "You've been a blessing to me ever since we met. I wish I could have brought you to something better than this."

"It wasn't too bad . . . until Vardeau showed up," said Marie-Clarice.

"I've been thinking of Vardeau. I don't think that he could have escaped punishment. He couldn't even run away," said Aimée, hoping that he'd finally pay for his crimes.

"I doubt it. He'll probably try to save his neck by confessing everything about everyone else," said Marie-Clarice, wtih sudden insight. "After all, he was colonel of Maximilian's guards and he knows everything that went on. He could be a valuable 'witness' against others in these trials."

Aimée's stomach lurched. She was probably right about Vardeau, and she was positive that he had no compunction whatsoever about lying or betraying anyone in order to save his own miserable life. Marie-Clarice slumped down on the floor against the wall and said, "I'm going to try and sleep." She closed her eyes and Aimée sat there beside her. But sleep wouldn't come. . . .

They were rudely awakened by screaming and then a volley of rifle shots. Marie-Clarice and Aimée huddled together and wept.

The sounds of men marching were heard in the corridor. They came to an abrupt halt in front of the bedroom door. Frightened, Marie-Clarice and Aimée rose, but it was the three women whom the soldiers had come for. The door closed and the soldiers marched off and then all was quiet.

Nothing more was heard for what seemed like hours. They did not know what had happened to those luckless women. Aimée hoped that whatever their sins had been, they would be spared. She suspected it was a rather futile hope.

Aimée judged it to be almost noon when they heard men marching towards the room. Again they stood up, but this time an armed soldier entered, and then another soldier came in carrying a tray of food for them. At the door he turned and said, "Be ready in one hour, señoritas."

Marie-Clarice's teeth chattered wth fear at the soldier's announcement. Aimée was more interested in the food on the tray.

"Look. Look. It's not rice and beans or the miserable slop they fed us on the way here. It's fresh fruit, bread, tortillas and chocolate."

"Last meal," Marie-Clarice dubbed it, turning away.

"I don't believe that. Anyway, I'm hungry and I'm going to eat my share, and if you don't eat yours, I'll have that, too," Aimée told her matter-of-factly.

Marie-Clarice soon changed her mind when her stomach rumbled and the two of them finished every crumb of their meal. Somehow the food made them feel more confident and they fixed themselves up as best they were able before the soldiers came to take them away, too.

They were led downstairs to the same room where they'd first been the day before. This time several people were seated there and a man in the uniform of a Mexican colonel sat behind the desk.

"Please sit down," he told them, waving at two chairs. "I am Colonel Pedro Vargas, in charge of criminal proceedings. Which of you is Angela . . . or Aimée . . . ?"

Aimée stood up. "I am Aimée Gaudin."

"*Gracias.* You may sit down again. You will understand that this is not a formal trial," he addressed them coldly but politely. "There's no time for that. We're deluged with enemies of Mexico and cannot devote hours to trials or meaningless debates. However, you will be treated fairly and you will be given a chance to speak in your own behalf. Before the witnesses are called, it is my duty to ask you this: Are you or are you not guilty of aiding and abetting the French occupation forces?"

Aimée stood up and looked him straight in the eyes. "I am guilty. However, I wish the right to explain the circumstances. My personal maid, however, is innocent. She is an indentured servant and knew nothing of what went on. I beg you to set her free."

"We shall see," he answered vaguely, as if the matter was of little importance.

Aimée felt that despite his formal attitude, he seemed compassionate. She felt a surge of hope, a surge that flickered and died when the first witness was brought into the room.

Vardeau was brought in. No longer the suave, well-tailored man she'd known in France or the self-confident officer of the royal guard, he looked dirty, sweat-stained and had a three or four-day old subble of beard. Any air of arrogance he had once possessed was gone. He moved slowly, almost painfully, like an old man and his powerful grace had disappeared along with his arrogance. One arm was suspended in a bloodied sling. He gave Aimée a hard-eyed stare and she knew she was doomed. He was an evil man, this Vardeau, and he would say whatever he could to see that she was sent to a speedy end.

"I still say I wish I'd killed him," Marie-Clarice hissed in Aimée's ear.

"Be quiet!" Aimée silenced her.

Vardeau stood before the colonel. He identified himself by saying, "I'm Colonel Roy Vardeau, late commandant of the royal guard."

"You have charged that this woman, Aimée Gaudin, is a proven traitor to Mexico. What are the details of this charge?" the colonel behind the desk inquired impassively.

"She lived here with a wealthy family pretending to be their niece and thereby gained control of their estate under false pretenses," began Vardeau. "She also supported Maximilian and the French regime. She was Maximilian's mistress and went to his bed whenever he sent for her. She did this willingly and became well known by the palace guards, who were ordered to protect her and to bring her to her lover's trysts."

"You know these matters to be factual?" questioned the colonel.

"I swear to the truth of every word I've uttered— and I defy this woman to prove otherwise." For the first time since entering, Vardeau turned to Aimée and shot her a smug, malicious glance of triumph.

Aimée glared at him and stood up. "May I speak now, colonel?"

"No. There are others to testify first and then you will be given your chance to try to defend yourself. Bring in the next witness," he said to the guard, who escorted Vardeau out and brought in Renato, Lino, Antonia, Melania and Della. They lined up before the colonel. Lino assumed the role of family spokesman and when he was ordered to begin his testimony, he spoke out in an angry tirade:

"This woman came to us as our niece and cousin. We believed her to be who she said she was. But since then we have learned that she is a French girl who is wanted in Paris for treason. This is the kind of woman you are dealing with," he said scornfully.

"In your opinion, señor," said the colonel quietly, "Did she do anything against Mexico? That is all this inquiry is interested in."

"She slept with Emperor Maximilian many times and she did so gladly. She often said she admired him and hoped that he would remain to rule Mexico forever. She lived with us, used our money, demanded obedience from us, and all the while she was an impostor, a traitor to Mexico," he ended righteously.

"Do all of you agree as to the truth of what has just been said?" asked the colonel.

The women, who hadn't glanced at Aimée even

once, replied that it was true what Lino had told the court.

After they were shown out of the room, the colonel told Aimée, "Now you may speak." She thought his manner was cordial, even encouraging, despite the damning evidence that he had just heard. And his seeming impartiality and willingness to hear everything gave her the courage to begin her defense for her life.

She stood up, took a deep breath and began speaking in a calm, modulated voice. "I admit that I passed myself off as Angela Fuchard and that in her name I assumed control of the estate. However, the estate was willed to me by a man who knew who I was and who asked me to take the place of his niece—to cover up the fact that he had murdered her. Thus, while his property was willed to his niece, it was with his full knowledge and blessings that he promised it would all go to me. So to the family I am an impostor. That I impersonated Angela Fuchard, this is true. That I illegally took control of the estate is not true. However, only a court might ever be able to decide that issue.

"Sir, I know this may all sound very strange, and you may wonder why one woman would agree to take over the identity of another. The reason was very simple: I was wanted in France. It was not that I personally had done anything wrong, but it was my father whom they sought. You see, he was once the ambassador to this country, in fact, to this very city. And I lived with him here as a child. He came to know and understand the Mexican people, and their need for independence. When he learned of Louis Napoleon's plan to take over Mexico, he actively campaigned against it. He publicly denounced the plan, saying it was all wrong. For this he was brutally gunned down in a Paris alleyway without a trial." Aimée paused dramatically, waiting to see if this announcement had any effect on Colonel Vargas.

"And my father's whereabout on that particular night were revealed to the French by a man whom he thought

was his most trusted friend and ally. That man was . . .
Roy Vardeau." A startled look passed across the colonel's face for a split second. Otherwise he remained impassive but listening intently to Aimée's story.

"My father trusted Vardeau, and his last words to me were to find Vardeau and to go to him for help. But Vardeau found me. He took me to his apartment under the guise of being a friend of my father's. He held me prisoner there and raped me and abused me. He did nothing to help me escape. When finally I found some incriminating evidence against him, and confronted him with it, only then did he make plans for me to escape." By now Aimée could see that the colonel was listening with great interest.

"Vardeau," she continued, "put me on a clipper ship bound for Mexico and assured me I was a first-class passenger. But after I was aboard and the vessel had sailed, I learned that I had not been booked as a first-class passenger but in steerage—that my fate was to be sold on the docks of Veracruz as an indentured servant. This was his revenge on me.

"But on the very first morning I was approached by Nemecio Miranda to have breakfast with him. And later he made his proposition that I pretend to be his niece. He told me that she had preferred to remain in France, where she had lived since the age of two. The truth was that he had brutally murdered her in a drunken passion. I discovered her body and he threatened to kill me too. He threw her body overboard and I became Angela Fuchard. Later that night, when I was asleep, he must have fallen overboard himself. At least that is what the captain believed. And that is how I came to Mexico, not as an indentured French servant but as a Mexican heiress. Who would not have taken advantage of this unexpected turn of luck?"

Not really pausing to wait for an answer, Aimée went on to explain how she had become involved with Maximilian and how it had been until Vardeau had been sent to Mexico City as punishment. She ended by saying, "And when he tried to rape me, he was shot by my maid. Monsieur Vardeau didn't lie when he told you his story, but there is much much more to the story, as you have just heard. And I swear that is the true story as to what has happened," she concluded simply, sitting down.

There was silence for a minute. The colonel said noncommittally, "What do you say about what your so-called uncle said?"

"He didn't lie, colonel," she admitted.

"Did you or did you not become Maximilian's mistress voluntarily?" he asked.

"Who can refuse a royal command and live?" she answered simply.

"This personal maid of yours had nothing to do with all of this?" he continued.

"She was ignorant of everything that went on."

"With regard to this family you lived with, there was a great deal of gold involved when they fled. What do you know of this?"

Aimée told him everything, including how she had been stranded in the city. "Lino saw to it that he escaped with all of it, but I wouldn't have taken it anyway, because it was never mine to begin with. I do not know where the gold is now."

Colonel Vargas wrote something down on a piece of paper. Then he carefully put his pen down and said to her: "We know what you say is true, señorita. And perhaps you would like to know that the gold is in our possession. Your 'family' was captured, along with their gold, when they tried to cross our border to the United States. Taking gold out of Mexico is a crime," he added ominously. "Now, we have a final witness, señorita." The door opened and this time Renato stepped in. He walked in, almost jauntily, smiled at Aimée and stood before the colonel.

If looks could kill, Renato would have died a painful death from the dagger-like stare Aimée shot at his back. She could just imagine what he'd have to say. She sighed, knowing whatever hope she had held onto had just vanished. Colonel Vargas nodded for Renato to begin his account.

"Ever since the French conquered Mexico, I have acted on behalf of Benito Juárez. I belong to his secret service. This I can prove."

"It is not necessary," the colonel obviously wanted to get this over with, Aimée noted. "Please proceed with your testimony of this woman's activity in Maximilian's court."

"There is one matter I would like to clarify first, with your permission," Renato asked the colonel. At a nod of approval he went on: "Once I arranged for a spy wanted by the French to change places with the regular driver of the carriage used by Aimée Gaudin. She was accused of helping him because the other members of my family found out about my activities and plotted to use them to their advantage by trying to place the blame on Aimée. They informed on her so the French would arrest her. They hoped she'd be shot, but at the very least they were certain she'd be imprisoned. Then, they would have the estate all to themselves, as Uncle Nemecio had cut them totally out of his will. Maximilian intervened and saved her. A second time my family implicated her as a spy and she was arrested. Again, Maximilian interceded on her behalf."

Aimée was perplexed. Evidently Renato's loyalty to Juárez was such that he had no compunction about incriminating even his own family. But what did this have to do with, her as all he'd accomplished so far was to say that she'd had no part in helping the *Juárista* spies? However, he had established that while she hadn't helped the *Juáristas,* neither had she been a French informant.

"And as the emperor's mistress," went on Renato, the word "mistress" bringing Aimée out of her speculating, "she gained the emperor's confidence and had full run of the palace. In that way, she learned many important things that were vital to our cause. She transmitted information to me, which was passed on to the appropriate parties. By being Maximilian's mistress, she was doing what she could to aid Mexico and Juárez."

Aimée almost gasped. Renato was lying in her behalf. But it really wasn't a total lie because she'd always trusted him and she had told him of incidents or of conversations she'd had at the palace. To her they had been innocent, inconsequential bits of gossip or news, but perhaps they had not been so unimportant after all.

"I'd like to also say, colonel," went on Renato, "that when Mexico City was about to fall, she transported the widows of three of the most important men in Juárez' forces. At great personal risk she drove them herself from Mexico City to her own home, kept them there overnight, gave them food, shelter and horses and sent them on their way. They are willing to testify on her behalf, if need be. She saved their lives for they were actively being sought by the French and would have been shot on sight. Juárez knows of this act of heroism on the part of Mademoiselle Gaudin, a girl who is not even Mexican."

There was now silence in the room. A fly buzzed near Aimée's ear, and she realized that even in the summer heat her hands were icy cold. The grim fate that awaited her only a few hundred yards away made her dizzy with fear and yet when she was ordered to stand, she stood there tall and straight.

"It is my duty to sentence this woman," began Vargas, "although I am not sure she deserves to be punished at all. She admits her liason with Maximilian, who was an enemy to our country. However, she did this in order to obtain information, a fact which has been attested to by one of Juárez's most trusted aides. However, before this trial is brought to an end, there is someone else who must address this court."

Aimée was now totally confused. What did all of this mean? Was she going to die? Who else could possibly testify against her? The colonel nodded toward the aide stationed at the door and someone walked briskly into the room and stood before the colonel. All the color drained out of Aimée's face when she realized the final witness against her was to be . . . Alex Mooreland!

Alex glanced only briefly in Aimée's direction and spoke to the colonel in a clear, low voice that carried throughout the room. He began by saying, "I owe Aimée Gaudin a sincere apology. I saw her being arrested after Colonel Vardeau told the Mexican authorities that the emperor's mistress was still in the country. I could have joined her or tried to defend her, but I did not."

This was the final blow. Aimée had been so strong throughout all her worries, the fear of imminent death, but to know that Alex, the one man she had ever truly loved was about to betray her confidences was more than she could bear. She felt dizzy and the room spun. She grasped the seat of the chair until her knuckles turned white. If she was going to die, she would conduct herself with all the dignity she could muster. Beside her, as though a thousand miles away, she heard Marie-Clarice, who had been quiet as a mouse throughout the trial, curse Alex under her breath.

Alex's voice continued and he was now saying: "Colonel, if I had tried to rescue her I would have been arrested, and if that had happened I would not have been able to locate Benito Juárez and explain to him the circumstances that brought Aimée Gaudin to Mexico. He did not know that Angela Fuchard was in reality Aimée Gaudin, the daughter of Émile Gaudin. Her father had not only provided Juárez with valuable information and advice, but had been a vocal opponent of Maximilian's regime. And it is true that he died for this belief. And it was her father's "crime' that led to Aimée's arrival in Mexico City, betrayed by Vardeau. All of this is true. She also risked her life to save those three widows. And so I bring word from Benito Juárez himself that this woman, Aimée Gaudin, is to be found innocent of all charges and to be released. This is so ordered in these documents. She is also to be allowed to proceed to the United States without opposition." At this, Alex handed to the colonel some very official looking sealed documents, which the colonel opened and quickly perused.

The colonel nodded. "It is as you said. You are free, Señorita Gaudin. Colonel Vardeau is to be held for trial. The Miranda family is free to go—without the gold—which is now ordered confiscated along with all other family holdings here and abroad. I believe this ends the proceedings. I congratulate you, Señorita Gaudin."

With these words, the colonel stood up and left the room. Aimée was totally dazed, almost unable to comprehend the total turnabout the entire trial had taken. But she didn't have time to think before Alex swept her up in his arms and said, "I'm sorry, my darling. I acted the only way I could to be sure that you would be freed. Also, the trial had to be held so you could not be brought up later on charges of spying. And your trial provided valuable evidence against Vardeau."

Aimée rested her head against his shoulder. "I can't believe it's over—all those months of deception and worrying."

"I have a carriage waiting. Unless you and Marie-Clarice have business here, I think we should leave at once."

"We?" replied Aimée uncertainly. Did this mean Alex really cared for her?

"Of course. Do you think I'd let you go anywhere without me?" he answered. "And Marie-Clarice goes with us. How could we do without her?"

Alex took both of their arms and gallantly escorted them out of the room and down the hall, past Lino, Antonia, Della and Melania. Antonia raised a hand as if to implore Aimée to stop and talk, but this time it was Aimée who ignored her and kept on walking. Near the exit they met Renato. Aimée kissed him fondly. "Thank you for what you did. It wasn't exactly the truth. . . ."

"In a way it was," Renato said firmly. "I did learn several interesting things from you, although you weren't aware you were telling me anything important. I'm glad it's over. And I'm sorry you aren't my cousin. I truly wish you were. And I hope you don't judge my family too harshly, Aimée. They come from a long line of people who were greedy and who were always willing to compromise their values if it meant they could live in luxury."

"Believe me, I will try not to think of them at all," said Aimée honestly.

To Alex, Renato said, "You're a lucky man, señor. I wish you well. The journey to the border has been arranged and you should encounter no problems."

Aimée kissed him again, and Renato gave Marie-Clarice a kiss that made her face turn red. Then all together they walked to the waiting carriage. Aimée was relieved to see that not only had a driver been provided so they could all sit and talk and relax, but that it was a large and comfortable coach that would make the long journey all that much more endurable.

As the carriage rolled down the avenue and away from the palace, Aimée glanced back only once to recall the days of Maximilian's splendor, of his lion-like good looks, the royal court, and the gilded coach. Things had changed so. The French pomp and glitter had been replaced by bandoleered Mexican soldiers. In a way, Aimée was glad Maximilian was dead, for he could never have submitted to defeat.

Aimée rested her head against Alex's shoulder, still shaken by recent events. But a tremendous burden had been lifted from her shoulders. The anxiety and tension she had learned to live with were gone. She was Aimée Gaudin again and she was on her way to a new life— and with the man she loved.

While Aimée was lost in her private reveries, Alex said, "Marie-Clarice, what are you doing to that turban?"

Aimée opened her eyes dreamily to see that Marie-Clarice was methodically taking apart the turban that she had spent so many hours laboriously sewing.

"Some day I'll understand you," she said to Marie-Clarice.

Marie-Clarice arched her eyebrows slyly and said, "I think you'll understand a lot sooner than that." As she continued her cutting, there was a little clunk, then another and another. Both Alex and Aimée leaned forward to see exactly what Marie-Clarice was doing. And there in her lap was a pile of stones—diamonds, rubies, emeralds, pearls—all sorts of gems began piling up as the turban unraveled—to reveal the jewels the emperor had given Aimée.

"I kept this in a safe place because I did not trust the family. And I was right. They searched your room from top to bottom for these precious gifts, but they never searched me. . . . I had to hide them somewhere, so I began sewing the turban. It's only too bad that I had to sew them on the inside instead of the outside," she sighed. "Think what a wonderful turban it would have been if they had been on the outside."

"Marie-Clarice," Aimée said, almost at a loss for words, "how can I thank you for all that you have done for me and for the way you have stood by me in the good times and the bad times? And now this! There are times when you are far more clever than I," marveled Aimée "And I thought we were penniless, except for that small bag of gold. . . ."

"It wouldn't have mattered if you just had the clothes on your back," Alex interrupted, seeing tears brimming in Aimée's eyes at the revelation of Marie-Clarice's friendship. "And I mean both of you."

"All three of us?" Marie-Clarice said happily.

"All three of us," agreed Alex.

"Except—" began Aimée.

"I know," Marie-Clarice cut her off. "Except in the bedroom. I know my place, madame. Besides, who knows, in America, I may find a man of my very own."

And with that, Marie-Clarice closed her eyes and pretended to sleep while Aimée and Alex kissed passionately as the carriage took them on to freedom and a new life—together.